See You In My Dreams

by

Marie-Nicole Ryan

A Ryandale Publishing
Paranormal Romantic Suspense Novel

Ryandale Publishing
Re-edited re-release
Cover art: Mary Varble

Ryandale Publishing
Copyright 2003 Mary Varble
ISBN-13 978-0615627267
ISBN-10 0615627269

Published in the United States of America 2003, 2012

Library of Congress Registration Number: TX 0005-854-545 10/29/2003

What they're saying about See You In My Dreams

2003 Golden Wings Award Winner
"Ryan's tale of star-crossed lovers who have loved and lost is a poignant—and sometimes gritty—tale that will resonate in readers." Faith V. Smith, Romantic Times Magazine

"This book is well written, fast-paced and thought provoking. It is full of suspense, mystery and action; a page-turner from start to finish." Coffee Time Romance

"This may be the first Ryan book I've read so far, but it won't be the last. Whether the characters were living the dreams, or experiencing the pangs of life and love, I was caught up in this story." Road to Romance Review

"SEE YOU IN MY DREAMS reminded me a lot of Judith McNaught's first contemporary romances.... [It] was very engrossing and it was extremely difficult to stop reading, even to do something important." The Romance Studio

"SEE YOU IN MY DREAMS is a definite fairy tale with heroes, villains, far off countries and dramatic rescues. Romance lovers will be in for an absolute treat with this book." In the Library Reviews

"Marie-Nicole Ryan has written a magnificent story about a hero and heroine who are destined to be with one another.[...]Once you start SEE YOU IN MY DREAMS, you will not be able to put it down. Come and experience a world where fairy tale dreams really do come true." Romance Junkies' Blue Ribbon Reviews

"*See You In My Dreams* is jam-packed full of suspense, mystery and action. A page turner from start to finish. Strong characters abound in this riveting novel about two people whose lives are connected both in the past and present. This story explores two souls that always find each and leave the reader thinking of the possibilities "could this really happen?" Fallen Angel Reviews

"SEE YOU IN MY DREAMS is well written, fast paced and thought provoking read. This reviewer looks forward to future books by the gilded pen of Ms. Ryan." Love Romances Reviews

Dedication

To my mother from whom I inherited my love for reading. And to my undaunted critique partners who slogged through the even longer first draft.

BOOK ONE: THE RUNAWAY

"Society is a masked ball, where everyone hides his real character, and reveals it by hiding."

Ralph Waldo Emerson,
The Conduct of Life,
"Worship" (1860)

One

October 1989

Nikki looked from left to right and over her shoulder before sliding into the dark, shadow-filled alley. Anyone with a smattering of brains avoided dark alleys. But for now, this one looked safe enough. Three street kids had disappeared in the last month, and she didn't plan on being number four. Like her, they were runaways who preferred living on the streets to home—not-so-sweet—home.

She reached into her jacket pocket and grinned when she located the match and a half-smoked cigarette. Scratching the match against the concrete block wall behind her, she lit the butt and took a long drag on her second smoke of the day. The tang of menthol flooded her throat. Swearing, she flung the butt away.

Shivering, she pulled her jacket tighter around her chest. She leaned against the rough concrete wall and wished it were August instead of early October in the Big Apple. The fall days were still warm, but the temperature dropped at night. Better find a place to stay pretty soon before she froze her butt off.

Her only friend was a seventeen-year-old hooker who worked for a pimp everyone called The Professor. At least her friend had a warm place to take her johns. Fine, if you were willing to pay the price.

But Nikki wasn't—not yet, no matter how The Professor pressured her to become one of his girls. And in spite of the way her friend made her living, and as pathetic as it might seem, Nikki was grateful for the hooker's friendship. The older girl had been on the streets for a couple of years, and it was Kayla who'd given Nikki a quick street-culture education. She hadn't glossed over anything—who to watch out for, which places would give her leftovers after closing and where she could crash for the night without having some buggy pervert decide she was the girl of his dreams.

She took a deep breath. Time to head for the shelter and find a warm bed for the night. Maybe she could even make it to the shelter without running into him. But no, as she stepped into the light, someone grabbed her arm. "Hey!" She tried to jerk away from the last person in the world she ever wanted to touch her—The Professor.

His watery blue eyes looked her up and down like she was at the top of his dessert menu. The old fart had to be at least forty years old—a real geezer—dressed like he thought he was something special—navy blazer, maroon tie and sharply creased white slacks. His blond hair hung in lank strands over the collar of a pale blue shirt. His preference for wearing blazers and ties had earned him his nickname—that and his stuck-up way of speaking.

Fancy duds aside, the man plain scared the bejeezus out of her. It wasn't just the way he looked at her. There was something deep-down evil about him—like maybe he tortured puppies when he was a kid.

"Need a place for the night, Nikki? I could find you a warm bed—or two," he said, his face wreathed in a smarmy smile that didn't quite reach his cold, fish eyes.

"No way. I'm headed to the shelter."

The Professor laughed. "I'm afraid you're too late. The shelter's full. But my offer still stands. Think about it."

She straightened herself to her full five-feet, ten-inches. "I know what your offer stands for. I'd rather freeze to death than work for you."

"You might just do that, little girl, and it would be such a terrible waste. I'm sure I could find you quite a few clients." His icy gaze traveled up and down her body, giving her the absolute creeps. "Think about it. You could be making good money, you know. Ask your friend. She doesn't spend the night huddled on a cot," he said, nodding toward the shelter.

She shook her head, trying to shut out his voice. She'd heard it all before. He was a total perv, just like the rest of the men who cruised looking for a good time. Only he was worse. The Professor might try to hide his true nature behind fancy speech and clothes, but he was still the slimiest piece of work she'd ever seen.

Cold, and more than a little scared, she couldn't help but consider it. A warm bed would be nice for a change, but the cost was too high. Sooner or later, her mama'd said, Nikki would end up selling her body if she dropped out of school. Damn. And she just hated for her mama to be right about anything.

I'll show her. One thing for sure, she'd never go back home; Mama didn't want her back anyway.

The touch of The Professor's hand on her arm wrenched her into the present. "No. Leave me the hell alone." She struggled to free her arm, but this time his grip held firm.

"No? Stuck-up little bitch." His voice roughened as he dropped his fancy speech. "You need to learn your place." He drew back as if to belt her one. "You might even like it."

Feeling his grasp loosen, she yanked with all her might. Freed, she took off, running in long strides down the crowded street, weaving in and out, looking over her shoulder as she did, until she bumped into an immovable object.

She turned, looked up and found the immovable object was the chest of a tall, handsome man. Gazing into clear, green eyes twinkling with amusement, she remembered her rusty manners and uttered a single word, "S-sorry."

"Watch what you're doing!" exclaimed a mink-draped brunette who stood alongside another elegant couple.

"It's all right, Jolie," Green-eyed and Handsome told the brunette, then he turned back to Nikki. "Are you all right, *mademoiselle?*" he asked.

She gaped. Without a doubt, he was the best-looking man she'd ever seen. When she drew herself to her full height, her eyes were nearly level with his, but his broad shoulders and muscular chest made her feel almost small. Her hands slid down his chest. She felt the coiled power in his body, as well as the fine wool of his overcoat. She stepped back, but couldn't keep her gaze off him. Dark brown hair waved back from his face and hung nearly to his shoulders. An irresistible impulse seized her. She reached out to run her fingers through his waves, but stopped short.

To cover her confusion, or maybe because of it, her words tumbled out as if they weren't connected to her brain. "Yeah, I'm fine. Sorry. I was—uh, just trying to get away from that—uh, someone." She cast another hurried glance over her shoulder. The Professor stood about ten yards away, leaning casually against a lamppost, watching her and smiling his freakish smile.

"Was he trying to hurt you?" Green Eyes asked.

Heart pounding, she pulled her gaze away from the pimp. "Yeah, but I'm fine." She looked up into the man's vivid eyes again and her pulse gave a strange kick. "He won't bother me any more—at least not tonight."

The man's elegant companion stepped forward and touched his arm as if she owned him. "Don't get involved, Maxim. This has nothing to do with us."

So that was his name. *Maxim.* She rolled it around in her mind and decided she liked the sound of it. Different. It suited him.

Maxim turned and frowned at his companion. "Jolie, I shall see he doesn't annoy her further. Can you not see she is frightened? It will take but a moment."

The woman huffed and shot Nikki a look of disdain. Trying not to be intimidated by the other woman's sleek elegance, she shrugged and glared back.

What was he doing? Her rescuer strode toward The Professor. The pimp might make his living intimidating and selling women, but he was obviously no match for Maxim, who stood at least four inches taller than the pimp and had shoulders twice as wide. She giggled at the sight of The Professor's shrinking, while Maxim spoke quietly to him.

Although unable to hear what her hero said, she observed the intensity with which it was delivered. Maxim's imposing manner and fists clenched at his sides left no doubt he could—and would—act on any threat he made. A white knight had come to her rescue, but it looked like her hero might be going home with the Wicked Witch of the West. Couldn't have everything, Nikki told herself with a heavy sigh. But just once she'd like to have something... or *someone*.

Maxim strode back to where she waited. "I don't think he will bother you again tonight," he said, while fishing in his inner jacket pocket.

Dumbfounded, she watched as he pulled out a business card and scribbled on the back of it with a gold pen.

"If he does, call me." He thrust the card toward her. "Here, my cell number is on the back."

She took it, feeling her mouth drop open. Was he for real? Was he on drugs?

His companion let out a showy gasp. "Maxim."

Deciding it was time to make a quick exit before she was forced to wipe her feet on a certain mink coat, Nikki shoved the business card into her jeans pocket without taking time to look at it. "Thanks. Guess I'd better get going." Without another word, she took off in a dead run.

Maxim might be a hunk, but the broad hovering at his side was a flat-out bitch. Tempted to look back at him just one more time, she resisted. Okay, so she was afraid she'd see them laughing at her, but so what? Maybe her life was pathetic compared to theirs, but it was her life, and she didn't care to be the butt of their jokes.

Max didn't laugh. He stared after the girl, still stunned by his rash behavior. "Wait here," he ordered his friends, leaving them in a confused huddle as he sprinted to catch up with the tall, willowy blonde who was already halfway down the block. He felt a strange compulsion to ensure she would be all right—at least for the night. He had already formed half a plan, but first he had to catch her. "Wait," he called. "I want to help you."

The runaway came to a dead stop, turned around and stared at him with the widest blue eyes he'd ever seen. Eyes full of distrust. Not that he blamed her.

"Look, get outta my way. Thanks for getting The Professor off my back, but I don't need any more help. Not your kind anyway."

"What do you mean, *my kind*?" A flash of irritation swept over him. Her youth and her beauty were at odds with her cynicism. But then, he supposed her life had been difficult.

"The only kind men down here offer."

Her husky voice made her sound older than she appeared. Just how old was she, and how long had she been on the streets? She was tall and extremely slim. Perhaps she was an addict. "I'm sorry, *mademoiselle*. I meant I could give you a job."

"A job?" Her mouth fell open; her blue eyes widened. "Just what d'you think I can do? I don't know how to do anything." Then giving him an impudent smile, she added, "But I'm getting pretty good at it."

Unable to hold back, he laughed at her saucy response. Unaffected, yet cynical beyond her years. Would she be able to adapt to the world he had in mind? And did he even have the right to ask her to try? No way could he abandon her to the streets. She had too much potential. "I'm sorry. I didn't mean for you to think I was… " He began again, "I own a modeling agency. I think you…"

"A model? Get real. I didn't fall off the truck last night," she laughed, then nailed him with another skeptical stare.

His professional eye found her entrancing. Unforgettable azure eyes, the singular geometry of her face—the camera would love her.

"But, *mademoiselle*, I can help you." He struggled for inspiration. He didn't blame her for not trusting him, but neither could he allow her to run down the street and out of his life. Once again, he noticed how thin she was. "Have dinner with me tomorrow night, somewhere around here so you'll feel safe. A free meal, no strings attached, as they say. You may choose the place."

The blonde appeared to consider his offer, then shrugged. "I don't know. I guess dinner would be okay, maybe, but…"

Frustrated, he threw up his hands. "Are you always this stubborn when someone is trying to help you?" Unbelievable. Why would the skin-and-bones beauty before him actually refuse a meal, much less a serious job offer. "Fine." Disgusted, he turned and walked away.

"Sally's," she called after him.

He stopped and glanced over his shoulder.

She pointed. "Over there, 'cross the street."

He nodded, noting the location of the hand-painted sign. "Seven, tomorrow night?"

She gave him another long, appraising look and nodded. "Yeah, I'll try to be there."

Her desultory response gave him serious doubts he would ever see her again. He fumbled for his wallet and removed a hundred-dollar bill. "Here. Use it for food and lodging... somewhere safe." While he accepted he might never see her again, he found his concern for her safety overwhelming and a trifle baffling. Was it because...?

The girl took the bill, held it up to the light and then, to his great surprise, handed it back to him, shaking her head. "It's too much," she said simply. "A twenty's enough."

Astonished, he insisted, "Please keep it. I want to help you. No conditions, I promise. Besides, you'll need it if you change your mind about meeting me tomorrow night."

Tears formed in her wide blue eyes. He took her hand and placed the bill in it, folding her long, slender fingers around it. A disturbing jolt of sensation hit him. She was just a kid. What was it about her? It was more than her potential as a model. He didn't want to leave her, but he struggled against his surging base instincts. "I have to rejoin my friends now, but if you come to Sally's tomorrow night, we'll talk more. All right?" He resisted the urge to touch her again, forcing his hands into his pockets.

She nodded, but continued to stare at him as if he were from another planet. She'd probably seen little kindness in her young life. Inexplicably he wanted to change that. It was a compulsion he didn't quite understand. In the past, he'd supported charitable causes, but never before had he felt compelled to do anything so personal. *Merde*. He forced himself to admit the truth. The girl was the double of his late wife.

So he left her standing on the street. Whether she would take the money and spend it on drugs or alcohol instead of food and shelter, he had no idea. But given the circumstances, he'd done what he could. Tomorrow, perhaps she would allow him to do more.

He remained thoughtful as he rejoined his friends in front of the small, very off-Broadway theater. Ignoring Jolie, he turned to his friend and attorney, Ned Landry. "What do you think? I'm going to offer her a job."

The lawyer shook his head and gave a wry laugh. "Only you would consider hiring a street kid for your modeling agency." Then shrugging, Ned admitted, "Cleaned up, she'd be pretty enough, but I still think you've lost it."

His date's response was more to the point. "I cannot believe you made such a scene, running after a prostitute."

Taking a deep breath and counting to ten, he turned and faced Jolie. "I don't believe she is a prostitute. She has an air of innocence about her."

"You're a romantic fool, always seeing things in people that aren't there," she said with a sniff, smoothing the lush fur of her mink.

Exactly. What had he seen in Jolie? True, his booking agent was beautiful, sensual and, most of all, persistent, but she lacked the intriguing combination of natural beauty and innocence he'd witnessed moments earlier. "She has quite a unique presence, in spite of her circumstances. I see great potential, and I'm never wrong. She and the agency will prosper together."

"You never sleep with your models," Jolie hissed. "Making an exception in her case?"

"Don't be ridiculous." Jolie had gone too far. "She's too young. She'll need to be guided and groomed carefully."

"You're already in over your head," Ned's wife, Laura, interjected. "However, given the right circumstances, I agree with you…about her potential anyway."

He sketched a bow to Laura, one of the agency's top models until her marriage to his best friend. "*Merci*, for your vote of confidence, *madame*."

Thankfully, further discussion was halted by the arrival of a taxi. Before stepping into the cab, he glanced around, hoping for another glimpse of the bedraggled beauty who, only minutes before, had caused him to brace a pimp in her defense, then chase her down the avenue like a demented Sir Lancelot. Disappointment laced through him. Not a sign of her.

Still, she might meet him at the diner. Hopefully she would—before something bad happened, as it most assuredly would if she stayed on the streets.

He ushered Jolie into the cab. Sliding in beside her, he realized he had no feelings whatsoever for his booking agent and wondered if he'd ever had any.

"Max?" Her whining tone grated on his ear.

"Yes?"

"Do you really mean to turn that homeless person into a model?"

"I do."

"Well, I suppose I was a little rash," she began, patently trying to appease him. "I mean, the agency could probably provide her with something in the way of a living. Maybe some catalog work?"

"Never mind. Time will tell," he said, brushing her off. He was determined…and he was the boss. Next he would call *Maman* and tell her of his plans. He would need his mother's approval. More than her approval, he needed her cooperation if they were to transform his street waif into a supermodel.

The next morning Nikki reached into her pocket and made sure the hundred-dollar bill was still there. That little piece of green paper was a warm reminder that someone gave a damn—enough to see she wouldn't go hungry or freeze to death. She'd never had so much cash...ever. Instead of paying for a room for the night, she'd pulled her jacket tighter and headed for the safest place she knew, St. Anne's Shelter. It turned out that The Professor'd lied. The shelter had room after all.

Par for the course, the director, Sylvia, had encouraged her to call her mother and go home, but Nikki wasn't having any of it. That was the main problem with shelters. The do-gooders always tried to tell her what to do—like go home—and that was the last thing she'd ever do. So later that afternoon, after much discussion about her upcoming dinner plans, the director reluctantly allowed Nikki to take a long, hot shower.

Afterwards she dressed, then ran a comb through her damp hair. It felt good to be squeaky clean for a change. Sylvia had even given her a pale blue sweater to wear. True, it had a couple of small holes, but they weren't visible, as long as she wore her treasured, black leather jacket.

She dug in her jeans pocket and pulled out his business card. His job offer better not be his idea of a sick joke. Yet she remained leery of his true motives. Suspicious? Definitely. But being suspicious had kept her alive, 'til now. More likely, he wanted something else. Why else would a swell guy like him just up and offer to help someone right off the street? Crap. He probably wouldn't even show up, but at least, she was a hundred bucks ahead...and she could make that last a long time.

At seven, Nikki opened the fingerprint-smudged glass door of Sally's Diner. She stepped onto the chipped black and white tiles and took in the evening dinner crowd. At least twenty customers were hunched over their plates, hoovering their dinners. Sally's food was supposed to be pretty good, and she could personally vouch for the quality of their scraps. She glanced around and saw faded pink walls highlighted with touches of graffiti. At least the steel tables and countertops looked clean. Booths, covered in cracked maroon vinyl, ran along the side wall and in front of the window.

What a dump. She really fit in with the rest of the losers.

Then she saw him.

The man named Maxim stood and signaled for her to join him. He wore a black suit, with a black overcoat that almost reached his knees. Taking her time, she walked to the rear booth, checking him out as she did. His face was angular and thin, and he didn't look as if he were a happy man. But he had a hint of a dimple in his strong chin, as if someone had taken a fingertip and lightly touched warm wax.

As she moved closer, she saw crystal green eyes glowing under thick, dark eyebrows. His dark brown hair was brushed behind his ears, but a curling strand had escaped and lightly skimmed his right temple.

His hair made him look romantic, like a knight from a fairy tale. Of course, she was a little too old for make-believe, and there was that wicked witch who could still foul things up. Maybe she'd mixed up her fairy tales with *The Wizard of Oz*, but it didn't matter.

She drank in the sight of her hero as if he were her last drop of water on a hot day. While she walked toward the booth he'd claimed, she felt some curious glances from Sally's patrons. Maybe they wondered what she was doing in the diner and if she had the money to pay for her meal. More likely, they were curious about why the hunk in the back booth was wasting his time with her. So what? She wondered the same damn thing, too.

"*Mademoiselle,* we weren't properly introduced last evening," he said in the silky, accented voice she remembered from the night before. "I'm Maxim Devereaux."

She stared for a moment, unsure how to respond. "Nikki," she said tersely. Then, deciding she sounded rude, added, "...short for Nicole." She extended her hand, the unaccustomed gesture awkward. Jeez. What if he didn't want to touch her?

He took her hand and held it in his strong one, his solemn expression never changing. "I'm sorry we didn't have the opportunity for introductions earlier. Shall we sit?" He gestured to the open booth. "I would like to discuss representing you."

Representing her? What did he mean by that? She jerked her hand from his. "I don't do that kind of thing." Okay, she'd sit down and listen to whatever line he was getting ready to lay on her. Like Mama always said, *If it sounds too good to be true, it probably is.*

"No." He shook his head. "I mean no disrespect. My business is a legitimate one. I gave you my card last night." He pulled the card case from his pocket and removed another card, which read DEVEREAUX AGENCY, Maxim Devereaux, CEO.

Running her fingers over the card, she felt the thick, textured stock on which it had been printed. The engraved lettering felt rich even to her, as uneducated as she was in the finer points of such things.

She shrugged. "I know where I can get a thousand of those printed for twenty bucks. Your fancy card doesn't mean squat to me."

The first hint of a smile came to Devereaux's face. "Of course, but will you stay and dine with me so that we may talk about your future? Surely you understand your life here on the streets is dangerous and limited. I can offer you something better."

"Yeah, right. And all dogs go to heaven, it never rains in Southern California, and the check is in the mail."

"Nikki. May I call you Nikki?" he asked, the corner of his mouth twitching.

"Sure, call me anything you like, just don't call me late for dinner." As soon as the words were out of her mouth, she wanted to crawl under the table. She had this awful tendency to crack jokes whenever she was nervous. Of course, on the streets that nervous habit had saved her butt a time or two.

However, she managed to look him in the eye. His mouth had quirked up on one side, as if maybe, just maybe, he understood how uneasy she felt, right here, right now, with him.

"Please take me seriously. Models are my business, and I think you will earn a great deal of money and my agency as well. But since you are so reluctant to discuss business, shall we have dinner first?"

She gave him a half-hearted smile and nodded. At least, she wouldn't have to go without dinner. In spite of major misgivings, she found herself relaxing in his company. He seemed sincere in his desire to help her. Besides, they were in a public place. She could always leave if he got out of hand. She picked up a grease-spotted menu.

"You should have something substantial," he suggested. "Choose whatever you like."

She'd often fantasized about her all-time favorite meal. Hadn't had anything like it since leaving home. Mama'd been a good cook, no quarrel about that. She eyed the menu; she was in luck. "Roast beef, gravy, mashed potatoes, green beans and rolls," she replied quickly, before he could change his mind. She licked her lips, thinking of an entire meal and all she could eat. Then he smiled again. Damn, she wished he'd stop. It made her nervous—like maybe Nikki was his all-time favorite meal.

A short, heavy-set waitress in a wrinkled, pink uniform took their order, but he ordered just like they were in a big fancy restaurant. At least, that was the way it seemed—so polite and genteel—even the waitress was giggling and batting her eyelashes at him by the time she left to give their order to the cook. Suddenly aware that she and Maxim were alone, she chewed her lip, while her heart turned cartwheels.

"You are a lovely young woman," he said, watching her with his piercing gaze.

She shifted uncomfortably under his gaze and shrugged. "I guess I'm all right."

He smiled at her again and said in an incredulous tone, "You're more than all right. Has no one ever told you before? I can't believe it."

"Just men trying to get me to fuck 'em. I'm still wondering if you're any different."

He blinked. "You haven't decided yet?"

"No." If telling the truth lost her the dinner—tough. She wasn't going to lie. And just because he turned her insides to jelly, she wasn't about to let down her guard either.

"But I am too old for you, Nikki. Besides I don't make it a habit to get involved with my models."

"Really?" She eyed him cynically. "My age doesn't seem to mean much to the men down here."

Her companion's face hardened for an instant, then turned sad. "No," he agreed, "I don't suppose it does."

"How old are you?" She drummed her fingers on the plastic tablecloth and continued to study him closely. "I mean, you don't look all that old to me." She studied him a moment longer, then added, "I'd say you're maybe thirty-five."

His eyes widened at her response. "I'm twenty-eight. I guess my hard life shows." He shrugged, a wry expression crossing his face.

"You don't look it." She snorted, then grinned. "Gotcha."

A smile flashed across his face. "And you? How old are you? Must I guess?"

"I turned sixteen in August," she said, tilting her chin proudly.

"So young," he murmured, frowning. "How long have you been on the streets?"

Her answer was interrupted by the waitress serving their dinners. Once the waitress had left, he asked again, "How long?"

She paused long enough to swallow her first bite of roast beef and replied, "Three months." Too hungry to care about manners, she attacked her plate of food. Sister Mary Luke from school would've been right pissed to see the way her worst pupil was stuffing it down.

Once her hollow belly felt less empty, she stopped and took a deep breath. She watched him while he ate. After a bit, she attempted to copy his precise, polite manners. He chewed with his mouth shut and didn't try to eat it all at once. No elbows on the table, either. She remembered having better manners, but they were a bit rusty. In her world, elbows were good for knocking someone out of the way from the best garbage cans.

He intrigued her, but she tried to hide it. While she ate, she remained undecided about his true motives. She supposed he would show his true colors soon enough. In the meantime, he seemed a little on the quiet side. Maybe he was shy. He'd appeared confident enough on the street when he'd gone after the pimp, but now he was sort of...well, different. His hands looked strong, but manicured. He probably had other people to do his dirty work or whatever passed for dirty work in the modeling biz. His mouth looked gentle and kind, but she'd been on the streets too long to be taken in by looks alone.

"You will need a place to stay," he announced suddenly, pausing in the act of buttering a piece of roll, "until you are old enough to support yourself and live alone."

"Oh, yeah? And just *where* did you have in mind?" A pang of regret sickened her. She'd been right all along. Another letch, just like all the others.

"No, you don't understand." He reached across the table and touched her hand. A decided tingle slithered up her spine and down again.

"I want you to live with my mother, Renée, for the time being. I have already told her about you, and she is willing to accept you as her protégée."

"You want me to live with your mother?" Was he nuts?

He nodded. "*Oui*, I mean, yes. My *maman*—my mother—was a mannequin in Paris, before she founded the agency, but she is retired."

"A mannequin, like in a store window?" Nikki asked, puzzled.

A quick smile crossed his face. "No. In French, mannequin means model. Forgive me, but I still sometimes use the language of my birth. My English is not perfect."

"Well, it's a lot better than mine," she replied quickly, feeling shy. She didn't want the man seated across from her to think she was criticizing him.

"Thank you. I have been in New York only since the fall of last year, and the language is a challenge."

She hesitated, then asked, "Why did you come to New York? Like, Paris is supposed to be one of the most beautiful cities in the world."

"It is true. Paris is my home." He glanced down at his plate for a moment. "But Paris holds too many memories for me—unhappy ones—you understand?"

She rushed to apologize. "I'm sorry. I didn't mean to stick my nose into something private."

"It's all right. My wife died two years ago…a traffic accident in Paris." Her dinner companion's gaze darkened, and he appeared to retreat in time. "After my wife died, my mother retired, and I took over the agency. I often think she retired to keep me from dwelling on my loss." He gave her another of his sad smiles. "Since then, she has devoted herself to caring for my daughter, Alexa."

"You have a kid? Wow." She tried to picture this stylish and elegant man as a father. In spite of her earlier teasing, he really didn't seem that much older than she was. Jeez. Her knight in shining armor was a daddy too. Her fairy tale was getting more screwed up, the more she thought about it.

"Yes, my wife and I married when we were young, but our families had known each other for years. She was very beautiful—tall and blond, a little like you," he added, glancing down at his plate again.

"Was she a model?" Tall and blond? Uh-oh. Now he was getting weird. She continued studying him while he talked. *Just don't let him be some kind of perv.*

"No. Our daughter was only two when my wife died. Alexa doesn't remember her mother, at all—only the photographs."

Tears welled in her eyes as she thought of the young husband and small child. "That must've been awful."

He nodded his agreement. "There were many nights my daughter cried for her *maman*. She was too young to understand." He paused and laid his eating utensils across his plate, his dinner half-eaten.

Poor man. He needed someone to talk to more than he needed a meal... or a new model.

"A year after my wife died, I moved to New York," he continued. "It has proved to be good for the business, but there is still an office in Paris. Things are, as you say here in the US, 'looking up'."

She giggled at his use of American slang. "Yeah."

Soon however, he shifted the focus of the conversation to her. He began questioning her background. "Why are you on the streets? You are so young. Why did you run away from home?"

"No big deal." She kept her response short, not wanting to go into the details. Instead she toyed with the small amount of food remaining on her plate.

"You can tell me," he pressed, his voice encouraging confidence, as he offered her a crooked smile. "I'm not easily shocked."

Sighing, she gazed into his eyes. She chewed her bottom lip for a minute, then let the truth out in a rush. "I didn't like school, so I ditched. When Mama found out, she told me to get a job or get out, but nobody would hire me 'cause I was still fifteen. So, I got out."

"That's terrible. Are you sure your *maman* wasn't using the reverse psychology to encourage you to return to school? She must be very worried."

She bit back a bitter laugh. "Well, I haven't seen my face on any milk cartons, if you know what I mean." Noticing the puzzled look on his face, she hastily explained. "They put pictures of missing kids on milk cartons, signs on buses, stuff like that."

"Yes, I see. I'm sorry." Again he reached across the table and touched her hand. This time, she didn't pull back from his contact. "You must have a very rough time."

"The drug dealers and pimps are the worst part," she admitted, trying to sound nonchalant. "The drug dealers are always trying to get me to work for 'em—the pimps too." She shrugged. An everyday occurrence—no big deal.

"And...have you?"

She didn't take offense. He needed to know, if he was really serious about her living with his mother. She might even be around his little girl. "No, I couldn't."

"Why not?"

She grimaced, then gave a little laugh. "I guess the nuns at school had too great an influence on me. I was afraid of going to Hell."

He chuckled, and a moment later, related one of his own early transgressions in school.

As she listened to his story, she realized she'd never had a boyfriend, and she'd certainly never known anyone like the man sitting in front of her. Excitement and confusion struck her at the same time. She'd grown less wary, and that worried her too. Her survival the last few months had depended, in large measure, on her sense of caution. Now here she was, ready to follow him to the ends of the earth...or at least to his mother's house.

What would it feel like to kiss him? Man, was that a stupid idea. Why on earth would he ever want to kiss her? She was just a kid, and he was the most beautiful man she'd ever seen. Men were supposed to be handsome, but somehow handsome seemed inadequate for Maxim.

His eyes—she couldn't keep from gazing into them. Acting like a deer in a car's headlights, she was, but his eyes were so green and so full of emotion. In spite of his self-deprecating laughter, she sensed the pain behind those green depths.

Pain she understood—but there was something mysterious, something he held back.

"Nikki?"

"Yeah," she whispered. She'd been so involved in staring into his eyes she'd forgotten to breathe. Her face grew warm. "I was gawking, wasn't I?"

"A bit," he admitted, shifting about on his side of the booth. "Are you finished? Do you want more to eat?"

She looked at her plate. It was empty. Had she eaten it all? Where had the time gone? "No. I'm full, really. First time in a long time too," she added, smiling.

"I'm glad." He returned her smile with one of his own.

That one smile undid her completely. The sight of his curving lips exposing his even, white teeth sent her heart rate soaring into outer space. She hoped he couldn't see it pounding through her sweater.

He motioned for the waitress to bring the check. All too soon, it was over. In another minute, the safety of Sally's Diner would be a memory. She'd be alone with him—for the first time.

Excited. Scared silly. What if he really was like all the other men and what he really wanted was a quick grope? What if it was all a dream? She did *not* want to wake up.

He stood. "Shall we go?"

Nikki stood on legs that promptly refused to support her. Her stomach grew queasy, probably from an unaccustomed full meal. The room spun, and she grabbed the table for support. He reached out and caught her before she could fall, easing her back into the booth. Being in his arms made her heart start to race all over again. Jeez. She really needed to get a hold of herself.

"Are you all right?"

From a distance, she could hear the concern in his voice. What was the matter with her anyway? She wasn't the fainting type. "I'm fine. Just got dizzy." Panicked was more like it. "Really, I'm okay now. It's gone," she reassured him.

"I'll hail the taxi, then I'm taking you home." He hesitated for a moment, then asked her, "Will you be all right, if I leave you...just for a second?"

Nodding, she didn't trust herself to speak. He was going to dump her after all. He was going to hail a cab and take off. She'd ruined everything with her dizzy spell. She watched him leave the diner and hail the cab. She held her breath. The taxi pulled up to the curb and stopped. He spoke to the driver for a moment, then turned...

Thank Heaven. She heaved a loud sigh. He was coming back for her.

Various patrons in the diner turned their heads and stared as Maxim led her from the diner. This time, she felt like a princess walking beside her handsome prince. Outside, he opened the door of the taxi and slid in beside her.

Moment of truth time. What would he do? He stayed on his side of the taxi. How did she feel? Surprise. Relief. Disappointed? She continued watching him, but he stared out the window, apparently deep in thought. Maybe he already regretted his generosity. Ha. She guessed it wasn't every day he picked up a girl out of the gutter and took her home to his mother.

The driver maneuvered the taxi through the busy streets—for miles and miles it seemed. The grungy streets gave way to ethnic neighborhoods, then to upscale, expensive townhouses in the East Sixties.

Without warning, Max turned to her and asked, "Your dizzy spell? Could you be *enceinte*?"

"What?" she asked puzzled by the word.

"Having a baby?"

Mortified, she responded with a definite, resounding "No!"

"Are you sure? I need to know the truth," he insisted. "It would affect the timeline of our plans."

"Very sure." She'd never been with a man that way. Her face burned with embarrassment and anger. Unable to bear his seeing her humiliation, she turned away from his piercing gaze.

"I... I'm sorry. I didn't mean to judge you. I needed to know," he finished in a flat tone.

"So now you know." She kept her gaze averted and stared out the window.

"Now I know."

Hearing the forlorn note in his voice, she turned back and saw the abashed expression on his handsome face. "'S'all right." She shrugged and offered him a smile.

"You're very forgiving." He took her hand and patted the back of it. "Thank you. I was rude to ask."

"Uh, anytime," she managed. She stared at the hand he'd patted— her hand. She relished the soft warmth of his strong hand against hers. And that warmth spread up her arm to her heart, which revved into overdrive for the umpteenth time that night. She looked from her hand to his face. One corner of his mouth had kicked up. Damn. He was staring at her again with those gorgeous green eyes of his. If she died on the spot, she doubted she'd ever have a happier moment. But she didn't want to die on the spot. She wanted to make him proud of her.

"Nikki." The sound of his soft voice brought her back to reality. "We're here."

Looking up at the three-story, brick townhouse with tall windows, her chin dropped. The entrance was well lit and welcoming. Although the sky was dark, she could see there were other houses, just as fine, on each side. It had to be a dream, and if she didn't wake up real soon, she was going to live in the most magnificent place she'd ever seen with the most beautiful man in the world.

She let out a sigh. "Oh, my."

Two

"*Mon Dieu.*" Renée Devereaux paced the foyer of her townhouse. "Maxim must be out of his mind. What is taking him so long?"

Patience had never been one of her virtues. And taking a street urchin and turning her into a model would be a formidable task, possibly requiring more patience than she had. And he expected her to do it—just like that with a snap of the fingers. He must think her a magician. And nothing would do but for the girl to live right here, in her very own house, alongside his daughter. What kind of person was this girl anyway? It wasn't like her son to be this rash and impulsive. The runaway must have something special; otherwise, he would not expect such a great accommodation from his family.

Ah well, her questions would soon be answered, but it didn't make the waiting any easier. Her son had been through so much in the last two years—first, Solange's death, then the police and the rumors.

By good fortune, The Devereaux Agency had thrived in New York. The rumors followed, naturally, but in New York, they only added to her son's mystique. The Americans did love bad boys. Never, not for one moment, had she believed her son had arranged his wife's death. But as long as people thought he was guilty, it made little difference.

She heard the squeal of tires and rushed to the door and held her breath while she watched her son exit the cab. He turned and held his hand to… "*Mon Dieu,*" she gasped. The girl had taken his helping hand from the cab and now stood staring up at the house. The street lights permitted enough illumination to see the look of wonder on the runaway's lovely face. The girl was tall, blond and very young. Yes, indeed, Maxim had been correct. This girl had something very special—a more than passing resemblance to poor, dead Solange.

What was he thinking? Was he trying to re-create her in the form of this child? Her uneasiness mounted as she watched them ascend the steps, her son's face unreadable. Whatever her son felt, he hid it adeptly.

She opened the door. "Welcome," she said with forced enthusiasm.

Maxim allowed the girl to enter before him. "*Merci,*" he said, giving Renée a quick kiss on both cheeks. He began the introductions. "*Maman,* this is Nikki. Nikki, my mother, *Madame* Devereaux."

She reached to take the teenager's hand in greeting and gave it a squeeze. "I'm very happy to meet you. I've heard so much about you from my son." She raised an eyebrow in his direction. A faint wink was his only response. Cheeky youngster.

"I'm very pleased to make your acquaintance, Ma'am," Nikki responded awkwardly, but correctly. The girl continued to look about in apparent awe of her new surroundings.

Nikki's eyes were the clearest blue Renée had ever seen. Up close, she could see the subtle differences between the girl and her son's late wife, but the basic facial architecture was quite similar. Same square face, slightly short chin, fabulous cheekbones, but Nikki's nose was more refined.

Her heart filled with conflicting emotions. Dear heaven, what was she to do with this child? If it weren't for the ragged clothes, she would never have taken Nikki for a homeless person. With her cloud of blond hair, she looked like an angel. Appearances could be deceiving, yet as she gazed into the girl's sky blue eyes, Renée inexplicably sensed innocence. Her maternal instincts warred with her usually logical disposition. Intuition, perhaps?

"I must go," Maxim said as he leaned over to kiss Renée on both cheeks. "I have an early meeting for which I must still prepare. The two of you will be all right?" he asked, raising an eyebrow.

"*Oui*." She nodded, then turned to Nikki. "We will be fine, no?"

The girl's gaze widened, as she cast an apprehensive glance toward Maxim and chewed her bottom lip, then finally an uncertain smile. "Yeah, we'll be fine."

Nikki stood at the beveled glass door and stared at Maxim's retreating back, a sense of desertion overwhelming her. What if his mother didn't like her? Why should a woman who'd never laid eyes on her give her the time of day, when her own mother had kicked her out? She turned to the tall, slender woman. "Where's he going? When will he be back?"

Max's mother ran a graceful hand through her short, red hair, then smiled. She took Nikki by the hand. "He's going home, but he'll be here Saturday to spend the day with his daughter."

"He doesn't live here?" Somehow, she'd just assumed...

"No, my granddaughter lives with me," she explained, "but Maxim is a man. He needs his privacy. Besides, he's very involved in running the business here in New York, so I am quite happy to have my granddaughter with me all the time. I am a widow, and I would be alone if not for Alexa."

"May I see her?" Nikki asked, her curiosity aroused. "His little girl, I mean?"

"Not tonight. She's in bed asleep." The older woman patted Nikki's shoulder. "Tomorrow morning will be soon enough. You both need your rest. And you have a very big day ahead."

Maxim's mother guided Nikki upstairs to a room she could only describe as Heaven. The walls were covered in a blue and white fabric. Reaching out, she touched the wall. To her amazement, it was soft. "Wow. It's padded."

"Yes."

"I'm used to wallpaper falling off at the seams. Never seen padded walls before, for Pete's sake." The windows were hung with the same material, as was the tall, old-fashioned bed. Taking a deep breath, she tried to tell herself it wasn't a dream. She almost pinched her arm, just to make sure.

She ran to one of the two tall windows and looked down into the small courtyard at the rear of the house. "Oh," was all she could say. She'd never seen anything like it before in her entire life. The tiny garden, lit by old-fashioned streetlights, was a jewel of emerald green in a city best known for its traffic and skyscrapers.

Between the two windows stood a tall, carved chest topped with dried flowers arranged in an old, woven basket. "This is my room?" she asked, still unable to believe her good luck. Maybe fairy tales did come true. If they did, Maxim's mother was her fairy godmother, for sure.

"But, of course. And you have your own bath," the elegant woman replied, gesturing to the door on the right wall. "And there in the armoire," she added with another graceful gesture, "are nightgowns in the drawer on the left side. My room is at the end of the hall if you need anything."

A bewildering combination of gratitude and shyness gripped Nikki as she stood in front of the lovely Frenchwoman. "I don't know what to say, except, 'Thank you.' No one has ever done anything like this for me. But y-you don't have to worry. I'm not a thief. I promise. I ran away from home, but I never did anything bad. Honest." Almost honest, if she were truthful. She had stolen once or twice, but only to survive, and she would never do anything like that again. Never.

Suddenly it was important that this woman believe her. No, it was more than important. She craved Renée Devereaux's approval. After all, her entire future rested in the hands of this one woman. Tears welled up in her eyes at the thought of being rejected again.

"My poor child, you have had a difficult time, no?" She pulled Nikki to her breast and hugged her.

The hot tears stung Nikki's eyes and spilled down her cheeks. No one had hugged her in years. Overwhelmed, she inhaled the clean, flowery scent of the older woman's perfume.

She pulled away, hurriedly wiping the tell-tale tears from her face. "Sorry. I'm messing up your blouse." Here she was, blubbering like a baby. On the streets, tears were a luxury and dangerous...and a sign of weakness.

"Now, now. No harm done. Dry your tears. Your bathroom is there." Renée motioned again to the door on the right. "I think you will find everything you need."

"Thank you." Awkwardness consumed her. Renée? Mrs. Devereaux? *Madame* Devereaux? Summoning her courage, she blurted, "What should I call you?"

The Frenchwoman pursed her lips, appeared to think for a moment, then smiled. "I think Madame Devereaux is much too formal. If you wish, you may call me Renée or *Maman*. Yes, I would like it if you would call me *Maman*. I never had a daughter, only a son." Her next words came in a rush. "Of course, I do not mean to take the place of your real mother."

"My real mother kicked me out." Nikki raised her chin a notch. "She doesn't have a place."

"You may wish to reconsider someday, but for now, I will be whatever you need." She hugged Nikki again. "Now, off you go. Get ready for bed. You have had a very big day, no?"

Nikki nodded. "A very big day, yes."

Max slammed the door to his apartment. All the way home, he'd tried to shut out the confused rush of memories of his dead wife. He knew what his mother must think. He'd wanted to reassure her he wasn't confusing Nikki with Solange, but the girl's presence had made that impossible.

Hell. Perhaps he *had* confused the two women.

No. The resemblance—it was a coincidence, nothing more. Nikki was simply a beautiful product for his agency. And that was all.

He pulled off his jacket and threw it across the leather sofa. Striding over to the bar, he poured himself a double shot of vodka. He tossed back the contents and gasped as the one-hundred-proof alcohol burned its way down his throat and exploded in his stomach like a stick of TNT.

He poured another, then walked to the sofa and sat while he considered what he should do next. His sudden fascination with the young runaway worried him. He knew what he must do—he must stay away from her. She was a child—a minor, for pity's sake. Sixteen, but still... What was the appalling, American term for it? Jail bait.

The sight of her shy, yet knowing, face, so like Solange, disturbed him on a primal level. Of course, he felt protective—nothing wrong in that—but the flickering of desire, that was something else. He actually longed to touch her, claim her. What kind of perverted creature was he to be attracted to a girl as young as Nikki? It had to be her resemblance to Solange. It was difficult to suppress his old feelings for his wife when he looked at a younger—and very alive—version. Yes, that was it.

At that moment his stiffened his resolve, vowing he would guide her career from a distance—like any other of his agency's models. His mother would make the perfect mentor and buffer. Never again would he allow passion to rule his life. Never again would he suffer the loss and pain of another betrayal.

Time passed, and the alcohol took effect. Warmth crept through his body and eased the tension he'd felt since he'd first seen Nikki on the street. A chance meeting and the runaway's life would never be the same. Would his?

Inevitably, his thoughts turned back to the horrible night Solange died.

After treating herself to a bubble bath in the white-tiled bathroom, Nikki washed her hair again. She inhaled the berry-scented shampoo—no more of that strong stuff from the shelter for this girl. After drying with the thickest towel she'd ever seen, she changed into a soft, pale blue nightgown, then left her new bedroom and floated down the hall to Renée's door. She gave a tentative tap.

Maman opened the door, wearing a long, black negligée. "Ah, there you are. I was waiting for you. I see you found everything."

Nikki nodded. "I… I wanted to say good-night…uh, and thank you for being so good to me. I won't let you down."

"First of all, I am glad I have a place for you. Second, I trust my son's judgment. He has offered you a tremendous opportunity—something he has never done before. I am sure you will not disappoint either one of us." She wrapped an arm around Nikki's shoulder. "Now, off to bed with you. I shall see you in the morning."

Once back in her bedroom, Nikki hugged herself in wonder. In a matter of hours, her life had turned into a fairy tale, and this time she was the fairy princess. She swirled around the room and glimpsed her reflection in the long mirror. In the billowy, soft nightgown, she even looked like a princess. Content for the first time in her life, she climbed into the bed, pulled the comforter to her chin, and sighed. It looked like mama was wrong about things being too good to be true. That night she dreamt of a French palace and a handsome green-eyed soldier.

***

Nicole swished down the long, mirrored hall of the royal palace at Versailles. She looked over her shoulder, fearing someone might stop her. She hurried past the green marble pilasters, carved in the Corinthian style, which lined the magnificent room. The walls were pierced by tall, arched windows, alternating with arched mirrors, but she had more important matters on her mind than palace architecture.

A certain royal guard was the reason for her haste. And he was a magnificent specimen of manhood. Poor, dead Papa would be calling out the lieutenant for a duel if he weren't already gone from the Earth. Indeed Papa would not rest easy if he but knew she was to meet a gentleman without a proper chaperone. A scandal, but in the court of Louis XVI, such things occurred all around her. Luckily Mama had no idea of the things her daughter saw every day.

She caught a glimpse of her reflection in the large mirrors as she sped past them. She stopped in her tracks before one of them to preen, thankful it was no longer necessary to wear the stiff corsets and wide panniers or the elaborate wigs and makeup. Such formal trappings were now worn only on Royal Sundays. Her blond hair curled attractively around her face and hung in soft natural waves to her shoulders. The bodice of her white lawn dress had been cut to show her neck and bosom to their best advantage. The skirt swept nearly to the floor, skimming the tops of her kid-leather shoes. More than pleased with the image she presented, she smiled at her reflection, then set off again. The lieutenant would think her irresistible.

At court for a mere three weeks, she had been elated by her *Tante* Renée's invitation to attend her at the royal court; Mama was not. However, Mama had been beholden to her aunt on other occasions and felt to refuse her would not be politic. Besides, her aunt was a great favorite of the Queen, and any influence, no matter how obtained, was prized, not scorned. Even Mama accepted that fact of life.

Five minutes later, she reached the formal rear gardens. She looked around for her lieutenant, but not seeing him, she contented herself with wandering amongst the flowers and fanning her warm cheeks with an ivory fan.

Mon Dieu. But it was hot. The flowers put forth so many wonderful scents, it was difficult to tell which fragrance was her favorite. The many varieties of roses were at their peak, and they all vied for her attention as she walked past. Occasionally, she stopped to bury her nose in their gossamer petals, like a butterfly after their sweet nectar.

Quick steps clicking on the brickwork walk made her turn. She smiled at the sight of her lieutenant hastening toward her. She gave him a petulant smile, warning him of her displeasure with his tardiness.

"*Mademoiselle*, I must apologize for keeping you waiting. I was held up by my captain. It could not be avoided."

She knew she shouldn't forgive him so easily, but he was so handsome, it was difficult to breathe, much less pout effectively. Still she tried, tapping her fan in her gloved palm. "Lieutenant, I had all but given you up, but since you are finally here, I suppose we might walk a while in these lovely gardens."

"Pardon, *mademoiselle*, I would never have kept someone as lovely as you waiting without good cause."

His face assumed an expression so intense it nearly made her lose her breath. Perhaps it was the July heat—no, it was the young officer himself. After all, he did possess the loveliest jade eyes she had ever seen. While she debated on her response, the misery in his face became so apparent, she relented. Any moment now, he would be dropping to his knees, begging her forgiveness. And she couldn't have that.

"Your tardiness must not be repeated, Lieutenant Du Mont. I fear I would have to turn my attentions elsewhere, to some other more punctual companion." She opened her fan with a snap, then gave him her most coquettish smile over its pierced-ivory design. "I forgive you this time."

"*Merci, mademoiselle. Merci.* Then may I have the honor of accompanying you to view the fountains?"

"*Certainement.*"

Duly chastened and forgiven, the officer offered her his arm. She placed her dainty gloved hand on his well-muscled forearm, relishing the strength of it. Indeed, merely touching him made her feel quite giddy.

Together they walked about the garden; her reserved companion fell silent. She, however, had no problem maintaining the flow of conversation, prattling about the fountains, the flowers and the greenery. "This is so inspiring, Lieutenant Du Mont. It is difficult to believe gardens this beautiful exist at all. I never dreamed I would ever see anything so magnificent."

"*Oui, mademoiselle*, it is a very beautiful place," he said, smiling down at her. "Made more beautiful only by your charming presence."

She fluttered her eyelashes and gave him her sweetest smile. "*Merci*, Lieutenant."

After they toured the gardens for thirty minutes, he halted and took her hand in his. "*Mademoiselle*, my presence is required in my barracks shortly. May I escort you to your suite?"

She nodded. "*Mais oui.*"

At the door of her aunt's suite, he stopped, clicked his heels together. Bowing, he took her hand in his. "*Mademoiselle*, I shall always treasure the memory of this day."

"It was most enjoyable, Lieutenant du Mont."

"It is my fervent hope you will save a dance for me at the upcoming masked ball, *mademoiselle?*"

"*Bien sûr*, Lieutenant." Quite intelligent of him to reserve his dance early. After all, she had every intention of being the belle of the masked ball.

The young guard bowed over her hand and brushed his lips across the back of it. He pivoted on his heel and cast one last, longing glance over his shoulder. He straightened his back and marched away, his footsteps echoing against the marble floor.

She entered her aunt's suite and leaned against the door. Fanning her face briskly, she tried to calm the rapid beating of her heart. The tall, handsome officer was quite enthralling, and if she allowed it, she could easily fall in love with the dashing royal guard. Already there had already been two frantic missives from poor Mama, filled with an abundance of admonitions. She did not trust her daughter's ability to form the right associations or make the correct decisions. Well, Mama would discover her daughter knew exactly what she was doing.

With the connections and assistance of her aunt, she would make a good marriage. Living a meager life in the country as someone's poor relation didn't suit her one single bit. A count or a duke would do quite nicely. While it was true the lieutenant was extremely handsome and a royal guard, he did not have a title which would assure her a comfortable life. She could, however, practice her wiles on him, and no doubt, his would be the first of many hearts she would break.

Trying to forget about his green eyes, she decided his older brother Henri, *le Comte* Du Mont, would be a more suitable choice. The royal court had moved to Versailles only two days earlier, and a masked fête had already been planned for five nights hence. Perhaps the occasion would provide the perfect opportunity for her introduction to his older brother. Perhaps Henri would prove as companionable and exciting as his younger brother. And maybe his eyes would be just as fine. *Mon Dieu*. Henri might be even more handsome.

Later that evening, a gaily wrapped parcel was delivered to her quarters. She pounced on the package, tearing off the covering in great haste. "Aunt, look. A mask." Nicole withdrew the white, gold-trimmed mask; there was an arrangement of blue feathers positioned on each side of it. Picking up the mask by its ivory wand, she held it to her face, then rushed to the nearest mirror and posed, turning her head first one way, then the other. "It is beautiful. The blue feathers accent my eyes, no?" she asked.

Her aunt let out an indignant huff. "Who would presume to send you a personal gift? You must return it at once."

"Lieutenant Du Mont has honored me with a token of his esteem," she replied saucily, placing her hands on her hips. "I will not offend him or his family by returning it."

Her aunt took a deep breath and reiterated, "You and your family are the ones who should be offended. He has overstepped the bounds of propriety. A young lady may not accept a personal gift from a gentleman, unless they are affianced."

Nicole stamped her foot. "No. I think it lovely, and I will not return it, no matter what you say."

"I forbid you to wear this mask, and if you persist in this heedless manner, you shall not attend the ball."

"You will have to keep me under lock and key if you think to keep me from going." Nicole stamped her foot. Unbelievable. This old woman was trying to ruin her life.

Renée drew herself up to her full height and shouted, "That can be arranged."

Her aunt's tone made Nicole stop and reconsider. Perhaps she had better make an attempt to placate her aunt, who after all had power over her. "Now, now," she began. "If I promise to return the gift, may I at least do so in person? The lieutenant is from an honorable family, and he has a right to know why I may not accept his lovely gift."

"And when were you introduced to him, pray? I do not remember him ever presenting himself to me as he should have."

Nicole thought for a moment. "Surely, *Tante* Renée, you remember? He was a guest at Honoré DuPre's salon only last week. He is very well thought of, I am told. He is a member of His Majesty's Royal Guard, after all."

A puzzled expression crossed her aunt's face. Nicole hoped a slight exaggeration of the truth would suffice to eliminate her aunt's misgivings.

"Well, there were so many at the salon, how can I be expected to remember every young officer?" Renée frowned. "Was he short and rather rotund with a washed-out coloring?"

"No, he is tall, very muscular, and he has beautiful green eyes that seem to change with his mood—sometimes gray, sometimes crystal green, sometimes dark as emeralds," she murmured.

Her aunt's sudden scowl told Nicole she had gone too far in praising her young Lieutenant.

"Yes, I remember him. He has no inheritance, you silly girl. He is a second son," her aunt replied, her tone exasperated.

"But he has an older brother, does he not? The one with the title, no?"

"*Mon Dieu.* I refuse to discuss it further. Return the mask and forget about both of the Du Mont brothers. Maxime Du Mont has no money or lands. *Le Comte* Du Mont is not suitable, either."

"He has a title and lands, so he must be suitable," Nicole insisted.

"No, he is not, and never mind why." Her aunt turned, gathered her voluminous skirts in hand and swished from the room.

Nicole turned to her mirror once again, raised her chin a notch and vowed, "I *will* wear this mask to the ball."

Three

Nikki awakened with a start. Confused by the lingering vision of massive palace gardens , she looked around, then gave a contented sigh. She was safe—and in a comfortable, clean bed. As she watched the bright morning sun streaming through the sparkling windows, she felt a big smile spread across her face. She allowed her gaze to travel around the room, taking in all the details. Never in her wildest dreams, had she ever expected to live in a place like this.

Like a cat, she yawned and stretched, luxuriating in the feel of fresh bed linens and the flowery fragrance pervading her room. "Now this is more like it. I don't miss the stink of garbage at all."

A soft rap sounded on her bedroom door.

"Nikki?" came Renée's soft voice.

"Yikes." She jumped from the bed and raced for the door. Breathless with excitement, she flung it open. "Yes, ma'am."

Renée Devereaux stood in the doorway, wearing a tailored, beige suit and a wide smile. "We have a lot to do today, *Mademoiselle* Nikki."

"I'm ready for anything." Nikki was way too excited, but she couldn't help it. "Move over, Cinderella."

Her mentor chuckled. "Shopping first, then we'll see Michel. He's the best hairstylist in the city. That should take most of our morning. But first, I shall find something for you to wear. I warn you. You probably won't like it. The style will be much too old for you, but it can't be helped."

"Sorry to be so much trouble."

"It will not be trouble. It will be fun. I do not know when I have felt such exhilaration. It will be like having a daughter again." A sad, but fleeting, expression crossed Renée's face.

"I'm sorry about your daughter-in-law. Ma—Mr. Devereaux told me she died."

"*Oui*, it was a great tragedy." Her expression grew troubled. "But we must not look back. We cannot change the past, but we may look to the future even if we do not know what it holds." Then her expression lightened. "But I am sure your future is going to be very bright."

"I hope you're right." Self-doubt washed through Nikki. What if she couldn't live up to Maxim and his mother's expectations? Her entire future depended on them. Her life.

"You will be fine. Do not worry," Renée said. "First things first. Coffee and croissants for breakfast or a bagel, if you wish. You will find a robe in the armoire, then come downstairs to breakfast. We'll find you something to wear afterwards. *Hein*?"

"Yes, thank you."

After Renée left, Nikki flew to the tall, ornate chest and opened one of the doors. Inside she found exactly what she needed, a white terry cloth robe. She stroked the robe's sleeve and marveled at its thick texture. She'd certainly never seen a bathrobe so thick. Jerking the garment off the hanger, she pulled it on and rushed downstairs, ready for day one of her new life.

Renée leaned over and picked up her drowsy granddaughter, then carried her downstairs to the comfortable French-country kitchen.

"*Grandmère*, 'ongry," the four-year-old murmured, snuggling in a sleepy bundle against Renée's chest.

"Alexa, we have company. Her name is Nikki, and she's going to live with us while she learns to be a model." Although she and her son often dropped into French when they were alone, most of the time she spoke to her grandchild in English. Alexa would grow up in America. The more her granddaughter heard English spoken, the more natural it would be for her to speak.

Alexa reached up and patted Renée's face. "Nee-kee? Want to see Nee-kee."

She walked into the kitchen, resting Alexa on her hip. Nikki sat on a stool pulled up to the butcher block counter. She looked up at Renée and grinned. "These—uh, rolls are to die for."

Amused, she watched Nikki lick the butter from her fingers. "They're called croissants," she said, emphasizing the French pronunciation.

"Crah-sans?" The girl attempted to imitate Renée's accent. "I don't think I can twist my tongue around that word the way you do, but whatever they're called, I love 'em."

Renée nodded and laughed, agreeing, "You'll soon learn." While her new houseguest seemed quite inexperienced and innocent, her naïveté was fresh and quite charming. Although she might resemble Solange, there were no similarities in their personalities. She set Alexa on the floor and turned to pour a cup of coffee.

"Pick me up, please." Renée heard the child demand. Surprised, she turned and saw the four-year-old holding her arms up to an equally shocked Nikki. The runaway grinned and complied by bending over and picking up the insistent little girl. "Here you go, sweetheart." Nikki offered the child a piece of buttered croissant. "Want a bite?"

Then Alexa stunned her grandmother by gazing up at Nikki with a loving expression. "I missed you," the child murmured and snuggled close.

Renée swallowed, then blinked furiously, attempting to hold back the tears. Somewhere, locked deep in her subconscious, Alexa must have retained memories of her mother.

Nikki's eyes widened and her chin dropped. "She thinks I'm her...you know?"

Renée shrugged. "Perhaps a little. You are very similar in appearance." She bent down to her granddaughter's level. "*Ma petite*, this is Nikki. She's going to stay with us and be a model for your Papa's agency."

Alexa nodded. "Nee-kee. I love Nee-kee, *Grandmère*." The child stifled a yawn, then snatched the proffered bite of croissant from Nikki's hand, squealing as she did. Butter dripped down the child's chin onto her nightgown. Undaunted, the she swiped the back of her hand across her mouth, smearing butter over her chubby cheeks.

Nikki grabbed a soft, linen napkin and wiped the tyke's mouth. "Here, you're gonna be a mess if you're not careful."

The child giggled and reached for another bite of the flaky pastry.

"I think she likes you, Nikki. I've never seen her warm up to anyone so quickly." Nor did her son, as a rule, invite strangers off the street into her home. But both he and his child apparently felt an immediate connection with the beautiful waif—as did she. Was it merely the resemblance or something more?

Initially on hearing her son's plan, she had been skeptical—very skeptical—but difficult as it was to understand, Nikki had won her over quickly.

The teenager gave the little girl a quick hug then brushed the curls back from her forehead. "She's so cuddly. I've never been 'round kids much. Never had a little sister or brother."

"Well, she's certainly seems comfortable with you." Renée sat, studying the cup of coffee in front of her. "Now we have a great deal to accomplish today."

"Yes, ma'am."

The runaway nodded and shoved half a croissant into her mouth. Renée watched while Nikki chewed and smiled at the same time with apparent pleasure. What were they going to do with this young woman? Besides assisting her in her early career, what else did her son have in mind? For once, she wished she could foretell the future. This was no ordinary girl—no indeed. She was a runaway with a mother who must be consulted, no matter what the girl wanted.

***

By the time Nikki and Renée reached Michel's salon, Nikki had degenerated into a bundle of nerves. She balked at the front door, shaking in her borrowed shoes. She just knew the world-famous hair stylist would throw up his hands and declare nothing could be done with her. He might even throw her out of his shop. Oh, God, she'd never get to be a model if he did.

"Don't worry. Michel is an old friend of mine from Paris."

Warily, she cut her gaze to Renée's. "Uh, didn't know you read minds."

Her new mentor merely laughed—a merry, tinkling sound. "You are not the first young woman I have taken for her first styling. Most girls are a little nervous."

"Wh-what if he…"

"Never fear, he will be enchanted by your youth and unspoiled beauty."

Nikki felt a gentle nudge in the middle of her back. "Let us go, *Chèrie*. The one thing we must *not* do is keep Michel waiting."

"Right."

Out of breath, the hairdresser Michel rushed into Nikki's private cubicle where she'd been waiting for what seemed like hours. The dapper little man ran his fingers through her hair, testing the weight of it and announced, "Virgin!"

"Wh-what?" she asked, looking for somewhere to hide. How did he know?

"Virgin hair, *ma chère*. Never colored, never permed either, *n'est-ce pas?*"

"Uh, no. My mama always said it was a waste of time." Nes pah? What the heck did that mean? Guess she'd have to bone up on her French.

In no time at all, she and Michel were joined by a shampoo girl and a colorist.

"First, the shampoo, then the cut—which I will do myself as a favor to Mme. Devereaux," Michel said, smiling and bowing in Renée's direction. "But no color," he declared, waving the colorist away. "Her hair is quite fair. We won't change it—at least not today."

Hours later, Nikki walked along the busy city streets with Renée. She couldn't believe the difference in the way she looked…or felt. She stopped to gaze at her reflection in the window of an antique store and wished her mother could see her now. But her reflection didn't hold her interest, not when there were so many lovely things inside the shop. "Can we?" she asked. "I've never been in an antique store before." Shifting her bundles from one hand to the other, she hoped Renée would agree.

"Of course, but for a few minutes only. I think we have shopped until I am ready to do the drop."

She grinned at the older woman's mangled slang. "We have, haven't we?"

She grasped the shiny, brass door knob, opened the door and bounded into the antique store. She inhaled the musty smell of old things, but she didn't care if they were old. In awe, she wandered through room after room. Everything caught her eye—from furniture to antique post cards. She ran her hand across the satiny surface of an ornately carved table, the oak so aged, it appeared black. The table legs had fat, bulbous protrusions covered in carvings of leaves. "I've never seen anything like it. So much stuff."

"You don't have to see everything today. You may come back as often as you wish."

Nikki took in Renée's tired expression and felt guilty, selfish even. "I guess that's a hint."

"Well, it is late. We have had a very long day."

"All right. Just let me see what's in this box." She opened it and handled the objects carefully; some seemed quite fragile. "Look. It's a mask. Like one of those theater masks, the sad and happy faces. Y'know what I mean?" She pulled out a smiling mask.

"Yes, the masks of comedy and tragedy."

She continued her rummaging. "Wait, I want to see if the other one is here too." She picked up the next object. "I found it." She held up the tragic partner to the first. Realizing she didn't have a penny to her name, she quickly set the masks down.

"Do you not wish to purchase them?" Renée asked.

She shrugged. "Sure. Like when I get my first paycheck—if I ever get one, that is."

"They are not very expensive. We shall bargain with the dealer for them."

"Oh, no. You've done so much already. I don't want to take advantage."

"It will be my gift to you."

Hesitating, she chewed her bottom lip." She really wanted the masks, but... "You've already done so much.

"It's settled." Her mentor took the masks and walked to the front of the store.

What else could a future supermodel do? She followed, restraining her desire to skip like a nine-year-old kid. After all, did supermodels skip? Not that she was one—or ever would be—but maybe it wouldn't hurt to act a little more dignified once in a while.

At the front of the store, a short and slightly round man stood smiling at them. She tried to think just who he reminded her of—someone she'd seen on television.

He bowed over Renée's extended hand. "Ah, *Madame* Devereaux, you have made a very wise choice. Masks are very collectible, but still relatively inexpensive."

"*Bonjour, Monsieur*. Bonpland. The masks are for my young friend, Nikki."

The antique dealer raised his eyebrows and smiled. "*Mademoiselle* Nikki, you collect the masks? You should only collect them, never wear them. You are much too beautiful to hide behind one."

"Yes, thank you." It occurred to her she did collect masks, even if these were the first in her collection. "Yes, I do."

"I am sure, *M'sieur*, that we may come to agreeable terms for these two masks?"

"*Madame*, of course. The bargaining is the best part of the buying, no?"

Renée agreed, "But of course," then offered, "one hundred."

Nikki gasped. A hundred dollars for a couple of masks? After all the money Renée had spent on her today with the makeover and clothes.

The dealer pursed his lips and held the masks up for closer inspection. "But, *madame*, look at the fine workmanship. The masks are in mint condition. I could, perhaps, allow them to go for... say, two hundred?"

Nikki couldn't swallow. "That's too much. I don't need them now. I can wait."

The dealer gave Nikki an appraising glance, then shrugged. "You drive the hard bargain, *mademoiselle*. For you, because I see how badly you want them, and because I have the soft heart for the young lady—one hundred fifty."

"No, sorry. Still too much." Nikki swallowed her disappointment and shook her head.

"You have a deal, M. Bonpland," Renée agreed, ending Nikki's torment.

The antique dealer's face broke into a wide smile. "But of course, *madame*." He tapped his temple. "The gray cells told me you would buy the masks for the beautiful young lady."

"Thank you." She couldn't help but grin; she couldn't ever remember having such a wonderful day. And surely no one else knew an antique dealer who looked like Hercules Poirot.

"You are welcome, my child." Renée turned to the dealer. "And now, I am going to take the young lady home before she finds something else she must have—something you will no doubt wish to bargain away—eh, *monsieur*?"

The dealer hung his head as if ashamed, then smiled. "*Madame*, you know me too well." He quickly wrapped the masks and handed them to Nikki. "Will you be able to manage all those packages, *mademoiselle*?"

"*Oui, Monsieur* Bonpland," Nikki replied, attempting a French accent.

The antique dealer smiled. "*Charmante, madame, n'est-ce pas?*"

"*Oui, trés charmante, Monsieur.*"

Nikki grinned. She knew a compliment when she heard one, even if it was in another language. "*Merci beaucoup.*" Then she added with a wide grin. "That's all the French I know."

The antique dealer brought the finger and thumb of his right hand to his lips and kissed them, then tossing them he echoed, "*Trés charmante.*"

"You have made quite a conquest. Treat him gently, my child." Renée laughed, a merry sound that gladdened Nikki's heart.

Four

A week after her make-over, Nikki walked into the Devereaux Agency, her stomach flip-flopping like it had all morning. She'd dreaded this meeting with her mother, ever since Renée insisted on it. *Maman*, in an elegant, turquoise silk suit, glided beside Nikki. She knew for a fact she'd never pull off a look that stylish—never in a million years. But both Renée and Max must think otherwise, or she wouldn't be here, would she?

They stopped at the receptionist's desk.

"Good afternoon, *Madame* Devereaux," the receptionist greeted Renée, aiming a friendly, if curious, smile in Nikki's direction.

"Good afternoon, Karen. I believe Maxim is expecting us."

"Yes, *madame*. I'll let him know you're here. Please, go right in."

They walked down a hall carpeted so thickly the heels of Nikki's shoes sunk in what seemed like an inch, adding to her feeling of imbalance.

"Crystal." Renée nodded, acknowledging Max's assistant.

"Good afternoon, *madame*. Mrs. Prentice and Mr. Landry are already here." Crystal rose and opened the door.

"Thank you." Renée placed her hand on Nikki's elbow, steadying her. "Everything will be fine. You'll see."

"I sure hope so. I'm not looking forward to it." Uh-uh. No way did she want to confront her mother. Mama'd been a bitch during their telephone conversation and no doubt would be a real pain today. She just knew it.

Don't blow this for me, Mama.

What little self-confidence she possessed deserted her as if someone had pulled the stopper from a drain. And the sucking sensation didn't feel so hot. Yes, there sat her mama in a nice, comfortable chair across from Max.

"Hi, Mama."

"Nicole, my baby," she gushed. "You look so beautiful."

"Thank you." She glanced downward. She wasn't used to hearing compliments, especially from her mama.

Max stood and spoke. "Mrs. Prentice, this is my mother, Renée Devereaux. Nikki, you may remember meeting Ned Landry?"

With a start, she did recognize him. He'd been with Max that night—the night her life changed. "Yes, of course. Nice to see you again."

Her throat closing with emotion, she took a deep breath. Besides, she found keeping her gaze off Max difficult. Her benefactor wore a black, pinstripe suit, which fit his broad shoulders perfectly. She looked down at the floor and tried to count the flowers in the Oriental rug, but failed. Sneaking another glimpse of him, she caught his eye. He winked.

Yes, he did.

"Why don't we assemble at the conference table?" Max suggested, gesturing toward a highly polished, oval table.

"Just what do we need a lawyer for, Mr. Devereaux?" Her mother asked, glancing at Ned Landry. She stood, brushed the wrinkles from her skirt, then walked to take her seat. Nikki and Renée followed, with men sitting last.

Max continued in a deliberate, patient manner. "As I explained earlier, it's a formality. Nikki is a minor, and you, as her parent, will have to sign any legal documents. We need to apply for a work permit and passport, in case she has an assignment out of the country. I trust you brought the documents my assistant requested?"

"Yes," her mother Jessie replied, patting her black, patent-leather purse. "They're right here."

"Good," Ned Landry replied. "Let's get right down to business." He opened his briefcase and removed a stack of papers.

"Fine, business is good," Jessie began. Leaning forward, her elbows on the table, she continued, "I want to know what I get out of this deal."

"Mama!"

"You hush," her mama hissed. "I'll handle this."

Nikki shrank back. Right. Her mother would ruin everything.

This time, the lawyer took over. "We've drawn up papers which say Nikki's earnings, once she generates them, will be placed in trust until she is of age to manage her own affairs. For the present, she will continue to live with Mrs. Devereaux. Her room and board are free. She will receive a generous clothing allowance, as well as spending money— an allowance, if you will."

"Excuse me. I guess you've got a Harvard education, but I don't think you understand plain, old English. What's my cut?" Jessie pursed her mouth and tapped on the table with her forefinger.

"Your cut?" the attorney asked, his eyes widened.

"Yeah, let's talk percentages. Either I get a commission, or my daughter comes home with me, and I'll find her another modeling agency."

"There's no need to be rash, Mrs. Prentice," Max began and cast a sideways glance at the lawyer.

She considered crawling under the table. Oh, crap. Classic Mama at her worst.

"Look here, I know you fellas get a healthy commission. You're bound to. I just want a fair share. After all, this is my little girl we're talking about. What it boils down to is this, if you want my Nikki to sign with your agency, it's gonna cost you."

Her face grew hot. Forget crawling under the table. Maybe she should just slash her throat with a fingernail. She glanced at Renée, whose gaze narrowed.

"It will be all right, Nikki," Renée reassured her. "We will work it out."

"First of all," Max started, "we don't even know what kind of earnings Nikki will generate."

"Hmph. You must've thought she'd generate something, or you wouldn't have moved her into your house." Nikki watched, her horror growing, as an ugly expression crossed her mother's face. "Unless this is all about something else—not modeling at all."

Jessie pushed her chair back and stood. "Come on, Nikki, you're coming with me right now. You're not staying in that foreigner's house another minute."

Max's chin dropped, but it was Renée who rose majestically from her chair, her face red from the other woman's insinuations. "One moment, if you please. You daughter lives with me in *my* house. If it were not for my generosity, your daughter would still be living on the streets and eating out of garbage cans." Renée's voice deepened. "Your insults are outrageous. If I were a man, I would be sorely tempted to strike you."

Nikki swallowed. Hold on. Renée's fists were actually clinched at her side. Out on the streets, someone would be calling, "Cat fight."

"Now, now, ladies," Ned Landry cautioned, with a placating smile. "Let's remember that we're here to do what's best for Nikki, not start World War Three."

Nikki giggled and looked at Max. He winked again, ever so slightly. Visions of cat fights aside, it was time she took control. "Okay, everybody, here's the deal." She slapped her hand on the table, guaranteeing everyone gave her their full attention. "Whatever you're going to put in trust for me, give my mama half of it…until I'm of age."

"Fifty percent? Too much," Max said. "Not to mention reckless."

"That's the deal." She straightened her shoulders. "That and I stay at Mrs. Devereaux's until I'm at least eighteen."

"After that," Nikki turned to her mother, "you won't have any say in my life, my career or my finances."

"But, Nicole…" she whined, but Nikki recognized the dollar signs in her mother's eyes—Mama was already counting the money.

"Fifty percent of my earnings for the next couple of years isn't too much to pay for my freedom."

Landry shrugged, looking back and forth between Max and Renée. "The girl's got a point."

Max raised his brow. "Are you sure, Nikki?"

"Oh, yeah. Never been so sure."

"All right then, people, we have a deal," the attorney declared. "Let's do it."

Max hit the intercom. "Crystal, we need a clause added to the Prentice contract." He dictated the simple clause.

Within minutes, the revised contract had been signed. It was official. Nikki Prentice might belong to the Devereaux Agency, but she'd taken her first step toward independence.

Remaining silent, rather than say too much, she walked to the door with her mother.

"You're cold," her mother said.

"I learned from the best, Mama. I learned from you."

"Oh, to think that you could talk so mean to me." She sniffed and pretended to wipe a tear from her eye. Crocodile tears.

"I'm not mean, just realistic. You were glad when I ran away. One less responsibility. You didn't even look for me, did you?"

"Of course, I did, baby."

"Yeah, right."

"You'll never know how I worried about you." Her mother stopped and shot Nikki a cagey look. "But I should've known you'd land on your feet."

"Okay, whatever."

Her mother glanced at the door. "Look, I gotta go. Call me sometime?"

"Sure, Mama. Two pieces of advice: Don't count it before you get it, and don't spend it all in one place."

"You're downright mean. I don't care what you say. You may have them fooled, but I've known you a lot longer than they have. These fine people will find out what kind of person you really are and turn on you in the end."

"B-bye, Mama." She waved. Her mother took the hint, shaking her head as she left.

She turned. Renée stood behind her, an apologetic smile across her face. "I am sorry. I know this has been a difficult situation for you."

"It's worth it to be free of her." She shrugged. "No big deal."

"Then, you are ready to come home with me?"

She nodded, then turned to Max and his attorney. "Bye, guys." She waggled her fingers at them. They both had curious expressions on their faces. Guess she surprised the heck out of them…herself too. It felt good to stand up to her mother for once. Before closing the office door, she cast one more look at Max. Couldn't help it. Her old street friends would've said Max was "one righteous dude."

"That's that," Max declared. Walking over to his desk, he placed Nikki's file in his out-going stack. He sat, but he was still edgy. His fingers seemed to have a will of their own, nervously drumming on the top of the desk. This new Nikki—more confident and attired in stylish clothing, flawless makeup—stunned him. Her blond beauty was ethereal, touching him on some visceral level he'd never before experienced, but strangely feared.

Mon Dieu, but she'd taken charge as if she did business deals every day. In spite of her waif-like beauty, she possessed plenty of savvy when the situation called for it.

"You're going to have a problem with her," his friend warned. He sat very relaxed in his chair, his lawyer persona suspiciously absent.

"Mrs. Prentice will be content with her cut." Max shrugged, dismissing Ned's statement with a wave.

"I didn't mean her avaricious mother. I meant tall, blond and only sixteen."

"Don't be ridiculous. Nikki is…"

"Head over heels. She couldn't keep her big baby blues off you."

"Enough," Max warned. Surely, he wasn't so transparent. It was Ned's imagination.

"Yeah, just like what runs through your mind every time she comes around." Ned stood and leaned both hands against Max's desk. "So, what're you going to do about it?"

He exhaled, impatient to change the subject. "Nothing."

"Like I said, you're going to have trouble with her."

"She's a kid."

"But, you *are* attracted?" He cast Max a skeptical look over his glasses, as if daring him to deny it.

Max straightened the legal papers for the second time."Drop it."

"Okay, pal. Have it your way." Ned grabbed his briefcase, gave Max a smirk and two-fingered salute. "Gotta go."

"Right. Gym tomorrow?"

"Yeah."

Without another word, his friend left, still shaking his head. But his friend knew Max too well, but his game plan was in place. He wouldn't budge from it. Distance, he swore—he'd keep his distance.

Five

"But you *have* to go," Nikki pleaded, pacing up and down Renée's elegant bedroom.

Renée squeezed her eyes shut. "Nikki, it is the migraine. I must go to bed. Don't' worry, *Cherie*, you look beautiful. Your gown, your hair, your makeup are *magnifique*."

"But I *need* you. I've never been to anything like this party. People will *look* at me."

Rubbing her temples her mentor said, "Of course, they will. You are the latest sensation. I will call Jolie at the agency. She will provide an escort. It is short notice, but it is certainly within her skills."

"Jolie can't stand me. She's always reminding me of where we met."

"Nonsense. She will do as I say." Renée reached for the telephone.

"Please let me stay home. Y-you're not feeling well. I shouldn't leave you like this."

"No. Now I know you feel uncertain, but please believe me, there is nothing for you to be insecure about. It is a party, not a trial."

But a trial is exactly what it would be. A trial by fire.

"But—"

Renée held up her hand. "Not another word."

She listened as Renée called Jolie and made her request. "*Merci beaucoup*, Jolie. I knew you would not fail me." Her mentor smiled as she hung up the telephone. "See there. She was more than agreeable to finding you an escort for the evening."

"Yeah, I'll just bet she was thrilled all the way to her toes."

"Nikki, enough. I am retiring for the evening." She kissed Nikki on the forehead. "Please try and enjoy yourself."

She stuck out her bottom lip in a pout. Whatever *Maman* said went in most situations. "Yes, *Maman*." Might as well go.

Maybe Max would be there too.

Nikki paced back and forth, her stilettos clicking on the black marble floor of the Ladies Room. She couldn't hide all night. The attendant had already given her some curious glances, offered to assist her with her hair, make-up, whatever. She hated facing all those society broads and tried to remember all the lessons Renée had tried, so patiently, to instill. She should've paid more attention. She didn't want to disgrace the agency or... or Max.

She smoothed the front of her gown. From the first moment she'd slipped the elegant white designer original over her head, she felt like a princess, however momentarily. But the sad fact remained, she was out of her league.

Tonight it was a stranger who stared back. She pouted, then wrinkled her nose and stuck out her tongue at her reflection. Jeez. Still, she felt like a little girl playing dress-up in her mama's Sunday dress and high heels.

Only a few months before, she'd dined a la garbage, and now she was hobnobbing with people who expected her to know a shrimp fork from a demitasse spoon. If she made it through the evening without tripping or spilling wine down the front of her gown, she'd consider it a pretty good night. Why, this night of all nights, did *Maman* have to come down with one of her headaches? She took a deep breath and sighed.

The attendant rose to her feet. "Are you all right, Miss?" she asked.

"Uh-yes, thank you." Taking another deep breath and gathering her courage, she turned to leave.

The door swung open, and a petite young woman with a riot of curly hair swayed in and sank onto the brocade chair. "Is the bartender heavy-handed or what?" the young woman asked.

Nikki walked toward her, hesitating. "Is there anything I can do?" she asked, afraid her offer would be refused.

The woman opened one eye and looked Nikki up and down. "Who are you? God, you're beautiful."

"I'm Nik-Nikki Prentice," she stuttered. "Thank you."

"Marti Lodge," the young woman announced, indicating herself with a dramatic curtsey, then added, "I should've known. You're the new model everyone in town is buzzing about. What are you doing hiding in here? You should be out there breaking hearts and making men drool." Marti gestured in a not-so-graceful wave.

Before Nikki could reply, the color drained from the young woman's face.

Marti clapped a hand to her mouth. "'Scuse me." She scrambled to her feet and rushed for the nearest stall, leaving the door open in her haste.

Nikki followed and found the young woman on her knees, heaving into the enamel throne. She rushed back to the attendant. "She's ill. I need a wet cloth."

"Of course." The attendant had one ready and handed it to her.

She took the cloth. Throwing a hurried, "Thank you," over her shoulder, she rushed back to the stall. No longer retching, Marti sagged against the toilet bowl.

"Here, let me bathe your face with this."

"Thanks, sweetie, I guess I should stick to wine." Marti wiped her mouth and placed the cold cloth against her neck. "Hard liquor has always been my downfall, ever since I contracted hepatitis on my first honeymoon." She rolled her eyes, before adding, "In Borneo."

"Borneo? You went to Borneo on your honeymoon? I'm not even sure where that is."

Marti nodded her head. "My first one. He was a rock star, and we ran away. It was so romantic, until I drank the water and turned yellow as a pumpkin."

"Your *first* honeymoon? Did he take you on another one later?"

"No, I meant my *first* husband. My second took me to Africa on Safari. I picked up malaria there." She shrugged and gave a half-hearted laugh. "Guess that'll teach me to stay single."

Nikki stifled a giggle. "Maybe you should think about staying single—or forget about honeymoons. Want to try and stand up? You're ruining your lovely dress."

"I guess I might as well." The young woman held up a petite, well-manicured hand. In comparison, Nikki thought her own were large and ugly. She gave a tug and Marti struggled to her feet.

"Feel any better?"

"Better than I did." Marti shoved her frosted curls back, but her face remained pale. Together they walked over to a love seat and sat. Marti rubbed her nose and asked, "Now, tell me why you're skulking away in the ladies room, instead of partying with the other young-and-restless beautiful people?"

Nikki looked down at her folded hands, "I don't really like parties. I'm not used to them," she admitted shyly, feeling the blood rush to her face.

"Good Lord. How old are you anyway?"

"Seventeen, almost. Come August."

"Good grief. Sixteen and someone turned you loose in this bunch? Given the chance, some of these people would have you for dinner."

"I know. One already tried," she admitted with a slight grin.

Marti leaned forward. "Is it true? Were you really a runaway when Max Devereaux found you?" She waved in a dismissive manner. "I mean there's so much hype in publicity you never know what's true and what isn't."

Nikki nodded. "It's true."

"Well then, this bunch shouldn't be so scary. You've handled worse situations, I'm sure."

"Well..." She couldn't help but grin. "... I'm supposed to be on my good behavior. A knee in the crotch and an elbow in the ribs might be a little extreme."

"Not always, but I do see what you mean." Again, Marti brushed hair back from her face, her color improved. "It's obvious you need a chaperone, not that I'm such a good one, but I can certainly make things easier for you."

"That's very nice, but it's a lot of trouble. You don't have to—"

"But I want to. Look, hon, I'm Martha Lodge. My blood is bluer than blue, and I cut my teeth on Emily Post. Now, let's drag your buns out there and have some fun."

Nikki shook her head. "I'd rather go home, but *Maman* would be disappointed. She's been so good to me I don't want to do anything to upset her."

"*Maman*—you mean Max's mother?"

Nikki nodded. "Yeah, she was supposed to be here tonight to sort of supervise from a distance, but she came down with a migraine. I tried to get her to let me stay home, but she wouldn't hear of it. She's pretty stubborn. So here I am."

"You-uh, live with her?"

"Yeah, until I'm eighteen, anyway."

"Hmm, cozy."

"What do you mean—cozy?" Nikki heard the edge creep into her voice, but she couldn't help it. She knew, or thought she knew, exactly what Marti Lodge meant.

"Sorry, I didn't mean to jump to conclusions."

"It's not like that. Max—Mr. Devereaux—he doesn't live with us. He has his own place, and he's a perfect gentleman. Besides, he's way too old for someone like me." She swallowed and added in a low voice, "He'd never looked at me twice."

"Sweetie, any man with an ounce of testosterone would look at you twice."

"Well, he isn't like that. He's a gentleman. Very old-fashioned and proper, actually," she said, affecting a high-toned accent.

"Really?" Marti raised a finely arched brow. "Well, old-fashioned or not, I've always heard Frenchmen make the best lovers."

She gulped. Lover? Max would never—

"Sorry," her new friend giggled. "Here I am corrupting you. I'll have to be more careful. How long were you on the streets, anyway? You act more innocent than some of the convent-educated girls I've known."

"'Bout three months, but I was lucky. Mr. Devereaux rescued me before anything bad happened. But I know what you mean about Catholic schools. I've attended a couple of them. myself. My mama always did her best to keep me in school."

"At least she tried."

"She did, but we fought about everything else. She had a real fit when I started ditching school, so I took off. That's how I ended up on the streets."

"I see." Marti hesitated, dropping her voice to a whisper. "I know this is so rude, and absolutely none of my business, but did you... I mean, were you...?"

"No!" She leaned close to Marti and whispered, "Tonight, my date offered to pay me, like he really thought I would...do it."

"That's when you should've applied your knee to his crotch."

She giggled and gave a vigorous nod. "That's why I came in here. My date—Jolie at the agency arranged it—he propositioned me five minutes after he picked me up."

Marti rolled her eyes heavenward and shook her head. "Do you know anyone else at the party tonight?"

"Mr. Devereaux's here—and a couple of models from the agency, but they still treat me like an outsider. Last I saw of Irena and Kathleen, they were having too good a time to pay any attention to me."

"Well, let's find Max Devereaux and tell him it's time he took responsibility for his newest protégée."

The last thing she needed was to be near Max. Everyone would see how she felt about him. She pulled back. "Oh, no, let's don't."

Six

Max sipped his champagne, half-listening to his socialite companion while she gossiped on and on about the latest fashions with one of her friends. He heard enough of that kind of chatter at the agency. How much longer would he have to maintain his pretense of interest. Joanne was lovely, but apparently without a serious thought in her head. Where the hell was Nikki?

Never again, would he allow Ned Landry to arrange a blind date. Horrible custom. But his mother had called, frantic and in pain from one of her migraines. She'd insisted he must attend the party and keep an eye on Nikki and her escort. Now he was here with a less than engaging companion, but no sign of his mother's ward.

He cast a weary glance around the crowd. Other than her splashy entrance with automotive scion Jason Kingsley, Max hadn't seen her. He grew concerned, given the state of Kingsley's reputation. Nikki was still quite inexperienced in social situations. He wondered why Jolie had paired the sixteen-year-old model with Kingsley. He hoped the former runaway wasn't overwhelmed. But his mother had assured him all would be fine and Nikki deserved the opportunity to have some fun as well. Still, he worried. To his way of thinking, she remained vulnerable and innocent, in spite of her time on the streets.

A flash of blond hair caught his eye. There she was. So lovely it hurt. He couldn't help but admire her shining beauty. The blonde was literally being towed toward him by a petite young woman—he d met her before. He was certain of it and struggled, trying to recall her name.

"*Bonsoir, M'sieur*. Devereaux," the diminutive woman said, in what he thought was a nice, if not perfect, French accent.

"*Bonsoir, Madame*." He turned and nodded at Nikki. "*Bonsoir, Nikki*."

A blush spread across those fantastic cheekbones. Poor darling. She appeared as if she'd like to fade into the background.

"Hi," Nikki responded, looking down at the floor.

Nikki's rescuer cleared her throat. "I'm Marti Lodge. You probably don't remember, but we met last year at the Kidney Foundation fund raiser."

"Of course. Forgive me for not remembering your name. But we had a very charming conversation, if I'm not mistaken." At least, he hoped they had.

"*M'sieur* Devereaux—"

He interrupted, tiring of the formalities. "Please call me Max."

"All right, Max. I found this young lady hiding in the Ladies Room. It seems her escort for the evening is something of a rat."

An unexpected rush of anger engulfed him. He scanned the room for Kingsley, then turned to his charge. "Are you all right?"

Cheeks still flushing, Nikki kept her gaze averted. "I'm fine, really. I'm afraid Marti's blowing everything out of proportion." Her body language altered. She straightened her shoulders, stiffened her neck, and jutted her chin. "I can take care of myself."

"But of course." He squared his shoulders, growing aware of his surroundings, once more. Everyone near them had turned to stare, including his companion for the evening. Actually, Joanne glared. Desiring to avoid a contretemps, he bowed before Nikki.

"Would you honor me with a dance, *mademoiselle?*"

Nikki bit her full bottom lip, then grinned. "*Mais oui, M'sieur* Devereaux." she replied and placed her right hand in his left.

At her delicate touch, he felt an unwanted current of excitement run up his arm... and down to his groin. *Mon Dieu. Deliver me from this madness.*

"Your French is improving," he said. Trying to ignore the sudden tightening in his groin, he led her to the dance floor.

"You really think so?" she asked him, her wide blue eyes gazing earnestly into his.

"I wouldn't have said so, if I didn't."

They reached the dance floor, and the band started an old-fashioned waltz. He gathered her somewhat gingerly into his arms. Considering the effect holding her hand had on him, he feared his body would betray his growing ardor, if he held her any closer.

He inhaled her scent. It filled him with the impulse to clasp her tighter in his embrace and place his lips on her slender ivory neck, but he resisted. The fragrance was light, French, of course, but one with which he was unfamiliar. It suited her perfectly.

He led her through the predictable one-two-three beat. At first, she followed his lead with careful, but studied steps. Then as she appeared to gain confidence, she relaxed in his arms, moving gracefully in rhythm to the strains of Strauss.

A tremor passed though his body. His arms shook with tension. Was his self-control so fragile that holding her was tantamount to losing his bearings?

Why did she affect him so? He'd been surrounded by beautiful women every day for years. Why did one shy sixteen-year-old girl screw up his equilibrium until he had trouble thinking?

Thankfully the waltz was a short one. The music stopped. He bowed, then led her back to the spot where Marti and Joanne waited. Again he surveyed the room, looking for Kingsley. "I still don't see your escort."

"I'm not leaving with him." Her chin went up a notch. "He's a pig. I'll take a taxi home."

A pig—leave it to Nikki to call it like she saw it. Amused, he offered, "We'll see you home." He turned to Joanne and asked, "If you have no objections?"

"Of course not." Joanne gave him a perceptive smile. "We certainly can't allow a social swine to take advantage of such a young girl."

"That's it then," he declared, only too aware of his companion's disapproving tone.

"Now that you have a way home, I'll call you tomorrow, Nikki," Marti interjected. "We'll have lunch."

Nikki gave a bemused nod. "Sure."

"Shall we go?" Not waiting for an answer, Max ushered Nikki and Joanne toward the door. Escape was all he cared about. Escape…and regaining his self-control.

The three of them rode along in an uneasy silence. At first Joanne made several attempts at conversation, but Nikki's distant, if polite, responses soon quelled any further efforts. Maxim withdrew, finding an unaccustomed comfort in the dark silence. His behavior was inconsiderate, but his emotions were too close to the surface. It had been years since he'd felt like a hormone-ridden teenager.

Despicable. That's what he was.

The limo stopped at his mother's townhouse, jarring him from his isolation.

Nikki placed her hand on the door handle. "Thank you for the ride."

"I'll see you to the door." He opened the door on his side and sprang out before the chauffeur could. He ran around and opened the door for her.

"You don't have to," she said with her gaze downcast. "It's only a few steps."

"No bother," he murmured, watching her long legs swing out of the limo. *Mon Dieu.* He was the worst kind of fool. Why hadn't he allowed the chauffeur to simply do his job? He gave her his hand and, once again, felt a flash of desire. At the mere touch of her hand.

What madness had overcome him?

He accompanied her up the steps to the front door, standing

patiently, while she fished in a jeweled evening bag for her key.

"Sorry. I know it's in here somewhere."

"Never mind, use mine." He fumbled in his pocket and retrieved his key ring. Selecting the one for his mother's townhouse, he inserted it into the lock and turned it. It gave a quiet click as the dead bolt opened.

Finally, Nikki met his gaze. "Thanks. Well—uh, good night."

"*Bonne nuit*, Nikki." Max kissed Nikki on both cheeks, in the European manner, more from reflex than desire. He heard her startled gasp and drew back. Her eyes were open and her soft full lips parted, as if expecting more...more than he could give and still retain any sense of honor.

"Sweet dreams, *Chèrie*. It's late." Unable to stop himself, before he turned to leave, he stroked the side of her face and felt her tremble in response. Turning quickly he fled down the steps and entered the limo.

"B-bye," she called after him.

He couldn't bear to look back. Instead, he settled back into the soft leather seat, determined he would never again risk touching the teenager. A *teenager*. *Mon Dieu*!

"You care for her, don't you?" Joanne asked, a rueful expression on her face.

"It isn't difficult. She is a very sweet girl. Quite innocent, despite her background."

"No, I mean you really *care* for her. What are you going to do about it?"

"Nothing." He gazed out the window, annoyed Joanne had read his emotions so accurately.

They rode in silence until they reached the entrance to her apartment building. He watched, without passion, while Joanne gathered her evening bag and wrap and turned toward him. "I think I'd better go up alone."

He nodded his agreement. "As you wish."

"I do."

He'd misjudged Joanne. Another time, another place, he might've been attracted. Then regretting his boorish response, he apologized, "If it's worth anything, I'm sorry."

The chauffeur had opened Joanne's door, but she turned to him, again. "You may have to wait a long time for her to grow up. And then what if she doesn't want you?"

Max shrugged. "I'll have to take my chances."

"Good luck, then."

"Thank you."

She exited the limo, leaving him alone with his thoughts. Passion had ruled his life, once. He wouldn't allow it free rein, again.

Sighing, Nikki shut the door to her blue and white room and leaned against it. Max had actually brought her home in his limo. Of course, his date hadn't seemed very pleased with Nikki's tagging along, but she didn't care. He'd even walked her to the door and kissed her cheeks. Made her feel special. And she would *never* forget how wonderful his lips felt.

If only she were older or more sophisticated, maybe he would really look at her like a woman, instead of the tarted up kid he'd rescued from the gutter. Someday, maybe…

Who was she trying to fool, anyway? He would never look at her that way. Oh, his manners were perfect, but that was as far as it could go. And she might as well get used to it.

Sighing, she removed her dress and hung it carefully on the padded hanger, then quickly stripped down to her panties and walked into the bathroom. She pulled her hair back from her face, twisting it into an untidy knot and began washing her face.

Free of makeup, she asked aloud, "Who is Nikki Prentice anyway? Will anyone ever love her?"

Resisting the urge to throw the balled up washcloth at her reflection, she walked back into her bedroom, pulled back the comforter and flopped down on the bed. It had been a long day and an even longer evening. She barely managed to pull on her nightgown before sliding between the cool sheets and drifted into sleep.

Time passed in a rush of activity. Nicole spared no time for the lieutenant. She had even received several missives from him, requesting her company for another walk in the gardens, but had refused him, saying she had no time, for she was entirely swept up in the preparations for the ball.

Her costume must be perfect, and it must be daring. After many frantic consultations with *Tante* Renée and her dressmaker, Nicole chose a shimmering mermaid costume.

"*Non, Non, ma petite,*" her aunt declared. "Not this one. It will not do for you at all. It is appropriate for an older, more experienced woman."

Nicole raised her chin a notch. "I will wear this to the ball. I *will*."

The dressmaker looked from Nicole to her aunt in dismay. "Perhaps, we should look through the other costumes again. Something more suitable for the young lady," she suggested.

"Yes, that is what we must do," her aunt agreed. "There is nothing on the top. You will be naked from the waist up. It is scandalous."

"A scandal in *this* court?" Nicole protested, pacing around the room with impatience. "Really, would anyone notice? The Queen herself wanders around Le Petit Trianon dressed as a milkmaid, taking lovers whenever and wherever she pleases."

"Hush. You do not know any such thing. You pay too much attention to scandalmongers who would ruin Her Majesty's reputation for their own ends. You will be their next reason for gossip, if you wear that shameless costume," Renée warned.

"Do not make such a fuss. Voila. There is a delicate silk bandeau the color of my skin. I will have my hair styled so it hangs free, and covers my bosom." She giggled. "I will not be exposed at all. My costume will be quite daring…and memorable." Her poor aunt was quite amusing and not nearly as sophisticated as she thought.

"If you wear this costume, I warn you, you will never find an acceptable husband. No proper courtier will have you—not in marriage anyway." Renée paced about the boudoir. "Your poor Mama will castigate me, for I have failed. You go too far, my girl!" She waved her hands in the air.

"I will wear it, and you will see. I shall capture the most eligible noble at the ball." So saying, she flounced from the room, leaving her aunt and the costumier alone in their dismay.

The night of the ball came, and Nicole had her way.

She stood before the ormolu mirror and admired her image, tugging and adjusting the brief bandeau that covered her small rounded breasts. Her midriff remained bare, while the lower part of her mermaid costume was form-fitting silk covered in sea blue beads. The bottom of the skirt was split and formed into the shape of two fins, edged in pearls. Her sea blue gloves, also trimmed in pearls, had webs of diaphanous silk between each finger. The costume had taken someone hours and hours of work, sewing each bead in place. Silk slippers, dyed to match the blue beading adorned her tiny feet. She held up the lieutenant's gift to her face. The lovely mask was the pièce de resistance and made the perfect complement to her costume.

With great care, she arranged her blond tresses, assuring her breasts were almost concealed. "Let the ball begin," she murmured to the lovely creature in the mirror.

Accompanied and guarded by her scandalized, but resigned aunt, Nicole entered the Hall of Mirrors. The crystal chandeliers glittered and blazed with thousands of candles. Never had she seen anything so magnificent in all her short life. This was where she belonged.

"Cover your face." Her aunt warned. "Your mask has slipped."

"I cannot believe it. I am at my first ball, and I am beautiful."

"Hush your drivel, girl. You are not bound by any necessity to expound every trivial thought in your empty head."

Nicole tossed her hair. "I will do as I please." Awareness grew. People were staring at her. *C'est bon. I want them to remember me.* She began making her way through the throng of people, then she saw Maxime coming toward her. Her mouth dropped open. She closed it quickly. He was attired in his formal Royal Guard uniform, white trimmed in a mountain of gold braid. He towered over her, and his dark hair, without a speck of powder or even a wig, gleamed in the candle light.

"*Madame* de Sombreuil, *Mademoiselle*," he said, making a sweeping bow before them.

"Lieutenant, you are not in costume?" Her aunt remarked coolly, by way of acknowledgment.

"No, *Madame*, as I guard I do not have that privilege." Maxime smiled, showing perfect white teeth. His green eyes twinkled with obvious good humor.

Nicole had never seen anyone, not even the King, who was more splendid.

"*Mademoiselle*, may I have the pleasure of the next minuet?" he asked, then cast a questioning glance at her aunt, who gave a crisp nod of consent.

Nicole curtsied and placed her hand in his. He led her to the area where the minuet was forming. The staid strains of music started, but no one had started the figure. Everyone was staring at her. When she returned the gaze of the man next to her, she was frightened by the intensity of his stare. For the first time in her life, she understood how it felt to be undressed by someone's gaze. The women turned their backs to her, signaling their disdain.

Her aunt had been right after all. Nicole looked down at her costume. She'd made a terrible miscalculation. Underneath the mask, her face grew warm with embarrassment. Plying her fan, she lowered the mask. What would he do?

"If you would permit, *Mademoiselle* de Sombrieul," Maxime began. "Perhaps, we should seek some refreshment, instead. I am quite thirsty."

"Y-yes, of course, Lieutenant," she said, faltering. "I find I am quite parched myself." His back straight and head held high, he led a grateful Nicole away from those who had shunned her. Following his lead, she managed to hold her head high and not slink away in total shame.

Wordlessly, he led her through the vast open windows into a small sheltered garden. "*Mademoiselle*, if you will sit here," he suggested, indicating a long marble bench, "I will bring you something to quench your thirst."

"*Merci*, Lieutenant du Mont. You are too kind. I fear I have humiliated myself and you as well."

"Not at all." He hesitated. "If you allow me the honor to say so, you are incredibly beautiful—by far the loveliest woman at the ball tonight. The dancers were simply bewildered by your beauty, nothing more."

"You are far too kind, Lieutenant. I realize my error too late." She looked down at her nearly bare breasts. "My aunt warned me—forbade me the wearing of this—this—" she stopped, unable to continue.

Her escort took an audible breath, then admitted, "It is very daring, true, but very ingenious. I thought my very heart would stop beating when first I observed your entrance, but it is less revealing than first appeared. It is an illusion, instead."

Her face grew warm again. Was it his nearness which caused her reaction or the well-deserved humiliation? Once more she raised her fan, and fanned her cheeks.

He straightened, then bowed. "A thousand pardons, *Mademoiselle*, I forget myself. I will fetch your refreshment as I promised."

"*Merci, Lieutenant* du Mont."

Nicole watched his back as he left her. His shoulders seemed incredibly wide, the rest of his physique very fit. She was jarred from her reverie by the arrival of an unknown, yet somewhat familiar man. He was attired in the flowing robes and turban of a Moor, while his skin had been darkened with some sort of preparation. His teeth flashed white in contrast to his swarthy face.

"Well, I see my brother has left his latest trollop in the garden where others may sample her favors."

"Sir, you are mistaken. I—"

He swaggered toward her, his eyes narrowing. "You are the loveliest whore I have seen in at least a fortnight. *Le Comte* du Mont, at your service." The count sketched a sweeping bow before her.

"No, *Monsieur le Comte*. I protest your forward manner. I cannot say I am pleased to make your acquaintance." She twisted about, anxious for Maxime's return. When she turned back, the count stood within inches of her. She flinched, her discomfort escalating.

The count tossed back his head and roared in laughter. "You protest? My brother's *whore* is not pleased to make my acquaintance." Then leaning forward into her face, he vowed, "Well, my pretty little *putain*, you will make my acquaintance, pleased or no."

He reached out and grabbed Nicole by the waist and shoved his large hands underneath the filmy bandeau, groping her breasts.

Stunned by the swiftness of his advances, she gasped, "No. Please." She pummeled his back with her fists. "Maxime. Help!" Until she heard the welcome rush of his feet and his shout—

"You bastard!" The lieutenant attacked his brother, tearing him off her. He followed with a quick punch to his brother's face and a knee to the groin, knocking him to the ground. "You drunken pig!" he yelled as his brother writhed. "Touch her again..." He drew his sword, brandishing it in the air. "...And I will run you through."

Unable to hear the count's response, relief flooded her when the roué crawled away.

Maxime hastened to her, kneeling at her feet. "*Mademoiselle*, did my brother harm you?"

She shook her head. "N-no, you came just in time. I fear he would have." She looked down at the top of her costume—aghast, her breasts were nearly exposed to the lieutenant's gaze.

"Here, you must wear this," he offered, removing his uniform tunic. "If you will permit, I will see you to your aunt's suite. I know a passageway which is not heavily traveled."

"*Merci*. Once more, Lieutenant, I find myself indebted to your kindness and gentle manners. I do not know what you must think of me, but I have learned valuable lessons this night."

Once again, he fell to his knees before her, taking her hand, he pressed it tenderly between his strong tanned ones. "Forgive my boldness, *Mademoiselle* du Sombreuil, but I fear I must lay my heart at your feet and confess that I have admired you ever since you first came to court. Your beauty is unparalleled. Your sweet, innocent nature has fair overwhelmed me."

She gasped and plied her fan, attempting to cool her flushing cheeks. The sincerity of his words was written across his handsome, nay, his beautiful face.

"I-I have fallen in love with you." His eyes glittered, reflecting the full moon that shone above them. "There you have it. My heart and my future are in these two sweet hands." Still clasping her hands between his, he pressed tiny kisses on the back and front of them. "Dare I hope that you have formed some tenderness for me as well?"

Tears welled up in her eyes. "I fear the same, Lieutenant du Mont, but I also fear that my aunt will not look on your suit with favor. She has already cautioned me you are penniless...as am I."

"Penniless though we may be, we will find a way," he swore, placing his coat around her shoulders. "Now, let us return you to your rooms. Then we will consider how best to bend your aunt to our will."

She looked over her shoulder at *le Comte* du Mont, who lay on the ground, snoring. "What about your brother?"

"Leave him. He has had too much wine. It is doubtful he will even remember his disgraceful behavior."

Before they walked away, she stole another glance over her

shoulder. "The *masque*? I must not leave it behind. It was your first gift to me."

"There it lies, beside my disgraceful brother." He strode to where it had fallen and picked it up. Returning to her side, he pulled her into his embrace. "Here my sweet. It will not be the last." He grazed her lips with his.

"*Mon coeur*," she murmured, feeling the warmth of his breath in her hair, while the hard muscles of his chest pressed against her breasts. Had she been standing at the gates of heaven, it could not be more transcendent than this moment. She felt as if the entire purpose of her life had been to find this one man, fall in love with him and be loved by him in return. Her previous thoughts of finding a rich husband had vanished like the morning dew with Maxime's heroic rescue. How could she ever look at another? Who needed money? They would live on their love.

Nikki yawned and stretched as the sun rose and cast its early morning rays onto her face. She smiled, remembering her dream of the night before. Her brief dance with Max was even better than her dream. The impulse to melt into his arms was overwhelming, but he kept her at a distance through the entire dance, before returning to his date.

Dammit.

She had to get over her stupid infatuation with Maxim Devereaux. Dreams were nice, but dreams weren't real.

Seven

July 1990

The next month was a hectic one for Max. For the most part, he managed to stay away from his young protégée, but not from this particular shoot. The photographer, Ian Stark, had a reputation for being particularly difficult, as well as having some unsavory habits. Max dropped by the photo session—just in case.

From the back of Stark's studio, he watched Stark put Nikki through her paces. Posing for the famous British photographer was considered a real coup for such a fledgling model. As a rule, Stark only photographed the supermodels. While her bookings were increasing steadily, she wasn't at the top, yet.

This advertorial for Vogue would certainly make others take notice. He had to give the photographer his due; the lighting was perfect and brought out the dramatic angularity of her face, making her appear more mature than her sixteen years. She wore a scarlet evening gown that left little to the imagination. The V-necked bodice was cut deep to the waist and displayed the inner curves of her small, but exquisitely formed, round breasts. The skirt was slashed on one side as far as the upper thigh, revealing her sinuous legs. Gold stilettos were held on by straps around her slender ankles.

Off-camera, a fan blew Nikki's blond mane away from her face. In a word, the former street kid presented a ravishing sight. So beautiful. So incredibly lovely.

The forceful driving beat of techno-rock filled the air. She moved to the music, becoming seduction incarnate. Glad of his dark vantage point, he found it difficult to breathe. He shifted his stance, uncomfortable from the sudden tightness in his trousers. For the hundredth time, he wondered why this one girl fascinated him so. It was more than her beauty. It was...indefinable.

He checked at his watch. Would the shoot never end?

As if on cue, Stark called out, "That's it, luv. Let's call it a night. You were great. The camera loves you."

She stopped posing, shaking out her hair with a sigh of apparent relief. "Thanks, Mr. Stark."

"Now, now, remember wot I told you. The name's Ian. Call me Ian." He walked toward her, placing an arm around her shoulder. "'Ow 'bout you coming with me to meet some blokes I know? We're going to party at a private club in Soho."

To Max's consternation, Nikki's eyes widened with interest. "Sure. Just let me get out of this stuff."

No way was she going with Stark. "Nikki, you're a little young for his crowd. Why don't you let me take you out for a late dinner or home?" Too late. The words had left his mouth. He'd made a mistake, and if he had any doubts, she quickly dispelled them.

"I'm *not* hungry," she declared, jutting her chin at him. "And I haven't been to a party for at least a month."

"Well, we mustn't 'ave that." Ian grinned, first at Max, then at Nikki. "Come on, luv. We'll have some fun, won't we?"

"Sure. Why don't you join us, Max?" she asked, with a toss of her hair.

Max hesitated, sorely tempted. "Sorry. I have an early meeting."

Her cheeks flushed, but she shrugged and flipped her hair back over her shoulder. "Suit yourself. Ian will see me home, won't you?"

"O' course, doll. O' course."

"See, I'll be fine." Her blue eyes narrowed, challenging him, again, "You could still tag along, be my chaperone, my older uncle or something."

Inwardly he seethed. That girl. Trying him. Testing him. Tempting him. Against his better judgment, he ground out, "I'd better not. As I said, I have an early meeting." Truly he did have an early meeting, but just as truly, he feared losing control if in another social situation with her, so soon after the last.

Dammit. He'd been out-maneuvered by a sixteen-year-old girl who would have her way or know the reason why…and he wasn't about to let her know the reason why.

"Fine." She stalked off to the dressing room, never giving him another glance.

"Didn't mean to poach on your territory, guv. I didn't know you were 'ot for 'er too."

"I'm not. Nikki's a minor. Remember that."

"Sure, mate, no problem."

He stepped into Stark's personal space and leveled his gaze on the Brit.

"Better not be," he warned, then spun on his heel and strode from the studio. Misgivings? He had plenty. But he couldn't live the girl's life for her. She had to make her own choices, whether he approved of them or not.

***

Nikki looked around the dimly-lit private club. Terry's Jazz Corner was little more than a dive, but the band was top-notch. There was Elena, another model from the agency, as well as a couple of celebrities.

She looked at her cocktail. No one had bothered to card her. It made her feel grownup. Here she was hanging out with a famous fashion photographer, and all he wanted to do was grab her ass. She'd managed to shame him into keeping his hands to himself, for a while, but now he was at it, again. "Look 'ere, mate," she said imitating his East End accent, "keep your bloomin' 'ands off me bum."

"Isn't she cute?" Ian asked his friend on the left. "I don't know w'en I've 'eard a better Eliza Doolittle." He leaned over and attempted a smacking kiss, but she turned her face away.

"Cool it." She stood. "I tell you what, Ian. I'm going to the Ladies Room, and then I'm calling a taxi."

"Aww. Don't be a spoil sport. I guess old Max's got you under his thumb."

"I don't give a fu—" she paused, hesitating to use the most appropriate obscenity. "Think whatever you want. I'm outta here." She grabbed her bag and headed for the rest room.

Five minutes later, she'd called her taxi from the pay phone. She made her way to the door, walking past Ian and his friends.

"Look doll, no 'ard feelings. Finish your drinkie, and I'll be'ave meself. Really, I will."

He gave her a charming smile. Being strict and straight-laced really wasn't her style. She relented, smiling back at him. "Okay, but only 'til my taxi comes. Then I'm going home."

"Sure, luv. Wotever you say."

She picked up her drink and swallowed the remaining contents, puckering her mouth at the taste. "It's really kind of gross, you know."

Ian leaned forward and whispered in her ear," You don't 'ave to rush off, y'know. I'll be on me very best be'avior, if you stay a little longer. Look, doll. You're a grownup now, so don't pull this little girl routine. Won't work. Not if you want to be taken seriously as a model, I mean."

"Just keep your hands to yourself, and we won't have a problem."

"Y'know 'ow it is? A bloke's got to try, otherwise, 'e's not much of a man, is 'e? See wot I mean?"

"Well, you've tried. So get over it."

"Yeah, yeah. All right."

A wave of nausea hit her. She grabbed for the bar to steady herself.

"I say, wot's wrong? You're looking a little pale, all sudden like."

"I-I don't feel so good." She looked toward the door. "Is my cab here yet?" She tried to focus, but her eyes didn't want to cooperate. Ian seemed to be wavering. Was he drunk, too? Couldn't he sit still? Another wave of nausea hit her. She just had to close her eyes for a minute. She reached out and felt someone grab hold just in time to keep her from falling.

Nikki opened her eyes and rubbed the sleep from them. Funny, she didn't remember going to bed. Had she fallen? Passed out? She stretched and...freaked.

She wasn't wearing a stitch.

And someone else was in the bed.

She rubbed her eyes again. No, this had to be a nightmare.

No. Still there. She jumped out of the bed, yanked the comforter off the bed and wrapped it around her. Taking a deep breath, she fought the panic threatening to choke her. She reached out and gave the sleeping male form a tentative nudge, then jumped back when the no-longer-sleeping person turned toward her and gave a bleary grin.

Ian Stark.

"What am I doing here?"

"Don't worry about it, luv. You were great."

"What do you mean 'I was great'? What the hell happened?" she shrieked and retreated to the far side of the bedroom.

Ian threw back the covers and swung his long skinny legs over the side of the bed. Her chin dropped. Sonofabitch. He was naked too.

She backed up against the wall. "Where's the bathroom?" She looked around, frantic...suddenly aware of discomfort...and an unpleasant stickiness between her thighs.

"Omigod." Tears formed and rolled down her cheeks. "What have you done to me? Oh, God, oh God." She spied her panties beside the bed and snatched them up along with the jeans she'd worn the night before. The pain told her what Ian had done, but she couldn't take it in. How could he?

"Nothing you didn't beg me for, ya know." He stood and walked toward her. Tall and thin, he loomed over her. "Listen, luv. Not like it was your first time. I mean I can tell."

"Stay the hell away from me," she cried. "You bastard. You drugged me."

"No way, doll. You might've been a little shaky on your pins, but, trust me, you were 'ot for it."

"No. No, no, no, no, no!" She grappled with the bathroom door, flung it open and stumbled inside. After slamming it shut and locking it behind her, she leaned back against the door and slid down to the floor, the cold tile floor a shock to her butt.

Sobs racked her entire body. 'Not the first time.' What did he mean by that? Until last tonight she'd been a virgin.

Pull yourself together. Get out of here. She stood, wincing from the stab of pain between her thighs, aware of Ian's pounding on the other side of the door.

"Come on, luv. Let me in. We can shower together, save on water usage. You know, save the planet. Come on, Nikki."

Save the planet? She shivered. "Rot in hell, you no-good bastard!" She brushed away the tears, anger fueling her emotions now.

Dress and get the hell out of here. And a shower. God, how she wanted one, but no way was she going to hang around this creep's apartment long enough to take one.

It was then she looked into the mirror. Two purple-red blotches on her neck and one on her breast. They stood out like stains on her fair skin. She bit her lip to keep it from trembling. The SOB had certainly left his brand on her.

Ian banged on the door again. She jumped.

"Come on, luv. We both 'ad a good time last night. You're blowing this all out of proportion."

She swallowed her rage. Damn good thing she didn't have a gun. She'd blow him into next month. Instead, she pulled on her jeans and yanked her sweater on over her head.

Didn't give a damn how she looked. Escape. That was the ticket. Summoning every ounce of courage she possessed, she squared her shoulders took a deep breath, unlocked and opened the door.

Ian jumped back then reached for her. "Now see here—"

Unable to stomach the sound of his whining voice, she shoved him away and stalked from the bedroom. If she kept her back straight and head high, she might just make it without dissolving into tears.

Home, she had to get home. Renée would be so worried. God, what kind of excuse could she give for staying out all night? Her mentor was strict, but fair. No way was she about to tell her what had really happened. No way, whatsoever. She was too ashamed.

Once out of Ian's apartment, she met no one in the hall. At the elevator, she jabbed at the down button several times, as if that could make it come any faster. The elevator doors opened. Her path of escape was empty. Entering the elevator, she leaned against the back wall and took a deep ragged breath.

The sides of the elevator car were covered in a highly reflective bronze tinted metal, revealing her ravaged image. She'd come a long way since leaving the streets and pursuing a modeling career.

Oh yeah, a long way, baby. How would she ever face *Maman*...or Max?

With a sickening lurch in her stomach, she felt the elevator slow as it reached the ground floor. Again, she squared her shoulders and held her head high. The doors opened. She rushed out and made a straight line for the doorman. "Taxi," she told him, staring at a point over his shoulder, attempting to ignore his knowing glance.

"Right away, miss." The doorman gave her another look, a slow appraising up-and-down glance which seemed to take forever, then turned and opened the door for her.

At least his reply was polite, even if his facial expression left a lot to be desired. Right now, she was grateful for small favors and followed him outside. The early morning air, crisp and clear, she wrapped her arms across her chest and shivered. Where the hell had she left her jacket? No way would she go back to that bastard's apartment. No way.

The doorman stepped to the curb and blew his whistle at an oncoming cab. The cab screeched to a halt, scrubbing its tires against the curb.

"Idiot," the doorman muttered and shook his head in apparent disgust. "They're all idiots. No pride."

She mumbled something she hoped was appropriate. All she cared about was getting home. At home, she could scrub to her heart's content—but would she ever feel clean?

The doorman opened the rear door, gesturing for her to enter. And enter she did. With a great sigh of relief, she plunged into the dank back seat. She gave the driver the address, then buried her face in her hands and sobbed.

In the townhouse foyer Renée paced. Hours ago, frantic with worry, she'd actually dug out an ancient pack of cigarettes and now puffed furiously on the last one. Should she call Maxim, or should she give her charge a little longer to turn up? Why hadn't she called back when paged? Were all teenagers so inconsiderate? While the battles over smoking and coarse language had been easily won, she had often wondered when the young runaway's independent streak would re-assert itself.

Apparently now, it had. She checked her appointment book. The only entry for the day before was the afternoon shoot with the English photographer. Even though she offered to accompany the girl, she stubbornly refused. "I can take care of myself, *Maman*. Really, I was on the streets. No Limey photographer is going to mess with me."

What worried Renée most was Stark's reputation for seducing his models, but surely he wouldn't be so stupid as to try anything with one as young as Nikki.

If the girl didn't show up by nine, she would call Maxim and let him decide what to do. She felt so helpless. What she would do if something terrible had happened, she didn't know. She had become quite fond of her protégée. In spite of the girl's street-wise facade, she was really very sweet and quite devoid of artifice.

After walking back to the kitchen, she poured another cup of coffee. She stubbed out the remainder of her cigarette, sat and looked at her watch for at least the twentieth time that morning. Seven-fifteen. She hadn't had more than an hour of sleep the entire night. Oh, she'd dozed off several times, only to awaken suddenly when she thought she heard the girl come in. But it hadn't been Nikki. It hadn't been anyone. Only the thought she might be with Maxim kept her from calling the police.

She reached for the phone, sorely tempted to call her son, but it rang the moment she touched it. Frantic in her haste to answer the telephone, she dropped it. "*Merde.*" Grabbing the receiver, she managed a ragged, "Nikki?"

"*Non. C'est moi,*" Maxim replied. "What's wrong?"

Near tears, she cried, "Nikki didn't come home last night. I'm so worried."

"Dammit! I knew I should have kept her from leaving with Stark."

"Surely, you didn't allow her to go out with him?"

"Short of slinging her over my shoulder like a Neanderthal, I couldn't stop her. She was very determined."

"She's never done—" She broke off. "Wait. I hear her key in the door. She's home," she said with a great sigh of relief. She laid the receiver on the counter. "Nikki?"

No response—save the sound of rapid footsteps, first in the entryway, then up the stairs.

"Nikki!" Renée called again. A door slammed.

She grabbed the telephone, again. "She's home, but something's wrong. I have to go." Without waiting for his response, she hung up.

At least Nikki was alive. A new sense of unease caught in Renée's throat. The more she considered what could have happened, the worse her fear became. Dreading what she might learn, she took a deep breath and walked slowly from the kitchen into the hall. She paused at the long stairway, crushed by a sudden feeling of profound weariness. It had been a very long night.

She climbed the stairs and walked to Nikki's door, knocking tentatively. "Nikki?" Through the door she heard the sound of water running. She hated to intrude, but staying out all night was not acceptable behavior. They might as well have it out, right now.

She tried the doorknob. Finding it unlocked, she opened the door and walked into her bedroom. "Nikki," she called again and stepped to the bathroom door. "When you're finished with your shower, we need to talk."

"G-go away. Please." Her voice was muffled as if she were crying.

"What's wrong?"

"J-just go away."

"*Non.* I'm coming in." She opened the door. Nikki hadn't bothered pulling the shower curtain. Water from the shower had splattered onto the tile floor. She crouched in the corner of the shower stall, red-faced and crying. A scrub brush hung limply from her right hand. Renée took in the red scratches, marring the former runaway's body...and the passion marks.

"P-please, l-leave me alone." Nikki hid her face against the shower wall. At the same time, she resumed scrubbing her body with a brush never meant to touch human flesh.

Sick at heart, Renée grabbed a white bath sheet and held it toward her charge.

"Stop it, *Chèrie.* You're hurting yourself. Please, come out of the shower," Renée coaxed, keeping her tone soft and nonjudgmental.

Nikki shook her head and cringed, putting up her hands as if warding off evil.

"Shh," Renée murmured, gently taking the brush from the girl's hand, then wrapped the soft bath sheet over the girl's head and around her shoulders. "It is all right. Everything is all right. You are safe." She cradled the sobbing girl in her arms and walked her into the bedroom.

"S-stupid. I'm so stupid." Nikki shivered.

"No. No, you're not." She guided Nikki to her bed, pulled back the duvet and sat her down on the side. "I'm going to get you a fresh nightgown and a comb for your hair."

"Just go away and leave me alone. You're too good to me. I—" Nikki dissolved into shaking sobs and fell against Renée's shoulder.

She stroked Nikki's damp hair and crooned, "What has happened, *Chèrie?*" Regretfully, she had a very good idea what had happened, but needed to have it confirmed. "Now, now." She cradled the girl in her arms, rocking her back and forth.

After a few minutes in Renée's comforting arms, Nikki stopped crying. As if from a distance, she watched her mentor stand up, walk to the armoire and remove a nightgown. After picking up a comb from the bureau, *Maman* came back and sat on the side of the bed.

"Here, stand up while I put this on you."

Like a small child, she stood and held up her arms, allowing Renée to pull the gown over her head and down her body, removing the bath sheet as she did.

"There, *ma petite*. Now, sit down and let me comb your hair." Her soft accented voice soothed Nikki's raw emotions.

She sniffed.

"Here." Renée handed her a corner of the bath sheet. "Blow your nose."

Obediently she blew.

While Renée continued combing Nikki's hair, she closed her eyes, wishing she could block out the last twenty-four hours as easily. The older woman's touch was gentle, just what she needed.

"Will you tell me what happened?"

She hung her head. "I can't."

"You don't have to tell me, but I wish you would."

"I-I'm too ashamed." She pulled away and lay down on her side, and drawing her legs up to her chest, she hid her face in the pillow. "I just want to go to sleep."

"But you need a doctor, and we must notify the police."

Panicked, she bolted upright. "No hospital. I won't go. No police. I'm fine."

"You're anything but fine."

"I-I'm all right. Please don't. Don't call anyone."

"Then tell me. Whatever we need to do—we'll decide together."

She looked away from her mentor's sympathetic gaze. She couldn't face anyone, much less tell what happened. "I—uh, went out after the shoot with Ian. Max tried to talk me out of going, but I wouldn't listen."

"Maxim was at the shoot?"

"Yeah, I didn't know he was coming, but he was there—watching. I guess he wanted to see how it went. He tried to stop me from going out with Ian. Even said he'd take me to dinner."

"You didn't want to go with Maxim?"

"Well, I did, but he was being so weird about it."

"Hmm, I see."

"Anyway, I went with Ian to this jazz club in Soho. We met a couple of his friends there. They were all older. I ordered a drink. I know I shouldn't have, but I didn't want them to think I was a kid."

"The club served you a drink?"

"Yeah, they didn't even card me."

"*Incroyable.*"

"I only took a sip or two, and Ian got real grabby. Wouldn't keep his hands off my butt, so I told him I was going to the restroom. I called a taxi."

"That was very smart of you."

"Not really. When I came back, Ian was all apologetic and said he was sorry and why didn't I finish my drink, no hard feelings. I didn't want to act like a hard-nose, so I did. After a few minutes, I got sick at my stomach and dizzy. The next thing I r-remember is waking up."

"And?"

Nikki buried her head in Maman's shoulder. "I-I was in b-bed with him. Ian. I don't remember, but we must've h-had s-sex."

"Are you sure?"

"Yes," Nikki wailed. "I didn't have any clothes on. And he said we did. He said awful things. How could he? I don't remember anything," she wailed.

"*Ma pauvre petite*. Undoubtedly, he put something in your drink."

"I feel so stupid. I should've listened to Max."

Renée patted Nikki's back, comforting her. But her next words were anything but comforting." You *must* be seen by a doctor, and we *must* call the police."

"No!" She pulled away, tears streaming down her face once more. "You can't call anyone. Please don't." She looked around anxious to escape. "I'll run away."

"But there are things to be considered. You don't know what happened, if he used protection. You must see a physician."

"Protection? I never thought about that." She collapsed onto Renée's shoulder and wept.

"Now, now. We'll work this out, but that's why you need to be seen."

"No. Hospitals report stuff like this to the police. I don't want anybody to know, *Maman*. No one."

"I will call a doctor. Perhaps my personal physician will come here, but no matter what, you have to have medical care. You simply must. I'll call Max."

"No! You can't tell him. Please, please. I don't want him to know. I beg you, please don't call him."

"Maxim already knows something's wrong. He called just before you came home. I'm afraid I hung up on him when I heard your key in the door."

"I don't care what you tell him. Just don't tell him what really happened. Please," she begged. "H-he tried to stop me, but I wouldn't listen."

Eight

Forty-five minutes after his mother hung up on him, Max stood in the foyer of her townhouse. "*Maman*?" He started to bound up the stairs, but saw his mother standing at the head of the staircase, holding a finger to her lips.

"Shh. Do not come up."

"Why not? What's happened?"

His mother descended the stairs. Always graceful, she seemed awkward in her movements and stumbled two steps from the bottom. He caught and steadied her. "What is it? Please, you must tell me."

She closed her eyes and shook her head. "The worst," she told him wearily. "Let us go into the kitchen. I want to make sure she cannot overhear."

His imagination soared into overdrive. Given Stark's less than salutary reputation, 'the worst' could only mean one of two things, neither of which he wanted to contemplate. He took a deep steadying breath and led his mother to the kitchen, but not before giving a last glance up the stairs toward Nikki's door.

He eased his mother into a comfortable chair, but growing impatient, he insisted, "Tell me."

Maman hid her face in her hands and dropped into French. "Nikki went out with him. He became obnoxious, so she left him at the bar long enough to call a taxi. When she came back, he was apologetic and encouraged her to finish her drink before her cab arrived." She took a ragged breath. "That's all she remembers," she paused, "until she awakened this morning—in his bed. She's…" Unable to continue, she shook her head.

He listened. Rage and horror mounted with every word. Engulfed him. He clenched his fists, needing to lash out and break something—anything. "The son of a bitch. He drugged her." Trying to stay in control, he closed his eyes. "How is she?"

"She is asleep, or at least, she is trying."

"Should I go up?"

"No, absolutely not. She is terribly ashamed. Does not want you to know at all, understand?"

"But—"

"She blames herself."

"It's not her fault. I'm as responsible as that slime ball Brit. I should've picked her up and carried her out of there."

"But you said she was determined to go with him."

"She was."

"Then you cannot blame yourself, *mon fil.*"

"I went to the shoot because I was concerned about Stark's reputation. I didn't do enough."

His mother sighed. "I know. But we are faced with what must still be done."

"It's simple. We're taking her to the hospital and calling the police. That photographer should be in jail."

"No—no, she will not hear of the police becoming involved. She became hysterical when I merely mentioned it. I shall call my personal physician and ask her to come here."

"Good. At least that's something. He walked over to the counter took a cup from an upper cabinet, then poured a cup of coffee. He watched his mother pick up the telephone. Anger alternated with disbelief. And what a nightmare for Nikki. And most of all, the responsibility was his. Indeed, he'd assumed that sweet, and at times heavy, burden the night he'd rescued her from the streets.

Nikki lay quietly, rolled up in a fetal position, pretending to sleep, wishing like hell she could wake up and it would all be a bad dream. She'd never feel clean again, not after a thousand showers. Max was downstairs. Thank God, he hadn't come up. She didn't know how she'd ever look him in the face, again.

A light tap sounded on her bedroom door.

"Nikki?" It was *Maman.*

Maybe she should just pretend to be asleep. No her mentor deserved better. "I'm awake."

The door opened. "May I come in?"

"Sure."

Renée entered, but Nikki stared at the wall, unable to face her mentor. The bed gave as she sat. "My physician, Charlotte Davenport, is outside. I want her to examine you. I have already told her what happened. She has seen cases like yours before, and she understands how traumatic this is."

Nikki's throat closed. She couldn't get enough air. She clenched a corner of the sheet. Her lifeline.

"Nikki?"

Maybe if she didn't answer, Renée and her doctor would just go away.

"Will you see her, please?"

She heard the misery in Renée's voice and regretted she was the cause of it. Wordlessly, she nodded, then afraid of being left in the hands of a stranger, clutched the older woman's hand. "*Maman*, please stay." Her voice was so hoarse she didn't recognize it as her own.

"But of course, *Chèrie*." Maman sighed. "I will bring in Charlotte. The examination will be over quickly. I promise."

She held her breath until the doctor entered.

"Hi, Nikki, I'm Charlotte Davenport." Her voice sounded soft...and kind, but Nikki squeezed her eyes shut and kept her face averted.

"I'll tell you what I'm going to do before I do it, and I'll wait for your permission. Just nod your head or squeeze Renée's hand before I proceed. All right?"

She nodded, but kept her face to the wall.

"First, I'll draw some blood from your arm. It'll be tested for various diseases your partner might've had as well as for any drugs he used. You'll need further blood tests at six and twelve month intervals."

Nikki nodded again, extending her right arm in the direction of the doctor's voice.

"Have you ever had blood drawn before?" the physician asked.

She nodded.

"All right then, you know what I'm going to do. I'll wrap this rubber tourniquet around your arm. It'll be tight. I'll swab the inside of your elbow with alcohol. It'll be cold. Then there'll be a slight stick."

Again, Nikki nodded her assent. *All right already, just do it and get it over with.* She winced as the needle slid home. No big deal, really.

"That's it, for the blood-letting. Next, I'd like to examine you for any injuries or marks."

Biting her lip, she nodded her assent once more, but when the physician touched the sheet covering her, an involuntary tremble shook Nikki from head to toe.

"These scratches?"

Renée explained, "A scrub brush...in the shower."

"I see. Not terribly surprising."

The doctor's touch, gentle and soothing, encouraged Nikki to take a peek at the woman who was so kind and understanding. A middle-aged woman with short gray hair...and a kind face. Just as she imagined. She shut her eyes again.

"I'll leave a prescription for an ointment. There'll be minimal scarring. The scratches look angry, but they're superficial."

"Thank you so much, Charlotte," she heard Renée say.

"The next part of the examination will be the most uncomfortable for you, but it's necessary. I'll be as gentle as possible, but I must be thorough—with your permission, of course. Have you ever had an examination of this type before?"

"No. Just get it over with," Nikki croaked, hating the sound of her own voice. Talking, any response, made it seem more real. She just wanted to be left alone. Would they never leave?

She clenched her jaw and clung to Renée's hand when she felt the sheet being adjusted. Her legs jittered at the physician's first touch.

"Take some slow deep breaths, dear. It will help you relax."

She tried. The deep breaths did help. Before she realized it, the exam was over. She heard the snapping sound of the doctor removing her gloves.

"I've done swabs for STD's and DNA traces, though I doubt there'll be any DNA evidence left."

Renée rose slowly, but Nikki continued clinging to her hand. "We understand. Thank you, Charlotte. I don't know what we would have done without you."

"One more thing. Nikki, I understand you don't want the authorities involved, but you must have counseling. It's essential."

Furiously Nikki shook her head. No way would she spill her guts about this to anyone else. It was so over.

"We'll keep that in mind." Renée nodded. "You've been so kind."

"I'll leave you some numbers. I'm so sorry this happened." The doctor paused, then stressed in a quiet, firm tone, "She really must talk to someone—a therapist, or at least a rape-victim support group."

As comforting as Renée had been—truthfully, Nikki couldn't have made it without her, but now she was ready for both women to clear out.

"All right then," the doctor continued. "Call me, if there are any problems. I'm leaving a prescription for some pills. They will function like the morning after pills you are familiar with in Europe. She should take a dose today and again tomorrow morning. They'll prevent the chance of pregnancy."

"We understand," Renée said.

"Nikki, you do understand you aren't to blame for this," the doctor said. "You're young and someone older took advantage of your innocence. He, and no one else, is at fault. More than likely, you aren't the first and won't be the last."

Oh, patronize me, why don't you? The longer she listened, the more her anger mounted, but she wouldn't give way again. She wanted to scream her rage. Every cell in her body wanted to scream.

"Perhaps…" Renée began, "…we could continue instructions downstairs. I think Nikki would like some time to rest."

"Of course. Good-bye for now. And again, I'm so sorry this happened."

She's sorry? That's rich. Get out of here. Get out of here. Get out of here.

Then finally, sounds of their retreating footsteps, the door opening and closing.

Alone. She'd had enough of being poked and prodded. She'd be damned if she'd see a shrink who would try and unscramble her brain. As far as she was concerned, Ian Stark didn't exist...and the night before never happened.

I'm not looking back. It's over. A done deal.

Downstairs in the kitchen, Max paced, stopping only long enough to pour his fourth cup of coffee. Hearing the sound of his mother's voice quietly conversing with her physician, he looked up. Dr. Davenport was a slightly-plump, middle-aged woman with fine skin and kind blue eyes.

"Well? How is she?" he asked in a level tone. Unfortunately his stomach had tied itself into a knot. Whether from worry about Nikki or the caffeine—not that it made a damned bit of difference.

The doctor lifted a finely arched eyebrow and looked at his mother.

"Sorry. Charlotte, my son Maxim Devereaux. Maxim, this is—"

The physician extended her hand and interjected, "Charlotte Davenport, Mr. Devereaux. Physically, Nikki will be fine. She has no serious physical injuries."

"That's a relief," he murmured, feeling powerless, not allowed to see Nikki—but he could well understand why she didn't want to see anyone. And at the moment, he was definitely the wrong gender.

"However, I'm not so sure about her emotional state. She is very fragile, which is to be expected. She'll need counseling. It doesn't matter that she's refused, right now. She'll need it sooner or later—but the sooner the better." Charlotte pulled a day planner from the black leather satchel she carried. "I have some numbers you might need, once she agrees to counseling."

He handed his mother pen and paper from the nearby counter.

Charlotte rattled off the numbers while Renée scribbled them down. "*Merci*, Charlotte. I cannot say it enough."

"I'm glad I could help."

"Is there anything else we may do in the meantime?" Renée asked.

Charlotte frowned, looked back and forth between them, then smiled. "She will need a great deal of love and patience. This is a life-altering event for her. She will never be or *feel* the same again."

"She will recover?" he asked.

"If she has counseling. Whether she does or not, she'll go through the stages of grief: denial, anger, bargaining, depression and finally acceptance. She might be emotionally labile—you know—angry one minute, depressed, the next. She may withdraw from those who care most about her. She might even continue as if nothing has ever happened. Denial is a powerful weapon in the arsenal of coping mechanisms. It's difficult to predict how Nikki will respond. And…" she paused, "… I must warn you, she is at greater risk for being raped, again."

"What?" He shook his head. "I would think just the opposite."

"No, I'm afraid it isn't unusual for a victim of rape to engage in further risky behaviors."

"*Mon Dieu*." His mother sighed, then sank down into the nearest chair. "I don't know if I'm up to this."

"Well, actually, it's not your problem. She has a mother, true?"

"No—I mean yes, Nikki does have a mother, but they don't get along," he rushed to explain. "I am certain she won't want her mother involved in this. The woman is cold, calculating."

"That's too bad. However, she's still a minor, you could turn her over to the juvenile authorities," the doctor suggested.

"No." He shook his head. "That's not an option. Besides, my mother has legal custody of Nikki."

His mother nodded vigorously. "Nikki has been with us for nearly a year. She's very dear to me. I suppose I am a little overwhelmed at the moment." She continued in a firmer voice, "Her place is here with me. I will do everything I can for her."

The doctor nodded and smiled. "Good. As I said, she'll need all the love and support you can give her. I warn you, it won't be an easy. The most important thing you can try to get across to her is it wasn't her fault. Her innocence and trust were callously betrayed, but she can, *must* in fact, learn to trust again, but more wisely."

"Of course."

He extended his hand to the doctor. "Thank you for your kindness."

Charlotte returned a rueful smile. "I'm so sorry it was required. I don't envy you the next few months. Please call me if there's anything else I can do."

"We will, Charlotte," his mother murmured, "Thank you for everything."

"Sorry, I can't do more. I will call you with the test results." She reached into her bag and pulled out a small envelope. "Here's the prescription. Call me if there are any problems."

"Pills? *Pourquoi?*" He demanded.

The physician ignored his question and kept walking toward the front door. "I'll call you tomorrow, Renée."

"Yes, tomorrow."

His mother ignored him too. What kind of conspiracy was this? Puzzled he waited, anxiety mounting, until his mother returned. "What are the pills for? If she's in pain, I should get them filled now."

"Maxim, the prescription is to prevent pregnancy."

"Oh." What else could he say? Pregnancy had been the last thing on his mind.

First things first.

His mother would take care of Nikki. He would take care of Mr. Ian Stark.

Antonio's Grill and Cigar Bar advertised itself as one of the few places where a man could still smoke and dine in New York City. While Max seldom indulged in the pleasant pastime of smoking a cigar, he'd chosen the Little Italy restaurant for its location. Besides, the sidewalk café section of the restaurant reminded him of Paris. Antonio's was also known for its grand humidor and excellent selection of cigars. He savored one of them, rolling the aromatic cigar back and forth between the fingers of his right hand.

It was unlikely anyone would notice or disturb his meeting with a prominent attorney from the D.A.'s office. He glanced at his watch. Already ten minutes late. Patience, not being one of his virtues, he shifted in irritation. In order to have a clear view of everyone coming and going, he'd chosen a table in the sidewalk café. He flicked the slow-growing ash from his cigar into the brass receptacle.

From his table he observed a man walking toward him who fit the description Ned had given. He was tall, whippet-thin, dressed in a well-tailored, gray-silk suit. The newcomer stopped and looked from side to side, as if searching for someone. Max stood and gestured, catching his attention.

"Mr. Devereaux?"

He extended his hand in greeting. "Yes."

"Roy Parsons," the man responded, shaking Max's hand. "Ned Landry told me you have a problem. Something to do with your agency, I believe."

"Yes." Max sat and motioned for the attorney to be seated. "One of the younger models." He dropped his gaze and studied his drink. Discussing what had happened to Nikki with a stranger wasn't something he relished. Thinking about it was difficult enough. "Ned suggested you because of your experience with cases—like this."

"He didn't go into any details." Parsons raised his brows.

Max forced himself to say the words. "She was—uh, drugged, then raped by a photographer after a photo session."

The DA frowned. "She'll have to file a complaint."

Max shook his head. "She refuses. Can anything else be done?"

Parsons leaned back and shook his head. "First of all, date rape is both difficult to prove and prosecute. I assume she was examined at an emergency room?"

"No, she wouldn't hear of it. My mother's physician came to the house. Examined her, took blood tests, but, uh—" Max stammered, not wishing to reveal her identity unless necessary. "She became hysterical at the mention of the police."

"So what you're saying is there's no DNA or other evidence?"

Max shrugged, uncomfortable with the details. "She came home and showered before anyone knew what happened."

"Unfortunate..." Parsons admitted, "...but not uncommon."

"She's deathly afraid of anyone finding out, but it's more than that."

"What?"

"She's ashamed. Blames herself."

"Any witnesses?"

"Only friends of his. She doesn't remember what happened."

"Not good. They'll all swear she was with him willingly. Anyone do blood tests for the date rape drug—rohypnol or GBH?"

"Yes, she tested positive for something. He struggled to remember what the doctor had called it. "Yes, I believe it was the first one."

"At least there's evidence she wasn't willing. How old is she?"

"She's a minor—sixteen."

Parsons' eyes widened. "Good God. What about her parents?"

"There's only her mother, and her mother doesn't know."

"What?"

"She doesn't live with her mother. She lives with my mother, who has legal custody."

"Well, I have to be honest. If the girl does pursue it, it will certainly become a matter of public record. Let me tell you one thing. What the defense lawyer will put her through will be as much a violation as the rape. He'll drag her through the mud. He'll put her on display; her entire life history will be fodder for his defense. This young woman doesn't sound like someone who's ready to go through the legal hassles or the character assassination."

"No, she's very fragile, right now. I don't think she could stand it. But surely, this rapist can't be allowed to get away with what he's done?"

Parsons shrugged. "Be realistic. He already has."

"But—" There had to be a way. The photographer couldn't go unpunished.

Parsons cleared his throat. "The *last* thing I would ever do is suggest you take matters into your own hands." Parsons gave Max a narrowed glance.

"You mean—"

"I mean," Parson's paused, "the last thing I would tell you to do is handle this yourself." The attorney's gaze never left Max's.

He nodded. "I understand."

"You understand that I'm not telling you to commit a crime."

"Yes. You have made it very clear. I understand."

Nine

Two weeks after Nikki's rape, awakened in the middle of the night from a restless sleep. Too much coffee too late. She plumped her pillow, but the sound of someone crying invaded her awareness. She sat up in bed and listened. Alexa having a bad dream?

She threw back the bed covers, walked to her granddaughter's bedroom door, opened it and listened again.

Not Alexa. Must be Nikki. Yes, the crying was coming from Nikki's bedroom. Renée walked the short distance to the teenager's room, stopped and listened again.

Crying, whimpering. Her pitiful voice. "No, stop it. No. It hurts. Mommy."

Her heart clenched in her chest. A nightmare. The poor child did remember something. She knocked on the door. *"Chèrie?"*

No answer, but the whimpering continued. The sound of it broke her heart. As much as she hated intruding on the young woman's privacy, but how could she not offer comfort?

Not wanting to startle the sleeping girl by knocking, she eased the door open and walked over to her tossing form. *"Chèrie."*

"No, no," the girl whimpered. "Mommy, help me."

She sat on the side of the bed. "It's *Maman*. You're having a nightmare."

She pulled away from Renée's touch. The girl's eyes opened, but stared, unseeing. "No! Stop. Go 'way." She turned her back to Renée and drew herself into a ball.

Torn by the raw pain in front of her and by her inability to lessen it, Renée waited. Eventually the girl's twitching movements quieted, and her whimpering stopped. She stroked her charge's forehead, then stood and walked to the door. She stopped and cast one last glance over her shoulder. Surely, now Nikki would sleep the remainder of the night.

Nikki combed her fingers back through her hair, then shook her head, assessing the effect in the bathroom mirror, then nodded. It'll have to do, she told herself. A touch of taupe shadow, a hint of blush across her cheekbones, and a smidgeon of gloss were all the makeup she wore when not on a job. Tonight would be the first time she'd been out in two weeks. It was time. She was ready.

Before she could leave, she heard a knock on her adjoining bedroom door. "Come in." She stopped to shake her mane of hair, once more—for the casual effect.

The door opened and Renée peeked around it.

Damn. She'd hoped to make her escape before her over-protective mentor returned. "I didn't know you were back." She attempted a wide smile, knowing she seldom fooled Renée.

"I returned about fifteen minutes ago," Renée said, smiling. "Here, *Chèrie*, I have something for you."

Nikki took it and turned the flower-covered book over in her hands. The pages were blank. She looked at Renée. "For me?"

"For you."

"Why?"

"I have kept a journal for years, and I always have an extra one on hand. I thought you might enjoy it. Writing helps me sort things out," Renée replied with a small shrug.

Her eyes filled with tears. *Maman* knew…knew the fear and misery that stalked her dreams, night after night. And no matter how much she might deny it, her waking hours too. "Th-thank you. It's lovely."

She looked into her mentor's eyes. They shone brightly, as if she were about to cry.

She felt Renée's arms slip around her. She sagged into the embrace, then recovered. Straightening her back, she blinked away her tears. "I'm fine. Really."

"I know. I only want you to know how much I've come to love you. You are very precious to me."

Nikki wavered between collapsing into Renée's arms and pulling away. She ducked her head, unable to meet her mentor's honest gaze. "You've been good to me—better than I deserve," she whispered.

"Not at all, Chèrie. You are a very sweet—"

She took a deep breath and pulled away. "You don't have to baby me. I'll be fine."

"No one will think less of you, if you give in to your feelings."

"I'm all right," she insisted a little stronger than she meant to. "You don't have to worry about me."

"I heard you crying in the night. The first few times, I went into your room, but you were always asleep. I tried to comfort you, but it seemed to make your dreams worse. I want to help you anyway I can."

She pulled away. "I'm fine. I told you." She clasped the book to her chest, knowing she'd been rude. "Th-thank you for the journal. I'll use it, okay?"

Renée smiled. "Promise?"

"Yeah, sure. I mean, like I'm totally over this. I would've had sex with someone, sooner or later, anyway. So, no big deal. I've seen worse things happen on the streets."

"No big deal?" her mentor protested. "You could have—"

"But I didn't. No harm, no foul." She reached over and kissed Renée on the cheek. "Gotta go. Marti and I are going to a club downtown tonight." She pursed her lips and reapplied her gloss.

"But do you not think you should be careful? Please do not go out. Marti's too mature for you. She is—"

"Only seven years older. Old enough to be a chaperone, but young enough to be some fun. Give me a break, okay. I have to go out sometime."

Nikki fluffed her hair one more time, then placed her hands on her hips. "You can't keep me locked up in this house until I'm eighteen. No way!"

"I'm not saying you should. I won't forbid your going, but I wish you would think about it before you do."

"I have thought about it."

"You still have a curfew," Renée warned.

Nikki huffed. "What time?"

"The usual for Friday night, eleven."

"Eleven?" Nikki groaned. "I don't know anyone who has to be in by eleven."

"Eleven." Renée's tone remained firm.

"All right. I'll be here."

"Good." Her mentor's face grew tense. Her lips tightened. "Don't forget there is the fashion show tomorrow. You need your rest."

"Good." She whirled around, leaving her mentor behind and stalked back to her bedroom, muttering beneath her breath, "I need my rest. I'm fine. I'm fine. I'm fine."

But she wasn't, and she knew it.

Ten

Not wanting to attract attention, Nikki eased her way into the hurly-burly madness of the backstage dressing room. As fashion events went, it wasn't a big show, but it would raise a lot of money for the Juvenile Diabetes Association. About half the models were this season's debutantes, no doubt anxious to do their bit for the good of humanity. The others were girls like herself. Girls who worked for a living and didn't have a rich daddy picking up the tab for sports cars, college and fancy ski trips.

Renée had been a tremendous mentor. Lessons in etiquette, how to walk, talk, dress—things Nikki had to learn—things which didn't come naturally. Would they ever?

While envy was not one of her usual failings, life sometimes seemed a little unfair. A few had so much, and others never had a chance at all.

Damn. What a whiner she was. She should count herself among the fortunate, and most of the time she did. What she really envied was the ease with which some girls moved through life—from prep schools and expensive universities to marriages with equally privileged men.

Frankly, she just didn't fit anywhere.

She found an empty mirror and sat, quietly busying herself with her hair and makeup.

"Nikki…"

Hearing her name, she turned around, looking for the source. Two agency models were at the far end of the dressing room. And they were trashing her. Midway in applying blush to her cheeks, she stopped and listened.

"What about Nikki?" one of them asked.

"It's all the talk."

"Why? What's love'em and leave'em Max's little darling done now?"

"You haven't heard? Well, Ian Stark spread it around how easy she was, said she just about attacked him after their photo shoot.

"No shit."

"No shit. Ian told everyone within hearing distance she was the poster girl for Miss Roundheels."

"That's terrible," she heard one of them snigger.

Nikki sat perfectly still, her face burning as if she'd just stepped into a sauna. As unpleasant as it was, she had to hear the rest.

"You haven't heard the best part," the unseen model said with a giggle. "Apparently, Max heard about it and beat the hell out of Ian. Anyway, Mr. Ian Stark went chasing back to England. Urgent business, I hear." Their light laughter trilled.

Nikki shivered. Stop. She hadn't done anything wrong. She took a deep breath, squared her shoulders and lifted her chin. She'd show them...all of them.

One of the dressers rushed over to her side. "*Where* have you been?"

She opened her mouth, but the dresser didn't give her a change to answer. "Never mind, we have to hurry. You're on in five." Turning to one of the other assistants, she clapped her hands together and yelled, "Dawn, get me number seven. Get a move on."

Through their combined efforts, five minutes later Nikki stepped onto the catwalk and prowled down the catwalk with leonine grace. At the end of the runway, she turned, tossed her hair, all the while favoring the onlookers with the look. The look that said, *Look all you want. You'll never touch me.*

In the audience of well-heeled patrons and nearly overcome by Nikki's radiance, Max sat alongside his mother. Nikki's eyes blazed with fire, while her expression appeared to have been carved from the finest ivory. He'd never seen her quite so dazzling. Leaning his head toward his mother, he remarked, "You have done a marvelous job. Nikki is breathtaking."

"*Merci, mon fil.*" She nodded. "I have to agree." She added with a smile, "Even if I say it myself."

"How is she, really?" he found himself asking.

"I wish I knew. She seems to be all right, but she is a bit more temperamental—how you say, rebellious, at times?

"But that's to be expected, *n'est-ce pas?*"

"Expected, *oui.*" She gave a brusque laugh "But still she is not always so easy to handle."

"She's young."

"Hm, yes, but she's at the stage where she thinks she knows everything." Renée laughed again. "Never mind, she is headstrong, much like you were at that same age, I must constantly remind myself."

He emitted a low chuckle. "*Oui, Maman,* I remember." While he kept a professional eye on the other models from the agency, it seemed that none of the others created quite the same air of excitement Nikki generated with her duality of fire and ice.

His mother leaned her head next to his. "Yet she is wonderful with Alexa, so patient. And your daughter dotes on her new big sister."

Inexplicably, this bit of news warmed him on a deep level. "They really do get along, don't they?" He couldn't keep from smiling. "So there is more to the runaway than her pretty face."

"Indeed, even if she is the handful."

"I know I've asked a great deal. I hope you don't regret my impulsive gesture."

"Gesture?" His mother's elegant brows lifted. "Hardly a gesture, *mon fil.*"

"What else could I do? She needed rescuing...and I needed a new model."

"Of course, I understand your motives completely. Do you?"

He shot his mother a don't-go-there look. Smiling, she turned her attention to the runway.

After the fashion show ended, guests mingled, drank champagne and gossiped about the new designs. He threaded his way through the crowd and procured two glasses of champagne, then returned to his mother.

"*Merci,*" she said, accepting the crystal flute. "Did you know, Maxim, that Saturday is Nikki's birthday? I thought we might celebrate with an outing in the park, *en famille.*"

He hesitated, trying to think of a logical reason for avoiding the outing altogether. "I'm not sure the mixing of work and family is a good idea."

"Maxim," she interrupted, shaking her head in obvious disapproval. "That's exactly what you did that when you brought her home. Besides, she thinks you're angry."

"Angry? Why would I be angry with her?"

"The incident with Ian Stark. She thinks you are avoiding her."

"I am, and you know why."

She pursed her lips and cast him a knowing glance. "Perhaps you should tell *me* why."

He shrugged. Damn, he shouldn't have to explain to his mother. It was uncomfortable to acknowledge to himself, much less to her.

She arched a brow. "Then shall I tell *you* why?"

He sipped his champagne and looked around, hoping no one was listening to their conversation. "Fine, *Maman,* tell me why."

"You are attracted to her, and you are afraid of where it might lead, *n'est-ce pas?*"

"She's hardly more than a child. To Nikki I am an old man."

His mother gave a quiet snort and shook her head in disagreement.

"The age difference will not always be a factor. Sometime you will have to address this thing between you."

"There is nothing between us."

"You are very much mistaken, if you think to pull the wool over the eyes of your *maman*. I have known you too long."

He restrained a sigh. As always, his mother could see straight through him. He'd never been able to fool her as a child, and he remained transparent as a pane of glass, even now. "Forgive my rudeness, but let us not discuss this, anymore."

"You have done nothing for which to be forgiven." She hesitated, "But what you must do is forgive yourself—for the death of Solange. That was not your fault."

"I'm afraid this is something else on which we disagree." From the corner of his eye, he spied Nikki on the far side of the room. The haughty beauty from the catwalk had disappeared, leaving behind an elegant, but shy, waif. More than anything, he wanted to protect her, cosset her. He tamped down his impulse to gather her in his arms.

Damn. She had turned his way and caught him watching her. She gave him a brilliant smile and started making her way toward him.

He turned to his mother. "A picnic on Saturday is fine," he said hurriedly, looking at his watch. "Call me with the details. I just remembered I promised to call Ned about—uh, our tennis match." Such a coward he was, not to mention a liar.

His mother frowned. "But I thought—"

"*Désolé*. Have to go." Without another word, he kissed his mother's cheeks and left. One confrontation with Nikki avoided. One to go. Surely by Saturday, he'd have regained some self-control.

Nikki watched in disbelief as Max beat it. He must really be disgusted with her. All she'd wanted was to talk to him in private. There were things she needed to say. He'd defended her honor, after she'd made such a mess of things. At least, she owed him a 'thank you' for beating up that bastard of a photographer. Never in her wildest dreams would she ever have expected him to do anything so heroic. Maybe he was displeased with her for some other reason. Maybe she hadn't performed up to expectations on the catwalk. At least she hadn't tripped or fallen flat on her face.

She worked her way through the crowd to Renée, trying to avoid jostling anyone.

"You were lovely dear," a mink-clad woman told her in passing.

"Thank you," Nikki replied, over her shoulder, continuing on her way. As she grew closer, she saw her mentor was smiling. At least

Maman was pleased with her.

Renée held out her hands, clasping Nikki's, then kissed her on both cheeks. "Ah, *Chèrie*, you were *magnifique*. I am so proud of you."

"*Merci,* I'm glad you think so."

"And why would I not? What troubles you?"

"Oh, nothing. I just thought Max might hang around."

"He was so sorry to rush off, but he needed to call his attorney about something."

"Really?" She chewed her lip, uncertain what to say next. As a rule, the older woman was painfully frank, but she surmised Renée might just be telling one of those little white lies–to keep from hurting Nikki's feelings. "I thought he might still be upset with me."

"Maxim isn't upset with you. No, indeed. He will be joining us for your birthday celebration this weekend in the park. So you see, there is nothing to worry your pretty little head about."

"Really, a picnic? Wow." On impulse, Nikki gave her mentor a ferocious hug. "You're the best. You're so good to me. I don't know what I'd do if-if," she stammered, "if it weren't for you and Max. I mean I haven't done anything to deserve all this." She gestured, including the gathering with a sweep of her arm.

"Nonsense. You are exactly where you belong, doing exactly what you should be doing, except perhaps finishing your schooling," Renée cooed.

"No-o-o," Nikki groaned. "Not that again." The very thought of school made her want to run for her life.

"*Oui*, that again. But of course, you must get the GED thing. That is an absolute." She looked about the room.

Nikki glanced around the room as well. Luckily, no one seemed to be paying any attention to their conversation. After all, in two days she would be seventeen, and that was a lot more grown up than sixteen. At least it had always sounded like it to her...not that she felt any older.

"We promised your mother you would finish your high school studies, and I intend for you to keep that agreement."

"I know. I just hate the thought of it."

"But you will not have to attend classes every day. I know you are intelligent enough to study on your own and take the test. You will do brilliantly, I am sure."

"Okay. I give up." Renée Devereaux was one stubborn woman; Nikki learned that fact quite soon after moving into the townhouse.

"Good. That is a wise decision. Now let us mingle, and no champagne for you. The American law says you are too young to sample even the finest French Champagne. Such a pity." Renée gave her a wry smile. "But there is plenty of time for that."

"I'd rather go home," she said, before adding with a grin, "and study."

"Hmph," Renée replied with an elegant shake of her head. "Do not think to fool me. I am not so naive, *Chèrie*."

Nikki grinned. "Busted." She gave her mentor another quick hug. "Okay, I'll tag along beside you and mind my manners while I'm at it."

A concerned expression flashed across Renée's face. "Hm, I am not so sure I trust this new person in front of me. She is much too agreeable. Tell me, what have you done with my old Nikki?"

"She's on her good behavior, for once. Scary, huh?"

"To be sure."

"I know I've been a lot of trouble lately," Nikki began.

"*Chèrie*, things happen. Sometimes very bad things. What counts is that you have people who love you and want to protect you." She shrugged. "Sometimes this means I have rules you might not care for— like curfews."

Nikki nodded. "And no smoking. I guess I just want you to know I appreciate it, even if I don't always act like it."

"I know. I know."

Further conversation was interrupted by the arrival of a slender woman, dressed in an elegant black ensemble. "Renée, darling, how lovely to see you. And is this your new protégée I've heard so much about?"

Nikki's face froze into an automatic smile, as she acknowledged the introduction, her mind back on the elusive Max. Did he really have business or had he ducked out to avoid her?

Eleven

Saturday morning dawned bright and clear. Nikki ran to the armoire and started rummaging through her clothes. What would she wear? After all, Max would be there. She didn't want to be too dressed up. Not like she was trying to impress him, but of course she was.

Okay, what would she wear to a picnic, if Max weren't coming? The answer was easy: a pair of jeans and a T-shirt.

Now that she'd made up her mind, she pulled out her best-fitting Levi 501 jeans and threw them across the bed. She crossed to the dresser and yanked open a drawer. Ah ha. There it was, the brand new baby blue tee she'd purchased in the Bahamas after the swimsuit shoot. Small discreet navy blue embroidery spelled out Bahama Mama. Her wardrobe selected, she headed for the bathroom.

One foot in the shower, Nikki giggled. "Bahama Mama, yeah right." It'd been weeks since she'd felt this good. This was going to be a good day, she promised herself. A very good day.

By ten o'clock, the weather report warned of a possibility for rain and severe thunderstorms by late afternoon. Of all the days for the weather to screw up—her birthday. Restless, Nikki paced about the large airy kitchen, watching Renée prepare the picnic basket.

"But what'll we do if it rains? We can't have a picnic in the rain, much less a thunderstorm."

Renée looked out the tall arched windows that flanked the dining area, then shook her head. "I think the rain will hold off. Don't worry. The sun is still quite bright, and there are no clouds in the sky that I can see."

Nikki gave a loud sigh and slumped across the counter. "It's my birthday, and I don't want it ruined."

"It will be all right. You'll see." Renée said, continuing to scoop melon balls. "Here, here's another melon spoon. If you help me, we'll finish them quickly. I want to get them back into the refrigerator."

"Sure." She took the weird looking spoon and watched Renée's technique. It didn't look all that difficult. She took one half of a honeydew melon and attempted to copy Renée's actions exactly. The pale green fruit scooped up easily, forming a round ball. "Hey, not bad."

She scooped another one.

"See, *Chèrie*. Very easy, *n'est-ce pas?*"

"*Oui, madame*." Nikki chuckled. Maybe Renée was right. The rain would hold off.

"Let me see. Do just enough to fill that bowl, and I will see to the paté."

Nikki grimaced. "Paté? On a picnic? Eww."

"Oh, I have researched the American picnic. Never fear, there will be fried chicken, the Boston baked beans and even some of those potato chip things for you and Alexa." Her mentor wrinkled her nose and frowned in imitation of Nikki's.

Nikki threw her head back and laughed. "This is going to be some special picnic—fried chicken and goose liver."

"But of course," Renée chuckled, then added, "and I have not yet wished you *Bon fête*. It will be a very special day, I promise." Renée turned to Nikki and hugged her.

"*Merci, Maman*," Tears threatened to well up in her eyes. Not wanting to seem too immature, she blinked them away.

"Your French is coming along very well."

"Really?"

"Really."

"I'll never get the "R" right."

Renée's laughter trilled through the kitchen. "No, probably not, but it is the effort that counts. You will not be sorry you took the time for the lessons."

"No, it's a beautiful language, so romantic."

"Ah, *oui*, romance," Renée responded with a knowing look. "Something you have plenty of time for, much later. No?"

"Much later, yes." Like probably never, she thought, then gave a mental shake. Today was special. And she wouldn't let the other crap weigh her down. Today she and Max would be on a picnic *together*.

In the back seat of his limousine, Max had a long strict, albeit silent, discussion with himself. Rather than face Nikki, he'd been a jerk at the fashion show, running out the way he had. She deserved his support, as an employee and as a friend of the family. He'd been so upset by what had happened to her with that low-life Stark he'd given little thought to how she might have perceived his behavior.

The doctor had warned them Nikki would be fragile, perhaps for quite a while. But what he'd done was plain neglect. Typically, he'd left it to his mother to bind the girl's emotional wounds, preferring to enact a physical response where it would do the most good. Beating up Ian Stark had given him more satisfaction than he'd dared to admit, but the animal had deserved it. And worse.

Why was he always leaping to Nikki's defense? The urge to protect her was only part of it. More disturbing were the other urges. He'd done the usual. Focused on work and saw other women. It helped…to a degree.

Today was her seventeenth birthday and special because they would be celebrating together as a family. At seventeen she still dwelt in that nebulous universe—neither adult nor child. Another year and she would be legally an adult, able to strike out on her own and make her way in the world.

Until then, he vowed he would make every effort to treat his mother's protégée with friendship, because there could be nothing else between them. Today would be a test of his resolve. He closed his eyes and counted to ten, then twenty, but a kaleidoscope of images of Nikki and her blue eyes shining with love made him stop. What a fool he was.

Several times for the next hour, Nikki ran to the window and looked at the sky. Each time she did, all she could see were white cotton-ball clouds, which seemed content to float around like they had nothing better to do. To her mind's eye, these puffy good-natured clouds didn't look like the kind that would be so cruel as to rain on anyone's parade—or birthday picnic. So far, so good.

And each time she ran to the window and checked the sky, Alexa would run to the door. "Is Papa here yet?"

Nikki grinned. The little girl was as excited about seeing her papa as Nikki. Almost. "No, not yet, but soon."

"But how long is *soon*?"

"Well…" Nikki stalled, looking at her watch again. She was sort of anxious for Papa to show his face too. "Any time now." She pointed at the grandfather clock in the foyer. "Your daddy should be here when the big hand gets to the three."

Alexa tossed her head and stamped her foot, her blond curls bouncing. "Hmph, I can tell time. He better hurry."

Nikki wanted to giggle, but hid it. "No," she told Alexa, "not a long time, just fifteen minutes."

"Fifteen! That's too long."

Nikki knew when she was licked. "Okay, it's a long time, but in fifteen minutes your Papa will come right up those steps and take us to the park."

"Okay." Alexa put her hand on the doorknob. "I'm waiting for Papa on the step."

"Why don't you stay right here and watch through the glass for him. You'll be our lookout, okay."

A frown, then a grin occupied the five-year-old's face. "Okay, I'm the lookout."

"The inside lookout," Nikki insisted. As neighborhoods went, they lived in a safe one, but it was still New York. No sense in taking any chances.

"Yes, inside lookout." Alexa finally nodded in agreement.

"Okay, now, I'm going to help *Maman* finish packing our lunch, so you give a big shout when he pulls up."

"Okay." Alexa turned around, true to her promise, and gave a big shout. "He's here! Papa's here!" She jerked open the door and launched into her father's arms before he was halfway up the steps.

"Help. I've been mugged," Max said with mock terror, hugging his daughter tightly in his arms.

Nikki looked down into Max's clear green gaze and felt like she was drowning. What was it about him? Why this man?

Wearing cut-off jeans with a navy and green striped rugby shirt, he seemed younger. It was the first time she'd ever seen him wearing anything but a severely tailored black suit. Her eyes traveled upward. His calves and thighs were darkly tanned and muscular... Nikki gulped and shifted her eyes back to his face, hoping like hell he hadn't caught her checking out his equipment. His eyes twinkled at her, an amused smile on his lips.

Oh, God, he had. The blood rushed to her face.

"*Joyeaux anniversaire*, Nikki." Max said, his accented voice soft as a caress.

How did he do that? How could he make 'happy birthday' sound so—so sexy? Before she could think of a single thing to say, he kissed her lightly on each cheek. All in all, Nikki decided his European manner of greeting was a pretty good deal. She just wished she had the nerve to kiss him back—just to be polite, of course.

"Uh, thank you," Nikki replied, finally finding her voice.

"Are you ready?"

"Ready?"

"For your birthday, the picnic in the park?" Max reminded her, grinning.

"Oh, yeah, the picnic." *Right on dummy*. A couple of cheek kisses, and she couldn't think straight. He could see right through her with those crystal green eyes.

"Maxim, is that you?" Renée's voice called from the interior of the townhouse.

"*C'est moi, Maman*."

***

Nikki leaned back in the limousine and sighed. How many people went to a picnic in a limousine? Two large picnic hampers had been stowed away in the car trunk, along with a soccer ball and two large white linen tablecloths.

Max rode up front with his driver Albèrt, but he kept turning around talking to her and Alexa. She couldn't ever remember seeing Max in such a light-hearted mood. Maybe her apology wouldn't be so difficult, after all.

"I want to ride up front with Papa," Alexa declared.

"No, no," Renée responded in her no-nonsense voice. "You are already belted in, so you must stay back here with us."

Max turned around and flashed a smile at his daughter, showing white even teeth. "Papa will ride in the back with you on the way home, okay?"

Alexa gave her father a happy smile and nodded. "Okay, Papa."

While Nikki and Renée located the perfect spot for their outing, Alexa tagged along with her father and the driver as they retrieved the hampers from the limo. The area chosen was located on the edge of the large meadow, in the shade of nearby trees. An absolute necessity on the hot, mid-August day.

Renée directed the proceedings. "First the tablecloths, then we shall unpack the hampers. The food is in this one, the china, silverware, crystal and silver wine cooler in the other." Under Renée's precise instructions, lunch was laid out in no time.

"I've never seen such a fancy picnic, Maman," Nikki murmured in absolute awe at the display before her. It was elaborate enough to invite Martha Stewart, not to mention celebrate Nikki's birthday with crusty French bread, cheese, melon balls, tomato-basil penné pasta, along with wine chilling in the silver wine bucket. For the more American palate were fried chicken, baked beans and potato chips.

"I wanted the day to be very special for you." Renée brushed a straggling auburn curl off her glistening forehead. "It does become so warm in New York in July. I wonder that everyone doesn't melt. Next year, we will rent a cottage and spend the summer at the seashore."

Nikki gave a deep sigh. "That would be wonderful, but I'll probably be working."

"Oh, you won't have to work all the time, and it will do you good to get away from the city. When we lived in France, every August we went to my old family home in Provençe."

Summer in Provençe. It sounded wonderful. Nikki and her mother had never stayed in one place long enough for it to be home, much less have a vacation home.

"We've been so busy the last year with launching your career that we haven't had time to play, but next year will be different." Renée continued to tweak the display before her.

"I'm sorry if I interfered with your plans for the summer..." Nikki began.

"No, no, *Chèrie*, you must not think that. I have never felt as alive as I have the last year. It has been wonderful for me. I had forgotten how much I missed the business."

"I'm glad, 'cause you—you and Max have changed my life beyond my wildest dreams. One minute I'm running from a pimp and the next—there's M-Max."

"*C'est beau, Maman*," Max said, leaning over and kissing his mother's cheek.

"*Merci, Maxim*." Maman smiled, gazing at her preparations with apparent satisfaction.

Nikki's head swiveled, in surprise. She'd been too engrossed in her own thoughts and hadn't heard Max return. He held Alexa one arm on his hip and carried a soccer ball with his free hand. Quite a picture they made. One she wouldn't soon forget.

"She said she was tired," he explained.

"I'm not tired anymore, Papa," Alexa said, squirming out of his grip. Smiling, Max set his daughter down.

"I've never seen anyone use real china and silver for a picnic in the park before," Nikki commented, unable to think of anything remotely intelligent to say. Even to herself she sounded like a died-in-the-wool ditz.

Max nodded, his eyes twinkling with good humor. "*Mais oui*. It's because we're French."

"I guess that explains it, then," she replied, her natural sauciness returning. Max's easy-going attitude had thrown her for a loop. It made him seem too approachable—too sexy. She liked seeing him relaxed. Today, he reminded her of the way he'd been the night they'd had dinner at Sally's.

"But of course, Nikki," Renée agreed with a laugh. "It's your birthday."

"And," Max interjected, while pouring three glasses of white wine. He handed one to Renée and kept one for himself, "you're a special part of our family. Happy Birthday from all of us," he said and handed a half glass to Nikki. "Just a tiny swallow for the birthday girl."

"Happy Birthday, Nikki," Alexa squealed, hugging Nikki around her thighs.

Nikki accepted the glass, and uncertain what to do next, patted the top of Alexa's head in an absent-minded gesture.

With a wide, ebullient gesture, Max said, "Now, let's share this wonderful luncheon which *Maman* has so splendidly prepared." He sank down onto a blue-and-white plaid blanket. "Come on, I'm starving."

"Me too." Alexa chimed, plopping down next to her father.

Renée settled gracefully beside Alexa, leaving Nikki a spot next to Max. Nikki took a deep breath, and dropped to the ground, wondering what the aliens had done with the real Max Devereaux. She hoped they wouldn't reclaim the new one—not for a while, anyway.

Forty-five minutes later, Nikki, very aware she'd eaten more at the picnic than she had all week, gave a theatrical gasp. "Enough. I'll lose my job, if I eat more."

Max assumed a severe expression. "I assure you, *Mademoiselle* Nikki, that your indulgence today will not be held against you, but you must not make a habit of eating four drumsticks, three servings of pasta, a kilo of melon, and half a birthday cake."

"I did not," she protested.

"But you did. I counted," Max insisted, unable to control his expression any longer. Muscle by muscle his face betrayed him, his frown dissolving into a wide grin.

"No, Papa, I ate the drum sticks," Alexa piped.

"No, no," Max maintained, holding up four fingers. "I saw her. Nikki ate four drumsticks."

"Children." Renée warned them. "Why don't you take a nice long walk, while I clear up things?"

"I'll help you," Nikki offered.

"No, shoo-shoo, go on. Albèrt is coming back to assist me. See, there he is now."

Nikki turned her head. True enough, the limo driver had returned, just in time, carrying another cooler. It seemed to Nikki, Renée had certainly planned everything to a "tee."

Max jumped up and extended his hand to her. "You heard her. She's given her orders. She must be obeyed."

Nikki accepted his hand with a gracious, "Thank you." The romance novels had it right. The oft-described 'electric current' zapped right up her arm, left her downright breathless.

"Me too, Papa!" Alexa jumped up and down, tugging on his shirt.

"Of course, *ma petite*," Max offered his other hand to his daughter.

Alexa tugged on Max's left hand. "Let's go," she prompted. "Nikki too," Alexa insisted, grabbing Nikki's free hand, she positioned herself between them.

Nikki gave a helpless shrug. "Okay," she agreed. At the ripe old age of five, Alexa could be quite a handful. Very determined and everything had to be now. "I don't think we have a choice."

Max nodded. "I believe the die is cast. *Maman* and Alexa have decreed that we shall have a walk, and so we shall."

Renée watched her son and Nikki being pulled along by her granddaughter. She turned to the driver. Albèrt glanced at her then at the trio, his eyebrows elevated, nearly to the line of his scalp.

"Nice little family, *n'est-ce pas, Madame?*"

Renée shook her head, and dropped into French. "*Non*, not yet, Albèrt." Not surprised he would take interest in family affairs played out before them, since he had been with her family for twenty years. "Nikki is far too young."

"Pity, but she won't always be too young. They seem to suit, and I think she likes him, too. How does Maxim feel about her?"

Renée gave an amused smile. "I'm not sure even my son knows the answer to that question."

Albèrt grew thoughtful. "Maxim has had tragedy touch him once. By nature, he is cautious in such matters."

"Hmm, well, there is plenty of time, no?" Renée remembered when Maxim had cast caution to the winds with Solange. She shook her head. "I hope he remains so. Now, you have the cooler with the ice cream. And is there plenty of ice?"

"Of course, *Madame*." Albèrt gave a formal bow, still holding the cooler with both hands.

Only too aware of the heat, Renée looked closely at Albèrt's flushed face. "Forgive me, you must be roasting in your uniform. Remove your jacket and loosen your shirt collar. Here." She patted the spot beside her. "Sit next to me in the shade until the young ones return."

"But, *Madame*," he protested.

"We'll share some of the champagne, and I'll prepare you a plate."

"But—"

"But nothing, Albèrt. There is no reason to stand on formality. It is entirely too warm." Without waiting for any further protests or his assent, Renée busied herself, preparing his lunch.

Even in the shade, perspiration broke out across Maxim's forehead and the back of his neck. How much was due to the heat of the day and how much to the lovely young woman beside him?

His daughter had tired of holding his hand and now ran several feet ahead of them. "Not too far ahead," he warned.

"She's having a fun day," Nikki said.

Max turned to her. "This is *your* day. Are you having a fun day, too?"

He watched a cat-licking-the-cream smile creep across Nikki's face. She glanced at him from the corners of her impossibly blue eyes.

"Yes, I'm having a fun day too."

"I'm glad." He hesitated. There was so much he wanted to tell her, things he wanted to reassure her about, but neither did he want to spoil her day by reminding her of the rape.

They walked along, keeping an eye on Alexa.

"Uh—" Nikki started.

"Yes?"

"I wanted to apologize for the way I acted and say 'Thank you'."

Maxim held his breath. She was going to bring it up anyway. He finger combed his sweat-dampened hair, wishing he didn't care so strongly for the young girl beside him. "No need to apologize. You didn't do anything wrong."

Her voice dropped to a murmur. "I was stupid and reckless, and I've been a bitch the last few weeks. I don't know why *Maman* puts up with me. My real mother wouldn't."

Not knowing what to say, Max shrugged. "It wasn't your fault, Nikki."

"Yes, it was. I wouldn't listen to you. I thought I could take care of myself. I mean I lived on the streets, for Pete's sake. What a dumb ass I was."

"And I should have carried you out of there over my shoulder."

She chuckled at the image. "I'm a pretty big package."

Max grinned. "Tall, not big. Besides, I have to accept some responsibility for what happened. I knew his reputation. I even warned him, while you were changing, told him how young you were."

Nikki stopped in her tracks and look sharply at him. "Is that why you beat him up? Because you felt responsible?"

"You knew about that?" He should have known she'd hear about it. Modeling agencies were hotbeds of gossip. His was no different.

She nodded.

Max ran his hand through his hair again, stalling. His tactic failed. His words came in a rush. "Partly, but I was so damned mad. That he would drug you and take something he had no right to have—" He clenched his fists and shook his head, unable to continue. He felt as if he'd violated some code of honor—more likely his vow of never revealing his feelings to the girl—not yet a woman—who stood before him, her eyes wide, lips parted.

"I figured you were like everyone else who said I deserved it." Nikki ducked her head, then gazed back into his eyes. "Thank you, for not living up to my expectations."

"I-I." The words died. His power of speech failed him. So much he wanted to say, but couldn't. It wouldn't be fair.

No, He was kidding himself. He was afraid. It wasn't only her youth. He was afraid of loving anyone, especially her...not the way she needed and deserved to be loved.

"'S'all right, Max, you've done enough for me. Enough to last a lifetime."

He swallowed, trying again. "You're young and you have a wonderful life ahead of you."

Nikki returned his platitude with a rueful smile and a Groucho Marx wiggle of her eyebrows. "I know. And we'll always be the best of friends."

"We will."

She shot him a swift glance, then softened it with a broad wink. "Then I guess it's true what they say, you can't ever have too many friends."

He nodded. If only... he were younger or she were older.

Alexa ran up and tugged on his hand. "Papa? Time for cake and ice cream?"

He glanced at his watch and said, "Yes, it's time."

Together they walked back to the sheep meadow. At his shoulder, Nikki moved quietly along the trail, silent, but wearing an enigmatic smile. Deep in thought, he wondered what the future held for all of them?

PART II: THE MASQUE

Twelve

New York, January 2000

The sun shone in a myriad of colors through the stained glass rose window at the far end of the cathedral. Wafts of sandalwood incense curled upward toward the nave. Banks of lilies and roses added their fragrant scents to the solemn occasion.

Nikki gripped the lectern, hoping her hands wouldn't shake and her voice wouldn't break. The numbness which had settled over her since Renée's death hadn't lifted.

Time. Blind-sided by her mentor's massive stroke, Nikki'd had no time to prepare. Nothing she could do would ever bring back the only real mother she'd ever known. She cleared her throat and began.

"Renée Devereaux was the strongest woman I've ever known. She was the much-loved mainstay of her family, a loving mother and devoted grandmother. For all her consummate professionalism and forward-thinking, she still had time to take a street kid and mold her into a decent human being. She had a heart and the wisdom to see the good in those around her. It may sound trite, but the world I've come to know will be the dimmer for her loss. *Maman*, we miss you."

Purposefully Nikki had kept the eulogy short. She didn't trust herself to say more without breaking down. And that wouldn't help anyone, especially Max or teenage Alexa. The younger girl who'd been a little sister to Nikki sat next to her father, sniffling into a tissue while Max himself remained stoic and silent.

After the funeral, Max received friends and mourners at Renée's townhouse. Nikki joined them at Alexa's behest. Truly she didn't know what to say to Max to comfort him—or whether to even try.

Alexa slipped her arm around Nikki's waist. "Daddy's taking *Grandmère* back to France."

"Is he?" Not such a surprise once she thought about it. "She'd like that—being back in her own country."

"I know, but…" Alexa stopped, then sighed. "I can't visit her way over there. Who'll keep fresh flowers on her grave if we don't?"

"I'm sure your father will see that it's done."

Shaking her head, Alexa insisted, "It's not the same."

"But *Maman* had many friends in Paris too." Nikki's tears threatened to spill, but she held on to her composure for Alexa's sake. "Besides, she's wherever we are. She gave us both so much love, and that won't ever go away."

Alexa glanced at her father who was surrounded by those who'd come to offer their condolences. "After we get back from France, Daddy's going to move in here."

"That's wonderful. The two of you will be together."

"No! He's sending me away to boarding school. I know I'll just hate it."

Boarding school? What was he thinking? Still if that was his intention, she should support it. "No, you won't. Boarding school will be fun. You'll see."

"I wouldn't have to go away…" A speculative gleam appeared in the youngster's green eyes, "…if you moved in with us."

Nikki swallowed hard. The little minx of a matchmaker was at it again. "Alexa, your father might have something to say about that. You know I have my own place."

"But—"

"Shh, before someone hears you." *Like your father*. She looked around to see if he could've overheard them. Damn. Max was heading toward them.

Alexa didn't hesitate, grabbing his wrist. "Daddy, please don't send me away."

"Not now, Alexa," he said wearily, as though he'd heard it all before. "Why don't you see if Mrs. Landry would like something to eat? I want to talk to Nikki for a moment."

The teenager looked from one to the other, then winked. "Okay." Alexa spun around and advanced on Ned's wife.

Max turned to Nikki, taking her hand in his. "Thank you for coming and for your eloquent eulogy. *Maman* is honored by your words."

Confused by Max's touch, Nikki stammered, "I-I'm glad you think so, but I'd just rather have her here alive."

"We all would."

"Of course." She sighed. "I'm not very good at offering comfort, Max. *Maman* was…" Unable to continue, she stopped.

"She was so proud of you," Max said, his voice deepening with emotion and his accent thicker than she'd had heard it in years.

"I know. She told me. Never stinted on praise—she was good that way." If he said another word, she'd break down and blubber like a baby. "I have to go. Early call tomorrow. You understand?"

Still holding her hand between his, Max murmured a polite, "Of course."

Did she imagine it or did he seem disappointed by her leaving? To be honest, she didn't have an early call, but she couldn't hold it together much longer, especially if he insisted on holding her hand and saying nice things. She eased her hand from his. "I'll just say good-bye to Alexa."

Max Devereaux, who was still her boss—and therefore out of bounds—never failed to affect her. Dammit. It just wasn't fair. Why couldn't she just get over her infantile crush?

Thirteen

End of March 2000

Nikki's flight from Nice had been arduous with plane changes in Paris and London. The last leg from London to New York had seemed much longer than usual, leaving her with plenty of time to take stock.

Plenty of time? Make that too much time. On one hand, her career was solid, enabling her to maintain two homes, in addition to the condo she'd bought her mother.

On the downside, her friend and mentor's death in January had been a blow, unexpected and swift, shaking Nikki to her very core. She'd talked with the active sixty-one year old the evening before she died. They'd made plans to have one of their long gossipy lunches as soon as Nikki returned from her current assignment. But now...

Renée's passing had served to remind Nikki of the fragility of life. She'd always thought she had plenty of time, but one never really knew what life held in store. Maybe it was time she slowed down and smelled the proverbial flowers...and got involved with someone.

But there was only one person she trusted or wanted that much.

Max.

Max stood staring out the window at the city street far below. People were rushing home to be with their loved ones. With Alexa in boarding school, he was alone. Nearly three months since his mother had died. How could he have wasted so much time? Nikki was due back from the shoot in Nice. Maybe he should call and ask her to dinner. What would be the harm in that? Nothing ventured, nothing gained, right? If his mother were here, she would agree it was time. If she were only here.

He suppressed his grief and strode back to his desk and punched in Nikki's number. The phone rang four times, then clicked, signifying her voice mail would answer. Damn. "Nikki, this is Max. Please call me when you get home."

Two minutes later his phone rang. He grabbed it, hoping it was Nikki.

It was.

"Is something wrong?" she asked, a note of tension in her throaty voice.

"No, I—uh, merely wanted to ask if you would have dinner with me tomorrow night. I—" Embarrassed, he found himself stumbling over his words like an awkward schoolboy.

"Dinner? Another dinner at Sally's Diner?" The tension in her tone melted into one of teasing.

"Sally's? Oh, yes, *Sally's*." He'd almost forgotten the name of the diner, but recovered quickly, "No, not Sally's this time. L'Haute Cuisine," he said, suggesting his favorite small French bistro. "If that's all right?"

"Of course. Sounds great."

"Quarter till eight?"

"Yes, I'll see you then," she said, her voice dropping.

He replaced the receiver and let out a breath of relief. Nothing so difficult about asking Nikki to dinner. Finally, without the encumbrance of an unconscionable age difference... He couldn't resist a small smile. Perhaps, he might soon hold Nikki in his arms and tell her—what? That he'd been in love with her for years. Nothing so rash. He'd scare her off. No, this dinner would be more of a reconnaissance mission to learn the lay of the land, so to speak.

The following evening, Max walked up and down in front of Nikki's apartment building. So damned nervous, he was fifteen minutes early. A hint of spring was already in the brisk evening air. What if she didn't care to see him in any role, other than as her employer? What if she were involved with someone else? He knew when and where she went on fashion shoots, but on a personal level, she remained a mystery. If only his mother were still alive, she would've known.

The doorman had started giving perturbed glances in Max's direction, so he screwed up his courage and nodded at the doorman.

"Max Devereaux to see Miss Prentice."

"Certainly, sir." The doorman gave Max a calculating smile, then called Nikki on the intercom. "Miss Prentice, Mr. Devereaux's here."

"Thank you. Send him up."

On hearing her cheerful reply to the doorman, Max's heart hammered into overdrive. Damn. He felt like a teenager, instead of thirty-eight-year-old man. Stop it.

Max regained his composure and walked briskly toward the ornate brass-door elevator. He jabbed the UP button twice and waited. He looked at his watch. He was still early.

Ding.

Max looked up, startled, then stepped aside, allowing a tiny elderly woman and her, equally elderly, white poodle to emerge. He stepped into the elevator and hit the button for Nikki's floor. All the way up to the twelfth floor, he reminded himself, this was just Nikki. Nikki, the runaway he rescued from the streets. Not an ogre. Not a mean bone in her beautiful body. Merely a dinner with an old friend.

The elevator shuddered to a stop. He took a deep breath and stepped off the old elevator. How like Nikki to live in an architecturally important building, one that possessed the charm and grace of another time. There appeared to be four apartments on the twelfth floor, Nikki's occupying the southwest corner.

He walked to her door and rapped the lion's head knocker against the black enameled door. She opened the door immediately, in all her haphazard glory. Blond hair damp. No makeup. Only two buttons on her cream silk blouse fastened.

Mon Dieu. His mouth grew dry as cotton.

"Come on in. Sorry, I'm running late. I tried to reach you, but you must not've had your cell phone on," she explained, padding across the highly polished hardwood floors in bare feet. "I have to finish my makeup and hair. I won't be long. Have a drink," she told him over her shoulder. "The bar's in the black lacquer cabinet. Make yourself at home." Her voice faded away as she hurried down the hall to her bedroom.

Grateful she wasn't there to see his hands shake, he poured a glass of wine. He still felt like an adolescent boy and drummed his fingers against the black lacquer cabinet. Was he making a mistake? No, at best it was dinner with an old friend. At worst, it was still dinner with an old friend. His sipped the wine. An excellent vintage.

He looked around the room and marveled at the former street kid's taste in furnishings. His mother had been a great influence on Nikki, but the flair with which the former street kid had assembled the eclectic furnishing was unique. An antique mask collection occupied a place of honor. Next to the mask collection was a piece of graceful Favrile glass. A brightly painted piece of art furniture, stood next to an antique *bureau plat*. Somehow she'd made it all work admirably. It suddenly occurred to him that perhaps Nikki was the reason his daughter Alexa had recently declared her interest in interior design.

His daughter was much closer to Nikki than he. Nikki had remained with his mother for four years and doted on Alexa, and the bond between the two had lasted. He'd moved into the townhouse after his mother died, but Alexa still considered Nikki her older sister.

"Finally, I'm ready." Nikki rushed into the living room wearing a cream and khaki silk trouser suit, her wheat blond hair falling in loose waves to her shoulders. "You look wonderful, Max. I think you must have found the Fountain of Youth. You haven't changed since our dinner at Sally's." She gave him a wide smile that made his heart lurch in his chest. "Of course, you did get rid of your curls." She pouted, then grinned.

"Well, yes. GQ decreed long hair must go. So, what was I to do?" he teased, shrugging.

Nikki giggled. "But of course, you could do nothing else."

The sound of her unassuming chatter filled him with delight. He resisted the temptation to take her in his arms. Years of keeping her at arm's length had given him discipline. Instead, he contented himself with a compliment. "You are the one who's found the Fountain of Youth. You're lovely, as ever." He gave her a kiss on each cheek, then said, "Shall we go?"

Nikki nodded. "Why don't we walk? It's a lovely evening, and I've been inside all day with the Trump shoot."

"Of course." Max had the distinct impression that for Nikki this was dinner with an old family friend, not a date. Best proceed with care. After all, that's all it was.

They walked the few blocks to L'Haute Cuisine while Nikki chattered on about Alexa and related an amusing story about meeting the Donald.

The early spring evening was unseasonably warm. He wanted the night to last forever. Being with Nikki was comfortable. It seemed right.

"*Monsieur* Devereaux and *Mademoiselle* Nikki, how wonderful to see you both. I have a lovely booth for you," the waiter said as he led them through the small elegant restaurant.

"*Merci*, Guillaume," Max replied. It didn't surprise him the waiter knew Nikki. Her striking face had graced the covers of countless magazines. Placing his hand in the small of her back, he felt the muscles in her back tense through her silk jacket, but she turned and gave him a sideways smile. He relaxed. That wasn't so bad.

As they surveyed their menus, Nikki asked, "Do you ever think about our first dinner? I mean I was so—so ragged. I can't imagine how you managed to sit there and eat your dinner with me across from you. You must have been horribly embarrassed."

"Not at all. I was having dinner with a beautiful young girl, who, incidentally, has matured into an incredibly beautiful woman."

Nikki blushed. "Thank you. It's all due to you and Renée. I owe you everything."

"You owe me nothing. I saw a beautiful child on the streets and gave her an opportunity. You've done the rest. But you never would've stayed there. You would've succeeded on your own."

She shook her head. "Not like this. Renée took me in and treated me like a daughter. The life I have is a debt I can never repay."

Alarmed at the direction the conversation was taking, Max shook his head. He didn't want her gratitude. He wanted her love. "This is becoming much too serious a conversation. You have worked hard these many years. You deserve your success. I was happy to be—hmm, an instrument of fate, if you will."

Her eyes widening, she asked, "Do you believe in fate? Have you ever thought that—uh, maybe we were meant to be together?" Her tone pensive, she added hastily, "I mean in the sense that we are in the same business. Same city. Same planet. You know what I mean." She looked down at her menu.

"*Oui*, I believe in fate. The kind of fate which brought me to a stupid play in that section of town, where across the street from me, I would see a young beautiful girl in torn jeans, bumming cigarettes and running from a terrible man. Yes, I believe in fate, and I am thankful for it."

She gazed across the table at him, a small smile playing about her lips.

Damn. He'd said too much. He covered his confusion by quickly asking, "What do you want for dinner? Their *coq au vin* is the best I've ever eaten—in the States, of course."

She gave him a fey smile, suddenly appearing distant. "Yes, that's fine."

"Are you sure?"

Her faraway look vanished as quickly as it had come. "Yes, I love the *coq au vin*. It's my favorite." Nikki flashed him a smile, illuminating her entire face with an inner glow that never failed to affect him. His heart clenched in his chest.

Guillaume took their orders and left them. Again, they were alone. Time for the dreaded small talk. Max cleared his throat. "Uh, so how are things going?"

"Well, Mr. CEO, you should know that better than I." Her wide grin removed the pique from her tone. "The agency and I are both doing quite well, aren't we?"

"Of course, I meant…personally."

A trace of confusion crossed her face. "Personally? I'm fine."

"Are you seeing anyone?"

"*Moi*? No way, besides…" Nikki stopped, looked down at her plate, then at him again. Her eyes intensely blue, her gaze steady. "…my heart's already taken."

"B-but?" he stuttered. "I'm confused. I thought you said, 'no way'."

He inhaled, trying to act as if her answer didn't matter.

"Oh, you know him quite well," she teased, her face flushing.

"Someone at the agency?"

"The *head* of the agency," she replied with a smile that made a dimple appear at the right corner of her mouth.

The head of the agency? It took a second for her words to register. "You mean—"

"Of course, silly. I've had a crush on you for years." She laughed, sounding somewhat self-conscious.

"A... crush?" Max wasn't sure what he'd wanted her to say, but *crush* didn't begin to describe what he felt for her. Was she teasing him? Playing a girlish game? If she only knew the passion he held in his heart, she would never be so cruel.

"You were my first love. I know you never knew. Renée did. But I got over it. You were so much older than I was...and sophisticated. Of course, you were only twenty-eight, but to me..." She shrugged, a mannerism so like his mother's.

"I suppose I am ancient to you now—an old man of almost thirty-nine?"

A dreamy expression came into her eyes for a moment. "No, not at all. The gap is not so wide now." Quickly she took a sip of wine.

A flush spread from her ivory-columned neck to her cheeks. The tell-tale blush pleased him, more than he'd ever thought possible. He hoped her jocular tone was merely a cover for deeper emotions. Wasn't it Shakespeare who wrote "Many a truth is spoken in jest?"

"No, it isn't," he croaked, the words dying in his throat. He caught a whiff of her perfume. Intoxicating—it left him speechless.

A troubled expression crossed Nikki's face. "You know, I miss Renée so much."

"I do too." He swallowed the emotions that threatened to overcome him.

Her face lightened. "It's odd. When I first moved in, she was wonderfully kind, but so strict. She made me stop swearing and stop smoking. She was one tough lady. After the first few days I thought I'd run away again, first chance I had."

"But you didn't."

"No. I guess, even then, I was smart enough to know *Maman* was right about...pretty much everything."

"Yeah, she was."

"I'm sorry. I didn't mean to upset you."

"You haven't. She was important to both of us. It's only right we should remember...and miss her."

"I didn't really know what to say after the memorial service. I wanted to go to the services in Paris, but—"

"I understood. You grieved for her too."

"But still I wanted to offer you comfort. I just didn't know how." She folded, unfolded, then refolded her dinner napkin, smoothing the edges, her gaze somewhat unfocused.

"You were there for Alexa. That meant a great deal to me."

"It was only natural."

"I never thanked you for it."

"It wasn't necessary."

At the time, he'd been overwhelmed by his mother's sudden death. Without being asked, Nikki had taken Alexa home with her for a week, while he'd dealt with the arrangements for the New York memorial service and Parisian funeral.

The sommelier interrupted, "*Monsieur* Devereaux, the wine." Deftly, he popped the cork, offered it to Max, pouring him a sample.

He tasted then nodded to the sommelier, who then poured a glass for each.

He took another sip. "I think you'll like this. It's produced by a vineyard quite close to my farm in Provençe."

Nikki sampled the white wine. "Mm," she said, savoring it. "It's perfect. Not too sweet. Not too dry."

The tip of her pink tongue catching a stray drop of champagne from her lovely lips was almost more than he could bear. Dear heaven, he wished he could do the same. From the corner of his eye, he saw Guillaume bringing their dinner. Saved, from making a fool of himself.

"*Monsieur, Mademoiselle.*"

"It looks wonderful and smells like heaven," Nikki commented, looking up at Guillaume.

"*Oui, le chef*, he is in very fine form tonight, *Mademoiselle.*"

"*Merci*, Guillaume," Max added. Odd that he and Nikki frequented the same small restaurant and yet never crossed paths.

Guillaume bowed, "Enjoy."

Max watched her take a bite of the chicken. "Is it to your liking?"

Nikki swallowed. "Mm, yes, it's tender and juicy. And the sauce is mmm."

Aware he'd been staring at her mouth, again, he picked up his knife and fork and cut off a bite. The aroma filled his mind with memories. Years earlier, *coq au vin* was his father's favorite dish, and his mother prepared it frequently while he was alive.

"I guess you're all settled in the townhouse by now."

"Uh, yes. Pretty much. It's still a little odd, not having my mother there. Sometimes, I almost expect her to walk in the door."

"You must be lonely with Alexa in boarding school?"

"I am, but the agency takes up my time." He couldn't help but wonder if that was her subtle way of inquiring if he was seeing anyone.

Nikki reached across the table and touched his hand, her expression worried. And as always, her merest touch revved his heart.

"Please don't think I'm questioning your judgment for sending Alexa away to school."

"I never thought you were. Anyway, it's the best solution, for now."

"She likes the school. At least she does *now*. She's made some new friends. In fact, I haven't heard from her in several weeks. Actually, I think that's a good sign. When she first went away, she called me nearly every night."

"She did?" Guilt swept over Max. His daughter deserved a home, a real family. What had he done? He'd sent her away from the only home she'd ever known...at the time she needed it most.

"That's why I think she's adapting. She's having too much fun to call."

"Not too much fun, I hope." The thought of his little Alexa—and that was exactly how he thought of her—doing anything but studying worried him.

Nikki gave a short bark of laughter. "You do realize she's growing up, don't you? It won't be long before she's dating."

"Dating?" Max shook his head. "No, I don't think I'll allow that until she's at least thirty." He suddenly grinned. "I suppose all fathers say something like that?"

"Wouldn't know," Nikki said, her expression suddenly serious. "I never had one. I was only two years older than Alexa when I ran away."

"Y-you don't think she'd do something like that, do you? Has she said something?" He cringed at the thought of his daughter on the streets. He ran his hand back though his hair and took a large sip of wine.

"No, of course not. Her situation is very different from mine. She's had the love and support of her family. She would never run away like I did." Nikki frowned, looking down at her plate. "I don't even know why I said that."

"I-I'd be—I mean I don't know what I'd do, if she ever—"

"I'm sorry. I didn't mean to worry you."

"I *am* worried."

"That's only natural, but I'm sure she's fine. Wintercrest is supposed to be a wonderful school."

"It is."

Throughout the rest of the dinner, he grew so involved in watching Nikki eat and emit sensual little noises as she did that he ate very little.

"Aren't you hungry?" she asked, setting her fork across her plate.

"Not really." He took his napkin and wiped his mouth. Again,

Guillaume appeared and saved Max from another awkward moment.

"*M'sieur, Mademoiselle*, dessert?"

"None for me, thank you," Nikki replied.

"*Non, seulement deux cafés, s'il vous plaît.*"

"Very well, *M'sieur* Devereaux." Guillaume turned to Nikki. "*Mademoiselle*," he said, giving her a brief bow before leaving them alone.

Max drummed his fingers on the table, stopping abruptly, once he realized what he was doing. Looking up, he detected a note of amusement in Nikki's eyes. Dammit, she was enjoying his discomfiture.

"Has Alexa thought about where she wants to go after Wintercrest?"

Nikki's question snapped Max from his drift. "Uh, yes, Parsons I think. It's the best, after all."

"Mm hm. "She sipped her wine, then added, grinning, "If she doesn't change her mind at least five times in the next four years."

"*Mon Dieu*, you don't think she'll change her mind that many times, do you?"

Nikki chuckled, a low delightful sound that sent shivers up his spine. He'd always loved her voice, low and husky. It stimulated emotions, nearly kin to memories, in him. Unexplainable, really.

"You'll be lucky if it's only four or five times."

"I tell you, this is not a topic that warms my heart. Frankly it gives me the chills. Alexa is very stubborn when her mind is made up."

"Oh, yeah… just like *Maman*."

Max hoped she would think it was Alexa's future that disturbed him so, rather than the sound of her voice. "It is no laughing matter. Fatherhood is a very difficult proposition."

"You're a great father. Alexa worships the ground you walk on. It'll work out."

Relieved by her encouragement, Max sighed. "I hope you are right. The next few years are going to be interesting."

Nikki raised an eyebrow and smirked. "Mm hm."

Guillaume brought their coffee, steaming hot and fragrant, and poured it. Bowing again, he left them.

Still at a loss for words, Max struggled for a way to broach his feelings. He was sadly out of practice in wooing. For the past ten years, relationships had never been important, merely convenient.

"We must do this again—soon," he said, silently cursing his ineptness. He could be glib when it didn't matter, but when it did, the words jammed in his throat.

"Yes, I'd love to. Call me anytime. Leave a message on my voice mail, or the service can locate me," she'd replied, a little too quickly he thought.

"Of course." Max concentrated on sipping his coffee, thankful the very mundane act of drinking made conversation unnecessary. He glanced at Nikki. She sat, staring at her cup with fascination. Maybe she was as uncomfortable as he.

Later they walked back to Nikki's apartment, enjoying the brisk spring air. He stopped at the door to her apartment.

"More coffee, Max?"

His heart and mind battled for control. But old habits died hard. "*Merci*, but I'm afraid I have an early morning meeting." Way to go. Fall back on the old early-morning-meeting routine.

A wry smile crossed Nikki's face. "Well, I wouldn't want to keep you from your power breakfast."

Unable to resist, he reached out and stroked her cheek. At his tender gesture, her smile turned into a puzzled expression.

What the hell was the matter with him? Then, impulsively, he kissed Nikki on both cheeks—as if here were her damned uncle or something, then stammered. "I-I'll call you—soon."

"Okay," Nikki replied, her voice grown husky again. "I'll look forward to it. G'night, Max." She looked down and chewed her lip, as if suddenly shy.

"*Bonne nuit*," he managed. Damn, his throat was dry. Quickly he turned and walked away. He'd done it again—kept her at arm's length. He wasn't even sure he could call her as he'd promised. Old habits proved difficult to change. He'd take refuge in work—another old habit... just to give her more time, of course.

Who was he trying to fool? He cursed himself all the way to his empty townhouse, not wanting to return home. Before his mother died, the house had been filled with love and laughter. Now it was barren of warmth and held no respite from loneliness. Only Nikki could bring it back to life again...bring him back to life, again.

Nikki closed the door behind him and knew without a doubt that if he'd stayed a single second longer, she would've melted into a puddle on the floor. Bringing both hands to her face, she touched her cheeks, still warm from his light kisses.

Damn. Why had she prattled on and on about having a crush on him? No wonder, he still treated her like she was a teenager. She'd thought when he'd called her the day before that maybe, just maybe, it would lead to something...anything.

But no. She had to act like a goofy school girl and gush all over him at dinner. Very impressive—not.

Besides, Max wasn't known for his long-term relationships. "Love'em and leave'em" was his nickname at the agency. Rumor had it one society deb after another had tried to waltz him down the aisle. How could she ever give her heart and body to Max, only to be dumped a few weeks or months later? She knew the answer, she couldn't.

Unbuttoning her blouse and kicking off her shoes as she went, Nikki stomped into the bedroom, promptly tripped over a footstool and landed on the floor. "Damn."

Frustration mounting, she struggled to her feet. Still, he'd said he wanted to have dinner, again. Just dinner. And here she was trying to read things into the situation that weren't there. He wanted to be friends. Friends, she could handle that.

Take it easy. Take it slow, a calm voice in her head advised. *But it's already been ten years*, another more insistent voice shouted.

Now Max had her hearing voices. If she kept it up, they'd be putting her away somewhere...for a very long time.

Fourteen

Paris, May 2000

Max breathed in the gathering of scents that was uniquely Paris—freshly baked bread and the sharp fragrance of espresso among them. Late to meet an old business acquaintance, he strode along the wide boulevard past an antique store. A reflection glinting in the sunlight caught his eye. He slowed his stride and turned, curious to see what it was.

Displayed in the shop window, a mask.

Quite an old one too. White leather, edged in gilt. It had been the gilt reflecting in the sun that captured his attention. He glanced at his watch. Renaud could wait. Max opened the shop door and stepped inside. The musty scent of old objects met him.

An elegant woman stepped forward. *"On s'occupe de vous, monsieur?"*

"Je voudrais voir le masque qui est dans la vitrine, s'il vous plaît."

"Oui, M'sieur."

Max held his breath, while his countrywoman rushed to the window.

"Here you are, *M'sieur*. It has quite a lengthy provenance. Allow me to procure it for you," she said, handing the mask to him and walking behind the counter.

*"Merci, Ma*dame."

"This mask has an interesting history." She smiled. "I'm not sure I should tell you."

"Pourquoi pas?"

"Well, if you are superstitious, *M'sieur*, I might lose the sale. The mask has been said to bring bad luck. Of course, I do not believe such stories, but if you are faint of heart, I would suggest you pass on this item."

"Superstitious? *Non, Madame.*"

"Well, it is all there in the provenance."

"Of course, *Madame.*"

She named her price, "Ten thousand francs."

He countered, "Four thousand."

"Monsieur, you insult my intelligence. This mask dates from before

the revolution." She countered, again, "Eight thousand francs."

Max shook his head, warming to the game. "Five thousand."

"Tut, tut, *monsieur*, you have the gift of driving the hard bargain. I will make one more offer—a very reasonable offer I must add—seven thousand, five hundred francs."

"Seven thousand even, *Madame*. Not only are you a great beauty, but a business woman, as well.

"And you are a true Frenchman, *m'sieur*. It is my pleasure to do business with you. You may have it for seven thousand francs."

Max bowed. "*Merci, Madame*."

He left the store with the mask boxed and under his arm. It would make the perfect addition to Nikki's collection—and for her birthday as well.

Later the same night, Max felt a unique thrill course through him whenever he touched the old mask. He stroked the leather face and fancied he could see its previous owners in his mind. He hoped Nikki would be pleased. According to its provenance, the mask predated the French Revolution and supposedly had been worn by a young woman of the French nobility, who'd lost her head to the guillotine.

The next time it appeared, it had been worn by an Italian opera singer, who'd had a longer, yet equally tragic life. She'd lost her young husband to consumption, her son had nearly died from a riding accident, and her last lover, a ship's captain, had eventually been lost at sea.

The next time the mask was documented, it was purchased by a young Parisian artist as a gift to his fiancée prior to WWII. Apparently he had been killed by the Nazis. His fiancée had then taken her life. The possession of the mask fell to her sister, who kept it until her death. The sister's son sold it to the antique shop.

Max wasn't superstitious. Life was simply cruel at times. His own life was proof enough.

He would overnight the mask to Nikki. The minute he'd spied it, he'd known he must buy it. He wanted to give her something, even if he couldn't quite manage to give her his love.

Carefully he laid the mask back into the silk-lined box. He walked to the window and looked out at the Parisian skyline. There was nothing for him here anymore. He'd made a good, life in the States. He turned from the window, his heart heavy. Being in Paris brought back too many memories. Walking to his bed, he folded the bed covers back, ready for sleep. Long into the night, he stared at the ornate-carved ceiling. Finally, he slept.

***

The life of the Maquis in la Forêt de Plombière, north of Dijon, was difficult, but Maxime held the fervent belief he must aid the liberation of his homeland. There were some Dijon residents who joined the Maquis in the forest periodically and brought with them intelligence gathered in town, but the Nazis were most suspicious of young men. They routinely harassed them and attempted to recruit or imprison them without cause.

Now that winter had ended, the temperatures were bearable. The winter was cruel, but instead of snow, there was often the interminable rain, dripping down the inside surface of his tent made from parachute silks salvaged from a downed SAS pilot.

Tonight, at least, the weather was dry. Luckily, the Morvan region of France was a fertile one, and with the covert support of their countrymen, he and the other men of the Maquis ran no risk of starving.

An artist in his former life, he'd never lived under such extreme conditions before. Every day was fraught with danger. And never had he felt so alive. There were the Nazis to evade, and always the never-ending rain. But what tormented him the most was not seeing his beloved Nicole. There had been no time to marry before he left Dijon and joined the Maquis. *Mon Dieu*, how he missed their passionate lovemaking.

There were women who drifted in and out of the Maquisards' camps. One in particular had made it very clear she was available. Emilie had been most persistent in her pursuit. She was pretty enough; some even thought her beautiful. But when Maxime compared Emilie to Nicole's pale, ethereal beauty, Emilie fell short. She was petite, dark and buxom, while his Nicole was tall, slender and graceful.

One of Emilie's functions was to act as a conduit of intelligence between a certain Nazi guard named Gerhard and the Maquis. One evening she'd given the entire camp a laughing description of how she seduced the guard and gained the train schedule needed for the Maquis' next raid.

A rustle at the rear of his tent alerted him. He pulled his knife, prepared to defend himself. The side of the tent raised.

Incroyable. Merde. Emilie.

"*Bonsoir*, Maxime," she said softly. "I don't think you will need that knife, do you?"

Dismayed, he noted the top of her blouse was unbuttoned, exposing her considerable décolletage. "What do you want? I'm trying to sleep," he said, not caring that his irritation showed.

"Why would you want to sleep when we could be making love? Life is too short not to take advantage of all it has to offer."

He repressed a groan. "We've been through this before. I am engaged to be married. Don't do this. It's embarrassing."

The woman gave him a seductive look from beneath her dark lashes.

Others thought her very sensual, but he didn't. She was, however, incredibly persistent. She stepped toward him, and before he could stop her, ran her hands over his chest and down his abdomen. She laughed at his body's reflexive response as her hands wandered below his belt. Embarrassed by his body's betrayal, he barked, "Enough."

"See your body knows what it needs…and wants," she observed with a throaty chuckle. "Even if your mind doesn't."

He grabbed Emilie's shoulders and thrust her away from him. "I said, no. Find someone else to play your little games. Leave me alone."

"You'll be sorry." She spat on the ground. "I'm in town frequently. Do you honestly think your precious little Nicole is faithful to you? She's not. She's a tramp. You should see for yourself. It's the talk of Dijon. She takes a different German soldier to bed every night."

Maxime drew back to slap her, but stopped short. Her words were filled with spite, and he knew them to be false. "Out of here, now, before I do something I'll regret."

"Fool!" she cried, then bolted from his tent into the night.

He lay on his cot and stared at the ceiling of the tent. Never had he desired Nicole more than at this moment. Needing the reassurance of lying in her arms once more, he would sneak into town to see her. He needed to feel her silken skin against his. He would go out of his mind, if he didn't.

He waited an hour, then sneaked from his tent. He placed a heavy pistol in the waist of his pants and carried his rifle on his shoulder. Going into Dijon would be risky enough without traveling the countryside unarmed as well. His body burned from his encounter with Emilie, but it was Nicole he wanted.

He checked the area. No one was about, except for his friend Gaston on guard duty who let him pass with one proviso. "Be back before dawn. We change guard then."

Maxime smiled, nodded, and left to walk the few miles that would take him to his love. As he walked through the dense, damp forest, the moon shone brightly. He shook his head, realizing how rash he'd been in choosing this particular night to see her.

He made an excellent target in the moon's silvery light, but months of living in the forest had taught him to move silently and swiftly. When he emerged from the forest into the open country, he walked quickly with his rifle still slung over his shoulder. The German soldiers were afraid of penetrating too deeply into the forest enclave of the Maquis bands, but open country posed a grave danger.

Still aroused after Emilie's attempt to seduce him, he was now on a fool's mission to see his true love. He'd always insisted Nicole and her family avoid any appearance of collusion with the resistance. Seeing her now could endanger her and her entire family and his, if he were discovered. He stopped...nearly retreated, but he'd come this far. He *had* to see her.

He craved her touch, the heady scent of her musk, the indescribable pleasure of surrendering to her warmth. Images of her beauty in the throes of passion consumed him. He picked up his pace. No time to waste.

It appeared he lived under a charmed spell. An hour later, he slipped unseen into the city of Dijon. Thankfully, the streets were quiet, and he eluded a single German patrol with ease. He approached the three-story Mansard-roofed house where Nicole and her family lived, then cautiously surveyed the area for any sign of soldiers. Seeing none, he entered the rear of the house and tiptoed down the hall to Nicole's room.

He opened the door and found her asleep, the moonlight spilling across her slender form. His heart clutched in his chest while he watched her innocent slumber. Walking silently to her side, he placed a hand over her mouth as a precaution before waking her.

"Shh. *C'est moi*, Maxime," he whispered, his other hand already exploring the familiar contours of her body beneath the gown.

"Maxime," she murmured softly. "You're not a dream, *mon amour*. You're really here."

"Yes, *mon coeur*. I am here." Maxime buried his face in the fragrant sweetness of her neck.

Her arms went around his neck, pulling him into the bed. Her lips against his, soft and pliant, then demanding. Deepening the kiss, he surrendered to her urgency, sweeping his tongue into her honeyed mouth. Oh God, he lived for her touch, her lips, her taste. Heaven did exist—he held it in his arms.

She pulled his shirt from his trousers. He fumbled with the fastener at his waist, his lips never leaving hers. Finally, the desperation to join conquered the practicality of undressing. Maxime's erection sprang free, heavy with need.

"My love." Nicole opened herself to him, her ivory limbs pale in the moonlight.

"Not yet. Too soon," he gasped. His mouth found the roseate peak of her left breast. He circled it with his tongue, reveling in the way it hardened into a tight bud.

"Now, Maxime, now," she whimpered, her breath warm against his ear.

"No, not yet." He slid his tongue down her alabaster abdomen to the crisp nest of pale blond curls at the apex of her thighs. He buried his face in her body's musk, feeling her body tremble and twitch in response to his tongue.

She implored him, begged for release. "Maxime."

He could wait no longer, his need too great. Shifting his weight to his elbows and knees, he centered himself above her. Her hand grasped and guided him to her warmth. Home. Shuddering, he drove into her moist heat, praying for control.

Her muscles clenched around his length, as her legs circled his waist. Slowly, he thrust, delaying his release. Her head tossed back and forth, her nails digging into his back. She moaned...the sweetest sound he'd ever heard.

He quickened the pace. His urgent craving for release grew. Her frantic arching met him thrust for thrust. His breath came in rasps, hers in sobs. The skin on her breasts flushed, her climax imminent, he increased the pace.

For one brief tantalizing moment...time stood still. Together they hung at the peak of excruciating pleasure before exploding into the heights of total sensation; the beginning of her orgasm triggering his. He gasped. His seed pumped into her. Hips thrusting of their own accord.

Nicole moaned, cried, sobbed, "*Je t'aime. Je t'adore.*"

His passion and energy spent, Maxime collapsed. He rolled to his side, and pulling her with him, stayed within her warmth. "I've missed you so," he murmured. "*Je t'aime.*" She wept on his shoulder.

"You are my life, my love, my future. I can't live without you," he whispered.

"Nor I, you."

When he left her just before dawn, he thought his heart would split. Being with his lover made him feel as if he could climb the Matterhorn. Yet leaving weighted his heart with lead. It never became any easier, no matter how many times he'd done it. She was as much a part of him as his right hand. Surely, it was the same for her. It seemed as if they could sense each other's feelings without having to say a word. He supposed all lovers thought their love was timeless, but theirs truly was.

He eased from behind the house and surveyed the street before him. Another hour and the sun would break the horizon. He'd stayed too long. Seeing and sensing no one, he stepped into the street.

Without warning, he felt the shock of a hand on his arm. "Halt!" a soldier ordered.

"No!" Maxime struggled, elbowing the soldier in the stomach. Two more appeared and wrestled him to the ground. Lying on his back, he garnered all his strength and gave a mighty kick with both legs. Gratified by the resulting grunts, he saw that he'd knocked two of them down. He rolled sideways, then rolled to his feet like a cat.

"*Arret!*" The click of a gun being cocked behind him. He stopped. He turned.

Emilie. Her pistol was aimed at his head.

"No," he said in disbelief. He watched her face for a sign. No mercy.

She raised her lip in a sneer. "Yes." Her finger tightened on the trigger.

Max sat up and gasped. Death, violent and real. He shook his head. Be practical. Just a dream, stimulated by the mask's history. Nothing more.

This was no time for pondering unanswerable philosophical questions. But throughout the rest of the day, a feeling of unease remained, a nagging presentiment in the back of his mind.

Fifteen

Feet dragging and spirits low, Nikki walked into the agency. Fashion shoots were taking place in more and more exotic locations and the long trips were getting to her. Maybe she needed a vacation. Maybe she needed a life outside getting her face plastered everywhere.

"Good morning, Nikki, how was Bali?" the receptionist asked.

She smiled, answering, "It was paradise, unless you're on a fashion shoot." Actually it had been a trying shoot, mainly due to an over-enthusiastic fashion assistant, who'd badgered the photographer into twice as many shots as necessary.

"You poor thing. I don't know how you manage," Karen quipped, rolling her big brown eyes.

"I know. It's a tough life, but somebody has to do it." Switching gears, she asked, "Jolie in? She left a message she wanted to see me."

The receptionist rolled her eyes again. "Oh yes, Madame Jolie is in the building. Better watch out..." she warned, "... she's in a very good mood, and—uh, frankly that's pretty scary."

"Yeah. Know what you mean. Guess I'd better see what she wants."

"I'll let her know you're here."

"Is Max in?"

"No, haven't you heard?" Karen gave a furtive look around. "He's in Paris."

"So? Nothing unusual about that."

"He's *with* someone," Karen whispered.

"Really?" Nikki managed a casual shrug. "Who?" Maybe it was another of Max's flavors of the week. The affair wouldn't last long; they never did.

Karen dropped her voice. "Arianne Willoughby, the banker's daughter."

"Who?"

"You remember the tall redhead who decided she'd like to be a model. Max had a photographer do some head shots, just to please Daddy. Seems her daddy belongs to the same gym our hunky boss does."

Nikki nodded. Yes, certainly she remembered redhead. The redhead had done everything but fall at Max's feet. "From the Multiple Sclerosis Benefit?"

Karen nodded. "That's the one."

Stuck-up and spoiled too, if Nikki recalled correctly.

"Well, *M'sieur* Max left for Paris two days ago."

"With her?"

"Not exactly. She left for Paris the next day—hot on his heels. It was in several of the columns."

"Coincidence?" Nikki suggested, hoping Max wouldn't someone like the redhead of interest.

The receptionist lowered her voice even further. "Maybe, but one of the columns hinted her family would be making an announcement soon."

Nikki leaned in closer. "Married? We are talking about love'em and leave'em Max?" She forced herself to stop before her voice rose out of control.

"Well, you never know. I mean even Warren Beatty got married, didn't he? 'Course, it's just gossip."

Anxious to think about anything but Max's getting married, Nikki prompted, "Uh-Jolie?"

"Oh, sorry. Go on in. She's expecting you."

"Thanks." Nikki straightened her shoulders. She might as well find out what the V.P. wanted.

She walked down the hall to Jolie's office and tapped on the door.

"Come in," came the low breathy voice of Max's V.P.

Nikki opened the door, walked in, and glancing about, remarked, "The new office looks good." Very good, in fact. Jolie had obviously employed an interior designer.

"Yes, the other wasn't my style at all, darling—so fusty. Max is such an anachronism. He should have been born in the eighteenth century or something." Jolie gave a brittle laugh—one always guaranteed to raise the hair on Nikki's neck.

"Well, this is lovely too," she offered. Diplomacy had never been her strong point, but she tried. Truly, the austere Italian furnishings were sleek and spare.

Jolie smiled, putting Nikki on guard. Smiles were not Jolie's stock in trade.

"I wanted to be the one to tell you this," Jolie began. "It's over. Devereaux's no longer requires your services."

For a moment the words didn't register. "Excuse me?"

"I'm sorry, dear. I should've used words of one syllable. You're fired."

Nikki registered disbelief, then anger. "You're firing me? And Max agrees?"

"Max isn't here. I'm in charge. And if the rumors are true, he might not be back for several weeks." Jolie gave another brittle laugh. "Yes, darling. After all, you're nearly thirty years old."

"Twenty-six," Nikki replied through gritted teeth. Not quite twenty-seven.

"No matter." Jolie gave a dismissive wave. "We take models younger and younger all the time. It's time to make way. You've had a nice run of it, but you knew it had to end sometime, and that time is *now*." She leaned back in her white leather chair and watched with a cold, calculating stare.

Nikki bit back the bitter response that came to her lips and turned on her heel. No point in giving Jolie exactly what she wanted. On the other hand, if Nikki stayed any longer, she'd have to kill Max's V.P.

"Nikki," Jolie called after her.

She turned. "Yes?"

Jolie gave her a wolfish smile. "Best of luck in the future, darling. You'll need it, especially now that your former protector is occupied with his new friend. I hear they might even marry." She gave a casual shrug and continued. "It's time you know. He's been alone much too long. I suppose he's been a little reluctant to take the plunge again. Of course, after being suspected of killing his first wife... If I were you— well, I'd count myself lucky to be out of the running."

It took every ounce of self-control she possessed to resist flying across the glass desk and attacking the smug Jolie on her white leather throne. "That's crap. Max's wife died in a car accident." To hell with Jolie and her vicious lies. She spun on her heel and left the agency without speaking to anyone.

Her words had been brave, but later she couldn't erase the ugly scene from her mind. Jolie's remark about Max's first wife had been chilling. Oh, she'd heard the rumors before—and never believed them. The Max Devereaux she knew was kind and gentle, even if a trifle distant with her. And he absolutely doted on his daughter.

Max's reputation aside, she'd reached a crossroads. Perhaps, it was her own doing. Certainly her enthusiasm for being photographed and lolling about in the latest fashions had palled. Did she really have the guts to weather this change? So maybe her new life would turn out to be less luxurious than her current one. At least, thanks to her connections, she didn't have to worry about being homeless again. Losing her job might even be a blessing in disguise. She might actually discover if she had any gifts besides the ability to slink down a runway without falling on her ass.

The biggest difficulty she foresaw was Mama. After Nikki had started making good money, her first large purchase had been a condominium in Florida for her mother. She absolutely would not sell the condo out from under her mother. Plus, her mother depended on

Nikki for the extras her meager monthly social security check didn't cover.

Unfortunately, Mama might still have to make some adjustments. Not that Mama had ever really appreciated what Nikki had done for her. Mama was never satisfied. Why she still tried to please her mother, she wasn't sure. Maybe she was sorry because her mother's life had been pretty grim. Still she hoped for a sign of approval—just one.

Back at her apartment, Nikki quickly packed an overnight bag. She would head for the small beach cottage she'd refurbished and decorated on Martha's Vineyard. Hefting the bag on her shoulder, she walked the three blocks to the garage where she kept her seldom-used sports car.

A long drive, the last leg on the ferry, to the picturesque island was exactly what she needed to clear her head before she made plans for the future.

Sixteen

Martha's Vineyard

After two days at the beach house, two long days of running and walking for hours along the shoreline, Nikki sat on the deck overlooking the dark-green Atlantic and watched the sun rise. The rays of light illuminated the far reaches of the water and crept closer on feet of lavender and purple. She'd spent another sleepless night mired in a morass of decision making.

Definitely at a crossroads, she'd faced the truth. At twenty-six, with number twenty-seven looming, she was finished...and as Jolie had so bluntly put it, it was time to make way for the younger girls. Nikki'd never wanted an acting career as some models did. The very last thing she wanted was another career based on her looks. Besides, it was too difficult trying to pretend to be someone else. She had enough trouble pretending to be herself.

If she were completely honest, her love life was barren. She'd been in love with Max Devereaux from the moment she'd crashed into his broad chest. She wasn't sure why she still fancied herself in love with him. Heaven knew he'd given her little encouragement along that line. When she was younger, she'd assumed it was because of their age difference. But now there was no viable reason she could fathom.

There was the very real fact he didn't get involved with his models. Except for the night he asked her to dinner, he always seemed to go out of his way to avoid her. She never knew quite what to expect from him, and she didn't like being off-balance whenever he was near.

While she feared the intensity of her own feelings, she'd never been able to learn the depths of his. It had proven very difficult, keeping those feelings private. She'd tried, how she'd tried to hide them, but *Maman* had sensed, from the very beginning, how Nikki felt about Max.

And now, he was on holiday in Paris, accompanied by the daughter of a bank president. It was just too bad she kept having dreams about the unreachable Maxim Devereaux—lovely passionate dreams of limbs entwined and hearts that soared as one.

She closed her eyes and attempted to obliterate the images that plagued her ever since they first met. The peaceful dawn brought no serenity.

Nikki sighed, stood and stretched, then wandered back into the cottage. The Vineyard had been her haven from the chaotic life of New York, but now only served as a reminder of her failure to measure up in Max's eyes...and win his love.

Damn. In an instant, she made up her mind. She would sell her apartment and the beach house too. The income from the sales, along with a substantial portion of her antique collection, should give her a cushion while she reinvented her life.

She'd been given so many opportunities. Some might even say she'd wasted them. More than once, Max had advised her to invest in the stock market, but her life on the street had left her hungry for a better life and beautiful things. Instead of taking Max's sage advice, she'd surrounded herself with the trappings of beauty—art, furnishings and antiques—but they were only things.

She might as well start the inventory now. She walked from one lovely room to another and stopped in front of the mask collection she carted around no matter where she lived. Always drawn to masks, she experienced a deep kinship when she held one. Indeed, the masks symbolized everything she experienced in her career...a facade, hiding pain and insecurity. Modeling had enabled her to hide her real self from everyone. The only person she hadn't been able to fool was *numbre une*.

The arrival of the latest addition to her collection was stunning. All the way from Paris—from of all people—Max. His unexpected gift included a letter which explained how the mask caught his eye. He'd immediately recalled her collection and upcoming birthday and purchased it. Always thoughtful, he even included the mask's provenance.

The gift was been so out-of-character for him; he admitted as much in his letter. 'The perfect birthday gift.' And it was. But her birthday wasn't until August. She glanced at the calendar—May 1st. An *early* birthday gift.

Wonder what his new fiancée thought about his buying a gift for one of his models? Maybe the engagement rumors weren't true. Maybe he just wanted to get her birthday present out of the way in order to devote himself to his new love. Once again, the man had her stymied.

She stretched on tiptoe to remove the new mask from its place in the rustic oak display case. She ran her fingers over the curves of the mask, smiling despite her funky mood. The mask was in wonderful condition for something over two hundred years old. The white-leather face had turned to a creamy ivory, and gold trim was still visible in spots around the eyes. Remnants of pale, blue ostrich feathers trailed down the sides. An ivory wand still attached on the right side of the mask.

She held it by the wand and peered into a nearby mirror. As she placed the mask over her face, she was overcome by waves of vertigo.

The landscape was strange…yet familiar. Something about it said home. Tall rows of poplars lined the lane on both sides. Sounds of cannon fire thundered in the distance, but the vibrations were felt by those rushing to flee Paris. The Nazis had taken Paris, the City of Light. Unthinkable! Now, brazen Nazis strolled down her wide boulevards. Nicole and her fiancé fled Paris with little more than the clothes on their backs and the antique mask he'd given her on her last birthday.

If Maxime's ancient Citroën didn't fall apart before they reached Dijon, they would join their waiting families. Once she was safe in the bosom of her family, she feared he would slip into one of the surrounding forests and join the resistance movement. While he had yet to tell her, she knew him well enough to know he would never sit idly by while the Germans occupied their homeland.

"Are the guns closer? How long will it take us to reach Dijon?" she asked. "Do you really think we'll be safe there?" From the squaring of his shoulders and the faraway look in his eyes, she knew her questions disturbed him. "What are you keeping from me? What's wrong?" she demanded, forcing the issue.

He sighed. "*Ma petite*, you'll be safe, but I'm going to join the Maquis. I must," he said softly. Removing a hand from the steering wheel, he reached over and caressed her cheek. For a moment, he turned toward her, his green eyes, looking at her with a familiar hunger…and with an unspoken plea for her understanding.

There. He'd finally admitted it. "I knew it." Still, she must change his mind. "Please don't. I can't live without you. Stay with me." Her eyes filled with tears as she gazed into his darkening green ones.

"I have to go. My country needs me."

"I'll go with you. I'll join the Maquis too," she declared, raising her chin in defiance.

"You'll do no such thing," he replied, shaking his head, his tone firm. He watched the road, but cast darting glances toward her. "I'll be nearby, but it'll be too dangerous for me to see you."

"But, Maxime, I'll miss you so much. I'll miss your…" she faltered. His announcement had ripped her heart in two. "We must make the most of every moment until we are separated," she said, a renewed determination in her voice, "*N'est-ce pas?*" She reached for his thigh and stroked.

"You're crazy, my little one. We're running from the Nazis, and you talk of making love. I'm not made of steel. Hush. This isn't the time."

"Wh-what if there isn't another time?" She glanced at him from the corner of her eyes, then slipped her hand higher along his strong thigh. "I need you, my love. I need to feel your touch and your lips." she whispered. "*Je t'aime.*"

"Any other time, we would stop, right now." He looked at her, as if pleading for her understanding. "If Paris hadn't been invaded, we would have already been married. Our families are waiting for us." He groaned. "Why torture me this way?"

"I love you. I need you." She inched her hand further up his thigh, stopping short of the growing bulge in his trousers.

Maxime bit his lip. "Mmm," the moan escaped anyway.

She giggled. "*Désolé.*

Carefully he took her mischievous hand and replaced it in her lap. "Behave."

"Maxime."

He sputtered, "St-stop this silliness. Right now."

She saluted. "*Oui, mon capitain.*"

"This is war," he muttered through gritted teeth, keeping his eyes focused on the road ahead of them.

"I am certainly aware of that," she muttered, in a peevish frame of mind. Now he had spoiled her playful mood. She folded her arms across her chest and looked out her side window.

His words proved prophetic. Fifty feet away, a shell exploded, raining clods of earth on the window shield.

"M-Max." She screamed and hid her eyes. "Let's get out of here. Please."

"*Merde,*" he swore. "I am driving as fast as I can. I cannot run over people."

"I-I'm sorry." She began crying. "I just want to go home."

"I know, my love. I know."

Nicole hadn't seen Maxime for over a month. He'd left her in Dijon with her family and disappeared into the forest. She'd spent most of her time worrying about him. Occasionally, he would send her a message, and she would know for the time being he was safe.

Only the night before, rumors of a Nazi train being derailed nearby had reached Dijon. As proud as she was of Maxime and the actions of the Resistance, she lived each day with the unbearable fear she would never see him again.

The Trudeau and DuPuis families continued about their daily routines. They kept to themselves and tried to avoid notice of the Nazi soldiers, but she felt as if she were being watched. The soldiers seemed to be everywhere, and one soldier in particular always seemed to be following her. One day, he even followed her home from the street market.

Her height and striking appearance made her obvious in any crowd, so she attired herself as plainly as possible, wearing her hair pulled back in a no-nonsense chignon, but it did no good. The soldiers still stared at her as if she had 'available' emblazoned across her derriere. She hated their stares and suggestive remarks. They made her feel dirty.

She slammed the front door behind her. "Alexandra," she called to her younger sister. "Is he still there? That ape followed me home, again." She placed her basket of morning purchases on the oft-scrubbed oak table.

Alexandra called from the upstairs bedroom. "*Oui, Chèrie.* Wait, I'm coming down."

Her sister made a swift descent and rushed into the kitchen. Everyone said they made a pleasing contrast. One tall and the other short, but their kinship was obvious. They shared the same blue eyes and wide smiles.

"He's talking to that slut Emilie. You know it's whispered she's with the Maquis. So, why is she talking to one of the Nazis?" Alexandra placed her hands on her hips. "You should tell Maxime. She might be a traitor."

"You must not say such things, and you do not know it for a fact. Possibly she is trying to get information for the Maquis. Besides, I don't know when I'll see him again," she said, unable to keep the forlorn note from her tone.

Alexandra gave her a reassuring hug. "Do not fret. You will hear from your handsome Maxime soon. I'm sure of it."

One moonlit night, she awakened, startled to find a hand over her mouth. "Shh, *c'est moi*, Maxime." He kissed her hungrily, his hands roaming over her body. "I have missed you so much, *Chèrie.*" His voice grew hoarse. You are more beautiful than ever, my heart."

"Maxime," she whispered softly. "You're not a dream. *Mon amour,* you really are here."

"Yes, I am here."

She succumbed to his kisses and the pure exhilaration of his touch. His tongue blazed a trail of fire as he kissed her breasts. He nibbled and teased and licked her belly. When and how he divested her of her gown, she didn't know or care. He was here with her now, and that was all that mattered. She pulled and tugged at his clothes, consumed by a desperate longing to feel his body next to hers. Ahh, he had marvelous skin, so soft and smooth, beneath his clothes. Well, it wasn't all so soft. She touched the firm length of him.

He moaned, "Not yet. Too soon." His tongue found her center.

With mounting desire, she gasped, "Now, Maxime. Now." Maxime entered her quickly and smoothly. Their passion soared, expanded and exploded out of sheer need. Afterward, they crashed in total exaltation, laughing, kissing, weeping--celebrating their joy in each other.

They made love again, slower. "The night is too short, my love. I must go before daylight comes," he told her gently as he held her in his arms. "I miss you so much. I ache for you," he said, nestling his head in her shoulder and nibbling her neck with tiny tender kisses.

"Must you go? Please stay with me. Don't go back. Please," she begged. In the pale moonlight, she drank in the vision of his perfect body, his dark eyes, his new beard, his curling hair. Her man, the artist, now a rugged soldier, had the body of a Greek god and the face of a renaissance angel. She loved him so much. How could she ever live without him?

"You know I must," he murmured, still cradling her in his arms.

She grew desperate, her breathing ragged. "Then let me go with you. I know there are women in the Resistance. Please," she begged, tears filling her eyes.

"No, it is too dangerous. I should not have come tonight, but I could not stand another minute without seeing you. I love you more than life itself." He kissed her. Her tears wet his face, and his, hers.

Tears rolled down her cheeks unchecked. "*Je t'aime*, Maxime. *Je t'aime.*"

He stood and dressed quickly. "*Doux rêves*, my angel," he said, turning for one last glance before softly closing the door to her room.

She lay back and wiped at the tears streaming down her face. Finally, she turned her face into the pillow where his head had lain. She inhaled deeply, breathing in his lingering scent.

A muffled cry broke the perfect stillness of the night. A shout. Sounds of a scuffle outside her window.

A single shot rang out. She jumped from the bed and rushed to the window. A broken figure lay on the ground. A widening circle of blood, black in the moonlight, pooled on the cobblestone street below. The world crashed around her. Her cry of agony rending the night. "Maxime!"

Nikki awakened and found herself lying on the sofa in front of the mirror. She set aside the mask and wiped the tears from her eyes. Had she fallen asleep? The last thing she remembered was looking in the mirror, and then the dream so vivid she'd cried in her sleep.

She shivered as she recalled the fervent lovemaking…so real…so incredibly sad. Was she going crazy? Maybe all she needed was more sleep. A dream? That's all it was. What a silly fool she was, dreaming of a man she could never have. She sighed and returned the mask to its place.

Later the same night, as was her habit, Nikki wrote in her journal. Even in her dreams, she couldn't get away from Max. He was always there. His green eyes haunted her and his softly accented voice seduced her in her dreams, even if reality left a lot to be desired. Quickly, before she lost the phrases, she wrote them down:

Green eyes and a soft accent
Forever they plague my dreams
Striding through my memories
Leaving my heart with an emptiness
No other can fill.

Well, that was a piece of emotional drivel, if she'd ever read one. Her journals contained all the miseries, fears and longings of her last ten years. She, who'd hated school, would now feel deprived, if time didn't permit her to enter at least a few lines in her journal. It was a comforting routine, and one that allowed her to express the thoughts she could share with no one. In her journal alone, did she admit her desire and love for Max, her rescuer…her champion.

"Thank you for the journal, *Maman*," she murmured aloud. "I wouldn't have made it without you or your gift."

Twenty minutes later, she closed the journal, wondering if she would ever have the kind of love poets wrote about. Would Max ever see her as a woman instead of a project?

Until March when he'd asked her to dinner, she'd never thought it truly possible. But from that moment, she'd thought of him non-stop. She couldn't forget the tenderness in his touch. She'd longed for more, but lacked the confidence to act upon her desire.

Dammit. Max was such a puzzle. How would she ever know if he desired her? Her 'crush' remark during that one dinner was a test, and his response wasn't what she'd hoped.

Well, she had her chance, and she blew it. Now, he was in France with another woman. Mistake or no, Max wasn't hers. Never had been. Never would be. And he hadn't called as he'd promised either. Translation: Loser.

Tears stung her eyes, but she brushed them aside. "Wimp," she said aloud, reaching to extinguish the light. She was a stupid, romantic fool, and there was no getting around it. She punched her pillow into an acceptable shape, hugged it and tried to go to sleep.

At one o'clock, the telephone chimed. Still awake, she was tempted to let it ring, but her curiosity over who was calling got the best of her. "Hello?"

"It's Max."

"Max? Is something wrong?"

"I just wanted to talk to you."

"Do you know what time it is?" she asked wearily.

"*Désolé*. I forgot about the time difference. I'm guessing it's about one, and I've awakened you. I just didn't know who else— No, that's not it. I really wanted to hear the sound of your voice."

"Well, I'm flattered, but I hardly think Arianne would appreciate your sentiment."

"Arianne? What are you talking about? I was thinking, maybe you could fly over and spend some time with me here in Provençe. Maybe we could—"

"What's the matter? Did you and Arianne have a fight?" Who did he think he was? Calling out of the blue and expecting her to drop everything on the basis of one measly transatlantic phone call.

"By the way, Jolie fired me this afternoon, so forgive me, if I'm a little unsympathetic to your trials and tribulations right now. I've a lot to sort out here, so I'm a little preoccupied."

Max chuckled, "Why don't you tell me how you really feel, Nikki? Don't try to consider my feelings. First of all, there is nothing between the Willoughby girl and me. She simply showed up in Paris."

"That's not what I hear."

"I mean it. Forget about her. As for Jolie, I'll take care of her. You're not fired unless *I* say so. You're taking this too seriously."

"Taking it too seriously? I don't have a job. That's pretty serious in most places."

"Calm down. You're just tired. Look, neither one of us has had a vacation, and Alexa is coming over after her school term. We could have a wonderful time—the three of us." His voice softly caressed her ear.

Vacation in Provençe with Max? Oh God, was he serious?

Long practice at hiding her feelings enabled her to take a deep breath. No way could she make decision like that over the telephone. "I'm going to hang up now and go to sleep. I suggest you do the same. We can talk about this tomorrow or next week. Besides, don't give up on your banker's daughter. She'll come back."

"Nikki." She could hear the exasperation in his voice. "You're totally off the mark about her, but you're right about one thing. We will talk about it soon. *Au revoir*."

Soon? Just like he'd called her soon. "Yes, Max, *au revoir*."

Nikki disconnected. "Dammit." She reached for her pillow and punched it once more. Who did he think he was? He'd ignored her for two months, then expected her to drop everything and take a vacation. Who made him master of her itinerary?

"*Merde.*" Exasperated, Max punched another number on his phone. He'd wasted enough time in France. If she wouldn't come to him, he'd go to her.

"Information."

"*Air France, s'il vous plait?*"

Seventeen

Nikki awakened slowly and stretched. Had Max really called her in the middle of the night? Never a morning person, she dragged from bed and staggered into the kitchen, then started the coffee. While her caffeine fix brewed, she headed for the shower, dropping her Mickey Mouse sleep shirt on the terra cotta tile floor.

After showering, she sipped her coffee and gazed around the cottage and enjoyed—for maybe the last time—all the work she'd done so feverishly when she'd first bought it With Marti's not-so-able assistance, she tiled the kitchen in terra cotta and hand-painted the sisal rugs herself. There wasn't a decorative element in the room she hadn't chosen or actually created herself. She'd even painted the wooden cabinets in the kitchen and bathroom, refurbishing them with crystal knobs. The effect was old-fashioned and charming.

White mosquito netting was casually draped over wooden rods at every window. Pale aqua walls had been ragged with an overlay of cream and white, giving them depth and texture. It made a simple background for a couple of modern paintings and the few *objets d'art* she carted around with her where ever she lived.

For five years, the cottage had been her refuge. She would certainly miss its casual comfort, even more than her city apartment.

As Max stepped from the Concorde into the jetway, he gave a hurried glance at his watch. He had made it in record time from the farmhouse in Provençe to Paris in order to catch the Concorde to New York. He rushed toward the luggage carousel, wondering how long it would take him to drive to Martha's Vineyard. By then Nikki should be in a better mood.

He grabbed his single piece of luggage and headed for the car rental counter. Even as he talked with the young woman at the counter, he changed his mind. Two-hundred and fifty miles to Martha's Vineyard. It would take him hours to drive. He walked to the nearest airline counter and asked for the first flight to Boston. Boston was only eighty miles or so from Nikki, a much shorter drive.

"The flight leaves in fifteen minutes, Mr. Devereaux. You'll have to hurry. The concourse is quite a distance."

"*Merci*. I'll hurry." Max laughed, dashing down the crowded corridor. The moving sidewalk too slow, he dodged happy families, slow-moving senior citizens and one punk rocker and finally ended up at Gate E45. He'd made it, but barely. The steward was closing the gate as he arrived. "Wait!" he shouted and ran through the jet way to catch his flight.

Throughout the short trip, Max drummed his fingers on his knees. The closer he came to seeing Nikki, the more anxious he became about how she would receive him. This hurried flight across the Atlantic had seemed like a stellar idea in the beginning, but now the words reckless and more than a little foolish came to mind. She might just slam the door in his face—*non*, she'd never do something so rude, no matter how angry she was.

After her cup of coffee, Nikki pulled on a pair of faded cut-off jeans and a turquoise sports bra. The run would give her some a much-needed exercise…and time to think.

She set a brisk pace, feeling her long strides on the sand pull at her calves. She continued for three miles up the beach, her breathing settling into an easy rhythm. At her usual turnaround point, she slowed her pace to a walk and continued beyond for another half mile until she reached an outcrop of rock. She climbed up on the boulder, sat and watched the relentless waves crashing on the rocks below her. The waves never faltered. They simply were. If she could only be as constant.

Beads of perspiration formed across her forehead. She wiped them away. It was time find out what Nikki Prentice was really made of.

Being in the public eye had its advantages. Only six months earlier at a gallery opening, she'd been approached by a young editor with an intriguing offer. He'd suggested she write her autobiography. *Runaway on the Runway* was how he'd pitched it. She hadn't taken him seriously at the time, but now the more she thought about it, the better she liked the idea. But could she actually write an entire book? One that people would actually plunk down their hard-earned dollars to read?

Another idea! If the book did well, she could donate a portion of the proceeds to a shelter for street kids—like St. Anne's.

Hold on. Here she was donating the profits before she'd ever put pen to paper. And her future was damned uncertain. But the more she thought about it, the more appealing the idea became. She could make it happen. She would.

Ten years before, Max had taken a chance on a street kid. It was time she gave something back.

***

Max rented a Lexus and drove as if he were taking part in the Gran Prix. But once he reached the ferry to Martha's Vineyard, he was stymied. He smacked the steering wheel with his fist. There didn't seem anything he could do to make the damn ferry move any faster.

As soon as he drove off the ferry, he zipped down the road toward the south end of the island. All he could think about was finding Nikki. He was damned tired of keeping his distance and playing it safe. At least there were no traffic lights to slow him down.

After an endless drive, he strode down the crushed shell walkway to Nikki's front door. He knocked on the barn red door.

No answer.

Her sporty red Mercedes was parked in the driveway. She had to be home, unless she'd gone out with friends. Maybe she was on the beach. He walked around the house and followed another path down to the beach. He glanced in both directions and saw only two small children playing under the supervision of a petite blonde.

He waved to draw the woman's attention. "Excuse me, but have you seen Nikki?"

The woman rose and wiped the sand from her hands onto her jeans. "Was she expecting you?"

He smiled and shook his head. "No, I wanted to surprise her. I flew in from Paris this morning. I'm a friend of hers, Max Devereaux."

"Hi, I'm Tamara," she said, extending her hand.

He shook it briefly. Her grip was firm, in spite of her fragile appearance.

"Let's see. I saw Nikki when she left for her morning run, but I haven't seen her since."

Alarmed, his muscles tensed, ready to spring into action, he asked, "Do you think she could be injured? Which way did she go?"

The neighbor shook her head and grinned. "Relax, she often spends the day jogging or walking up and down the beach. Anyway, she headed north this morning, so I imagine you'll find her without any trouble, unless she walked all the way into town. Then she could be anywhere."

Max nodded. "North?"

"Yes." She pointed. "North."

He thanked her and strode away in long purposeful strides, trying not to run. Of course, Nikki was fine. He was anxious for no reason.

As the sun reached toward the western horizon, long shadows formed in front of Nikki. She was suddenly aware of hunger—ravenous hunger. No food all day, and now her butt seemed to have formed a permanent bond with the rock.

Climbing down from the outcrop, she saw a man running toward her. Even though he was still quite a way off, the powerful, yet graceful, way he moved reminded her of Max.

Although her benefactor would be sure to deny it, he walked with a certain swing to his shoulders which proclaimed his self-confidence to all.

It wasn't just her opinion either. The *boss* was a favorite topic among the women at the agency. No doubt he'd be mortified if he ever heard the perfection of his butt discussed. She giggled. Yeah, he might just take issue with the female locker room terminology.

A frisson of uneasiness shimmered from her spine to her neck. Except for the man, the beach was deserted. She glanced about, then laughed at her own paranoia. Yet better be safe than sorry. She picked up a hefty rock to carry along with her—just in case.

The man continued jogging in her direction until... No, it couldn't be. "Max?"

It really was him. She dropped her weapon. Besides, the protection she needed couldn't be afforded by a simple rock. Her heart was in danger, not her life.

"Nikki. Are you all right?" he shouted.

Closer now, she didn't have to shout. "Of course, I'm all right. Why wouldn't I be?"

God, he looked so good, noting his hair hadn't been trimmed in a while. The sleek GQ style he'd sported for the last five years now curled about the front of his ears and on the back his neck. He wore jeans that fit his thighs like a second skin. A lightweight, pale blue, cashmere sweater topped off his jeans. She gave herself a mental nudge—best get her mind off the boss's bod and onto what he was saying.

"Your neighbor said she hadn't seen you since this morning. I was concerned, unnecessarily, I see."

She watched his gaze move up and down, then up again. She felt the blood rush to her face. "I must look a sight. I've been sitting on a rock, watching the ocean. Thinking."

"All day?" His tone sounded amused.

"Just about. Why don't we go back to the cottage, and you can tell me why you're here, instead of lolling around the south of France trying to iron things out with the lovely Miss Willoughby."

"I tried to tell you last night, but you weren't listening," he protested.

"It was the middle of the night." Dammit. She couldn't believe he'd flown all the way to the States on the basis of a telephone call.

And he had some nerve. No man had any right to show up looking so yummy in jeans and a sweater. His eyes searched hers, asking a question and looking for an answer. An answer she didn't have. She shivered.

"Cold?" he asked.

"No, someone must have walked over my grave," she replied with a shrug as they strode side-by-side on the beach.

"Shall we go out for dinner? Or shall I cook for you?"

Her stomach growled. "I haven't eaten all day," she said. "If you want to cook, I suggest something quick before I collapse."

"I trust you have something edible in your refrigerator?"

"Chicken and burgers in the fridge, salad stuff. I need to shower and change. Deal?"

Max smiled. "Deal."

She escaped into the bathroom. After she stepped into the shower, she turned the temperature control as high as she could stand. He'd flown from France to see and talk to her. There would be no dodging the truth of her insecurities…or how she really felt about him.

His showing up on the beach so unexpectedly confused her. Were the engagement rumors just that? None of it made any sense. He wasn't known for his long-term relationships, and she couldn't bear merely being the latest in a long line.

Twenty minutes later she emerged wearing white jeans and a navy tank top. Pleased, she found her guest very busy. She could already smell the heavenly aroma of chicken grilling. The wine chilled in a silver bucket. She opened the refrigerator door and found a salad already prepared.

Talented man. She wondered when or where he'd learned to cook. She walked out on the deck. "I see you haven't wasted any time." Leaning over the grill, she inhaled the delicious odors. "Vegetable kebabs too." She flashed a smile at her handsome cook. "I approve."

Max gave her a wide grin, showing his even, white teeth. "Yes, I've been busy. Couldn't take the risk of your starving here in the land of plenty."

The combination of his soft tone and his slight accent was a treat to her ears. A shiver of anticipation skittered down her spine—no matter what nonsense he uttered about her starving. She wished they were meeting for the first time, and that his presence didn't have such a powerful effect on her. How she would ever manage to eat dinner and not lose herself in the cool depths of his jade eyes?

"Shall we eat out here on the deck?" he asked.

His warm gaze glance covered her like a caress. The blood rushed to her cheeks, again. "Yes, the deck would be wonderful." Pacing on the deck, she tried to keep from wringing her hands. But she kept sneaking quick glances at him, while he turned the chicken.

"Won't be long now," he said, looking up from the grill.

"Uh, good." She tried to swallow, but her throat had dried. "I think I need something to drink."

He cleared his throat. "I think, perhaps, the chef could use a glass of wine, too"

She jumped, consumed by embarrassment. "I'm not much of a hostess, am I?" What an idiot she was. The most elementary courtesy and she didn't have enough sense to offer him something to drink. She retrieved the bottle of wine, her hands shaking as if palsied. The condensation on the surface of the bottle caused it to slip from her hands. "Shit."

"Here," Max leapt forward and caught the bottle before it could crash to the deck.

She grabbed for it at the same time. Their hands touched. Startled, she jumped, nearly dropping the bottle again.

"Maybe, I should see to the wine, since your seem to have, what you call, the butter fingers." His wry tone was playful. He removed the bottle of wine from her jittery hands, then set it aside carefully. He took her left hand in both of his and kissed the back of it.

"Uh—" she gasped. His eyes held hers, as if he could read her most intimate thoughts.

Not a good thing. Way too scary. Damn. This was hopeless. She would dissolve in a useless puddle at his feet, if he made another move.

"The chicken!" she yelled. "It's burning."

Max spun, grabbed a fork and poked the chicken. "The chicken, it is all right," he said, a sly grin spreading across his face.

Once again, he stared. Growing more and more uncomfortable under his unrelenting gaze, she rushed back into the kitchen, blurting over her shoulder, "I'd better set the table."

Five minutes later, the table was set. Max brought out some candles and lit them. "Voila. We work together well, no?"

Nikki's lips curved into a smile. "Yes, we do."

He pulled out her chair. "I hope you don't mind my chauvinistic behavior, but it's how I was taught," he said with a slight shrug.

She sat, feeling her face grow warm. "It seems natural when you do it." She gazed up into his eyes. "Thank you."

Max sat and speared a piece of lettuce. Still nervous, she picked at hers with a fork. "What's the matter?" he asked. "Don't you like it?"

"No, I—uh, guess I'm not very hungry, after all. Why are you here, Max?" There. She'd said it. Now he'd have to give her an answer.

His dark brows raised in seeming disbelief. "Not hungry. You have not eaten since this morning. The sun is now setting. You must be hungry." Max tilted his head and spoke in falsetto. "Remember what *Maman* would say? *'Les discussions sérieuses gâtent l'appétit. La conversation de dîner devrait amuser'*."

Nikki giggled at his imitation. "Yes, she did. And quite often too. I still miss her." She picked up her glass of wine and swirled it, her mind suddenly awash with memories.

He nodded. "As do I, but she would not approve of your cavalier handling of this most excellent wine," he teased, his expression soft, his gaze never wavering from hers.

"You're right," she agreed. "She certainly wouldn't." She retrieved her fork and sampled the grilled chicken. "Mmm. This is wonderful. So how was your flight?"

Nikki managed to get through the rest of dinner without any further serious discussion. Together they cleared the table. She loaded the dishwasher while Max lit a fire in the fireplace. From the living room she heard the strains of chamber music—one of the Brandenburg's if she wasn't mistaken. Her hands trembled slightly. She took a deep breath to steady her nerves and carried two glasses of wine into the living room and placed them on the coffee table. The sight of Max crouched before the fireplace weakened her knees. She half-sat, half-collapsed on the sofa.

He turned from the fire. "I am a reasonably good cook, and I can build a fire. Pretty good qualities, no?" He stood, walked toward her, his eyes never leaving hers, then sat beside her. He leaned back and placed his arm across the back of the sofa, close enough for her to catch the charcoal scent from where he'd grilled their dinner.

"For a caveman," she blurted, then amended with a grin, "Yes, dinner was wonderful."

Max's eyes crinkled at the corners. "You were very hungry, after all."

The amber and red flames reflected and sparkled on the rim of her wine glass. Nikki stared, fascinated by the images, then took a deep breath. Her breathing slowed. Max leaned toward her. *Omigod.* Was he going to kiss her?

Panicked, Nikki leaned back, blurting out, "Well, let's have it. Why are you here?"

He groaned, "You are impossible. I am here because I want to be with you."

"And you're really not engaged?"

He stood and started pacing. "Don't you ever listen? I told you I went to Paris on business and met some old friends. When she showed up at my hotel, I made it very clear that I had no intentions whatsoever— good, bad or indifferent."

Max, pacing about and running his hands through his wavy hair. Comical...and utterly gorgeous. Her heart swelled with emotion and indecision. Why didn't she simply fling herself into his arms and have done with it? "I don't understand. Other than my career, you've never shown any real interest in me. I—"

The shrill ring of the telephone interrupted. Saved by the bell—yes. She reached for the telephone. "Sorry, I'd better answer it."

"Nikki?"

The sound of the voice on the other end raised the hair on Nikki's neck. Wonderful. Less-than-perfect timing, as always. "Hi, Mama."

"Is it true? I heard you were fired. It's on Entertainment Tonight."

"Yes, it's true. I'm no longer with the agency."

"You could've called me."

"I was going to, but I've been busy trying to get the apartment and beach house ready to sell," she lied. Well, not quite a lie, but almost.

"What about my condo? Are you going to sell it too?"

"No. No, we won't have to sell your condo. Really, I'll be fine. I just need to make some adjustments."

"What did you do to get fired?"

"I got too old. It was personal between the V.P. and me. Look Mama, I'm sorry I didn't tell you before you saw it on TV, but everything's going to be okay."

"But what are you gonna do? You don't know how to do anything else."

"Gee, thanks for the great vote of confidence."

"Well, do you?"

"I'm not sure what I'm going to do yet. I may write a book. Don't worry, Mama, you won't have to support me!" Nikki slammed the phone.

"Dammit!" She jumped up and started pacing. "She makes me so mad. Never satisfied. Nothing I do pleases her. I don't know why I try." Tears formed, threatening to fall. She swiped at them and gave a little sniff.

Max took Nikki in his arms. "She's your mother. It's only natural you want her love and approval, but you are an adult. You've supported her for the last ten years, so you have nothing of which to be ashamed. She should be proud of you."

She attempted a weak smile. "Thank you for understanding," she replied, her thoughts still on her mother.

He cupped her chin in his hand and dabbed at her eyes with a handkerchief. "Now where were we, *Chèrie?*"

Nikki pushed him away, shaking her head. "I'm sorry. I just can't deal with you and my mother at the same time. I've a splitting headache. Will you think me terribly rude if I just go to bed."

"Of course not." He glanced toward the door. "I shall leave and come back tomorrow, perhaps?"

"No, no. You don't have to leave. I have a spare bedroom. Besides, the ferries don't run this late. You'll never find another place to stay at this hour."

"If it's not too much an imposition?" he said, giving her an ironic smile.

"Don't be silly. Just make yourself at home." Realizing how abrupt she sounded, she apologized, "I really am sorry, Max." She fled down the hall to her bedroom. While she undressed, she cursed her mother's rotten timing and unerring ability to say exactly the wrong thing at the wrong time.

And what was he up to, anyway? His sudden appearance on the beach had thrown her for a loop. It was one thing to fantasize about a romantic relationship with him, but another thing entirely to have him right there in front of her, leaning in for a kiss. Something told her— maybe it was the sultry look in his eyes—he wasn't aiming for her cheek this time.

Naples, Florida

Jessie Prentice turned to her friend Maude. "Can you believe that? My precious supermodel daughter hung up on me."

"Oh, no, surely not. Nikki's such a nice girl."

"Hmph. She may have everyone else fooled, but not me. Just because I'm worried about her future. You know, being a mother is such a thankless job."

"Now Jessie, our children grow up. Have to lead their own lives."

"Why she's too busy to tell her own Mama she's been fired. I don't guess she thinks how it might make a difference to me. Just imagine having one of my friends tell me before she did." Jessie sniffed, continuing to ramble on, while she busied herself with tidying up an already immaculate living room adorned with her favorite Elvis-on-black-velvet paintings.

Jessie stopped in front of the mirror, patting her silver-blond hair into place. "Not bad for sixty-four. Nikki got her height from me, and her good looks from her no-good father. Such a handsome devil, always chasing after other women. Didn't like being tied down with a child."

"Really?"

"Yes. I know I've never talked about him much. It was such a painful time of my life–when he ran off and left us. You wouldn't believe how many jobs I took to keep that little girl fed, but she's such an ungrateful little wretch. She's never once treated me the way I deserved. Here she's made millions and nothing to show for it but an apartment and a beach house and bunch of fancy antiques that never did anybody any good."

"But I thought Nikki bought you this condo and sent you money every month."

Maude's memory was a little too sharp. "Well, it's true, she did buy the condo for me, but I earned it. After all, I worked my fingers to the bone for her."

"Now, Jessie, there's not many kids who do that much. Believe me, I know."

Jessie ignored Maude's protests. "I guess she'll find out what it's really like to work for a living like I did. It won't hurt her a bit to have to dirty her lily white hands. The only thing I ever asked that girl to do was get a job when she quit school. And what did she do? She ran off—just like her no good daddy—and lived on the streets, doing who knows what.

"Then that rich foreigner scoops her up and turns her into a supermodel. Like I don't know what *that* was all about. Let her live with his mother. Huh. Well, he didn't marry her, did he? No, he's not the marrying kind—not him."

Jessie continued to walk back and forth. "Nikki's been a problem all her life. It was Nikki's fault her father and step-father both ran off. They couldn't take the responsibility of having a whining brat in the house. Left *me* stuck with a little girl to raise all by myself." She'd been so mad when Donnie, her second husband, left that she'd taken back her maiden name Prentice. Except for Nikki, there wasn't a single thing left to remind Jessie of Nick or Donnie. "I really tried to do my best by that girl, even sent her to private school whenever I had the money."

"Now Jessie, don't you think you're blowing this all out of proportion?"

Mad enough to spit nails, Jessie turned to her friend. "Maude Dillon, either you're on my side or you're not my friend. Make up your mind."

"Now Jessie—"

"Don't now Jessie me. You're just too mealy-mouthed. I can't believe you'd take Nikki's side over mine."

Maude drew herself up to her full five-feet, one-inch. "I'm not mealy-mouthed. I'll tell you exactly what I think. You're a miserable old woman, trying to live your life through your daughter. I don't blame Nikki for not coming around more than she does. You're always complaining and carrying on when she visits. So there! Mealy-mouthed—am I?" Maude spun around and headed for the door.

"Now, Maude, I'm—"

The slamming door stopped Jessie's tirade. Her chin dropped. "Well, I never saw anyone so rude in all my life."

Nikki stirred, restless and unable to sleep. Max was only a few feet away. Her bedroom had grown stuffy with the door to the hall shut. Normally she left it open; tonight she thought it best to keep it closed.

God, but it was hot. She kicked the sheet to the foot of the bed, but it didn't help. Finally she climbed out of the bed, walked to the French doors and opened them, allowing the sea air to enter the room. She took a deep breath of cool, salt air, then walked through the open doors and onto the deck. It was late, maybe one in the morning. The full moon was high in the night sky. Its brilliance illuminated the night, reflecting on the water and the white sand beach. She took another deep breath and exhaled slowly. She leaned her elbows against the intricate wood rail. Max must be asleep. Too bad. It was a night made for love.

She heard a crash and turned. He must be awake after all. She tugged at her Mickey Mouse sleep shirt, feeling self-conscious—no, just a little ridiculous. She caught a glimmer of movement from his room and motioned for him to join her.

He opened the French door and walked onto the deck.

"Did I wake you?" she asked softly. "I didn't mean to. I just needed some fresh air."

"No. I didn't know if you wanted company. I'm afraid I made a mess with the vase."

"'S all right." She tried to ignore his bare chest. She covered the distance between them in two strides. "It was in an awkward place. I'll clean, and you can go back to sleep." She walked past him and through the open door into the guest room.

They knelt down simultaneously to replace the scattered marbles in the vase. Their knees touched. Knocked off balance by the suddenness of the contact, she fell in a sprawl. Her face grew hot. His erection strained against his loose white athletic shorts. Her mouth grew dry. Her nipples tightened at the sight of his arousal. Had she caused that?

Pretty damn obvious. He wanted her. She wanted him. Their eyes met. In that moment, they acknowledged their desire. She extended a languid hand to him, feeling time had slowed to a crawl, or as if she were moving underwater. He took her hand and held it to his heart; she felt the bounding rhythm beneath her touch.

"Max, I—" she began, uncertain and unsure.

"Shh. Nikki, do you want me?"

"I—" She didn't know what to say. Of course, she did. She always had, but...

"Do you desire me? Answer me," he demanded, his voice grown hoarse.

She felt his body quivering with desire. His dark green eyes glittered with it, as he waited for her answer. She nodded her head, unable to say the words.

"Do you want me to make love to you? Now?"

If she was going to say no, she'd better say it, because he appeared to be seconds from losing all control.

"Yes. Oh, yes," she heard herself say. She reached for him and pulled him to her on the cool pine plank floor.

Max lifted her sleep shirt over her head revealing her body in the pale shafts of moonlight. "You are so beautiful."

His lips crushed hers while he caressed her breasts, then ran his lips to the hollow of her neck. He found the cleft between her thighs. "I've wanted you so much," he gasped between breaths. "I have never loved anyone since I first saw you."

Waves of warmth and pleasure erupted throughout her body, gathering, centering between her thighs. Coherent thought—impossible. His hard arousal nudged her thigh. She moved against it. Soft moans of pleasure escaped without volition as he licked her abdomen. As his tongue moved lower, she began trembling with need.

Instead he groaned and rose from the floor, pulling her with him. "Not here," he gasped.

"Why not?" she could barely speak.

He gathered her in his arms and carried her to the soft, old-fashioned feather bed. "Here." He lay her gently on the bed and renewed his caresses, imprisoning her hands above her head, whispering, "*Je t'aime.*"

Her senses on fire, she surrendered. Max...making love to her. He *loved* her? She'd dreamt of it for years. Only reality was better. The heightened nerve endings in her fingers seemed to sizzle as she ran her hands over his strong back. His skin felt like satin, wondrous and unblemished, his muscles, dynamic and rippling as he moved over her.

Running her hands down to the waist of his shorts, she eased them over his buttocks, freeing his manhood. She touched the silken hardness of him and was rewarded with a groan of unabashed desire. His tongue plundered her mouth, twining and battling.

She couldn't breathe. Another wave of desire swept over her. Every cell in her body ignited by his lips on her neck and breasts.

"Tell me what you want," he whispered. "I want to please you."

"Just love me," Nikki murmured, "Just love me and don't leave me."

"Leave you? Never. *Je t'aime.*"

Finally, he stopped talking. Lost in the pleasure of his lovemaking, her body shook craving his deeper touch. "Please." A moan ripped from her throat.

Centering himself over her, he drove into her warmth. She wrapped her legs around his waist, the waves of pleasure building. He thrust, setting a furious pace, each stroke sweeter and hotter than the one before until they were swept up by the inferno of their desire.

Eighteen

Nikki awoke with a start, her heart racing. She looked at the empty half of her bed and realized... Damn. A *dream*? A dream so intense, even now it was difficult to reconcile the dream with the obvious reality. "No-o-o," she moaned.

There was no Max, only the pillow she cradled in her arms. Frustrated, she lay back on the bed and shut her eyes, reliving the touch of his strong hands against her body. The memory of his lips claiming hers sent her pulse skyrocketing into the stratosphere.

Stop it. If I keep this up I'll go crazy. Nikki sat up and swung her legs over the bed. The hardwood floor felt cool to the bottom of her feet. Too late she remembered the sensation of the floor against her back from her dream. A shiver ran up her spine. "Dear heaven. I have to stop this."

The ceiling fan above her bed spun lazily, leaving her skin clammy. Her hands still shook from the adrenaline rush. How would she ever face him over breakfast? The only thing on her mind would be her dream and his hard body.

What time was it anyway? She glanced at the clock beside her bed—five. Plenty of time for an early morning run. With some time and distance, she just might be able to pull herself together without drooling into her cereal bowl.

She pulled on a pair of blue sweat pants and T-shirt. Hurriedly she dragged a brush through her tangled hair, then walked onto the deck and took a deep breath of fresh sea air. After performing a few desultory warm-up stretches, she had one foot on the sand when she heard a door open.

Crap. No time. No distance. She'd have to face him now. She turned, and there he stood in all his bare-chested, firm-muscled glory. A pair of athletic shorts was all he wore, leaving precious little to her imagination. Her mouth grew dry as she dragged in a ragged breath.

"Good morning, I hope you don't mind my borrowing these," Max said, looking down at his shorts.

"No, not at all. Uh, I—uh, have an extra T-shirt, if you want. It's kind of cool." She shivered and rubbed her upper arms for emphasis.

He grinned. "I'm hot-natured." He bent over, stretching his hamstrings, an action that did nothing to steady the erratic rhythm of her heart.

Hot-natured? Just how was she supposed to take a remark like that? "Yes, it's a beautiful morning. Did you sleep well?" Better than she had…probably.

He shrugged, giving her a crooked smile. "Not really. And you? Did you sleep well?"

Nikki shook her head, "Not really. I was going for a run, but if you'd like some coffee, it won't take a minute."

"No, I could use some exercise. I'm still jet lagged. A run might help…if you don't mind my company?"

"Of course not." She struggled to keep from breaking out in a nervous giggle—and failed miserably. "Why would I mind?" Why indeed? Just because she couldn't look the man in the face without remembering last night's dream. Maybe he wouldn't want to talk. Maybe he'd forgotten about where their conversation was heading last night.

And maybe she'd sprout wings and fly to Mars.

Fortune was with her. Apparently he wasn't in a talkative mood. They jogged the sandy beach at a brisk pace, dodging errant waves. After a half hour of jogging in companionable silence, Nikki slowed her pace and turned to new running partner. "I think I've had enough," she told him. She stopped to catch her breath. And regain her composure.

He reached out and touched her shoulder. "May we talk…now?"

Not again. In spite of all her misgivings, she nodded. "I guess."

He brushed the sand from a flat rock, then gestured for her to have a seat.

Reluctantly she sat and watched him while he stood, gazing at the ocean. It seemed now he didn't want to face her. His dark wavy hair stood in irregular rows, as if he'd finger-combed it in a hurry. Her fingers fairly itched to reach out and touch him.

"I am perhaps precipitous, rushing like this." He paced a small path on the sand. "In spite of everything, I'm drawn to you. I always have been."

"'Drawn to me' means what?" She hesitated, still unsure. "You act like it's something you're fighting."

"I'm not explaining myself very well. Nikki, what I'm trying to say is…I care for you."

Panic, surprising, but panic nonetheless, mushroomed and lodged in her throat, threatening to render her speechless. She looked down at her feet, studying them intently, before taking a deep breath. "I need time to think."

Time to think? What was there to think about? That's all she'd done for the last ten years.

"Either you care for me or you don't. It's not a difficult question. I just want to know if you care for me too."

A peevish tone had crept into his voice. Fine, now he'd made up his mind, it was time for her to get with 'his' program—just like that.

"I-I told you, Jolie fired me. I have some adjustments to make, and I need to—" She broke off, then added in a rush, "I guess it sounds cliché, but I need to find out who I am."

He stopped pacing and dropped to his knees in front of her. Taking her chin between his thumb and forefinger, he raised it, forcing her to face him. "I told you to forget about being fired. *I'm* the boss, remember?"

His voice, soft as a sigh, made her want to melt into his arms, but she couldn't. Something held her back. Maybe it was the old insecurity, maybe something else. She forced herself to meet his gaze. "I know, but maybe being fired is what I need at this stage in my life. I'm considering a publisher's offer to write my autobiography." Her voice faded away, and why not? It was a damn poor evasion, even if it was a partial truth.

Max took her hand in his and pulled her to her feet. "That's wonderful. You should do it, but you don't have to sell your apartment or the beach house. Let me help you."

"I-I want to do this on my own." As soon as the difficult words crossed her lips, she realized she meant every single word. "You've been wonderful, but you've done enough. I'm not a kid anymore. After all you've done for me, I don't want to confuse gratitude with love." Nikki shrugged away from him, unable to continue. Had she lost her mind?

He stiffened and turned away, then with a parting glance, he said. "I see. Since you are determined to do this your way, I wish you the best of luck. I'm sure you'll write a wonderful book. Now if you'll excuse me, I have an appointment in New York." His curt words, once said, hung in the air. Taking long angry strides, he left her, stunned and alone.

Go after him. Go on, run. In spite of her heart's command, she couldn't. She simply couldn't. She'd meant what she'd said. She wasn't his charity case, not any more. Of course, he'd taken it the wrong way.

"Damn all men." Hot tears formed and trickled down her cheeks. Furious, she wiped them away. Maybe—just maybe—if she walked slowly enough, he'd have time to dress and leave. She walked slowly and cursed herself for being such a coward.

The cottage came in sight when she heard the roar of his rental car. Her eyes welled up again, and her nose started running. What was wrong with her? Why couldn't she just let it happen? What was really holding her back?

She stepped onto the deck. Lying on the table was a single red rose.

How sweet. Where had he found the rose? She unwrapped the paper around the stem, flattened it out against the table and read, *You don't need him.*

Chilled, Nikki looked around, then up and down the beach. Seeing no one, she dashed into the cottage and locked the door behind her. After making a hurried check of the remaining windows and doors, she took the rose and tossed it and the note into the trash.

Once again, Max cursed the slowness of the ferry. He'd lied about his New York appointment. As far as the agency was concerned, he was still in France. Yes, he'd out and out lied. Damn Jolie for firing Nikki and precipitating this crisis. And damn Nikki for being so stubborn.

And why he wasn't in Provençe lolling in the sun with the first available female he could find, he didn't know.

How could he have made such an error in judgment? It would be long time before he laid his heart at any woman's feet. A wave of grief swept through him. It was exactly this type of situation when he missed his mother most. She'd always been so level-headed and understanding of the female perspective…and she'd been so close to Nikki. His mother had been the glue that held their small family together. Her death had been a greater shock than he could have ever imagined, leaving him adrift, coping because he had no choice.

After all, that's what men did. They stood strong, no matter what happened. But now, he didn't feel capable or strong…not after Nikki's rejection.

Family.

It dawned on him that he hadn't heard from his daughter in the last week. Alexa was supposed to join him in France as soon as her school let out for the summer, but a week was too long to go without talking to her. He reached over and unzipped his carry-on bag, scrounging around in the bottom for his cell phone. He retrieved it and hit the speed dial, calling her school.

"Wintercrest Academy."

"This is Max Devereaux. I wish to speak to my daughter Alexa. I have just returned to the States."

The receptionist placed him on hold. He waited, drumming his fingers against the steering wheel. Finally, he heard the plummy tones of the headmistress.

"Mr. Devereaux, we've been trying to find you. Alexa is missing. We think she's run away."

His daughter missing? How could he lose someone else he loved? "Have you called the police? When was she last seen? What's happened? Why would she run away?"

"Please Mr. Devereaux, this is not a matter to discuss over the telephone. Where are you, and how soon can you be here?"

"I am between Martha's Vineyard and Boston. I will be there in an hour or so. At least tell me if the police have been called?"

"Yes, they have, as a matter of procedure, however we don't suspect foul play."

"Why not?" he asked. What else could it be? "What are you not telling me?"

"We'll discuss it when you arrive, Mr. Devereaux."

"I will be there as soon as I can, and I will expect a *complete* explanation." He disconnected, then immediately dialed Nikki's number. It rang five times, his anxiety level rising with each ring. Finally, she answered.

"Nikki, Max. I'm sorry to disturb you, but there's a crisis. Alexa has run away from school. Has she contacted you at all in the last week?"

"No, I told you last night, she hadn't. Where are you? Are you going to her school? What can I do?"

Nikki's quick offer to help gratified and relieved him. He wouldn't have blamed her if she had refused to talk to him after the way he'd stormed off.

"I'm on my way to the school now. I hate to ask this, but would you mind going to the townhouse, and see if she's gone there. Do you still have a key?"

"Of course, I will. And, yes, I still have a key. Renée made me keep it when I moved out."

"Wonderful." He hesitated, knowing an apology was in order. "I- I'm sorry for the way—"

"Never mind that now." Her tone was gentle. "We have to find Alexa. I'll catch a flight to the city. That'll be quicker."

"As kind as you are beautiful," Max murmured, the words slipping out before he could call them back. "I'll call you at the townhouse, after I've talked to the school and the police."

"And I'll call you as soon as I get there. Okay?"

"*Oui. Au revoir*, Nikki."

Max felt a thump as the ferry reached the dock. Anxious to find his daughter, he turned on the ignition.

Fifty-five minutes later Max strode into the Wintercrest Academy. The mild-mannered receptionist showed him into the headmistress's richly furnished office.

The headmistress, a plain, but well-dressed, woman in her early forties greeted him with a grim expression and an outstretched hand. "Mr. Devereaux, I'm glad you were so close at hand."

He gave a dismissive wave, not caring about meaningless

pleasantries. "What's happened to my daughter?"

"We have reason to believe your daughter has run away."

"Why would my daughter run away from this school? What have you done to her?"

"Please allow me to explain. Alexa confided in another student she was about to do so. Naturally, we have filed a police report because of the age of the young man she is thought to have joined.

"A young man?" Images of his daughter under the influence of someone much older chilled him. "This gets worse and worse. Does this school have no supervision? I must speak with this other student immediately."

Alexa was only fourteen, too young to be interested in boys. There had to be some mistake.

Wintercrest's headmistress gave an audible sniff. "Very well." She leaned over, and spoke into the intercom, "Have Elizabeth Elliott brought into my office."

An uncomfortable five minutes later a tiny brunette, dressed in the blue-and-gray school uniform eased into the office. Elizabeth appeared barely twelve. Her blue eyes were wide, and she gave Max a nervous glance, before looking down at the floor.

"Elizabeth, this is Mr. Devereaux, Alexa's father. I want you to tell him all you know about her disappearance," she said. Her firm voice brooked no nonsense.

The girl licked her lips with the tip of her tongue, looking first at him, then at her headmistress.

"It's all right. Tell him exactly what you told me yesterday."

Elizabeth swallowed, then began. "Alexa and I are really close, and when we went to the village a couple of months ago, we met a couple of cute guys at the mall from the local military prep school. They accused us of being stuck-up. So we had to show them we weren't. Anyway, Mario really liked Alexa, and I guess she really liked him too, because she told me last week that she'd been sneaking out to see him after lights out. I told her she'd better stop, because that kind of thing isn't allowed here. This is a really strict school." Elizabeth glanced at the headmistress, who nodded that she should continue.

"Anyway, Alexa laughed at me and said, 'Bitsy, you're just a baby,' but I'm not. I'm actually older than she is. I know I don't look it—"

"Continue," the headmistress said.

"So, she said she was going to run away with Mario to New York and meet his family. I told her she'd get in trouble, but she made me promise not to tell."

He held his breath during the girl's recitation, asked, hoping against hope, "Then you know where she is?"

"No, not really. I just know she's with Mario. He's really nice and cute, but I was afraid she might get into trouble, so I waited a couple of hours, and then I told Ms. Arnett."

"How old is this Mario?" he asked gently. He wouldn't learn anything if he intimidated her.

"Uh, eighteen."

"Eighteen. That's—"

The headmistress cut him off. "That will be all, Elizabeth. You may go," the headmistress said, shooting him a warning glance.

He took a deep breath. He'd been very close to shaking the child until her teeth rattled, which wouldn't accomplish anything. "Thank you, Bitsy," he said through gritted teeth.

As soon as Alexa's friend left the office, he leaned forward on the headmistress's desk. "So, who is this Mario, and where do I send his body when I find him?"

The headmistress's face turned pale. "Mr. Devereaux, there is no need for mayhem," she protested, her tone growing obsequious. "I'm sure the police will find them quickly. They have a composite of both this Mario and his friend. The police indicated they hoped to locate the other young man and through him find Mario and Alexa." She paused for a breath, then continued, "You must remain calm. After all, the teenage years are often difficult for girls who have an appropriate role model, but even more so for one like Alexa, who doesn't."

Max took a deep breath, but never made it to ten. He exploded, "I'll have you to understand my mother was an excellent role model for Alexa, but she had the temerity to die. How thoughtless of her." His accent became very thick, as it did in moments of emotional stress.

"I'm so sorry. I never meant to imply she wasn't. It is entirely possible Alexa's acting out is in reaction to the loss of her grandmother. I would recommend perhaps professional—"

"I will take care of my daughter once I find her. After I have spoken to the police, I shall return to the city, since that is where you say she's supposed to be. I have someone waiting at home to see if she calls or goes there. You already have my numbers. I trust you will notify me if you hear anything."

"Of course, Mr. Devereaux."

He turned on his heel and left the headmistress's office, still unable to believe his little Alexa had run away with an eighteen-year-old. His little girl. Walking to the rental car, he recalled Bitsy's remark about Alexa's seeing the boy after lights out.

Incroyable. Methodically, he unlocked the car door, stepped inside only to sit staring ahead at…nothing. His fists clenched around the steering wheel, for the very thought of anyone laying a hand on his daughter made his stomach churn. He remembered clearly the upheaval Nikki had experienced after being date-raped. He prayed history would not repeat itself.

Nineteen

Several hours and a flight later, Nikki paid the cabby, shouldered her bag and climbed the steps to the brownstone. She couldn't help but recall the first time Max brought her here. The memory left an emptiness in her heart that only Renée could fill. After unlocking the door, she walked into the kitchen and checked the answering machine. Great. The red light blinked. After locating pen and paper, she hit the play button and listened to the messages, hoping to hear from Alexa. After multiple calls about social events, which she impatiently recorded, she was rewarded by the sound of Alexa's cheerful voice.

"Hi, Daddy, I'm in New York. Don't worry about me. Talk to you later. Oh, I forgot. You're in France. Well, I'll try to reach you there later."

At least there was no indication of distress in the teenager's voice. Nikki let out a sigh of relief, but the stinker hadn't left an address or phone number where she could be reached. The answering machine logged her call at eight the previous evening. How ironic. Max's daughter had called while he was with Nikki—if he'd only been home instead. Why hadn't Alexa called his cell? Probably because she didn't want to have to explain herself and knew full well her father was in France.

The ringing telephone interrupted her train of thought. She grabbed it, hoping it would be Alexa.

It was Max instead. "Is she there?"

"No, but she left a message last evening. She sounded fine. Just a little put out when she remembered you were in France. She said she would call you there."

"All right. I'll check. I've talked to the police, and I'm on my way home. I'll tell you the rest when I arrive. Make yourself comfortable."

"Sure," she managed to say before Max rang off.

Hearing the exhaustion in his voice touched her. He had to be out of his mind with worry. Might as well unpack. She took her bag upstairs to her old room and opened the door.

Nothing had changed, and truthfully, it seemed as if she'd never been away.

After she unpacked and stowed Max's birthday gift on the top of the armoire, she wandered down to the kitchen and opened the refrigerator. Nothing. She picked up the phone and called the market for a delivery.

Alexa would be hungry when she returned home. And there was absolutely no doubt in her mind that the girl would show up unharmed. Well, there was a niggling fear, but she shoved it away.

Think positive.

Across town, in a comfortable living room in a sunny apartment, Alexa, Mario and his mother stared each other down. Alexa looked from Mario to his mother and back again to Mario. She wasn't sure what she'd expected to find, when they returned from the matinee, but it certainly wasn't Mario's mother, mad as a hornet and foaming at the mouth.

At the moment Lorena Judson's brown eyes flashed as she berated her son. "What were you thinking? How could you have been so—so stupid?" she sputtered. She stopped long enough to eyeball Alexa. "How old are you?"

"Sixteen?" Alexa answered, but the rising inflection gave away her lie.

Mrs. Judson's eyes narrowed. Alexa backed away. "I don't believe it. Tell me the truth. How old are you?"

Dying on the spot seemed desirable, but since that wasn't likely, she hung her head. "Fourteen, ma'am."

Mario's eyes widened in shock. She'd embellished her age for him too.

"F-fourteen? Omigod!" Mario's face darkened. "Mom, I didn't know, honest."

"It makes no difference. Sixteen is still too young to be running away from school. Mario, you crossed state lines with a minor. At eighteen, you're an adult. In the eyes of the law, you're guilty of kidnapping. They'll call the FBI, you dolt."

Mario snickered. "That means they'll be calling you, Mom."

"This is *not* funny." Turning to Alexa, she said, "I want the name of your parents, their phone number and address. Now!"

Never had Alexa seen any one human so angry. She could barely get out the words. "M-my father's supposed to be in France. I tried to call him last night, but he isn't there. I think he might be on his way back to the States, but I'm not sure."

"And your mother?"

Alexa hung her head. "She died when I was a baby." Maybe that would soften the woman's attitude.

"I'm sorry," Mario's mother said, her tone down a couple of decibels. "Your father's name, please."

"Maxim Devereaux." She rattled off her home address and phone number. "But there's no one at home, so it won't do any good to call."

"We'll just see about that. Otherwise, a trip to the police department is next on the agenda for you, young lady. I'm sure your school has already notified them." She turned back to her son, her hands on her hips. "In fact, I'd better call them now before someone comes here to arrest *you*!"

Alexa's heart lodged in her throat. She attempted an explanation. "I didn't really run away. It was just to visit for the weekend. Mario wanted me to meet you. I'm sorry. I didn't mean to cause so much trouble."

Mrs. Judson shot Alexa a look of dismay, then snapped, "You have no idea how much trouble you've caused."

"B-but nothing happened. Mario thought you'd be home, but we found your note saying you were out of town on a case, so we went to a movie, and I spent the night in the guest room." She started sniffing, then broke into sobs. Overwhelmed, she desperately wanted her father. She didn't care how mad he'd be. She needed him *now*.

Mario's mother patted Alexa's shoulder "Don't cry. I have to let the school and the local authorities know you're safe, and we have to find your father. This is going to be okay." Then added, "I hope."

Mario put his arm around Alexa. "See, Mom says it's going to be all right. You know, Mom, you're being really nice about this."

Mrs. Judson turned to her son, her brown eyes flashing. "You! Even if Mr. Devereaux doesn't press charges, you are still in very big trouble with *me*, young man."

After the market delivered her grocery order, Nikki set the box on the kitchen counter. When the telephone rang, she grabbed it. "Alexa?"

"No, this is Lorena Judson. I need to speak to Mr. Devereaux."

"Mr. Devereaux isn't here, but I expect him shortly. May I take a message?"

"Are you a member of the family?"

"No, this is Nikki. I'm a friend of the family—is this about Alexa? Do you know where she is?"

"She's fine. She's here at my apartment with my son."

"Thank goodness." Relief surged through her body. "May I speak to her?"

The next voice she heard was Alexa's. "Daddy?"

"No, it's Nikki. Are you all right?" She held her breath. Please let her be all right or Max would never forgive himself.

"Of course, I am. I'm really sorry. Where's daddy? I tried to reach him—"

Nikki cut her off. "Your father's talking to the police, calling out federal troops, you know—the usual."

"I'm so sorry. Is he really, really mad at me?"

"Scared out of his mind is more like it. Put Mrs. Judson back on. We need to get you home ASAP."

"Sorry. Here she is."

"Uh, this is a little complicated. My son Mario brought Alexa home for the weekend, without my knowledge, of course. I'll bring her home, if you'll give me directions."

"Of course. We're on East 65th Street."

"No problem, that's easy enough to find. We'll be there shortly."

"Thank you."

After Mrs. Judson rang off, Nikki tried reaching Max, but he didn't return her page or answer his cell phone. She wouldn't feel comfortable until she saw Alexa safe and sound. Restless for something to do, she returned to the kitchen and prepared tea and sandwiches in a mechanical manner, still disturbed by Alexa's rash behavior. It was something new, but fourteen was just the beginning. Gradually an idea formed—one which would keep Alexa occupied during the summer and, at the same time, give the teenager a taste of what it was like to really run away. Of course, it would take Max's approval and cooperation.

Forty-five minutes later, the doorbell rang. Nikki raced for the door and was more than a little relieved to see the wayward Alexa standing there with a sheepish expression across her pretty face.

"We've been so worried."

Alexa immediately engulfed Nikki in a bear hug which she returned with enthusiasm.

"I'm so-o sorry. I didn't mean to worry everybody."

After disentangling herself, Nikki stood back and offered her hand to Mrs. Judson. "I'm Nikki Prentice, You must be Mrs. Judson." She looked at the handsome Hispanic youth, standing beside Alexa. "And you must be..."

"Mario, ma'am."

"Mario." She acknowledged him with a nod. "Please come inside." She led them into Max's study. It was less formal than the living room, which was filled with French antiques.

She motioned for them to be seated. "Alexa's father will be here soon. He'll be so relieved."

Mrs. Judson sat on the leather sofa. "I've already notified the local authorities Alexa has been located, and that it was a mistake of sorts. I don't know if Mr. Devereaux will want to press charges or not, but if he does, Mario will have to accept the consequences for his actions."

Alexa turned pale. Wide-eyed she glanced at Nikki. "Oh, no. Daddy won't press charges, will he?"

Nikki tried to reassure Mario and his mother. "Naturally, I can't speak for Max, but I hope not. It all seems to have been a whim. But Alexa's only fourteen."

"I lied to Mario. I told him I was sixteen," Alexa confessed, hanging her head. After a moment she looked up at her erstwhile bodyguard and told him, "I'm sorry. This is my fault."

Mario shook his head. "Nah. I knew better, but it seemed like a good idea at the time."

Lorena Judson glared at her son, then turning to Nikki asked, "Exactly, what is your relationship to the family?"

"I'm a friend."

"Mr. Devereaux's *friend*?" The inflection in the woman's voice told Nikki what she was really asking.

Puzzled, by the woman's interest, Nikki answered, "As I said before, I'm a friend of the Devereaux *family*. When Max discovered Alexa was missing, he called and asked me to come here and wait, while he dealt with the school and the police."

"I see. Have you known Alexa and her father for very long?"

Okay here we go. "Ten years. I was a runaway. Max found me on the streets when I was sixteen and brought me here," Nikki explained. "His mother became my mentor, friend and surrogate-mother. Under her tutelage I became a model for the Devereaux Agency. While I lived here, Alexa and I became very close, like sisters."

She hesitated, wondering why she felt the need to detail her past. It seemed strangely important that Mario's mother should understand the situation.

"Of course, I recognize you now. Mrs. Devereaux no longer lives here?"

"No, she passed away in January."

Mario interrupted, "Geez, mom. Enough with the interrogation."

His mother's eyes flashed, but the sound of a key in the door alerted them to Max's return. "Nikki?"

"In the study."

"Have you heard anything?" Max called from the foyer.

At the sound of her father's voice, Alexa sprang from the sofa and ran to meet him, "Daddy, I'm fine."

He rushed into the study, relief written across his face. "Alexa!" He grabbed and hugged his daughter, then pulled a stern expression. "What did you think you were doing, young lady?"

"I'm sorry, Daddy. I didn't really run away." Alexa hung her head.

"Well, I did sneak away, but—"

Nikki interrupted, "Mrs. Judson, this is Max Devereaux, Alexa's father. Max, this is Lorena Judson and her son, Mario."

"Mr. Devereaux, I am sorry to meet you under these circumstances. I assure you my son is not in the habit of spiriting little fourteen-year-old girls away from school."

Max turned and glowered at Mario who seemed to shrink under the older man's gaze.

Hoping to defuse the difficult situation, Nikki nodded toward the kitchen. "Why don't Alexa and Mario come with me? I'm sure they'd like something to eat or drink."

Alexa gave her father a questioning glance. He nodded.

Taking the two teenagers out of the line of fire would give Max time to calm down and give them all some breathing space.

Max shook his head and sat in a leather arm chair facing Mario's mother. Lorena Judson was of medium height and had dark brown hair, cut short and waved about her face. She was quite attractive—not a beauty like Nikki, of course—but quite attractive nonetheless.

"Mr. Devereaux," Lorena Judson began, "I'm appalled my son has caused you all this worry. I'm so embarrassed. I really don't know what he was thinking, but then I guess not thinking clearly is part of being a teenager."

"First of all, I'm Max, and I'm very grateful you brought my daughter home. Thank you for remedying the situation so quickly. I will need to talk with Alexa privately, but I don't think any charges will be placed, as long as this event is never repeated."

The boy's mother gave a sigh of relief. "Thank you, Mr.Dev—uh, Max. I assure you, to the best of my ability, it will *never* happen again. Unfortunately, I'm called out of town frequently on business, and when Mario isn't away at school, he's there alone with the housekeeper. She has been with us since before my husband died. I'm afraid she spoils my son."

He nodded. "I understand the difficulty of raising a child without both parents. My mother brought up Alexa after my wife died, but she passed away earlier this year. We are still trying to adjust. I thought boarding school was be the answer, but now...after this." He gave a rueful laugh. "I don't know if I'm going to make it through these teenage years."

"Please, call me Lorena." She relaxed her posture, apparently relieved her son wouldn't be brought up on charges. "I agree. It is very difficult. Once I could control everything my son did or where he went.

Now, very little. Letting them go isn't easy."

"Well, I have no intention of letting Alexa go. She's only fourteen. How old is your son?"

"Eighteen last month. I'm afraid it hasn't dawned on him, that in the eyes of the law, he's an adult. He's had a difficult time since his father was killed in the line of duty, but he's never done anything like this before."

"Your husband was a policeman?"

"No, we were both with the FBI."

"FBI? Both of you? I would have guessed you were an attorney."

Lorena smiled. "Isn't it odd...the choices we make?"

"Fascinating," Max replied. "I have never known anyone from the FBI."

"And what do you do?" she asked.

"I have a modeling agency—commercials, print, and high-fashion. It varies."

She nodded in the direction of the door. "Nikki's very lovely. She's one of your models?"

"She was."

"She seems to care a lot about Alexa."

"Yes, she's been a family friend for a long time. Alexa and I are both very fond of her."

A smile played about her mouth, before she answered, "I see."

Twenty

The sound of low laughter reached Nikki who stood outside the study. With Alexa and Mario in tow, she found Max and the boy's mother chatting comfortably like old friends. A sharp twinge of jealousy stabbed the pit of her stomach. The young man's mother was attractive and polished.

Perhaps rejecting Max at the beach house was a mistake. After all, the man flew all the way from France just to see her.

"Everything okay, Mom?" Mario asked, appearing anxious.

"You and I still have to talk, young man." Her dark eyes still flashing. "But Mr. Devereaux isn't going to have you arrested, if that's what you mean?"

"Yes, Ma'am. Thank you, sir."

The tall, well-built teenager had dark wavy hair, dark complexion, a deep dimple in each cheek, and expressive, dark brown eyes like his mother's. At the moment, he acted very respectful, in awe of his mother, but Nikki wondered how long his mother would be able to control him. With his dark good looks, Mario had heartbreaker written all over him.

Mrs. Judson rose to leave, offering her hand to Max. "I want to thank you for being so reasonable. It's been a pleasure meeting you, considering everything that's happened. Now all I have to do is take my son home and decide how I am going to keep from killing him."

"Mom," the teen protested, rolling his eyes, but his mother gave him a stern glance.

Max took the woman's hand and said, "My relief at finding my daughter has outweighed my anger, but I too, am in the same situation. I wish you the best of luck."

Feeling like a voyeur, Nikki watched the interchange between Max and Mario's mother—her hand lingering in Max's, her engaging smile. Chalk up another Devereaux conquest.

"I think we'll both need it for the next few years," the woman replied, her dark eyelashes fluttering.

Crap. Max and Mario's mother had so much in common. Nikki didn't have any right to be jealous, but she was. Her face grew hot, but luckily no one was paying her any attention. She watched Max and Alexa walk the Judsons to the door. Unless she was mistaken, Max appeared quite taken with boy's mother. Well, why shouldn't he be? He was a strong and virile man, who had every right... She'd had her chance the night before and, again that very morning, and she'd completely blown it. Max seemed to be ready for a relationship. Why wasn't she?

By the time Max and his daughter returned to the study, Nikki regained a semblance of self-control. "I guess I'd better get out of here so you two can talk."

Alexa grabbed Nikki's hand and begged, "Don't go." She turned and grabbed her father's hand too. "Daddy, she doesn't have to leave, does she? She can stay here, tonight, at least?"

"Of course, Nikki may stay, if she wishes?" He lifted a questioning brow. "Do you?"

She glanced from one Devereaux to the other. Part of her wanted to stay, but she hedged and replied with a shrug, "I think the two of you might need some of that quality father-daughter time."

Max fixed his gaze on her. "But you are a member of this family." He stuck his hands into his pockets, a wry grin on his lips. "Actually, I have a proposition for you."

"A proposition?" What was he up to now? The glimmer of mischief in his eyes...and the half-smile playing about his lips held a warning. A proposition, indeed.

"Since you're selling your apartment and beach house, I thought maybe you might like to move in here and be Alexa's companion—for the summer."

"What?" she gasped. Never in a million years...

"Daddy!" Alexa squealed at the same time, clearly delighted by the idea. Her green eyes dancing with excitement, she turned to Nikki. "Say yes. Please, please say yes."

"You would really be doing both of us a tremendous favor. We've been at loose ends since *Maman* died, and since you are going to find another place to live, anyway..." He shrugged. "You would be free to write, and it would be a more homelike atmosphere for Alexa. You would have your privacy. In fact, Maman's suite would be ideal. Alexa really needs you."

Please say yes," Alexa persisted. "I hate being away at school."

Nikki looked from one pair of green eyes to the other. One set implored her to say yes. The other sent a more obscure message—one she wasn't quite sure how to interpret. Trapped—that's what she was. Max wasn't playing fair. "I'll think about it," she said slowly. "Will Alexa finish the school term at Wintercrest?"

He nodded. "If they'll take her back."

"I need time to close the condo and cottage."

"She has three more weeks of school. Is that enough time?"

"Barely." An unexpected chill skittered from Nikki's neck down her spine. Misgivings be damned, she thought. "All right. I'll do it. Just for the summer."

"Cool!" Alexa squealed. "I promise I'll be an angel. I won't be any trouble, and we'll have such fun."

"Thank you," he said with a smile, then turned to his daughter. "Nikki and I need to talk. Why don't you go upstairs and find something to do. Afterwards, I'll take you both to dinner."

"Okay, Dad." Alexa gave her father a hug and skipped from the room.

Max waited until his daughter left then sat behind his desk, a self-satisfied smile across his handsome face.

Unbelievable. The man had manipulated the situation like a pro. Once there was no risk of Alexa's overhearing, she turned on him. "You don't play fair."

His gaze narrowed, but the half smile softened his expression. "No, I don't. And you will do well to remember in the future," he warned, still grinning, his voice seductive.

She sputtered, "W-we're going to have some ground rules. This is not a permanent situation. You need to know that right up front."

"Don't you want to help us? This is such a difficult time."

His tone was 'poor pitiful me,' but damn, if she couldn't see the twinkle in his eyes. She hesitated, remembering how much she owed him. But this was emotional blackmail. "Of course, I want to help you, but I don't like being manipulated. You used my feelings for Alexa, and you know it."

"Yes, I did. So, tell me about these ground rules." He jutted his chin, challenging her, then leaned back, with his hands clasped behind his head.

Damn the man. He had her over a barrel and he was enjoying it. What's worse, he didn't care that she knew. "Well—uh—"

"Just say yes."

"I-I have to have time to write."

"*Pas de problem.* I have a cleaning lady once a week. All you have to do is be here for Alexa. Be her friend and mentor." He paused, smiled crookedly. "Do for her what *Maman* did for you."

Playing the *Maman* card, was he? "You really know how to apply the screws, don't you?"

"*Naturellement.*"

Did he have any idea how his use of French discombobulated her? The very timbre of his voice changed, became softer...sexier. Oh yeah, definitely sexier.

"Well..."

He shrugged and smiled. "It will also give us time," he paused, arching a brow, then continued, "to become better friends. What do you think?"

What did she think? He'd maneuvered her until she was between a rock and a hard place. Wrong term, best not go there. Difficult, yes, that was what she meant.

"What do you say?"

Instead of speaking her mind, she nodded. "I suppose it might work, but if it doesn't? What about Alexa? We have a wonderful relationship, but I don't want her to end up hating me."

He pooh-poohed her with a dismissive wave. "I don't think that's likely to happen."

Nikki's will weakened. Okay, maybe it was his reassuring smile that did the trick. "I had an idea about a project for Alexa this summer, but I wanted to clear it with you first."

"Really?" His expression grew curious.

"Yes, I planned on volunteering at one of the homeless shelters downtown, and I'd like Alexa to go with me. Sort of find out what it's like for others not as fortunate as she is."

His eyes widened, then he smiled. "You never cease to amaze me. It's a wonderful idea."

She couldn't help but be pleased by Max's approval. "It's time I gave something back. To the community—and to you. This way, I can do both."

"If that's what you want, then you should do it." His expression grew thoughtful. "You know I've never regretted your knocking me down."

"I never knocked you down and you know it."

His gaze locked with hers. The atmosphere changed, felt charged, as though lightning were about to strike. Nikki broke the silence first and changed the subject. "Alexa is a beautiful young girl," she said carefully, knowing she broached a very touchy subject. "Mario is just the first."

He shut his eyes for a moment and shook his head slowly. "I'm not ready to think of my daughter as other than my little girl." He stood. "According to her friend at school, Alexa has been sneaking out to meet this young man for the last month." His mouth tightened with disapproval. "He's entirely too old for her. I shall forbid her to see him."

Nikki laughed, then shook her head. "No. That's the quickest way to guarantee she'll fall in love with him. I'd suggest no unsupervised dates. That way Mario will get tired of being chaperoned and start dating someone his age.

He chuckled. "You have a very devious mind. I think you'll do very well at mentoring."

"Don't forget, I had a good teacher."

"We both did, although I'm afraid I didn't listen to her nearly as often as I should have."

"Neither did I." She let out a quick laugh, and amazingly she couldn't recall ever feeling so comfortable with Max. He was certainly doing everything to make her feel that way, asking her advice and offering confidences. In spite of herself, she found herself relaxing. "I can't imagine you did too much that upset her. The words pride and joy come to mind."

He seemed to relax as well. His expression softened, his gaze distant. "You know, Solange and I were married far too young. We wouldn't listen to our parents, either. I have always felt responsible for her death. I regret so many things."

"But she died in a car accident. Why should you feel responsible?"

"Now you sound like the inspector who interrogated me."

"The police were really involved? Now I'm curious." Nikki sat on the sofa and leaned forward. Max in a talkative mood? She found him entirely too charming...and distracting. "Sorry, I'm being nosy. It's really none of my business." She'd never believed the agency gossip about Max's dark past. Not her knight in shining armor.

Max sighed. "Solange was killed in an automobile accident...with her lover."

"Oh." What else could she say? Why did life have to be so complicated? Poor Max.

He sat in a chair across from her, then continued, "I was young. I concentrated more on my career than my marriage. I took my wife for granted. I worked long hours, usually seven days a week."

"But most successful business men work long hours. You did it for your family."

"It was the nature of my work which drove her crazy. For all her beauty, Solange was very insecure. She hated that I was surrounded by beautiful women all day, and she became irrational and jealous when I was late or missed a family dinner. I suppose it was inevitable."

He shrugged. "She turned to someone she met at school—one of her professors. They died together."

"But why the police? It was an accident."

His mouth tightened into a rueful grimace. "When the police investigated the accident, they discovered someone had tampered with the brakes. I had an alibi, but the inspector believed I paid someone. He hounded me for a year. Finally I moved the agency here to New York. There was nothing tying me to the accident, but it made no difference to the inspector."

She sat stunned. No wonder the man had never engaged in another long term relationship. "I had no idea the situation was so difficult. How terrible."

"It's over."

"Did they ever find…?"

"No, never."

She shook her head. "So, it's really not over."

He stood and walked toward her. "It's over because I choose to go forward and not look back."

"That's best." At his approach, her heart rate picked up, an insistent hammer in her chest. What was he up to now?

He took another step, taking her right hand in his. "I'm very glad you're coming to stay with us."

The sound of his voice, hoarse with emotion, the touch of his strong hands holding hers, sent her heart rate into the stratosphere. She swallowed. "I am too." Summoning her resolve, she withdrew her hand from his. "This is exactly what we have to guard against."

"What *this*?" he asked, an innocent altar-boy expression playing across his face.

"Touching. Getting too close. I'm here to help you with Alexa. That's all."

He took another step. "Are you absolutely certain that's the only reason?"

She took a step back, her voice faltering. "Y-yes."

"All right, I won't harass you, but I warn you," he said with a grin. "I'm not immune to your charm."

Unwilling to meet his gaze, she took a deep breath in an attempt to steady her ragged breathing.

"Can you truthfully say that I don't affect you?" Max asked.

"No. That's why we have to have rules. It wouldn't be proper, otherwise."

Max threw back his head and laughed. "No, my sweet urchin from the streets, it certainly wouldn't be proper." He took her face between his hands and kissed her lips, a long slow lingering kiss that left her weak in the knees.

She had to resist. "Max, please," she groaned. Damn the man. He certainly kissed like he meant business.

"I know. I guess we have to watch that too. I couldn't resist just once." He chuckled, then turned and walked away, leaving her standing in the study with her mouth gaping like an air-starved guppy.

Hopeless. She'd given Max her word, but he wasn't playing fair. One kiss and he had her trembling—from her dizzy head to her curling toes. What would happen if he stopped teasing and pursued her in earnest? She'd be putty in his hands, that's what.

***

Nikki fled to the safety of her old room. She leaned against the door, forcing herself to take slow deep breaths. The more she recalled the last exchange with Max, the angrier she became. He was insufferable and arrogant to boot. The nerve of the man. He'd appeared quite pleased with himself too.

Once again, he'd thrown her off-balance. Through the years, he'd been a kind man, a true gentleman. He'd always treated her with respect—sort of like a niece. Of course, if she were absolutely honest, she would have to admit she'd never thought of him as an uncle. Not with the dreams she'd had. No, Max was definitely not uncle material.

Now, he'd finagled her into an impossible position. And like a true dimwit, she'd agreed to move into the townhouse to be there for Alexa. Her word was given, but she wasn't about to let Max Devereaux translate it into a surrender.

Throwing herself across the bed, she hugged a pillow to her chest. The conflict might just tear her apart. The sight of Max chatting so comfortably with Mario's mother had unlocked pangs of jealousy. It was an unnerving experience, to say the least.

Okay. So she wasn't making sense, even to herself. Why was she so reluctant to accept his pursuit? Especially when she'd had X-rated dreams about him for years.

Granted, being date-raped had left her wary of the entire male gender. The other side of the argument was Max's reputation with women. Gossip was plentiful at the agency, but she'd never paid much attention—unless it concerned Max. The boss didn't date any of the agency models, but that left at least a million viable candidates in New York City alone. Over the past ten years, she'd often seen him in the society columns photographed with a variety of women. But 'love'em and leave'em Max' never committed and never took anyone home to meet *Maman*. That much she knew for sure. Renée or Alexa would've mentioned it.

Another thing for sure: she couldn't bear being another one of Max's flavors of the week. And she had no reason to believe she would be anything else, just because they'd shared a delightful dinner at the beach house. He'd been charming, but he was always charming. His smooth European manner was his most singular attribute. Women were attracted to him like flies to honey. And here she was trapped—and up to her knees in the honey.

She reached over and picked up the phone and dialed her best friend. *Come on, pick up the phone*. Marti could and would give a reality check like no one else. For all her distinguished forebears Martha Lodge

Alden was a very practical and down-to-earth person. Nikki held her breath as the phone rang four, then five times.

"Hello," came the breathless and familiar voice.

"Hi."

"Nik. Where are you?"

"I'm at Max's."

"Well, that's certainly an improvement over the last time we talked. Spill. What's happened? I thought luscious Max was in France."

"Long story. Why don't we have dinner tonight, and I'll tell you all about it?"

Marti paused. "All right. Why don't you come over here? Tom has a meeting, so we can have a real girl session. Simone's planning a cold dinner for me. She can just as easily make it for two. Around eight?"

"Great. Eight, it is." Nikki replied, unable to keep a note of satisfaction from her voice. She'd show Max Devereaux she was still an independent woman with friends and a life of her own.

Nikki walked into Max's book-lined study. "I'm having dinner with Marti tonight."

"Fine. Have dinner with whomever you wish." He watched her from behind his desk. "But, I thought you would enjoy—"

"Stop it right now. Don't you even think about laying a guilt trip on me, Max Devereaux. Alexa isn't in the room. You and I both know what this is about." She paced as she spoke, pointing a finger in his face.

She watched for his reaction. He arched an eyebrow. Damn the man. He couldn't keep the glint of amusement from his eyes.

"And what is this about?" he asked, his voice husky. The sound of it weakened her knees. What if he was thinking of kissing her again? What if he wasn't?

Max answered for her. "Yes, it's about you and me. For some reason you've decided you don't want a closer relationship with me. But..." he gave an exaggerated shrug, before continuing, "... I always thought that we had a certain connection—one that transcended our age difference." He rose from his chair and walked over to her. "Was I mistaken?"

He stood mere inches away. Concentrate. Breathe. "Stop it," she gasped. "I don't know. Don't you understand? I simply don't know what I want. Until I do..." She threw up her hands and ran from the study.

Puzzled, Max asked the empty room, "What next?" The more he pressed Nikki, the more she resisted. Maneuvering her into living with him and Alexa might not have been such a smart move after all. She seemed more determined than ever to place barriers between them. Had any man ever made his intentions clearer? "If you were only here, *Maman*," he murmured, gazing at her portrait, which graced the wall of his study.

The unalterable truth was his mother was not here. And he was a thirty-nine year old man, who ought to be able to win the heart of the woman he loved.

Some things were meant to be—karma, kismet or fate. Didn't matter what it was called. From their first meeting, he'd been haunted by Nikki—the wide blue eyes, the self-deprecating sense of humor; and last but not least, her pretense of being tough and unaffected by the deprivations of her early life. That night had changed their lives, but she'd been so young. Since then he'd marked time, waiting for her to grow up.

Had he waited too long? Had he wasted ten years of his life waiting for a relationship never meant to be? Had he overlooked other relationships which might have led to happiness? Was his fear of losing control so great he preferred to wait for the unobtainable rather than face life as it came? The questions he asked were difficult; he had no ready answers.

Max paced back and forth in his study. If Nikki wanted nothing to do with him, why should he postpone life? Let her struggle to find herself. She could damn well do it alone.

He walked to the desk and stared at the telephone. He reached for it, but still he hesitated. Should he make a phone call that might change his life, or should he be patient with Nikki a little longer? Recalling Lorena Judson's dark brown eyes and attractive face, he dialed Information and asked for her number. He made a note of the number, but was powerless to banish Nikki's image from his mind's eye.

"*Merde*," he swore softly and hung up the phone.

Twenty-one

Marti greeted Nikki with an enthusiastic hug. "It's been ages, sweetie."

"Yes, way too long," she agreed, following her best friend into the luxuriously furnished living room. "You've redecorated again," she said, admiring the entirely new, Spartan look.

"That's the best thing about having a sister-in-law who's an interior designer. Tom nearly had a fit, but when I told him about all the discounts, he didn't say too much. Besides, it's his sister who talked me into it."

Nikki giggled. "Tom never says too much about anything you do. You've trained him well."

"Yes, he's a keeper." Marti sat on the Italian leather sofa and motioned for Nikki to join her.

Nikki settled into the baby-butt-soft leather sofa. "Longer than the other two?"

"Well, I learned on Joel and Chris, and now Tommy reaps the benefit of my maturity."

A full-blow giggle erupted. "Maturity? You're thirty-seven."

"Mere details, darling. You know I've always felt older than my years, except when I was being very immature, of course."

"Of course."

"Besides you didn't know me when I was eighteen. I was such a wild child then." Her friend leaned forward, her eyes wide. "But enough about me, what's the scoop on you and Max? I'm not going to feed you any dinner until you tell me absolutely everything."

"Are you really going to make me rehash it all?"

"Of course. So spill."

Nikki made a face. She'd known Marti for ten years. Her oldest friend wasn't about to give up until she knew everything. "I was at the beach house. Max called from Provençe and asked me to fly over."

"Sounds great. That's what you want, isn't it, to be with Max?"

"Yes—well—I don't know. Nikki shrugged. "I'm so confused. I don't know what to expect from him anymore. I've idolized him since that first night we met. He's always been my knight in shining armor."

Marti laughed and gave an eye roll. "I think I might have heard this story once or twice."

"I guess you have at that," Nikki admitted then stuck out her tongue. "Anyway, he was always unobtainable. Now all of a sudden, he wants me to visit him in France? I don't understand. First, I'd heard through the grapevine he was in France with this Arianne Willoughby. When he called me, I assumed they'd had an argument. I—uh, wasn't very receptive."

Marti shook her head. "Not receptive. I suppose by that you mean you blessed him out in no uncertain terms."

"Sort of."

"Well, I do have a grapevine of my own, you know," Marti said. "Arianne's father and my Tommy both being bankers. I'd heard she was interested in him, but I never heard about any signs of interest on his part. I think you were upset for no reason."

"Well, to be fair, he said she followed him to Paris, and he told her he wasn't interested." She chewed her bottom lip, still uncertain. "But why would she act as if they are nearly engaged, if there's not some reason?"

"From what I know about Arianne, she's not used to taking 'no' for an answer."

"If he's telling the truth." Nikki shifted on the sofa.

"Is he in the habit of lying to you?"

"Not that I know."

"Just my point, Nikki."

"Okay, but wait, you don't know everything that happened. When Max called, Jolie had just fired me a couple of days before."

"Fired you? Is she nuts? You're the agency's top model. Don't you have other agencies sniffing around all the time?"

Nikki nodded. "That's a story for another day. But still I wasn't in a very good mood to begin with. I told him I was too busy with rethinking my life. He seemed to think that was amusing. Then he told me he'd talk to me later when I was in a better mood. The next day I'm out on the beach, and there he is, walking straight toward me."

"Impulsive...and determined. Oh, I like that in a man." Marti giggled. "Go on. Then what?"

"We had dinner."

"*You* cooked?" Marti's eyes grew wide.

Nikki grinned. "No, he did."

"This is better and better. Have to love a man who cooks. And...after dinner?"

"We were sitting before the fireplace about to talk and have some wine...and the phone rang."

"No." Marti groaned. "Please tell me you ignored it."

"If only I had. It was my mother."

"Oh, Lord."

"Yes. She felt it her maternal duty to call and read me the riot act because she'd heard about my leaving the agency on television. She also managed to get in a few digs about Max."

"And you hung up on her...I hope."

"Yes. She never fails to piss me off. By then, I had a headache, so I pointed Max toward the guest room, and I went to bed."

"You're kidding?" Marti shook her head in disbelief. "I can't believe you had the man of your dreams alone and in the same room, and you sent him down the hall to the guest room."

Nikki gave a rueful laugh. "I did."

The more she tried to explain about her desire for independence, the more her friend shook her head. Nikki concluded her story with Max's calling her about Alexa. "So that's how I ended up at the townhouse."

Marti sat with her mouth open for a moment, then said, "You are in quite a predicament, aren't you? He may have you right where he wants you, but it's still up to you to take advantage of it."

"Take advantage of it? Max and I can't start a relationship with Alexa there. It wouldn't be proper. I'm supposed to set an example, not seduce her father."

Marti seemed to consider Nikki's reservations. "Okay, think of it as an opportunity to know the real man. I mean, if you really want to get to know him, the situation is ideal. Keep some distance between you, but not too much. Drive him crazy with desire. That's what I'd do."

"*Au contraire.* He's already driving *me* crazy. The dream I had the night he was at the beach house. Whew!"

"X-rated?"

"Was it ever. The hard part about waking up was that it was so real. And it seemed so right. It didn't seem like the first time, either." Nikki grew contemplative, then asked. "Did I tell you Max sent me a gift?"

Marti leaned forward. "This just gets better and better. Tell me!"

"The day before he called, he sent me this old French mask he bought from an antique shop in Paris—for my birthday, which by the way, isn't until August. I put it on at the beach house, and I either fainted or went to sleep. I'm not sure which, but I had another dream. Max and I were lovers in France, but it had a tragic end. He was killed after making love to me."

"That wasn't very nice of you."

"I didn't mean I killed him. The Nazis did, after he left me. I think reading the mask's provenance must've made me dream that, because it referred to a similar incident."

"Interesting."

"It was anything but interesting. In my dream I saw him lying in a pool of blood, and I woke up crying."

"It must've seemed very real. Still it was only a dream." Marti's voice soothed, encouraging Nikki to continue.

"It was more like watching a movie than a dream, Marti. You know how dreams are usually all jumbled up? Well, this one made perfect sense. At least it did in the dream." Nikki worried her lower lip for several seconds, then decided to take the plunge. If Marti thought she was crazy, so what? She took a deep breath. "Do you believe in reincarnation?"

"Not sure if I do or not." Marti's perfectly arched brows drew together in a frown.

Nikki continued, "At first I thought it was just another one of my many dreams about Max, but now I wonder if wearing the mask stimulated some kind of—I don't know—karmic memory?"

Marti smiled and raised an eyebrow. "Well, you're getting pretty deep into the esoteric realm here. I guess it's possible that you and Max have been together in another life and are still trying to work it out."

"I don't know. I mean how can you really know?"

"True."

"On the other hand, maybe it's a warning. Maybe we aren't good for each other. Honestly, I want to be with him, but whenever he broaches the subject, I back off," she wailed. "I can't help it. Something deep inside makes me want to run in the opposite direction."

"It's more likely you're reacting to what happened with Ian Stark."

"That was a long time ago. I'm *over* it."

Marti reached over and patted Nikki's hand. "I'm not so sure about that. Still, you'll never know if you don't give Max a chance."

"Life shouldn't be so complicated." Nikki paused and sipped her coffee. "Something else very weird happened at the beach house too."

"What?"

"After he left the cottage, I walked back and found a rose lying on the wrought iron table. First, I thought Max had left it, but there was a note lying under it. Someone had scrawled, *You don't need him.* What do you think? It really gave me the creeps. I was already packed and ready to leave, when Max called and asked me to come to the townhouse."

A puzzled look crossed Marti's face. "Ever received anything like it before?"

"No."

"I don't like the sound of it. Did you call the police?"

"No, I threw it away. I mean, it didn't threaten me or anything. The police would've just blown me off."

"Well, I don't know, but if it happens again, promise me you will. I don't want to scare you, but it sounds like you might have a stalker."

"One rose doesn't a stalker make."

"I still think you ought to call the police," Marti said, giving an emphatic nod of her head. "By the way, have you tried on the mask again?"

"No. I mean—well, I hadn't slept the night before. I thought I'd fallen asleep, and dreamt it, but the more I think about it... Hell, I don't know."

"Just as an experiment, mind you, why don't you try it, again? I mean either you will or you won't. If there's something about the mask, which caused it the first time, then it might happen again."

She frowned as she considered the idea. The initial result had been pretty startling. "What if something worse happens?" she asked, uneasy at the thought of trying it again. "I'm not sure I want to experience those other lives, if that's really what's going on."

"What if you brought the mask over here..." Marti suggested, "...and I stayed with you? If it looked like you were having a rough time, I could just wake you up, and that would be that."

Nikki grinned at her friend. "I think you're more interested in this previous life thing than I am. I can't believe you'd even consider something like this. You're usually so levelheaded."

"I may be levelheaded, Sweetie, but I've had an experience or two that makes me think anything is possible." She rustled in her pocket for a cigarette. "I know, I know. I need to quit, and I will, but not yet."

Nikki watched her friend become very agitated, her hands shaking as she lit a cigarette. Marti took a long drag before speaking. "I don't think I ever told you, but when I was about nine or ten, my grandmother was sick. Mother had gone to Cambridge to stay with her, but she wouldn't let me go. Mother said Gram was too ill, so I was left home in Boston with my governess.

"Late one night after I'd gone to sleep, I woke up, and there was Gram standing at my bedside smiling at me. I said, 'I thought you were sick.' she smiled and shook her head. 'Not any more, child. I'm much better, and I wanted to see my little namesake. You go back to sleep now.' Then she sat in the rocker by my bed, and I went back to sleep."

"I think I know where this story is headed."

Marti shushed her. "Just let me finish. The next morning, everyone was rushing around, and my mother was back at home. I asked her where Gram was, and she told me Gram died the night before. I kept saying, 'No, she didn't. She was here last night, in my room. I saw her.' My mother became very upset and told me to be quiet and never mention it again. It wasn't until later when I heard of other people having similar experiences that I even remembered what had happened."

The hair raised on Nikki's neck and forearms. "I've heard of things like that too, but I've never known anyone who actually experienced it."

"That's not the only time I've had it happen, Nik. When I was sixteen, I was in the school library, studying for an exam. I kept seeing someone in my peripheral vision. I'd turn around and look, but no one was there. Finally, I heard my brother Eric laugh, as if he were playing a joke on me. Then I heard him say, as clearly as I can hear you, 'Bye, Sis. I have to go now.' When I turned again, he wasn't there. I called home, and mother said I was being silly, that Eric was with friends, and I needed to get out of the library and get some fresh air. An hour later, my father called and told me my brother had died in a boating accident. So, yes, I do believe there is more to life than we know. I don't think anything is impossible. Far from it."

Nikki shivered, rubbing her arms. "The hair is absolutely standing up on my arms. So you still think we ought to try this little experiment?"

"I do. Then if nothing happens, you'll know you were tired and it was just a bad dream."

Wary, but curious, Nikki took a deep breath and let it out. "Okay, let's do it."

Nikki and Marti made a quick trip to the townhouse. "Max?" Nikki called, listening for a response. She shrugged and turned to Marti. "Come on in. I guess he and Alexa went out to dinner. Now, we can get in and out without any questions. I'll be right back."

She bounded upstairs to her room and retrieved the mask from its place of safekeeping, an old-fashioned hatbox on top of the armoire. Lifting the lid, she looked inside the box. Yes, still there. A frisson of unease shimmered down her neck and lodged in her stomach.

Don't be silly. It's just butterflies.

She carried the box down to the foyer where Marti waited.

"You look like the cat that ate the canary. I take it your mission was a success."

"It's right here." She patted the hatbox.

"So, let's see it."

"Now?"

"Yes, now. Just for a second. Then home for the grand experiment," Marti said, the sound of excitement mounting in her voice.

"All right, but I don't want to be here when Max and Alexa come home." Removing the top, she revealed the leather mask.

"Oh. It's beautiful." Marti reached inside the box. "May I?"

"Sure." Nikki shrugged.

Marti took the mask, lifting it from the box, but then quickly dropped it. "Oh."

"What's wrong?"

Appearing dazed, Marti's eyes widened. She glanced first at Nikki and back again at the mask. "No, I—uh, I don't know. Something strange happened. Look, sweetie, maybe this isn't such a good idea, after all." She handed the box to Nikki. "Why don't you take that thing and—uh, put it away. Why don't we take in a movie instead? Forget all about Max and that silly mask."

"Marti? What happened?"

Her friend headed for the door. "Or we could go have a drink."

"Hold on." Nikki took Marti by the shoulders and gave her a shake. "What's wrong? You have to tell me because you're pale and this just isn't like you."

She flashed a quick smile at Nikki. "Let's go home and I'll tell you. I really need that drink."

During the taxi ride back to Marti's apartment, she tried explaining the sensations she'd experienced when she'd touched the mask. "It didn't burn, but the mask was definitely warm. Almost like flesh. I know it sounds silly. But when I touched it, I had flashes—visions of people running and shouting. It doesn't make a lot of sense right now, but maybe in time it will." She visibly shivered and Nikki noted the faraway expression in her friend's eyes.

Another chill zipped up Nikki's spine. She closed her eyes for a moment, but the twin images of a Royal Guard and a French Resistance soldier caused her to open them right away. She shook her head. Two Max's were too many. She had enough trouble with the Max Devereaux in the present, she wasn't signing on for any more.

Once back at the apartment, Nikki gathered her courage and opened the hatbox. "I'm going to prove all this nonsense about the mask is just that—nonsense."

Marti placed a restraining hand on her shoulder. "I wish you wouldn't. It was a stupid idea. I'm sorry I suggested it."

"I disagree. Look, I'm touching it, and I don't feel any heat. Nothing." She raised the mask. "Watch. I'm putting on the mask and nothing—"

Over his after dinner coffee, Max smiled at his daughter. "Lexxie, I promise we'll find you a school in the city for the fall. I won't send you away again. The townhouse is too lonely without you. I missed you more than I thought possible. I was selfish and thought only what was convenient. Didn't think how it would affect you."

"Is Nikki going to stay with us in the fall?" his calculating daughter asked, glancing up at him from under her spiky dark lashes.

"I have no idea about her plans. I doubt she does either."

A sudden wave of vertigo hit Max. He grasped the edges of the table with both hands.

"Daddy, what's wrong? You're pale."

He shut his eyes for a moment before answering. "I'm not sure. I felt like the room was spinning, but now it seems to be going away."

His daughter's eyes grew wide. "Are you sure?"

"It's nothing. In fact, I'm fine." He shrugged. "It's over." Looking at his watch, he said, "I need to make a call." The vertigo had passed, but a feeling of unease remained. Images of Nikki had come to mind and wouldn't go away. Something was wrong. He keyed in his home number, but the answering machine picked up. "She's not answering."

"Wasn't she going to Marti's?"

"Ah, yes. See how handy you are. I need you around to keep track of everyone."

"I know how you could keep track of Nikki." His daughter shot him a smug grin. "*Marry her.*"

Nikki would have fallen to the floor if Marti hadn't been standing by her side. She eased her friend down on the leather sofa and held her hand. What else could she do?

"Crap." Worried, she patted the side of Nikki's face. "Answer me, what's happening? Your color's good. Breathing okay?" She noted the easy rise and fall of her friend's chest. "Yes, breathing's okay." She continued watching, but Nikki didn't respond to any of Marti's feverish efforts to awaken her.

Should she call a doctor or 911? She wrung her hands. Maybe Nikki would come out of this spell without assistance. Marti held her breath and waited.

Nicola walked about the open deck and spied the Captain of the *Santa Elicia* at the helm. She made her way toward him, determined she would have her fears allayed... or confirmed.

"Captain, are we in for a storm?"

"Not much of one, *Signora*, but you should remain below in your quarters. My ship and I have weathered many such storms." The captain smiled, flashing his white teeth behind a dark mustache.

She found his presence virile and his sea green eyes compelling. She nodded her agreement, suddenly suspicious the handsome officer had merely placated her. Still, she would take his advice.

The swells grew larger and larger, a strong gust of wind blowing the ship suddenly leeward, caused her to stumble against him. Grateful he had kept her from falling, she looked up to thank him and felt the intensity of his gaze. The sudden contact of his body with hers startled her. Her hands lingered on his firmly muscled chest. His arms felt like iron bands as he steadied her. This was the first time she had felt a man's embrace since her husband died two years before…and it felt most pleasant. But because she was a lady, she backed away and tried to ignore the sensations awakened by his touch.

"First Mate, see to the helm," Captain Ramos ordered, "I will escort Signora Vincenza to her quarters."

Without further incident, she allowed the captain to assist her to her cabin. His manners perfect, he bowed over her hand and offered, "May I send dinner to you, *Signora*?"

"*Grazie*, but no, I am afraid I shall not be able to eat."

He smiled and bowed again. "Then *Signora*, please excuse me. I must attend to my ship."

"Of course, Captain."

Closing the door, she leaned against it, closing her eyes in contemplation, remembering the first time a man had looked at her with passion. Twenty years earlier, after quitting the stage, she had entered her dressing room, removed her mask, laying it with great care on the dressing table. It was a superb specimen of the whitest leather. She had been told it came from the hide of the last unicorn, but of course she had no faith in such myths. She traced her fingers around the gold outlining the eyes and finely arched brows. The feather trimming the mask was still colorful and full. She had no idea of its true history, but she had protected it, ever since her dresser Maria had unearthed it from storage.

A new face appeared in the mirror among those who thronged into her dressing room that night. Soft brown eyes watched her from a face that appeared kind as well as handsome. She had not been able to break away from his piercing gaze, though she had tried.

Maria entered, abruptly scattering the other admirers. "*Signorina*, do you want me to make him leave?" The older woman placed her hands on her hips and frowned at the newcomer, ready to do the prima donna's bidding.

"No, you may leave us, Maria."

Maria sighed. "As you wish, *Signorina*." The wardrobe mistress withdrew, casting repeated glances over her shoulder.

Later that same evening, she married the stranger in the mirror and never looked back until now. For two years after her husband's death she mourned him.

A sudden jarring of the ship flung her to the floor, interrupting her pleasant memories. The ship pitched and tossed with greater frequency. With great difficulty she made her way to the bed. Lying down she was able to quiet her heaving stomach, but only by clinging to the headboard was she able to remain on the bed.

For what seemed like hours, the ship tossed and heaved throwing her passengers about as if they were dice in a shaker, causing more than one of them to call loudly on Heaven's intervention.

Eventually, the sea calmed. Night covered the ship with a foggy blanket. The sea, without the light of the moon or stars, gave her a feeling of terrible isolation. She fell asleep almost as soon as the worst of the pitching ceased, a prayer of thanks on her lips. She had survived and rested not in the black depths of the ocean.

After a dreamless sleep, she awoke with the bright morning sun hitting her face, nearly blinding her with its intense rays. Pleased to find the ship still intact, she rose from the narrow bed and gazed out the small window. Sunlight struck the waves, causing a myriad of sparkling lights to dance in a dazzling array over the water. The sky was perfectly clear with only one large white, puffy cloud in sight.

A school of dolphins raced alongside the ship, their dorsal fins slicing the surface of the water as they swam, dived and raced through the watery depths. Occasionally, one would leap from the water and show his entire body, gray and glistening in the sunlight. So playful, they appeared to enjoy their capers in the jade sea.

It was a truly a beautiful morning to be alive. Only concern for her son clouded her heart. He had been injured in a horseback riding accident in England, or she would have had no reason for voyaging to such a cold, damp country.

After dressing, she decided to take a walk on the deck. She threw a lace shawl around her shoulders and left the already stifling heat of her small cabin. She found the captain watching the same school of dolphins she had watched earlier. He stood tall, as the wind blew through his dark curls. His wavy hair was clubbed back on his neck, but a few tendrils had escaped. A short, well-trimmed beard and mustache complimented his angular thin face.

She remembered their brief encounter the evening before and blushed. It puzzled her greatly, this feeling of passion for someone she barely knew. It was something she never expected to experience again. However, it seemed as if she already knew what he would be like. He would be tender and loving, but very passionate. Indeed, the vivid images shocked her. No modest woman should think such things.

But she had already made up her mind she would never give him any reason to make advances. Acting on her impulses simply would not do.

The captain turned toward her. In the bright sunlight, his eyes blazed an emerald green. Indeed, they were a sharp contrast to the soft green of the water surrounding the *Santa Elicia*.

When he saw her, he smiled showing white, even teeth through his dark mustache. "*Signora* Vincenza, I see you have suffered no ill effects from last night's little storm. Most of my passengers are still in their beds. I am happy to see you are an excellent sailor." He bowed low and kissed her hand, his lips lingering a moment longer than politeness dictated. All the while he gazed into her eyes, causing her entire body to grow quite warm. What manner of man was he to affect her so?

The waves of heat coursing through her caused her to withdraw her hand from his. Unable to explain her abrupt reaction without revealing the nature of her confusion, she attempted a feeble laugh. "You would not have thought me a good sailor last night, Captain. I fear I was as ill as the rest of your passengers. For one, I am very thankful we are standing here on deck this morning and not food for the fish below. I commend you for your skill in saving our lives. I did not think anyone could have brought us through the storm as you did."

Captain Ramos, his voice soft and seductive, replied, "The *Signora* does me too much credit for the sailing of my ship. I merely did what any captain would do."

Although he decried the necessity of praise, she knew, by his knowing expression, she had pleased him. Whether his pleasure was due to her expression of gratitude or her silly girlish reaction to his kiss on her hand, she remained unsure.

Nicola dawdled over her simple breakfast, then selected a book to read to while away the morning. They had been at sea for only five days, and had they not been blown off course by the storm, it would have been their last day. Concern over her son's fate consumed her. The delay and the uncertainty took precedence in her mind. Finally, she was able to dismiss her conflicting thoughts about the handsome Captain Ramos.

The loss of her son would be too much to bear. Antonio must not die, she willed. It was her son who had helped her though the horrible time after her husband's passing. It was Antonio who had kept her going, when she had wanted to stop living and join her husband.

"*Signora* Vincenza, pardon me for disturbing you," a soft voice said.

Nicola looked up from her book. Captain Ramos stood in the open doorway of her cabin. He was smiling and showing his fine, white teeth. He must be extraordinarily proud of them, for he certainly flashed them often enough.

"To the contrary, Captain, you do not disturb me at all," she began with unfailing good manners. "I am merely reading to pass the time. The book is not a very good one—very dull with scenes of battles and such. It does not interest me much." In reality, the book was a history on the politics of Italy and would not, in any circumstances, be considered proper reading material for a lady, but Nicola had always been encouraged to read books of all kinds by her late husband. Thanks to him, her innate intellect had grown sharp, and she had developed a great interest in politics. Too many world shattering events had occurred in her short thirty-eight years of life.

"I wonder if the *Signora* would do me the honor of dining with me in my cabin tonight?" he asked, his gaze holding hers. "Since it is the last night aboard ship, I have persuaded my troublesome cook to prepare something special." Smiling again, the captain's green eyes twinkled as he bowed over her hand and kissed it.

Nicola's tranquil manner belied her inner qualms. Although she smiled coolly and did not snatch her hand away as she had earlier, her knees weakened and would have given way, had she not already been seated. The same warm sensation ran up her arm and down to the pit of her stomach. With eyes out of focus and a brain which seemed to possess no will of its own, she assented, "Yes, Captain Ramos, I will." In spite of her misgivings, she would have dinner with the handsome captain. Her tell-tale heart pounded rapidly in her chest. Ridiculous. She must not act like a giddy school girl.

"Until then, *Signora*. I await your company with great pleasure," had been his bold reply.

Nicola could not believe the forwardness of the man. He kissed her hand again. She pulled a fan from her sleeve and plied it, cooling her warm cheeks.

Captain Ramos, his emerald eyes glittering, bowed gracefully, pivoted and exited her cabin, rubbing his hands together as he did. The nerve of the man. He thought to lie with her. Well, he would not find her favors so easily won.

The hours, which once had passed so slowly, now flew. Long before she was prepared for her dinner engagement, the faithful Maria had moved Nicola about like a sack of flour, finally managing to dress her in pale blue silk and arrange her hair in a becoming style. Maria held the precious glass mirror before Nicola.

Maria gave an exasperated sigh. "You must show some life, child. You are dining with a veree han'some man tonight. You have been alone too long. Eet ees time you have a man in your life. Thees captain weel not be aroused by a puppet. You mus' show some life."

Her cheeks grew hot at Maria's implications. "You go too far. You are my friend, but you go too far." With angry jerking motions, Nicola adjusted a ribbon here and a fold of the blue silk dress there. She took the ivory fan from Maria's gnarled fingers and used it furiously, pacing back and forth in the small cabin.

Maria chuckled and clapped her hands, "That's much better, *cara mia*. Now you are alive. You are mad, but eet ees a def'nit eemprovement. Ah, *Signora*, you are still so lovely."

She nodded. "Thank you, Maria. You have not lost your touch

"The chignon, it is perfect for you, *Signora*. The captain, he will want to make love to you tonight. I am sure of it."

"Maria!" she cried, her face flushing with heat. "I am joining him for *dinner*."

"In the han'some captain's cabin."

"I am too old for such foolishness. It is not proper."

"Hah. You do not look a single day over thirty. Your skin is smooth as a bambino's, and there is not a single gray hair on your head. I should know. I have dressed your hair for the last twenty years."

A knock at the door startled Nicola. "Oh no, not yet."

Maria opened the door. The ship's first officer had been sent to escort her to the Captain's quarters. Taking the first officer's proffered arm, she cast one last frantic glance over her shoulder. Panic rose in her throat. Visions of a lamb, being led to the slaughter, crossed her mind.

He greeted her formally in the presence of the seaman, "*Signora* Vincenza."

"Captain Ramos." She curtsied, as gracefully as possible with weakened limbs barely able to support her.

"Would you care for a glass of this very fine Bordeaux?"

"*Grazie*, Captain." Gratefully, she accepted the glass. Its glowing depths reflected the points of light from the candles burning in the room. She sipped the full-bodied wine and experienced a rush of sensation to her head. Dinner passed in a blur. The seaman acted as waiter for the many courses, while she attempted what she hoped were appropriate responses to the captain's conversation, but she would forever remain unsure of what transpired prior to his words, "That will be all, seaman."

They were alone...and there were fewer candles alight than when she had first entered. The flickering candlelight made their shadows weave and shimmer. Whether this was an illusion or the effects of the wine, she had no idea. She had consumed, possibly two glasses, but she had the distinct sensation of bobbing about like her shadow.

Powerless to move, she watched the captain. Her breathing quickened. He stepped around the table and walked toward her. Still, Nicola's body refused to move. Ramos's green eyes had darkened to emerald, yet glowed with light reflected from the candles scattered about the cabin. Giddy, she gazed into his eyes, her heart thudding louder with each second he continued to hold her gaze. Surely, he must hear her heart, pounding as it did.

Once he took her hand in his and held it, she could not turn back. It was simply too late. Ramos held her hand in his very gently and gazed into her eyes, a hesitant smile on his perfect lips. She gasped, "I—"

"Shh, *Signora* Nicola, you must call me Maximilian, and I shall call you my precious blue bird." Tenderly he placed his hand against her cheek, then caressed lightly across her lips. His touch left a red hot trail of sensation down the side of her face, making her lips ache to be kissed. Next he traced a line from her trembling chin to the hollow of her neck, causing her to feel she might swoon. He gently stroked the soft skin above the low neckline of her gown. A shudder ran throughout her body, but she was powerless to shop his gentle caresses. She told herself it was wrong, but her body gave silent permission and cried for more of his touch.

Maximilian seemed to sense her surrender, for he took her in both arms and pulled her close. He lowered his head, grazing her neck with his tender sensual lips. His manhood pressed against her. Dear heaven, he was very aroused. She opened her mouth to him. He deepened the kiss, sweeping his tongue against hers, battling for dominance, mimicking strokes of love.

Abandoning her mouth, he began slow, sensual kisses down her neck to the margin of her décolletage, moaning softly as he did.

"You are so beautiful, my blue bird. I must make love to you."

Panicked, she could take no more of his torturing kisses or his soft words. "You must stop, you must…"

Maximilian stopped, pulling away slightly, but still holding her in his arms. "Are you sure you want me to stop?"

Confusion reigned in Nicola's head and heart. "I-I do not know what I want. Your touch, your lips they set me ablaze." Unable to speak, she winnowed her fingers through his wavy hair. "I-I—" Uncertainty claimed her power of speech. She rested her head against his muscular chest.

"My blue bird, I would not hurt you. I only wish to make love to you…and bring a smile to your lovely face."

Raising her head, she looked into his eyes. "Then, make love to me, Maximilian. Make me smile, again."

He claimed her lips, once more—demanding, passionate kisses that left her unable to breathe. Her senses on fire, each kiss more excruciatingly sweet, she responded, her passion matching his. Wild tremors tore through her body and left her helpless under their assault. She grew bold. She unbuttoned his snowy white shirt, caressing his broad shoulders, tentatively at first, then with more confidence; her fingers discovered the fine hair covering his chest.

Hurriedly they undressed each other in a frenzy. Maximilian's white ruffled shirt hit the cabin floor first, her blue silk dress next. The ubiquitous stays and petticoats followed in a rapid succession. She was swept into a river of passion, passion too long denied her.

Once her clothing no longer hampered him, Maximilian brought his lips to play on her bare breasts. Her nipples tightened into buds, as his hands explored the flesh of her buttocks and thighs.

Maximilian took her in his arms and carried her to his bed in a symphony of movement and sensation. He suckled one pink-tipped breast, caressing the other with one hand, and exploring the moist valley between her thighs with his other.

His manhood pressed heavily along her thigh, and she longed to join with him. "Please," she moaned, opening herself to him.

He centered himself over her and thrust into her feminine core. Nicola welcomed him, arching to meet him, thrust for thrust, until time and place held no meaning—only the hot, sweet tremors, breaking like waves of the sea, again and again.

Their hunger sated, they slept briefly. Nicola, the first to awaken, watched her lover's body shining in a shaft of moonlight. Her lover— what wondrous words. Sweet, indeed. She stretched, smiling to herself. Maximilian's cat-like eyes opened.

Overcome by shyness, she snatched the sheet across her naked body, casting her gaze downward.

"Cara, you must not hide you loveliness from me."

He took her chin, pulled her face close to his and gave her a soft kiss. Again, she marveled at his sensitivity and snuggled closer into his warm embrace.

"You are so beautiful and so passionate. Your body is an instrument of delight for us both. True? You found pleasure with me, as I did with you?"

In a haughty voice, she replied, "Captain Ramos, I find you quite conceited and," she paused, then permitting a smile to cross her lips, she continued, "a most wonderful lover." She finished her pronouncement with a light kiss, which landed astray on the tip of his nose. He pulled her to him, again.

When Nicola disembarked at Dover the following evening, she wore a smile and a new lift in her heart. She had not felt so alive, not since her husband's death. Life was good again. Silently she thanked Maximilian Ramos from the bottom of her heart for awakening her, but she did not look back, for her remaining thoughts were only for her son.

Twenty-two

Nikki stirred and stretched with a wide yawn. "Now that was a much better dream."

"Well, you certainly couldn't tell from my point of view. You haven't moved for the last hour. I tried to wake you up, but nothing worked." Marti began to pace back and forth, chain smoking. "I was ready to call 911, but I knew they would never believe my story."

"It was wonderful." Nikki sighed, the languor of her vision still upon her. "So romantic."

Marti paced and shook her head. "You *never* should've done this. I shouldn't have suggested it. Promise me you won't do it again."

Nikki gave an easy and relaxed laugh. "If I could be guaranteed a dream about a certain handsome ship's captain again, I'd do it again, in a heartbeat."

"Really?" Marti sat and eyed her skeptically then sat. "Okay, tell me about it."

"I dreamt about Max again. We were both older, maybe in our late thirties or early forties. He was a ship's captain, and I was a former opera singer. We spent one wonderful night together. After that, I left the ship, and it was over." Her entire body seemed to radiate satisfaction. "This time it was nothing like the last one."

Nikki frowned. "Hold on. I just remembered something. The mask's provenance, said the ship's captain and the opera singer lived together, but he was lost at sea," she sighed. "I guess there aren't any happy endings, are there?"

"Not many, but enough to keep us all hoping for one."

"I think I've read too many fairy tales." Nikki squared her shoulders. "It's up to me to change my life, whether my handsome prince comes along for the ride or not."

Marti snorted. "Your handsome prince did come along, and you're already living in his house. I don't see what's stopping you. The man is obviously crazy about you. For Pete's sake, he flew over from France just to see you. Don't you realize you're this far," Marti said, measuring an inch with her thumb and forefinger, "from your happy ending."

"I don't know. I just don't know." Confused, she truly didn't. Her friend was right. All the ingredients for a happy ending seemed to be there, except Nikki didn't have much faith in happy endings.

"But—" Marti's reply was cut off by the shrill chirping of the telephone. "We'll continue this in a bit. You're not off the hook yet." She grabbed the telephone. "Hello."

"Yes, she is."

Nikki listened to the puzzling one-sided conversation.

"Yes..."

When Marti disconnected the cell phone with a frown, she gazed at Nikki with a curious expression, her finger tapping the back of the phone.

"Marti? Are you okay? You're shivering."

"It was Max," Marti said with a quiet and tentative smile.

"What did he want?"

"He wanted to know if everything was all right. He said he would talk to you later, sounded like he was in a restaurant."

Nikki nodded. "That fits. He and Alexa had dinner plans."

"I've got it! You and Max are psychically linked," Marti said with a knowing look in her dark brown eyes.

"And I think you're off-the-wall," Nikki replied with good humor, although Marti might actually have something.

"Max sensed something was wrong. You're linked. No two ways about it."

"What difference does it make, supposing for one minute I did believe in reincarnation?" She leaned back and finger-combed her hair.

Her friend paced about, puffing on a cigarette. "More than you might think. If you and Max didn't work out your relationship in past lives, then according to what little I know about the theories of reincarnation, you have another chance in this life."

"Oh, that's just great." Nikki took a deep breath. "You really believe this, don't you?"

Marti shrugged. "I don't know, but it answers a lot of questions. I don't think any of us can ever really know, but it makes as much sense as some other things I could mention."

Nikki rose from the sofa and hugged her dearest, if somewhat screwy, best friend. "You're deep. Honestly, I had no idea."

"Don't be a smartass."

"All I do know is, I've had this mask on twice, and twice I've passed out and had two dreams that were as real as any day in my current life. I don't think I *want* to try it again. You're right. It's too weird."

It was nearly midnight when Nikki returned to the townhouse. As she unlocked the door, she nearly stepped on a small bundle of three red roses tied together with raffia. The hair stood on her neck. Shivering, she recalled the last rose she'd found. She glanced around, but didn't see anyone. Again, there was a note attached. She unfolded it and read the hand-scrawled warning. *I don't like it when you stay out too late. You never know what might happen.*

She wadded the note into a small ball and stuffed it in her jacket pocket, then jammed her key in the lock, turned it, and stepped inside in one economic move. She entered the security code, then quickly re-set it. That was one advantage to living at Max's. He had one hell of a security system.

Whoever was playing games with the roses was starting to get on her nerves. She walked into the kitchen and removed a bottle of water from the fridge, uncapped it and took a long drink. removing the note from her pocket, she threw it in the trash, along with the roses.

"You didn't like the roses?"

Nikki screeched and jumped, then whirled toward Max. "*You* sent the roses?" She bent over and fished them from the trash.

"No, but obviously, someone did." An expression of displeasure marred his angular face.

"Doesn't matter who sent them." She tossed them back in the trash, growing uncomfortable under his intense gaze. She wished—hell, she didn't know what she wished.

"Did you have a nice dinner at Marti's?"

"Yes, she said you called. What was that about?"

Max's face went blank. "It was nothing—a whim. Sorry, I didn't mean to appear as if I was—"

"What—checking up on me?"

"I wasn't checking up on you. I," he paused. "It was nothing really."

"I see." Of course, she didn't see, not for a second.

"Good night, Nikki." Max turned and left the sunroom.

"G'night."

The wistful note in his voice left her more confused than ever. Max was assuredly the most frustrating man she'd ever known. She'd committed to staying with Alexa, at least for the summer. She owed him that much. Her feelings ran deeper than mere gratitude, but how much more? How much of what she felt for him was the remnant of a teenage fantasy? Even now, when she gazed into his eyes, she was mesmerized. And there were times when the urge to touch his proud face was unbearably strong. Just once, she wished she could trace the line from his high cheekbones to his sensual lips.

She shut her eyes and chewed her bottom lip, living the moment.

Max walked back and stood in the doorway, watching Nikki. A

shaft of moonlight bathed her in its shimmering pale beauty, rendering her long blond hair into tones of silver and the occasional streak of gold. He wondered who or what caused the soft expression on her face. Was it for him, or was it for the person who'd sent her the roses?" Not wishing to intrude, in what was obviously a private moment, he turned and tiptoed back to his study.

He sensed the passion lying beneath her cool beauty, passion that struggled with her iron will. The street kid still lurked within her psyche. There were times, when he looked into her lovely face, he imagined he saw the traces of insecurity that fame and fortune hadn't been able to erase.

He looked at his watch, eleven. Might as well go to bed. He pulled the latest Dick Francis mystery from the bookshelf and carried it upstairs. Perhaps, he could lose himself in a mystery and get Nikki off his mind for a time.

An hour later, he set the book aside. Dammit. She was all he could think about. He might as well admit it; he'd made a mistake asking her to move in.

Would she ever trust him? The violation she'd undergone years before had scarred her, but he'd never betrayed her trust. Why wouldn't she believe in his good intentions?

Possibly her reluctance was a simpler matter; the timing was wrong. They'd both denied their true feelings for too long. Maybe it was too late. The past seemed to be all they had in common. If he had the sense he was born with, he'd best look to the future and let the past go.

If only he could... It didn't matter. She wanted no part of him. She was here only because of her love for Alexa and gratitude to him. He'd didn't want Nikki's gratitude. He wanted her. All of her.

But it was time he faced reality. He and Nikki would never be together. It was his fault, of course. Too many times, he'd vacillated between losing control and giving in to his desires and maintaining his self-control—to what end? He'd been warned, and now he'd waited too long.

He'd passed on many opportunities over the years, unable to commit to anyone else because of Nikki's unspoken claim on his heart. Could he set his feelings for her aside and find happiness with someone else?

Max tossed and turned, punching his pillow in frustration. The same question came to him over and over. The past had ruled his life too long. Why did he dread a future without Nikki? That was the question he couldn't answer. Finally, his body's need for sleep overwhelmed him.

***

It had been a simple matter for Maximilian Ramos to remain single all his life, for few women desired the absentee husband he would have been. He could never relinquish the sea for a mere woman. The sea was unpredictable and beautiful in her fury. In her calm phases, she was the sensual lover any man could desire, for a mortal woman was never able to attain the mystery of the sea. Once you were married to one, the mystery vanished. They settled into their little houses and tried to suck all the joy from a man's life. He had seen too many men marry and attempt leaving the sea. But they always came back, for the sea was a mistress who would wait forever. Still, he was only human. Now, pleasure...another thing entirely.

Maximilian remained overwhelmed by the lovely Nicola Vincenza. Visions of ivory limbs, pale in the moonlight, a kaleidoscope of expressions on her face, crying out her passion. They faded until, once again, he stood on the deck of his beloved ship.

Downcast, he watched her depart. She never looked back. Inexplicably, he felt as if his very life were being torn from him, leaving a chasm, wide and deep. For the first time, he had met a woman he wanted to follow to the ends of the earth, but something stopped him. Not this time, either, an inner voice told him. Not this time? What could it mean?

Max awakened, the gut-wrenching sense of loss lingering. Another entirely too real dream. The captain's emotions washed through Max even though he was now awake. What could it mean? Again, frustration washed through him. The dreams left too many unanswered questions.

Twenty-three

The last three weeks of May passed in a flurry of activity. Nikki finalized arrangements for closing on her apartment, but decided against selling the beach house she loved so much, while Alexa returned to school for the final three weeks of her term.

Apparently Max had been busy too, spending long hours at the agency and not coming home until after midnight most nights. Most likely avoiding her, but it made their situation easier. No more opportunities to talk or to avoid talking. He simply wasn't there.

She also spent one long afternoon, shopping for a computer. If she was going to write her autobiography, she wasn't about to do it in longhand. After more than a few calls to technical support, she set up her computer in the bright sunroom which ran across the back of the townhouse. She'd even chosen an ISP; she was on the information superhighway.

Except for rudimentary typing skills, there was nothing to stop her from working on the autobiography. Where to start was the major stumbling block. Maybe she'd have a better direction tomorrow after her first official meeting with editor, Geoffrey McHugh. And day after tomorrow, Alexa would be home from school for the summer.

As for Max's daughter, Nikki had plans for that young lady.

Thursday morning dawned bright and clear. Nikki took a deep breath before walking into the building which housed Rafferty Publishing. She'd heard horror stories about editors. An editor could be an author's best friend or worst enemy. She wondered where Geoffrey McHugh would fall on the continuum. She'd dressed simply in a beige silk pants suit with a turquoise silk blouse. She wore her blond hair down, in soft waves. As for jewelry, she wore a watch, a gold rope necklace and gold-filigree hoops in her pierced ears.

She walked into Rafferty's reception area and stopped at the front desk. "I'm Nikki Prentice," she said, keeping her voice low. "I have an appointment with Geoffrey McHugh."

The receptionist responded brightly, "Yes, Miss Prentice. He's waiting for you. If you'll take the hall to the left, his office is the third on the right."

She thanked the receptionist and followed the simple directions. Geoffrey McHugh greeted her with an outstretched hand. He was about her height for they were eye to eye. His strawberry blond hair was worn short, but the natural curl couldn't be disguised. He was handsome with a square jaw and a nose that tended toward the aquiline. Dressed casually in jeans, open necked shirt and a camel jacket, her editor gave her a bright smile and flashed even, white teeth.

In truth, his blue-gray eyes fairly twinkled with merriment under heavy lids.

Bedroom eyes. At least that's what *Maman* would've called them.

"Miss Prentice, welcome to Rafferty's den of iniquity," he said with a decidedly rakish grin.

"Den of iniquity?" she asked, baffled at his reference. She'd done some research. If anything, Rafferty's was known for its somewhat stodgy literary reputation. The fact they were interested in publishing a book about her life was a departure from the norm.

"One can always hope," he replied, arching an eyebrow.

"I see." She suppressed a giggle and wondered how or why Rafferty's had managed to hire the maverick she saw before her. He must be someone's nephew.

"Nepotism," he replied.

"What?" She'd often been told her face was an open book. Apparently, it was true.

"I'm the great-great grandson of the original Ryan Rafferty, founder of this esteemed institution," he said, leading her into his office. He motioned for her to sit on a love seat placed at right angles to his own comfortable chair. His mouth twitched as he continued, "I'm being groomed to take over some day, but I've also been given the privilege of bringing our readership into the twenty-first century. It's going to be painful for some here at Rafferty's, since they're still operating in the mindset of the mid-fifties. You, Ms. Nikki Prentice, are one of our first ventures into the pop culture genre."

She swallowed, suddenly overcome by insecurity. "That's quite a responsibility for you... and me."

He scratched his head. "Hmm, I understand you don't want a ghost writer."

"That's right."

"You've written before?"

"Just my journals, but I love writing really." Doubts about her writing abilities already? No, she *could* do this. "I want the book to be all mine, not some ghost writer's version of me."

McHugh nodded, then grinned. "I need to get an idea of how much time I'm going to spend with you."

Was he flirting with her? "I hope I won't prove to be too onerous, Mr. McHugh," she said with a smile. He *was* flirting, and it was somewhat disconcerting, even if he was cute as the very devil. "I've been keeping a journal for the last ten years, which should provide me with plenty of back ground material for the proposed book...as well as familiarity with the written word."

She widened her grin to let him know she was on to him. "Well, then I'd like to know, other than your relationship to the founder of this company, exactly what are your qualifications to act as editor on my book?"

McHugh gave Nikki a sheepish smile. "I've a master's degree in comparative literature. I apologize. I'm usually more diplomatic."

"I'd be surprised if that were actually the truth, Mr. McHugh. I think you have a way of saying exactly what you mean, whether it's diplomatic or not."

"Touché. You're correct, of course. But I'd like to take a look at your journals, and we can go from there."

"No." Her refusal was automatic and unequivocal.

"No? What do you mean no?"

"I mean that they're too personal to just hand over to anyone. I mean we may come to know each other quite well before this book is completed, but there's no way, I can let you read my most private thoughts. If that's what you expect, then I'm very much afraid the deal's in trouble." Her face grew hot. All her adolescent longings spilled onto those pages. No way!

"Now, don't get all fired up. I assure you I'm not peeking into your most private secrets, but surely, there's some part of your journal you would allow me to read." He gave her a coaxing grin. "Just to get an idea of your strengths and weaknesses."

"I suppose there might be something, I could let you see," she conceded slowly, her nerves calming. She couldn't help but smile back at him. Geoffrey McHugh was a dangerously charming man.

"That's better. You know they might not let me take over, if I lose one of my first authors," he said with a disarming smile.

"Well, that would be a pity. I'd hate to be the ruin of your promising career." He definitely had a way about him. She found herself warming to his easy banter.

"May we start over then? First of all, please call me Geoff. May I call you Nikki?"

"Of course. Everyone does."

"I didn't want to presume," he said flashing his ready smile once again.

"Right." Presumption would probably be the least of his faults.

Geoff settled back in his chair, drumming his fingers on the chair arms. He seemed to have a lot of nervous energy. "Have you thought about how you would start the book? Simply starting with your birth and trudging to the present in ABC fashion is not always all that interesting. How are you going to hook your readers? I realize your gorgeous face on the cover will tempt a lot of readers into buying the book, but how are you going to keep them interested in Nikki the woman, who evolved from a kid on the streets to a famous supermodel?"

She settled on the settee, getting more comfortable. "I've thought about it. It would be nice if a message of hard work and hope would keep them turning the pages, but realistically, I know it'll take more. I've thought about starting with the night I was rescued by Maxim Devereaux. You know, starting with the fairy tale element before exploring what came before and after."

He nodded. "That would work. Don't be afraid to tell the truth. Some of the readers, bless their salacious hearts, will be attracted to any negative aspect of your life. There has to be some, surely?" he asked, his expression hopeful.

"I'm not sure what you mean. I was only on the streets for a few months. I wasn't a prostitute, and I didn't do drugs. Surely, you don't want me to make up something, just to increase sales?" A tiny bit of sarcasm eased into her tone.

"No, but we'll need to delve into your family relationships, the reason you were on the streets in the first place."

She took a deep breath, then shook her head. "I don't like talking about my mother. It's private."

Geoff sighed clearly exasperated. "You're writing an autobiography, not a text book. There has to be some guts to your story, or we could let my nine-year-old cousin write it on his computer from your press releases collected over the Internet. I warn you. I think you have a book in you, and I intend to dig in and pull it out of you—word by word—if I have to."

She stood. "*You* be warned," she said, still smiling, "You may have more difficulty with me than you think."

"Challenge accepted. I'm looking forward to it." He stopped, checked his PDA, then continued, "I'd like to see your opening chapter, one week from today, no later than ten A.M. Is that possible?"

"Yes. You'll have it." She extended her hand and received a firm grip in response, with none of those troubling electrical currents she received whenever Max touched her. Geoff McHugh, however, was a very tasty man. She liked his irreverent attitude, even the teasing adversarial way he treated her. No walking on eggshells with him.

"I'll see you then…and one of your journals?" he asked, raising an eyebrow in her direction.

"I'll go through them tonight and messenger something to you tomorrow. Okay?"

He nodded. "Fair enough. Until next Thursday then."

"Next Thursday." Surprised at how much she was looking forward to their next meeting, she flashed a wide grin and left his office. She'd just taken up residence on Cloud Nine.

Finally, she had a goal.

Twenty-four

Friday morning rush hour was long over, but even at noon Union Station was still quite busy. Nikki glanced at her watch, then at the enormous clock at the far end of the grand lobby. Both time pieces reported the time as five after twelve. Alexa's train was due in at twelve-ten and Nikki was anxious to see the young teenager again.

"Nik!"

She looked up and saw Alexa running toward her, lugging one tote, her other arm outstretched. Grinning, she grabbed the teenager and gave her a big hug. "It's so good to have you back. Where's the rest of your stuff?"

"This is all I brought. Daddy's having the rest shipped. So, what's going on with you and Daddy? Are you two—uh, you know?" The teenager's eyes danced with mischief.

"Alexa," she warned, shocked the girl would think such a thing, much less say it. "That's not what my being in the house is about, and you know it." Hesitating to discuss personal matters in public, she said, "Let's get a cab. We'll talk about it at home."

"Oh, come on. I was only kidding—sort of." A pleasant mixture of contrition and humor was written plainly across the girl's face.

"I know. You just took me off guard." She placed her arm around the girl's shoulders. At fourteen Max's daughter was only five-feet, four-inches, but the young teen was very pretty and showed every promise of being a beauty. Her light ash-blond hair was worn short in an attempt to control the wild ringlets she hated. Her father's crystal green eyes, ringed by spiky, dark lashes contrasted with her fair hair. A light sprinkle of freckles were scattered across the bridge of her pert nose.

Arm-in-arm, they threaded their way through the crowd to the busy street. Now that his daughter was home, maybe Max would spend more time with her. At any rate having her home would mean more company for Nikki, even it if cut down on some of her valuable writing time.

Once they were settled in a taxi, the teenager maintained a flow of nonstop chatter. Only half listening, Nikki supposed Geoff McHugh must have the journal she'd sent by messenger earlier that morning. How long it would take him to get around to reading it...and what he would think?

The night before she'd hurriedly scanned the stack of journals and finally selected one from one of the more stable periods in her life. Eventually people would read her autobiography and know most of her secrets, anyway, so she might as well get used to the idea of her editor delving into her past. But there just wasn't any point in overwhelming him with all her angst over Max right away.

"Nik?" Alexa's raised voice brought Nikki back to the present. "We're home and you haven't heard a single word I've said."

She cast Alexa a wan smile over her shoulder, while she paid the driver. "Sorry, kiddo. I've a lot on my mind. By the way, your dad is taking you out to lunch. I wonder if he's home yet," she said, changing the subject.

"Great. I missed him—well, a little. You know they kept me pretty busy with finals and stuff. Mario called me every day. I can hardly wait to see him, but he doesn't come home from school 'til next weekend. Do you think Daddy will let me go out with him? I mean, you know, movies, stuff like that?"

"That's between you and your dad. I'm not about to second guess his rules."

Together they ran up the stairs and entered the townhouse. In the entrance hall they found Max talking with great animation to a tall woman with short blond hair. At least five suitcases stood stacked to the woman's left. A sinking feeling struck Nikki in the pit of her stomach. Oh God. Please let it be anyone but…

Max and the woman turned.

Mama.

"Guess who's come to visit her favorite daughter?" Max asked, the corner of his mouth quirking upward.

Unbelievable! How like her to show up uninvited. Absolutely, the very last complication she needed in her already complicated life. Five suitcases. Damn. Looked like she planned on staying a month. Well, she'd see about that.

"Mama. What a surprise." She recovered quickly and rushed to her mother's side for a hug and a Hollywood-style air kiss.

"Well, I hadn't heard from my baby in so long I just had to see how she was doing. Max was about to take my things upstairs. I knew you wouldn't want me staying in a hotel."

The more her mother simpered, the more Nikki wanted to dig a hole and crawl in it. Oh, she wasn't surprised, just appalled. Her mother always acted that way around handsome men…even if they were fifteen years younger.

Nikki stared in disbelief. Her mother was actually fluttering her— they had to be fake—lashes at Max.

"Oh, no, Mama, I wouldn't want that," she said with more sincerity than she felt. And the dark gleam in Max's eyes. Damn him. He thought it was funny. But she knew her mother too well to think he'd be amused for long.

During this war of wills, Alexa stood stock still in the foyer. "Hi, Daddy." She walked to his side and gave him a quick peck on the cheek.

Max smiled and hugged his daughter. "Welcome home, *ma petite.*" Then turning to Nikki's mother, he said, "Mrs. Prentice, you remember my daughter Alexa? Alexa, this is Nikki's mother, Mrs. Prentice. You were only seven when you met before."

"Oh, little Alexa? Why she's all grown up, isn't she?" The woman advanced with arms outstretched to hug Alexa, whose eyes grew wide. "You're such a pretty little thing."

"Thank you. It's nice to see you again," the girl said, giving a tentative hug in return.

Looking askance at the pile of luggage, Nikki managed a stiff smile. "How long are you staying, Mama?"

"Oh, just long enough to do a little shopping and take in a few shows. You can get tickets, can't you, Max?" Jessie turned to him and smiled coquettishly.

"I'll be happy to obtain some tickets for you, Mrs. Prentice."

Again, it seemed that Max actually relished his role of host. As usual, her mother was oblivious to how grasping and ridiculous she appeared.

"Please, Max, just call me Jessie. Why we're almost family."

"Mama." Nikki warned, resisting the strong temptation to kill her mother… "I'm sure Max doesn't have time—"

"Of course, he does, hon. He just said he would."

Nikki closed her eyes for a moment and took a deep breath. It gagged her, seeing her mother acting coy. In the past, her mother never had a kind word to say about Max. What had changed?

Max intervened. "Let's get your mother settled. What do you say, Nikki? How about your old room?"

"Yes, that'll be great. It's a very nice room, Mama."

A crafty look crossed her mother's face. "Where do you sleep *now*, Nikki?"

Max, perhaps in an attempt to prevent bloodshed in his foyer, started retrieving suitcases, picking them up easily as if they held nothing. "Nikki has my mother's former suite. She has more privacy that way."

"Oh, I see. She has your mother's suite. How thoughtful of you. I really have to hand it to you. You certainly have taken good care of my little girl."

"Mama," Nikki protested, knowing it was useless. If she had a sock she would've gladly stuffed it in her mother's mouth. Better yet, murder was still an option. Surely, no court would find her guilty of murder…justifiable homicide, maybe.

Taking a cue from her father, Alexa stepped forward to take one of Jessie's smaller pieces of luggage. "You'll be in the room next to mine, Mrs. Prentice. Let's go up. I'll help you unpack."

Bless the child and her bright smiling face, Nikki could have kissed her. On her way up the stairs, Alexa turned toward Nikki and gave a sly wink.

Finally, alone. Time to regroup.

She sagged against the wall. Any encounter with her mother absolutely drained all Nikki's energy. Mama was much easier to tolerate at long distances and in very small doses. Oil and vinegar—that's what they were—and no matter how many times she counted to ten, a blow-up was inevitable as the sunrise each morning.

She sucked in a breath. Might as well get it over with. She climbed the stairs to the next level. Haunting specters of hesitation and dread sat on each shoulder, whispering to her, *This isn't gonna be fun. It's gonna be hell.*

Nikki rapped lightly on the door to her mother's room, then entered after hearing Jessie's, "Come in."

"Are you settling in okay?" she asked hesitantly. "Is there anything you need?" She didn't want to appear ungracious, but her mother's unannounced visit upset her more than she could ever have imagined.

"Why yes, Nikki, little Alexa has helped me quite a bit. This is a very nice room, and this is where you stayed when you lived here before?"

"Yes, Mama. This was my room." She looked at the familiar poster bed and the ornate French armoire. The walls were still covered in the same blue and white *etoile de jouy* with matching full draperies and comforter. Her old room had always been a haven, but now her mother was ensconced in it. It would never be the same.

"Well, it's certainly nicer than anything I ever had growing up."

The taut edge to Jessie's voice grated on Nikki's nerves.

Alexa shot Nikki a questioning glance. She nodded, relieved at the girl's perception.

"I'll leave you two to catch up," the teen said in a sprightly voice, as she eased from the room.

Nikki watched her mother's smile fade. Now what?

"Well, you've certainly got a nice little set-up here, don't you?" Her simpering, sweet tone had vanished.

"It's not like that, Mama, and you know it." She paced, hands clasped behind her back...mainly to keep from strangling her mother.

"I'll tell you what I know, Missie. Men are out for what they can get. The way I figure it, Max must be getting plenty of something from you, if he's got you installed in his dead mother's suite. You're the worst kind of fool," she said, with a sneer.

Nikki took a deep breath, turned toward her mother. "A fool?"

"Yes, to let him use you this way. Nothing will ever come of it. You're right here under his thumb, at his beck and call. He'll use you and toss you out when he gets tired of you. You can bank money on that, young lady." Jessie stood with hands on hips, nodding her head vigorously with each pronouncement. "Some fall in status, isn't it? From fancy supermodel to live-in nanny."

"He's not using me. I'm here because of Alexa. She needs someone."

"I guess you'll just have to find out the hard way. You've always been stubborn as hell, running off, living on the streets, moving in with his mother, like you didn't have one of your own who was worried to death about you."

"Worried to death about me? That's rich, Mama. You threw me out, remember?" Nikki struggled to keep her tone low.

"Well, I never meant for you to go. I-I was just trying to get you to go back to school, but no, you had to run away, and I didn't know where you were for months on end. Then out of the blue your fancy French boyfriend and his la-ti-dah mother call me, demanding I come to his office to sign a bunch of papers so they could make money off you."

"Well, you certainly didn't let it keep you from bargaining a pretty sweet deal for yourself, did you? I'm not stupid. I was there, remember. I gave you fifty percent of my earnings for two years."

"Well, it was my right. I'm your mother, after all. I deserved to have a good life too." Her mother's mouth twisted into a simpering smile.

"Yes, you certainly did." Nikki couldn't keep the ironic tone from her voice, but as usual, her mother was oblivious.

"Well, that's water over the dam. I just wanted to make sure you were happy here. I warn you, you better hold out for the little gold band. Then you'll really have it made. A rich handsome husband—even if he is a foreigner—doesn't grow on trees. Besides, if you divorce, you can really take him to the cleaners."

"I hope that's it for motherly advice today." Unable to take any more Nikki whirled around and fled down the hall—her mother would live longer that way.

All the way down the hall, she muttered obscenities under breath. She didn't see Max until he placed a warding hand on her shoulder.

"Sorry. Seems like I have a bad habit of not watching where I'm going."

"You all right?"

"No." She shook her head. "I'm on the verge of committing murder. I don't know what my mother was thinking…showing up like this."

"You don't have to apologize. She's your mother, and she's welcome to visit. She'll be treated as any guest would."

"Thank you."

"There's no need to thank me. I owe you. After all you're staying here for Alexa."

"No, *I* owe you so much," she protested, turning away from his soft gaze."

"We're not in a contest to see who owes whom." He took her chin, gently forcing her to look him in the eye. "We are friends, aren't we?"

She held her breath a second, before answering. "Of course."

"Then I don't want to hear anymore about how much you owe me. Our business arrangement was beneficial to us both. As a result we are, at least, friends. Friends do each other favors. You're doing me a favor by being here for Alexa."

Unable to think, much less speak, clearly, she nodded.

"Are you sure you're all right?"

She tried swallowing the lump in her throat, finally succeeding. "I'm fine."

"Good." He looked about the hall. "I have a daughter somewhere around here. Wonder if she's hungry yet?"

"Aren't all teenagers hungry?"

"I suppose you're right. Are you sure you'll manage…with your mother, I mean?"

"Really, I'll be fine."

Max left Nikki standing in the hallway. Her mother was quite a character, but she was Nikki's mother, and there was no changing that fact. Nikki had inherited her mother's fair skin, blue eyes and height. However, the resemblance ended there. Max had never met Nikki's father. Apparently, her father was a drifter who skipped out early in the marriage.

"Daddy," Alexa called from the upper landing.

Max looked up at his daughter who was neatly dressed in a jade green top and white jeans. "Are we still on for lunch?"

"Of course, what did you have in mind? I wasn't sure if you still wanted to be seen in public with your old man."

"Of course, I do, Daddy." She rushed downstairs and gave him a hug. "You're the best-looking of all the fathers at school. Why wouldn't

I want to be seen with you?" She paused, glancing around furtively. "Can we? I mean, shouldn't we invite everyone?"

"Not if we sneak out right now." Max suggested with at grin. "I think we ought to let Nikki and her mother have some space."

Alexa nodded her agreement, her eyes sparkling. "Right."

Having lunch alone with his daughter would give him the opportunity to talk to her about the future. Alexa would want Nikki to stay indefinitely, but living side by side with her was proving more difficult than he ever imagined. He'd hoped their proximity would be enough to sway Nikki in his favor. Instead, they were farther apart than ever.

"Where do you want to go for lunch?" he asked.

"Hard Rock Café."

"What?"

"You know," Alexa prompted, pulling him toward the front door. "It's a lot of fun. The waiters come out and sing the "YMCA" song. Everybody stands up and sings, 'Y M C A.'" She began forming the letters with her arms, giggling as she did. "Besides, they have great burgers."

"As long as you don't expect me to get up and sing, it's a deal," he said with a smile.

Alexa cocked her head to one side, giving a look he could only describe as calculating. Then she nodded. "Okay, you don't have to get up and sing, but you'll have to..." she paused, as if thinking of an appropriate bargaining point.

"I'll think of something suitable, Alexa. I promise." Max pulled the cell phone from his inner jacket pocket, flipped it open and called a taxi. "Can you wait five minutes, young lady?"

Alexa looked down at the floor in pretense of being demure. "Of course, Daddy. I'll just go tell Nikki we're leaving." She shed her charade, winked at him, then ran upstairs

Max laughed to himself. His daughter was an original. There was no doubt about it. In many ways, she reminded him of Solange. His wife had been spontaneity personified, always ready to party. He didn't want to run the risk of losing his daughter. She was at a difficult age and needed his attention.

Twenty-five

Friday afternoon

By the time Max and Alexa entered the Hard Rock Café, the luncheon crowd had started thinning out. He looked around at the rock 'n' roll paraphernalia. Guitars, shirts, autographs of everyone from the Beetles to The Grateful Dead were in abundance, in addition to T-shirts emblazoned with Hard Rock Café, New York City. Bouncers uniformly clad in red T-shirts, having little to do, hung about looking official.

Max and Alexa followed the waiter to a quiet booth—at least it was quiet for now. After taking a seat across from his daughter, he glanced around to see if anyone was going to jump up and start singing. His daughter would be disappointed if no one did.

She beamed at him, patting his hand, before speaking. "I wish Mario were here. He's the one who told me about it."

He cleared his throat, hating to start off with a list of rules for the summer. But since Alexa had mentioned Mario first, he thought he might as well. "About Mario. I'm not forbidding you to see him, but..."

"Daddy, you *have* to let me see him." His daughter's cheeks flushed red with pent-up teenage angst.

"All I was going to say is we have to have some rules. Mario is too old for you."

"You were older than my mother, and you're twelve years older than Nikki. I don't see what difference it makes."

"It makes a lot of difference where you are only fourteen and Mario is already eighteen. Your mother was nineteen when we fell in love. I know from experience what happens when you marry too young."

She fixed him with a cold stare. "Are you saying you're sorry you married my mother? Didn't you keep loving each other?"

He paused before carefully answering her question. "I always loved your mother, but we changed and grew apart. We were having some difficulties before she died. We never had time to resolve them." No, no time at all.

"It's different with Mario and me."

Mon Dieu. Was this the beginning of a total teenage rebellion or just a skirmish? "Young people always think they'll be different. I look at you and Mario, and I see myself and your mother. Only it is worse because there is even a greater difference in your ages."

"But, Daddy, I'm crazy about him."

"You're still a child," he said in as decisive a manner as he could muster. "No matter how grown up you think you are."

Alexa glared at him, her green eyes flashing, as she bit her upper lip.

"All I'm saying today is that we must have some ground rules."

"Fine. Whatever." Her words were followed with an indignant huff.

Max swallowed his pique, trying to keep his cool. His daughter was every bit as obstinate as he and Solange had been, defying and arguing every point.

Attempting to change the subject to a topic less volatile, Max picked up a menu. "What's good?"

She chewed her lip, then flashed him a grin. "Hamburger with everything, French Fries, and a chocolate milk shake," she announced with a definite nod of her head. "How about you? Their fries are the best, Daddy."

The waiter appeared and took their orders, his preference not as heavy as his daughter's. "Grilled chicken, house salad, fries and coffee." Try as he could, he couldn't do without the fries. They were his favorite.

"French fries and coffee? Gross, Dad, really gross."

He permitted himself a patently fake smile, aiming it at his only child. Alexa returned one that was equally phony, all in good humor, of course.

After the waiter left, Max wondered how to bring up the subject of Nikki

"There's something else."

Alexa rolled her eyes in mock horror. "What now?"

"I've been investigating schools and housekeepers for the fall."

"Why? Nikki—"

He shifted uncomfortably. "I don't think she's happy living in the townhouse. She's used to her privacy."

Alexa tried to stand, but the edge of the table stopped her. "But I thought you and Nik would—"

"Enough. Remember where you are."

"I *know* you love her. You *have* to stay together."

He glanced around the restaurant. People were turning to stare at them. "There's no point in discussing this further."

His daughter huffed, blowing the curls off her forehead. "You're the one who brought it up, Daddy. Not me."

"My mistake. Subject closed."

"You've ruined my special time with you. You've ruined my whole day, maybe even my whole life. I *hate* you." She folded her arms across her chest and refused to meet his gaze.

Stymied, he shook his head. Who was this baffling creature sitting across from him? Had aliens abducted his little girl? Every time he tried reasoning with her, he only made things worse. "Alexa, be reasonable." Somehow he needed to restore the day's early amiability.

His daughter responded with a sullen glare, then opened her mouth, but the waiter's approach with their lunches interrupted the beginning of another tirade.

She glanced down at the grilled hamburger and the crisp, browned-to-perfection fries. She swallowed. He watched her struggle to maintain her fit of temper. It was obvious his daughter was hungry, and the food had been prepared to her standards.

He looked at his own. The fragrance of mesquite-grilled chicken teased his nostrils, making his mouth water. Frankly, he was famished. Picking up a fork and knife, he carved a bite of chicken. He popped the tender bite into his mouth and chewed. "Mmm." He carved another bite. "You should eat." He motioned toward her lunch. "Mine is delicious."

His daughter looked up, twisting her mouth, admitted, "I guess it would be a shame to waste good food like this. I mean when so many people have to go hungry and all." Then she grinned sheepishly, picked up her hamburger with both hands and bit into the juicy sandwich.

"Mmm, this is so fab, Daddy," she mumbled with her mouth full. "It's really great to be home from school. Where will I go to school next year? And how long do you think Mrs. Prentice will stay with us?"

He laughed, relieved her mood had changed. "Please, one question at a time. I've found two schools. I'll take you to meet the headmistresses next week. As for Nikki's mother, she may stay as long as she wishes. We have plenty of room."

She rolled her eyes at him. "I know we have plenty of room, but don't you think Nikki seemed a little tense this afternoon?"

"Well, it's true they have difficulties, if they're around each other too long."

"Yeah, like five minutes," Alexa said, then wolfed another big bite of hamburger.

Difficult as it was to keep a straight face at his daughter's bluntness, she was extremely accurate in her assessment of relations between Nikki and her mother. "We shall let Nikki handle her mother. It's not for us to judge how well they do or do not get along."

Alexa helped herself to a long fry. Amused, he approved of his daughter's healthy appetite. She ate heartily, no signs of the eating disorders which often plagued the agency's models. "I don't know if you'd be interested, but I have tickets for a play tonight," he said. "Unless you have other plans?"

"A play? I'd rather go to a concert. 'NSYNC's new tour is in town.

Can't we go to that instead? I would die happy, if I could see them just once. They're *so* hot."

"Really?" What was happening to his little girl? She was growing up right in front of his eyes. Soon, there would be no traces left of the child. She would be a woman. *Mon Dieu*, but he couldn't bear thinking about it, not now.

Max reached into his front pocket and pulled out his cell phone. "Let me make a call. We'll see about this 'NSYNC thing." He quickly tapped in the number for Ramona, his assistant, who answered promptly.

"Ramona. Max. It appears theater tickets aren't what my daughter had in mind."

Ramona chuckled. "She'd probably rather see 'NSYNC."

"Yes, that's right. How did you guess?"

"My daughter Cyndi started whining for tickets two weeks before they went on sale. She stood in line for hours."

"Oh, I see. You have them already. Any chance of procuring a couple for tonight's show?"

"Sorry, but that show's been sold out since the first day."

"Well, do your best anyway. Call in some favors, if you have to."

"Okay, but it's not going to do much good."

"No pressure, but I'll be very high on my daughter's list, if you can come up with a couple."

There was silence on Ramona's end of the line. "Don't you need at least three? I mean surely she would like to take a friend. Or better yet, four?"

"Three, if you can, otherwise, I'll take whatever you can come up with."

Ramona snickered. "That's me, boss man. The miracle worker. No job too big. By the way, it's going to take a miracle."

He gave Alexa an uneasy glance. "All right. I'll hear from you later? Just call my cell."

"One way or another."

His daughter's eyes widened in anticipation. She took a sip of her milkshake, still questioning him with her eyes.

"Ramona's working on it. Nothing's certain yet."

"I'll simply die, if she does." She pushed her plate away. "I can't eat another bite. I'm too excited."

Once again, the thought he might not survive the next five years crossed his mind. Nikki knew exactly what she was talking about when she warned him. He didn't remember putting his parents through such ordeals. Now, his daughter sat across from him, grinning and squirming in anticipation over seeing a band of *hot guys* perform.

His appetite deserted him. He caught the waiter's attention and motioned for the check. After signing it, he turned to his daughter. "Ready? Let's go see how Nikki and her mother are doing." He winked and privately hoped murder hadn't been committed in his absence.

Alexa smiled widely. "Daddy, you are so bad. Nikki should punish you."

Being around Nikki without the ability to pursue her was punishment enough. Instead, he gave his daughter what he hoped was a stern, no-nonsense fatherly expression.

Together they left the restaurant, at truce for the present. How long it would last, he had no idea. But if today was any indication...not very long.

Nikki heaved a sigh of relief. Her mother had decided to take a short nap. With any luck, she would stay asleep long enough for Nikki to calm down. She might even get some work done. She'd already organized her journals. Geoff McHugh had called right after Max and Alexa left for lunch to ask if he could drop by. He sounded excited...and said he wanted to see what progress she'd made on the first chapter.

Since her autobiography started with the night she first met Max, she'd been very painstaking in her phrasing. What she feared most was giving away her true feelings for Max—that and looking like a damn fool in front of the entire world. More than anything, she wanted to be able to look him in the face after it was published. As pathetic as it sounded, she wanted him to be proud of her.

The doorbell rang, ending her brief moment of freedom. She took a deep breath and walked to the front door. Visible through the glass, Geoff McHugh stood on the front stoop, gazing up at the darkening summer sky dressed in business casual, consisting of a light blue shirt that intensified the blue of his eyes and khaki slacks, sharply creased. His brown loafers were shined to perfection, while his tan leather briefcase was slightly scuffed, but substantial. A superhero tie topped off his ensemble.

She opened the door and cast a worried look at the darkening sky. "Looks like it's going to storm. Better come in."

"I hope you don't mind my being so casual. I'd thought we'd work better, if we weren't so formal." Geoff ran a hand through his crisp strawberry blond hair.

He appeared nervous, and she wondered why. He wasn't about to spill *his* guts in a book. "Somehow, I doubt that formality is one of your strong suits, or is it?" She gestured at his superhero tie, then motioned for him to follow her to the sunroom.

He laughed. "Like my tie, do you? Now, we don't have to be

adversaries. We both have something to gain from your book."

She turned and grinned. "And what do you have to gain?"

A smile spread across his face. "A lot. For one, it'll be the first in an entertainment line I want to launch. If your book does well, then there'll be more to follow. I'll gain prestige."

"You certainly expect a lot from one has-been model," she said with a laugh. "I hope you're not disappointed."

"You can't fool me. You're bright. There's more to Nikki Prentice than her beautiful face."

She processed the compliment. "Thank you, I should hope so."

"See here, once your book is published, you'll have established yourself as an author. A whole new career will open for you."

His words sent a wave of relief through her. He'd said exactly what she wanted to hear, but the thought of it scared her too. Success or failure, it was in her hands…and Geoff McHugh's.

"I want to see what you've done so far. I don't care how rough it is. The journal you sent me was clear and concise." He sat on a blue and white ticking-striped ottoman and removed the journal from his brief case. "In this one journal, I see you have a sharp sense of humor. Of course, I already knew that from our first meeting." He awarded her with an engaging grin.

Her face grew warm. "I suppose I was a little nervous."

"Well, we both had a surprise then, didn't we?"

"Meaning?"

"Meaning, I expected to meet—uh, I don't suppose there's any way to say this without being offensive, but I didn't expect you to be so intelligent. I figured someone, who stood around all day looking beautiful, wouldn't have an original thought in her head. But I'm glad to say I was wrong. I'm looking forward to working with you."

She leaned back against the desk chair and folded her arms across her chest. "Are you aware of your tendency to make speeches?"

A guilty little smile tugged at his mouth. "I think it's been mentioned before. Guess it's a good thing you're around to remind me not to do it quite so often."

"I suppose I could take on that responsibility, in addition to everything else I have to do," she said, making a sweeping motion with her arm, encompassing the entire room.

"I'm sure you'll take it very seriously."

"I will." At this point, she couldn't restrain her laughter. "You weren't anything like I expected, either. I don't know exactly what I expected, but it wasn't someone like you."

Geoff's eyes twinkled. "I think I've just been damned by faint praise."

"I wouldn't be at all surprised."

The two of them burst into laughter. This was definitely going to be an enjoyable relationship. Something different and new. No history involved.

Alexa in tow, Max bounded up the steps to the townhouse, opened the door and stopped in the hall, leaving his keys on the Empire center table. He skimmed through the mail. Nothing of interest.

"I'm going up to my room to call Bitsy, okay Dad?" Alexa asked.

"Sure." Max was distracted by an unusual sound... Nikki's laughter. It surprised him. She'd been working much too hard on her book. He hurried to the sunroom, anxious to discover the cause of her merriment...and share it, if possible.

As he walked through the kitchen, another sound puzzled him—the lower rumble of male laughter. Incensed, he wondered who in the hell was here in his house...with Nikki?

He stood in the doorway of the sunroom. Neither of them noticed his arrival. They were too busy laughing. Nikki's face was slightly flushed, as she attempted to make some point or other with the young man.

He cleared his throat, not wanting to spy any longer.

Nikki glanced in his direction first. "I wasn't expecting you until later. Max, this is my editor, Geoff McHugh. Geoff, Max Devereaux, my—uh..." She waited a beat before adding, "...ex-employer."

Not trusting himself to speak, Max nodded. Besides, his throat had grown dry. He extended his hand to Nikki's editor, who stood and returned the greeting.

"It's a pleasure to meet you, sir. I've been reading about the night you and Nikki first met. It was certainly a fortuitous meeting, wouldn't you say?" The handshake became a contest, as each man tried to impress the other with his strong grip.

"Indeed, it was." He looked from Nikki to her editor back at her again. Their laughing camaraderie pissed him off. Dammit. Why couldn't she be that relaxed with him?

"It seems rather remarkable you should come out of a theater and find a future supermodel on the street, right there in front of you. Have you been back to see if there are any more undiscovered supermodels waiting for you?"

Already tired of McHugh's impertinent questions, Max asked one of his own, "Are you a reporter or an editor?"

McHugh chuckled. "I know. I know. Actually, I did entertain the idea of journalism at one time, but I regained my sanity and changed majors."

Nikki giggled. Max turned in her direction and shot her what he hoped was a pointed look.

McHugh turned to Nikki. "You've made a good start. If you work on the additions and revisions I suggested, your opening will be much stronger." He picked up his briefcase. "It's been a pleasure meeting you, sir."

"You also," Max muttered. McHugh's insistence on calling him sir aggravated him beyond belief. The editor's politeness was feigned and verged on insult. They weren't that many years apart in age.

"Nikki, we'll talk more tomorrow, okay?" McHugh said.

"Sure, I'll get started on the revisions right away." She stood. "I'll see you to the door," she said with what Max thought was a very self-satisfied smile.

Max watched them leave the sunroom. "Good riddance," he muttered, then looked down and discovered he'd clenched his fists. And his stomach felt like someone had used it for boxing practice. For the life of him, he couldn't understand why she was so at ease with McHugh, someone she barely knew. From the foyer he heard her giggle again. Didn't the she have anything better to do?

Finally, he heard the front door open and shut. Seconds later, Nikki rejoined him, her face flaming red. "I can't believe how rude you were to Geoff."

"Rude?" Why the hell was she so angry at him? What had he done now?

"He was here, a guest in your home…at my invitation. You did everything but beat your chest and hike your leg on the furniture."

"Nikki!" Damn. She had him pegged—not that he'd ever admit it.

"Your behavior was inexcusable. You embarrassed me."

She advanced on him and Max took a step back. If she continued in this vein, she'd be shaking her finger in his face. He stepped toward her and placed his hands on her shoulders. "You're overwrought," he said in an attempt to calm her.

"Keep your hands off me, Max Devereaux." She shoved him away. "I'm not overwrought. I'm pissed off." She flounced back and forth. "I was working with my editor. And you came in here acting like you caught us in the sack."

She whirled, but he caught her arm and pulled her to his chest. His heart slammed against his sternum like a blacksmith's hammer. Her nearness intoxicated him more than any liquor could have. The light scent she wore mingled with her own unique fragrance and rendered him senseless. He felt her breasts rise and fall against his chest with each rapid breath. Her lips parted. He bent his head to claim their sweetness. Finally, his lips touched hers. They were warm, soft…and so sweet.

204 *See You in My Dreams*

Caught up in the moment, her body molded to his.

"Oh. *Excuse* me," Jessie Prentice's harsh tones sliced through their brief moment of expectation, severing his fragile bond with Nikki as effectively as any knife.

Nikki reacted first, jumping back. He dropped his hands. He'd been so close. Now this.

Jessie pursed her lips, then sneered at Nikki, "I didn't mean to intrude, but the child could've seen you two, rutting like dogs in heat."

Dumbstruck, he resisted the urge to lash out and shake the silly woman.

"Mama!" Nikki's face reddened.

He had to say something, but his command of English failed him. "*Ça suffit. Désolé.*" He waved his hands in the air. At the agency—hell anywhere—he was in total control, but here in his own home? "*Merde.*"

Jessie's expression turned to one of puzzlement. "What's he saying, Nikki? You know I don't speak a word of that language? Why doesn't he speak English like usual?"

Nikki shifted uncomfortably from one foot to the other. "He's upset, Mama. He just said he was sorry and that he's heard enough."

"Are you sure that's all he said?"

Max regained his English. "Don't talk about me in the third person. I apologize, Mrs. Prentice. It was my fault. I...care for Nikki, but we're not lovers, nor dogs in heat. What an abominable expression." He swallowed dryly and continued, "If you wish to leave, I will understand. Your daughter is in no danger here, in spite of my crude behavior."

Mrs. Prentice looked from Max to Nikki, who occupied herself with looking at the floor and breathing heavily. "That might be the best solution, after all. I don't want to intrude," she said, then added with a smirk, "or be in the way."

"Mother! It's not like that."

"Oh, no? I'm not blind. You can't fool me, young lady. You've had the hots for this foreigner ever since he picked your sorry butt off the streets and turned you into a fancy model."

Nikki's her fingers curled at her sides. Fearing she would attack her mother, Max placed a restraining hand on her shoulder. She stopped short, but her eyes flashed her anger clear enough.

Jessie turned on him, her tone loud and shrill. "You! You've corrupted my daughter. Brought her into a world of drugs and wholesale sex. Had her parade around, strutting her stuff like she's better than anyone else. You should have left her on the streets. At least, being a whore would've been more honest."

"Left her on the streets? I took her *away* from the drugs and wholesale sex. For heaven's sake, your daughter was eating out of garbage cans and begging on the streets. I gave her the opportunity of a lifetime."

"You certainly didn't mind taking the money I earned, Mama." Tears ran down Nikki's cheeks.

Those tears sent a burst of anger through Max. "That's enough. No more. I want you to leave. Now!" He turned and grabbed the telephone and dialed information. "Loew's Carlton?"

Nikki stood watching him while he made reservations for her mother and called a taxi. He wanted so much to reach out and comfort her—but not in front of her malicious mother. What a nightmare. He'd been polite and gracious when the blasted woman showed up at his door uninvited, but she had more than worn out her welcome.

"Well. I can certainly see I'm not welcome here." Jessie whirled and rushed from the room.

"It's your own fault," Nikki called after the woman.

"Let her go." He gathered Nikki into his arms. Her shoulders heaved, as she sobbed.

"Sometimes I think I hate my mother. You've been wonderful to me. Why does she have such an evil mind?"

"She can't help being who she is, but I won't put up with it. Neither should you." He kissed the top of her head, breathing in her sweet scent.

"Hey, what's wrong?" Alexa walked into the sunroom and stopped, her eyes wide. "Did I miss something?"

"A little disagreement. Nothing for you to worry about," he said, hoping to soothe his daughter. No need to get her upset as well.

She cast him a doubtful look. "Heard anything about the tickets yet?"

"No. Don't worry, Ramona will call when she has news."

"Tickets?" Nikki stopped crying. "I thought you already had tickets."

"This teenager decided she'd rather go to the 'NSYNC concert instead."

Nikki grinned and nodded. "Yeah, I guess she would at that. The group's pretty hot, isn't it?"

Alexa pressed her hand to her heart and rolled her eyes heavenward, "Oh, yes. They're really, really hot. Bitsy will be so jealous."

The shrill of the telephone saved him from having to listen to more 'NSYNC adulation.

Alexa squealed and grabbed for it. "Ramona. Yes, it's Alexa. Tomorrow night, three tickets. You're wonderful. Here's Daddy." She thrust the telephone at him and began to dance around the room. "I'm going to see 'NSYNC. Omigod! I'm going to see 'NSYNC."

"Tomorrow night, Ramona?" he asked, still a little befuddled by the emotional scenes he'd just experienced. Only moments before, he and Nikki had been on the brink of something, and then her vicious mother interrupted. And now his daughter was on the verge of swooning over a bunch of semi-adolescent boy singers.

His assistant's, "Max?" brought him back to reality.

"Thanks, Ramona. Wonderful. Messenger them over." He turned to his daughter. "You have your wish." Turning to Nikki he asked, "Would you like to come with us? There are three tickets. "I'd really like you to go."

"Say yes." Alexa danced around the room."Say yes."

"Wouldn't you rather ask Bitsy to go with you? I still have a lot of work to do on my book—the revisions my editor suggested."

Max stiffened. "If that's what you'd rather do. Fine."

"Bitsy!" Alexa squealed again. "Oh, yes." Then she stopped and turned to Nikki. "If you're sure you really don't want to go?"

"I'm sure." Nikki shifted from one foot to the other. "Actually, I ought to get back to work."

Max bristled, but told his daughter. "Yes, let's leave Nikki alone with her work. Why don't you call your friend from the study? Maybe you could arrange a sleepover for tonight at Bitsy's? I'll pick up the two of you tomorrow night and take you to dinner and the 'NSYNC concert from there." He placed his arm around his daughter's shoulders as they walked out of the room, but glanced over his shoulder at Nikki, leaving her with a silent warning, our conversation isn't over.

Twenty-six

Nikki watched Max and his daughter leave, realizing her hands were trembling. The scene with her mother had been pretty bad, but the little scene her mother had interrupted had shaken Nikki more than she'd ever thought possible. Now, in one fell swoop, Max had cleared the house for the evening, leaving them quite alone.

Maybe it was just as well. She and Max could finally have it out. Clear the air, once and for all. If he couldn't accept her terms, she'd have to leave—in spite of her promise to Alexa.

For the present, she still had a book to write. She walked over to her desk and booted up the lap top. She'd only been online for a short time, and checking for email wasn't an ingrained habit. Her screen name wasn't very original. She was still plain old nprentice@aol.com. Probably ought to change it to something more anonymous, but it would do for now. She had a mountain of work ahead.

The sunroom had darkened, and she could make out the sound of distant thunder. A tiny shiver slid down her spine. She hated thunderstorms, always had. Shaking her head, she clicked on the touchpad and connected.

A chipper "You've got mail" issued from her computer. She clicked and found a long list of emails. Most turned out to be spam, but one looked interesting. She clicked on it, wondering who in the world knew she was online. After all, she'd only given Geoff McHugh her email address that afternoon.

She scanned the email. A sick sensation of fear clutched at her stomach. It wasn't from her editor.

Found you at last, but this won't be our last communication.

Quickly she deleted it. On occasion, she'd received weird mail at the modeling agency, but never one directly delivered to her so personally. Now that she thought about it, the Internet was kind of scary.

Immediately, she went to the members section, changed her screen name, then fired off an email to Geoff McHugh, advising him of the change.

Overhead the thunder rumbled louder. She gazed out the high arched window. They were in for a storm, for sure. The sky, darkening by the minute, was full of low fast-moving clouds.

Stop with the weather report, Nik. It's time to get some work done.

After disconnecting the laptop from the electrical source, she took a deep breath. She could still get a lot done before the battery needed a recharge. Maybe the storm would be over soon.

A commotion from the hall interrupted her before she finished the first sentence. The voice of her mother protesting, "I can carry my own luggage. Thank you very much."

The doorbell rang. Thank heaven. That meant her mother's cab had arrived. Should Nikki say goodbye or not? Apparently, Max was carrying her mother's luggage. Or attempting to. She heard him apologizing profusely for his churlish behavior. Jeez, did anyone use the word churlish anymore?

Damn. There was no reason he should have to apologize to her mother. It should be the other way around. Nikki walked to the hall and stood in the doorway watching as her mother huffed and puffed and performed her indignant mother routine. Poor Max stood behind her with a bewildered expression on his face.

"What should I do?" He mouthed the words from behind Jessie's back. Nikki shook her head, still feeling as if she should say or do something. She stepped forward, "Mama, I'm sorry."

She spun around. "I've never seen such an ungrateful child. You've never been anything but trouble to me since your daddy ran off and left us. Sometimes, I wish you'd never been born."

She'd heard it all before, but the underlying venom still had the power to wound. "Mama, you said that so many times, when I was growing up. But you know what? It doesn't hurt like it used to." Tears stung her eyes all the same. Yes, it still hurt. She just hid it better, now.

Turning on her heel, she walked back to the sunroom. She sat and shut her eyes to keep the tears from falling. The soft splat of raindrops hit the tall Palladian windows across the back of the sunroom. Finally, she heard the front door open and shut. She let out a sigh of relief.

"Are you all right?" Max asked, standing over her.

She gazed into his eyes and saw only pity. Dammit, she didn't need his pity. "No big deal. It's nothing new. She's always been like that. I've learned to brush it off and let it go." She shrugged and attempted a smile.

"But it's not that easy, is it?" His voice was hoarse with emotion. He reached out and touched her cheek. "I'm sorry. It's my fault. I shouldn't…"

The light touch seared her skin, as if he'd branded her. She tried to shrug his hand away, but he resisted.

"None of this is your fault. She's just the way she is," she told him, trying to regain a bit of self-control.

She caught a movement behind Max and stiffened. Alexa stood quietly, watching them. Max turned to his daughter. "Ah, there you are.

Did you talk to Bitsy and her mother?"

"Yes, she says I ought to come on over before it starts storming. I've already packed my overnight bag." She motioned to the purple nylon bag beside her feet. "They're coming over in a cab to pick me up, if that's all right?"

"That's fine," he said. "I'll call you tomorrow. The concert starts at eight, so I'll pick you up in the limo and take the two of you to dinner first."

The teen rushed to Max's side and threw her arms around him. "This is the neatest thing you've ever done for me, Daddy. I know you'll love the show." She looked over at Nikki. "I just wish we had a fourth ticket, so you could go with us. You'd love 'NSYNC, they're—"

"So hot!" Nikki and Max finished, in unison. Together the three of them laughed. The light-hearted moment eased the knot in Nikki's stomach.

The taxi arrived a few minutes later. While Max walked his daughter to the waiting cab, Nikki looked out the window into the small rear garden. The soft spatters of rain had transformed into fat, smacking drops which sounded almost loud enough to break the glass. She really did have work to do. Surely, Max wouldn't interrupt her, if he saw how focused she was on her work.

Assuming she could focus.

But more than once, she caught herself staring out the window. The heavens had opened with large, driving sheets of rain, slanting against the window.

Max stomped into the sunroom. "*Merde*."

She looked aware from the computer screen, ready to give him hell for interrupting her. Oh my, what a sight. Her chin dropped.

Soaked to the skin.

"You didn't take an umbrella?" she drawled unnecessarily.

"Obviously not." He finger-combed his hair, squeezing out the excess water. "The second I shut the taxi door, the sky opened up."

She watched dry-mouthed as he unbuttoned and peeled off his soaked shirt. The muscles of his chest glistened with tiny beads of moisture running down his flat abdomen. She didn't know whether to swallow her tongue or just surrender to the inevitable and drool.

Unable to sit still another second, she leaped from her chair. "Here, let me have that. You're dripping all over everything. I'll hang it in the laundry." She grabbed the sopping shirt from him and headed to the laundry room, but came to a dead stop.

This time she heard the unbuckling of his belt, followed

immediately by the sound of his zipper. She whirled around. "What do you think you're doing?"

"My pants are soaked too." A devilish smile spread across his face. "Don't you want them?"

"No. Max Devereaux, you keep your pants on." Her heart exceeded the speed limit and her cheeks heated.

He bowed and winked at her. "I think the appropriate term is, Gotcha."

"Very funny." She tried to swallow, but her mouth was too dry.

"I thought so." He walked toward her, his hand outstretched. "You're not here to be my housekeeper. I can hang up my own shirt."

"No problem. I was—"

"You were working and I interrupted you. Now," he said, taking her by the shoulders, he turned her around and guided her back to the computer, "sit down, and I'll see to my laundry."

A little befuddled, Nikki sat and stared at the still-blank screen. More than likely Max had never done his own laundry…ever. Actually, she'd be surprised if he even knew the location of the laundry room.

"No, it's the other door. The one on the left," she said, holding back a giggle.

He turned and gave her a sheepish glance. "I know which door it is."

She laughed. "Sure you do."

"Well, I do." As if to prove it he, disappeared into the laundry room and shut the door behind him. She imagined him peeling his wet trousers down his strong thighs. "Crap." No use thinking about his strong thighs…or his calves. He was taboo. Getting involved with him while living under his roof and acting as his daughter's chaperone wasn't on her agenda.

Outside, the weather worsened; the downpour continued. The rain still fell in sheets, while the wind blew the trees in the rear garden nearly double.

The temperature in the sunroom had dropped with the onset of the storm, but that wasn't the only reason for her shivering. No matter how hard she tried, she couldn't deny the effect he had on her. Only a few minutes before, he'd held her so closely, her breasts pressed hard against his heavily muscled chest, she'd felt the heat emanating from his hard body. The memory sent a wave of desire sweeping though her body weakening her resolve.

The laundry room door opened, and he emerged, clad only in a white bath towel, wrapped around his trim waist.

Holy shit. As if she needed any more temptation. "Max, really."

"*M'excuser*," he said, his eyes alight with mischief. "Everything I had was soaked."

"Yeah. You'd better get some dry clothes before you catch cold." How in the hell was she supposed to concentrate with his parading around in a towel. His body was sculpted with broad planes of muscle rippling across his back. And she did not want to think about his firm butt, except there it was, covered only by a towel which looked like it might fall any second.

Inspiring... To say the least. Too bad she wasn't writing a romance novel.

"I'm going. I'm going. I don't want to risk offending your tender sensibilities." Max bowed and turned to leave.

She sprang from the chair with a protest on her lips. "I'm not offended. I'm—" She stopped, stunned by what she'd almost said.

"What?"

"Never mind."

"Were you tempted, Nikki? Say you are, because I'm tempted every minute we're in the same room." He prowled toward her. "And when I'm not with you, I'm thinking about you." His voice deepened with emotion.

Her knees grew weak...as usual whenever he spoke in those soft, sensual tones, his accent grew stronger. Like a fool, she backed away.

Before she could say another word, the shrill peal of the telephone startled them both.

Hot damn. Saved by the bell. She rushed for the phone and grabbed it. "Hello."

"Saved by the—" He imitated the ringing of a small bell, a wry smile tugging at his kissable lips.

"Nikki? Everything all right? You sound kind of breathless. Is he making advances again?"

"No, Mama. Everything's fine." For once, she didn't mind her mother's timing.

"I just wanted you to know, I'm all settled in. The hotel is lovely."

"Great. You're settled in. I'm glad."

"Are you going to stay mad at me forever?"

Okay, a little whining goes a long way. Unfortunately, her mother never figured that out. "No, of course not. Look, I'll call you tomorrow, okay? We'll go shopping." Now why had she said that?

"All right, baby. You know how I am. Foot-in-mouth disease."

"Yeah, I know. It's okay. I've got to get back to work. B-bye." She set down the phone. "Will wonders never cease? That must be the first time she's ever almost apologized for anything."

"It's about time."

"Now," she said, anxious to change the subject, "Don't you have something to do?"

"I do have something in mind." He walked toward her, giving her that lazy-lidded sultry look again.

She swept her gaze up-and-down his body, then shrugged. "You know, you could use a little work on those love handles."

He looked down aghast. "Love handles?"

"Yeah, I'd say you're in serious denial if you can't see them."

"Think so?" He twisted and turned, stretching his awesome bod. "I guess I could use a workout."

She swallowed the emerging giggle and waved him from the room. "Shoo. Shoo. Go pump some iron."

"Okay, I'll go." Grinning, he snatched a pillow and threw it, which she dodged with ease. She returned the honor, but missed hitting him as he rushed from the room.

"Whew!" At least, tomorrow night, she could count on having the house to herself. She might even get some work done without the constant distraction of his presence.

Twenty-seven

Friday evening

"Mm, this is more like it." Nikki sighed and eased her body into the hot bath water.

After the stress of dealing with her mother and a half-naked Max, she deserved some downtime. She'd arranged an array of candles around the bathroom and tub. Outside the townhouse, a storm raged, causing the lights to flicker more than once. At least, if the lights went out, she wouldn't be left in the dark. Frangipani scent filled the bathroom, reminding her of a tropical paradise.

After soaking for nearly an hour, she stepped from the old claw foot tub onto a thick bathmat. Grabbing a thick towel, she twisted it into a turban around her head then grabbed another to wrap around her body. She walked to the vanity and picked up a square glass bottle, filled with her favorite Chloé body lotion.

As she smoothed the lotion on her arms and neck, a loud crack of thunder shook the bathroom windows, accompanied by a bright flash of light. "Damn!" The bottle of moisturizer flew from her hands and shattered on the marble floor into tiny slivers of glass. The lights went out—flickered on, then off…and stayed off.

She looked down. In the flickering candlelight, glass shards glittered all over the marble floor. She stretched and attempted to step beyond the broken glass.

"Ouch!" Her heel landed on a sliver.

A light knock sounded on the bathroom door, followed by Max's deep voice. "Nikki? Are you all right?"

"No. I stepped on a piece of glass," she told him through the closed door. Of all the bad luck. Now, she was the one wearing a towel, hopping on one foot, like a one-legged freaking bird. Only to be rescued once again. Fate and her warped sense of humor.

There was a pause, before he asked, "Are you decent?"

"More or less, come on in. But be careful," she warned. "There's glass everywhere."

The door opened slowly, and he peered through the opening. "I'm wearing shoes," he said with a cheeky grin.

"Fine. Now get me a pair, so I can get out of here."

He stepped into the bathroom. Gray athletic shorts showed his strong thighs and a white muscle shirt left little else to her imagination. He'd actually been working out. His chest and arms glistened with a fine sheen of perspiration. His gaze traveled around the room, taking in the candles, then finally rested on her. He folded his arms across his chest. "You are wearing a towel. This is your idea of decent?" he said, his mouth twitching.

She huffed. "It's as much as you had on a couple of hours ago. If my memory serves, you were parading around in a towel that barely covered your—you know what I mean."

He leaned against the doorjamb, threw back his head and laughed. "You're barely covered yourself."

She held out her hand. "Shoes, please." The longer he stood there staring at her, the more ridiculous she felt. "Do I have to beg?" she asked, starting to lose patience.

The scoundrel shook his head. "I don't think you should try to put a shoe on that foot. Here, I'll carry you." He took two crunching steps forward and swept her into his arms.

"Put me *down*."

He stopped and gazed thoughtfully. "Surely, not. There's glass everywhere."

"Do something. Don't just stand there." She struggled, but it was useless. His hold on her was firm, albeit cautious. She just hoped he couldn't feel how fast her heart was racing.

"Your wish is my command, *mademoiselle*." He kicked the door back with the heel of his shoe, carried her into the bedroom and set her down gently on her bed. To her amazement, he turned and walked back into the bathroom.

"Max?"

The intensity of the storm increased. Vaguely aware of the lightning which brightened the sky with nearly constant flashes, she held her breath.

He returned from the bathroom carrying two of the larger candles. "I need some light, if I'm going to get that splinter out of your foot." He took the largest candle and set it beside the bed.

She peered through the dim, although romantic, lighting it provided. "That's not enough light," she told him flatly.

"I have to try. You'll get an infection, if I don't get it out. Where are your tweezers?"

"Tweezers?"

"Let's get real here. I can't pull it out with my teeth," he said, his tone patient. "Although it might be fun."

In spite of the stabbing pain in her foot, Nikki giggled. "'Get real'? You're really picking up some slang. Next thing you know, you'll be losing your beautiful accent," she said, trying not to sound wistful.

He paused, in his search for the tweezers. "What accent?" he asked, elevating one of his thick, dark eyebrows.

"It has a certain charm," she admitted, casting a shy upward glance in his direction. The candlelight flickered, the flames reflecting in his eyes as dancing points of light. The effect—mesmerizing.

He shrugged. "It doesn't seem to have much effect on a certain resident in my house."

"You mean my mother?" she asked, grinning in spite of her attempt to keep a perfectly straight face.

"Your mother is no longer here." He leaned forward and brushed her hair from her face.

Quick. Distract him before things go too far. Dangerously close to surrendering to the desires incited by his warm, hard body, he was definitely crowding her. She swallowed, trying to regain her composure. "Tweezers—far, right-hand drawer of the vanity."

He nodded. Once more he retraced his steps to the bathroom. Casting a glance over his shoulder, he seemed reluctant to leave. She heard more crunching footsteps as he tread on glass shards in the bathroom. Over the sound of his rummaging for tweezers, the wind kicked up another notch in ferocity. The gusts whistled, shaking the windows in the townhouse.

"Shouldn't we check the weather report?" She shivered and rubbed her arms. "It really sounds bad outside. I don't think I've ever heard anything like this wind in the city. I've weathered a few storms at the beach house, but this is something else."

He returned and gazed down at her, causing her to pull the towel tighter. "What do you want me to do? Remove the splinter from your foot or find the battery-powered radio?"

She detected a tiny note of irritation in his voice. "The splinter, I guess. But be careful. It hurts."

"I'll be careful." He positioned the candles for maximum effectiveness. "Turn around and prop your foot up here, so I can see this terrible splinter." He patted the pillow closest to the candles and reached for her foot.

"Don't be so rough." She flounced about, attempting to keep the towel wrapped around her body.

"I haven't touched your foot yet. Stop acting like a big baby. Now, let me see."

Nikki sighed and finally allowed him to take her foot and hold it to the light, experimenting with the best angle. "I see it, but if you aren't perfectly still, it might break when I extract it."

"All right, already. Just get it out," she whined, in spite of herself.

"Patience. This is a very delicate procedure. I don't think you respect the skill it requires to accomplish it."

"Stop trying to be cute."

He grinned again. "You think I am cute?"

Before she could make a cheeky reply, there was a blinding flash followed by a deafening crash. She jumped and yelped.

"*Mèrde*. I almost had it."

"I'm sorry. I hate storms, and this one's been going on too damned long." Max ignored her, apparently intent on his surgery. Honestly, the man could care less if they were blown away by a freak storm. "Ouch."

He raised the splinter to the light. "There. Got it."

She heaved a sigh of relief and immediately was overcome by embarrassment. "Thank you. I was a pill, wasn't I?"

"Most definitely." He smiled, his eyes glittering. Her gaze followed his, down to the towel that had covered her.

"Just what do you think you're looking at...like that?" she asked, suddenly breathless.

"Merely the loveliest woman I've ever seen."

Flustered, she grabbed the towel and pulled it over her exposed breasts, leaving her thighs exposed along with the blond patch of curls where they joined. Hastily, she tried another arrangement of the towel, but it didn't work either. Damn thing was too small to cover everything. "Max Devereaux, you could've at least told me I was uncovered."

"No, no, *Chèrie*, I could not." He closed his eyes, as if not trusting himself to gaze on her any longer. He gave a heavy sigh. "Goodnight, I'll see you in the morning." He stood.

"Wait." She grabbed his hand. She didn't want him to leave her. Not now. "Thank you."

He turned. "You'd better put something on it and *le bandage adhésif* or whatever it is you Americans call them."

"Band-aid™," she finished for him. "Are you sure you got it all?" She waggled her foot toward him.

"*Oui*, but perhaps I should check again," he replied, his lips twitching with a poorly disguised smile.

Once more, he knelt down beside the bed and took her foot gently between his hands. His glittering green gaze, challenged her. Lightly, he kissed the arch of her foot. She moaned, powerless to suppress it. The soft touch of his lips sent waves of pleasure skittering up her leg to center between her thighs. She whimpered, aching for him to continue, yet still fearful of what would come next.

"Nikki?" he asked, his voice hoarse. "Do you want me to stop?"

Thunder crashed again, shaking the townhouse.

"No." She grabbed the straps of his shirt and pulled him to her.

"Don't leave me," she murmured, "I'm afraid... of the storm."

"Not here," he breathed into her ear, then picked her up, carrying her gently.

She wrapped her arms around his neck and rested her head on his shoulder. What was he doing? Why not there? Her bones had gone molten. No resistance, not after all this time. And she didn't care where he was going, as long as he took her before she came to her senses. She wanted him more than she'd ever wanted anyone. To feel his hands and lips discovering her body, to feel the strength of his need for her.

To feel whole for the first time.

Max carried Nikki down the hall to his room and laid her gently on the bed. Slowly, he pulled away the towel; she lay trembling before him, open to him for the first time. He placed a knee on the bed beside her, still hesitating. "I-I'm speechless before your beauty."

"Obviously not." She grinned and reached for him.

He sank down on the bed, overcome by a blaze of yearning...and disbelief. She was so lovely. So desirable. Her skin, a swath of pale ivory silk, displayed before him, was illuminated only by flashes of lightning from the storm. And this time she hadn't run from him or turned him away.

Her body arched toward him and pressed her lips against his, her unspoken commitment to whatever followed. He moaned. His tongue swept into her mouth sampling her sweetness. Somehow he had always known kissing her would be far sweeter than anything he'd ever imagined. Drowning in a maelstrom of fire, he covered her neck with tiny tender kisses.

She tugged at his thin shirt; he obliged by whipping it over his head. Her hands slid down his back to his butt. He kicked his shorts off the rest of the way, his manhood springing free.

She gasped and caressed his length. He groaned, then found her nipples. First one, then the other, they tightened into buds at the light scraping of his teeth. Burying his face between her breasts, he licked down her belly, slow tantalizing strokes down to the fair curls above her sex.

He cupped her hips with his hands and spread her quivering thighs. He tongued the sensitive core of her desire while her hips moved against him.

He smiled down at her, then took her hand in his. "Touch me. See how much I want you. How much I need you."

She writhed beneath him.

He reached for the drawer in the bedside table and removed a foil packet. Together they slipped the condom on his rigid length.

"You are so beautiful. I have wanted you for so long." He slid his fingers between her thighs, in and out, preparing her.

She moaned and gasped, "Now."

"So long," he whispered. He claimed her lips, his manhood prodding between her thighs. Fearing he'd hurt her with the strength of his passion, he entered her with gentle inching thrusts. Then as her body adjusted to him, he drove his full length into her sweet enveloping heat.

Arching her hips she met his driving thrust and moaned her need. "More."

"*Facile,*" he breathed in her ear, resting his weight on his elbows. He thrust slowly. "Not too fast. I won't last."

Her lithe legs wrapped around his waist and pulled him even deeper into her hot core. He struggled for control, slowing the rhythm, then increasing until feverish abandon threatened to send him over the brink. He slowed the pace again.

"No, don't stop," she cried, her breath coming in gasps.

"Never." He buried his face in the hollow of her neck and clasped her wrists high above her head. He drove home until he was desperate to come. Again, he slowed the rhythm, desiring to bring her to completion before he pursued his own release.

Her body trembled under his assault. "No!" she cried and refused his attempt to hold back. She screamed his name, her cries of pleasure, triggering his climax.

His body pulsed deep within hers. He never wanted to be with anyone but her. They were meant to be together. It seemed as if he'd had searched for her all his life because it had never been like this with anyone else.

Collapsing beside her, he kept her within his embrace. Gently, he wiped the tears from her eyes. "Did I hurt you?" Had he been too rough? The last thing he ever wanted was to remind her of what happened so many years ago.

Speechless, she could only shake her head and nuzzle her face into the breadth of his chest. Lulled by their lovemaking, she fell into a state of near sleep. He marveled at the sense of fulfillment. This one woman, arms and legs entwined with his, she was the woman of his dreams. For the first time in years, he knew peace.

Outside the storm raged. Max lay with Nikki's warm body still cradled in his arms. The moon shone through the window, lighting the face of his woman. The near-feral street kid still lurked beneath the passionate woman he held so tenderly.

Awakening from her nap, she stretched and gave him a blissfully feline smile of satisfaction. "Hi."

"Hi, yourself," he replied, kissing her forehead. "Are you all right?"

"Wonderful," she purred. "It's just I've run from this for so long, and now I can't understand why."

"I can't either."

She snuggled closer. "It could've been that you were always so unapproachable. We were worlds apart, and I knew I wasn't good enough for you." She nibbled the lobe of his ear, causing him to tremble.

Mon Dieu, but she was adorable; however, his body craved sleep. Now that her needs were sated, *she* wanted to talk.

"You were still a child. I forced myself to stay away from you." She rewarded him with another dazzling smile. He pressed a kiss in the palm of her hand, his heart filling with love.

She lay across his chest, tracing the muscles on his chest with teasing fingers. "Since I've been here, I've gone crazy trying to keep this from happening. I was so afraid, and I didn't know why."

"Perhaps, your fears had something to do," Max hesitated, fearing to mention the incident that had destroyed her innocence. "With what happened before."

Her face clouded at the memory. "Ian."

"Yes."

"There hasn't—I mean, I haven't..." she managed to say. Tears welled in her eyes; she turned away.

"*Ma pauvre petite*," He murmured, somehow he wasn't surprised she'd avoided men and relationships. That made her acceptance of him even more of a gift. Gently he touched her chin. "Don't turn away. Look at me."

"I was glad you beat him up," she replied, sniffing. "I don't ever have to be afraid again."

"What else could I do?" He pulled her closer. "I wanted to kill him."

"It's over." He stroked a strand of hair back from her face, tucking it behind her ear.

She let out a soft sigh. "It really is."

"He drugged you. He should've gone to jail."

"It doesn't matter anymore. Not now. Not with you in my arms."

"It mattered to *me*. He took something precious, something he had no right to take. And he kept you from trusting anyone, even me."

"I trust you now." She caressed the side of his face, ending with a her finger on his lips.

Her words were a balm to his heart, healing the scar left by Solange's betrayal. "*Ma chère*, the night we met, you changed my life. One minute, I was leaving an incredibly boring play, the next I was a knight rescuing a fair maiden. I'd never done anything like that before...or since."

Nikki worried her bottom lip, ready to confess something she'd never told anyone. "You saved my life that night. I was desperate and alone. And I ran from him because...I was tempted to give in."

"You never have to worry again, little one. We're together now."

Her eyes swam with unshed tears. "Are we? Are you sure?"

"As sure as I have ever been of anything. Do you still doubt me?"

She shook her head. "Not you, me."

He tucked a strand of hair behind her ear. "I have no doubts. I love you, Nikki."

"But what about Alexa? Do you think she'll mind?"

Laughter rumbled deep in his chest. "Alexa? She'll be thrilled. You know how much she loves you."

"I know, but our being together could change everything."

Max kissed her, effectively silencing her. "You worry too much. We were meant to be, I feel it here."

He took her hand and placed it against his heart. His heart beat strongly, the pace picking up at the touch of her hand. Tenderly, he stroked another stray lock away from her face, murmuring, "My love."

Again, he kissed her, his lips soft, but demanding.

Loving him demanded everything from her. She shuddered, in response as his hands slid lower. Flames of desire threatened to engulf her. She found herself a victim to the heady rapture that came with lying in her lover's arms.

The flames consumed her once more.

Twenty-eight

What should have been Max's first deep sleep in weeks evolved into a torturous night filled with images from the past.

Running. Running. Desperate to save Nicole from a sure death, Maxime ran. His young love had been imprisoned in the Temple Prison and condemned for the crime of being born into an aristocratic family. Disguised in the unkempt garb of a Citizen, he wore the tricolor cockade on his head. He'd escaped capture, but his brother, the count, wasn't so fortunate. The rest of his family had been executed by Robespierre's dictum. Now, his precious Nicole was under the sentence of death, as well.

He ran. The *Place de Guillotine* was filled with throngs of Citizens, shouting and crying for more blood, crying for the heads of innocent people. As one, a vicious shout emerged from the mob whenever the head of another unfortunate was held high. Minutes later, the head would appear on a pike to be marched around for the rabble to view and spit upon. He had to save Nicole from such a horrible fate. He would rather die himself than see her being hauled up those terrible steps in hysterics. The love of his life wasn't a brave person, barely more than a child. She had been at court a mere three months when the revolution began. Unless he could free her from prison and spirit her away to England, she would die—another victim to the madness possessing his country.

He ran. He wasted little time waiting for his contact. Armand never made the rendezvous. Heaven only knew why? Maxime rushed for the gate, intending to sneak inside. Somehow, he must save her.

His heart sank.

Too late.

He stood at the entrance to the prison and watched the tumbrel exit with his beloved among the prisoners. He barely recognized her. Her wavy blond hair hung in limp, oily strands. Her face was dirty while she clung to another prisoner, a woman as hapless as she. The vacant expression in his lover's eyes destroyed him. *Mon Dieu.* What had they done to her?

The mob pelted the cart with rotten vegetables and brick hard loaves of bread. "Let them eat cake, you *putain*," a toothless hag beside him yelled. His love never flinched.

"No, no," he yelled, running beside the cart. A blow to the head felled him. Trampled and kicked by dozens of people.

Pain...ribs broken. Each ragged breath he took burned like fire. He pulled himself along the rough cobbles, only to see Nicole hauled up the rough-hewn steps to the guillotine. "No!"

Deafened by the shouts of the blood-thirsty mob, as the bloodied blade descended swiftly on her neck, he shouted, "Nicole!"

A shout and another kick to his ribs. "Dirty aristo pig."

The last thing he saw was a rough staff swung with great force toward his head.

Max awakened, his head throbbing. Glancing at Nikki, he found her still asleep with the sweetest smile across her lovely lips. How had she managed to sleep though his nightmare?

He rubbed his temples. No sleep for him the rest of the night.

Night? His watch said three. Swinging his feet to the floor, he grabbed his hastily-shed clothes and carried them to the bathroom.

After dressing in the dark, he wandered downstairs to the kitchen, fighting an intense desire for his morning cup of coffee. Still no electricity.

The storm had abated. Wasn't raining. Perhaps a run? He looked toward the door. He hated leaving Nikki alone, but the nightmarish images haunted him. The desperation...and the pain. Gingerly, he touched his ribs, half expecting them to be broken. A measure of relief swept through him, but he still had to get out of the house.

Last night's storm had passed, but the storm inside had not. Making love with Nikki should've brought exhilaration and peace...and it had, until he slept. Now, inexplicably he was filled with dread...dread of what their love might bring. Dread of the future.

Dammit. He'd never been a coward. He'd taken what life offered like a man. Yet now his strongest impulse was run and run like hell—from everything he held dear—all because of a bad dream.

He stuffed his feet into a pair of running shoes and bent over to tie the laces. Maybe a run would exorcise the troubling visions. He walked to the foyer, grabbed a light jacket from the closet. With practiced economy, he disarmed the security system and then rearmed it before leaving the townhouse. Luckily the system had a battery backup; he wouldn't have left Nikki alone and asleep without it.

For a moment, he stopped and stood on the front landing. The pre-dawn sky was clear. Nothing moved. He was alone. All he had to do was go back inside the house and crawl in beside Nikki and enjoy her sweet warmth. Instead, he started his warm-up. Halfway, through his usual routine, he stopped and took off, impatient to clear his head.

"Mm." Nikki yawned and stretched, reaching for Max. He wasn't there. She looked over at the clock blinking 12:00. The storm was over and it had stopped raining. Whatever time it was, it was still dark. Puzzled, she sat up, swung her legs over the side of the bed and looked around the room. She was in Max's bedroom. She smiled, remembering how gently he'd carried her to his bed and the passion that followed. Her cheeks grew hot from the memory.

He was probably in the kitchen. She reached down and felt the bottom of her left foot. There was barely any residual tenderness and no sign of glass. She glanced around the bedroom and spied a robe thrown over the back of a chair. Hurriedly she drew it around her shoulders, cinching the garment in a loose knot at the waist, and ventured into the hallway. "Max?"

Carefully she tiptoed downstairs, the oak floors cool to the bottoms of her bare feet. Walking into the kitchen, she looked around, but still no Max.

She called his name, louder this time. She turned from the kitchen and hurried to his study. Where could he be? She checked the security system. It was still armed.

In her peripheral vision, Nikki glimpsed movement at the front door. The door with its Chinese-lattice, beveled glass made for a distorted view. She crept to the door to see who it was. By the time she reached the door, all she saw was the back of a man rushing down the street.

It wasn't Max; he was taller.

She shrank back and took a deep breath, then raced for the stairs. Holding up the hem of the robe to keep from tripping, she bounded up to the second floor. She checked the other rooms. No Max. Shit. Where was he?

Why did he leave? Her bottom lip trembled. Abandoned again. As if it were yesterday, she could hear her mother's shrill voice. "Bad girl. Your daddy's left us. And it's your fault. Why can't you learn to behave? He wouldn't have left, if it wasn't for you."

"No, Mama. Not me," she barely remembered whining. She'd cried herself to sleep for nights after her daddy left. She'd been so young, she didn't remember him—just her mother's angry, tear-stained face.

Max ran along the darkened streets toward the park with long loping strides that stretched his thigh muscles. Invigorated by the regular pounding of his feet against the pavement, the crippling tension eased. Sweat collected at his neck and ran down his back as he warmed to the run.

He had no idea what time it was. Frankly, it didn't matter. This was the second disturbing dream he'd had...his death...and Nikki's, as well in the last one. Had his dream been influenced by the mask he'd bought her in France? Or was there a deeper connection between the two of them—one that traced back over lifetimes?

If the theory of reincarnation were a reality, were they destined for another tragic end? Had Nikki somehow sensed they were bad for each other? Was that the real reason for her fear of commitment?

"*Merde*." He'd left her alone after making love. What would she think?

Still in the grips of the nightmare, he turned and headed back to the townhouse. What could he say? The truth? She'd think he was crazy.

Hell. Must be crazy to consider reincarnation as a plausible explanation. On the other hand, the dreams were so vivid he could almost believe they were glimpses of earlier lives. No jumbled landscapes, no surreal symbolism. Just desperation, fear, pain and...love, the same incredible longing he felt for Nikki.

As he ran, he visualized the scene. How could he just march in and tell her he loved her...but their being together was in all probability doomed. For her own good, he would give her up. *Mon Dieu*! How could he break her heart? And his own?

The alternative was continuing their relationship and throwing caution to the winds. Allow fate to run its course? Could he risk it? No, he couldn't. Not with Nikki's life possibly at stake.

After last night, she would expect more from him...as she had every right. He never meant their making love to be a casual affair. He loved her and wanted her with him, at all costs—except her life.

For the last five blocks before reaching home, he slowed his pace, stopping in sight of the stone steps leading to his front door. He bent over from the waist, then straightened up, gasping for breath. Still tempted to run in the opposite direction, he summoned his courage to face the woman he loved.

Nikki huddled on the bed in her room. After rushing upstairs, she became chilled and wrapped up in the duvet, pulling it tight around her shoulders. She'd never felt so alone...or frightened. Why had Max he left? Why...after they made such sweet love?

The empty house echoed with creaks and groans. All old houses did, but she jumped at every one. The sound of the front door opening reached her along with the insistent beeps of the security alarm. She listened…and breathed a sigh of relief when the alarm shut off. He was home. She heard him as he ascended the stairs and walked beyond her bedroom door to his.

"Nikki?" he called, then knocked on her door. A pause. "Are you awake?" He paused again. "May I come in?"

She pulled the duvet tighter. She'd have to face him sooner or later. "Sure. Come on."

He opened the door and waited, as if unsure of his welcome. His shorts and T-shirt were wet, and his hair was damp and curled at the nape of his neck. Was it raining again? Had he been running? Okay, he could say something. Anything. How about an explanation? Like where the hell was he? Why had he ran out on her?

His sea-green eyes were troubled as he walked to the side of her bed.

Okay, not feeling too good here. Something was definitely out of kilter.

He sat beside her, reached out and caressed her cheek. "Sorry, I'm a mess."

"A mess?" Who cared what he looked like? He was back. She wasn't alone anymore.

He leaned forward and touched her shoulder, then stopped short. "I apologize for leaving the way I did." Pausing again as if considering whether or not to touch her, his hand shook with a fine tremor as he ran his fingers through his damp hair. "After what happened, I had a lot to think about."

"Just what did you have to think about?" She struggled to keep the fear from her voice, but failed. "You said you loved me. H-have you changed your mind?"

"There are things in my past you don't understand…things I'm not sure I understand. This—us—may have been a mistake."

"A mistake?" She grasped the sheet tighter and grappled for control. "How convenient…after the fact." She watched the emotions play across his handsome face, the face she'd loved for so long. She believed his words of love. How could she have been so freaking stupid?

"It's not like that. You know it's not."

A wave of nausea roiled through her. She swallowed the bitterness welling in her throat. Don't let him see how much it hurt. "No, of course not. You're not like other men, are you?" Unable to meet his gaze another second longer, she averted her gaze. "Now, if you're through making excuses, I'm tired." Looking at the wall was preferable to seeing the pity in his gaze. Pity, where only hours ago was passion. "I'd like to get some sleep."

Again, he reached for her. "Let me explain."

"No!" She jerked away and lost all pretense of self-control. "Get out!"

He jumped up as if startled. "I'm sorry. I never meant to hurt you."

"You didn't? Like hell you didn't. You're no different than Ian Stark, except this time I won't have to listen to the laughter and gossip at the agency."

"I would never discuss what happened between us with anyone at the agency." He paced stiffly.

"Of course you wouldn't. You're too much of a freaking gentleman. And as humiliating as this is, you want to know what's worse? Mama was right about you after all. And that really pisses me off."

The bastard stopped pacing and squared his shoulders. "I see." He turned to leave.

"I'll be out by this afternoon." She swung her feet to the floor. "No point in prolonging the mistake."

He turned, anger flashing in his eyes, the muscles in his face tightening. No misconstruing that emotion. "You don't have to leave. I won't come near you again." He rasped out the words through clenched teeth.

"As if I'd let you!" She grabbed the nearest object and aimed it at his head.

Max ducked. The porcelain clock flew over his shoulder and crashed against the wall, shattering. He spun on his heel and left Nikki's bedroom without looking back. No point in it. He was too angry with himself...and heartbroken. She had a right to throw anything she wanted. He was the worst kind of heel.

And to make it worse, he was grateful she hadn't allowed him to explain, but ascribed her own interpretation to his actions. Better to leave things like that, than attempt an explanation he didn't understand. At least she'd be safe.

From the hall, he heard the slamming of drawers. He stopped and listened. Packing? She was leaving. "*Merde*."

They'd shared one beautiful night—one of passion and communication at the most sensual and ethereal levels. And he'd destroyed everything, all because of a nightmare he couldn't explain...or ignore.

If he'd been a woman, he would have wept. But no, a man hid his emotions behind a blank stare... and brooding silence. For once, he regretted being a man.

***

Nikki stalked from the bed and pulled two suitcases from the walk-in closet. She threw them on the bed and jerked at the stubborn zippers. She'd teach him to play with her feelings. Without a doubt, Max Devereaux was an absolute bastard. She'd never forgive him...never.

Yanking open a drawer, she swept the lacy contents into her arms and dumped the undies into one of the empty suitcases. Jeans and tops followed in rapid disorder. She could come back later and pack the rest after he left for the office.

Grabbing the telephone, she punched in Marti's number. "It's Nikki. Sorry to wake you, but..."

After making sure of her friend's welcome, Nikki lugged the larger of her two suitcases to the stairs. The other one could wait. Max's bedroom door opened. Halfway down the stairs, she hesitated and turned. He stood in the hall, silent, hands at his sides. She mustered her courage and fled down the remaining steps. Tears welled in her eyes, but she wouldn't let him see her cry.

Pride? False pride maybe, but right now false pride was all she had.

Twenty-nine

Stifling a wide yawn, Nikki sat in her friend's streamlined kitchen and shivered. Marti set a steaming cup on the bistro table. "Careful. It's hot."

Nikki reached for the cup, blew and then sipped, immediately burning her tongue.

"I told you."

"I'm not thinking clearly." She groaned and shook her head. "I need it to stay awake." She buried her face in her hands.

"Late night?" Marti prompted, the toe of her shoe tapping the floor.

She looked up at her friend. "You could say that."

"See here. If you're going to wake me at the ungodly hour of—well, whatever time it was when you called—you could at least have the decency to tell me what's wrong."

"Max and I—uh," Nikki stopped, not sure she could form the words.

"What?"

"We made love last night." She got the words out, even they were little more than a whisper.

Marti nodded. "Great. So what's the problem? Isn't that what you wanted?"

"Yes—I mean—no. I woke up early this morning, and I was all alone."

"Maybe he went out for a paper, or juice?" Marti suggested.

"No, he went out for a run to think. And when he came back he told me he'd decided it was all a mistake. A mistake." Nikki sobbed, unable to stem the flow of tears. She felt Marti's arms around her, when all she wanted was Max.

"Honey, you must've misunderstood. He wouldn't treat you like that."

"Would I be here like this, if he hadn't?"

"Guess not," Marti sighed. "But maybe you misinterpret something he said?"

"Oh, no. He made it very, very clear."

The telephone rang.

"Hm. Now I wonder who that is?" Marti asked. A wry smile on her lips, she reached for the phone.

Nikki shook her head furiously. The last thing in the world she wanted was having to talk to Max.

"Yes, she is, but I don't think… All right." Marti clapped her hand over the receiver. "He won't take no for an answer. You're going to have to talk to him sometime. Might as well be now."

She swallowed and held out her hand for the phone, her tone terse. "Yes?"

"You have to come back."

"Excuse me? '*Have* to come back?' Did I hear you right? Just like that? You demand I come back." Nikki's voice grew harsh. "How dare you?"

"Something's come up. I have to leave for Paris Sunday morning. You will be here for Alexa—as we agreed."

"So hire someone. Someone you can play games with when Alexa's sleeping over."

"There's no time. I have to spend the morning at the office, then I'm taking Alexa and her friend to the concert. I expect you to be here when I leave on Sunday. There's no one else to whom I can entrust my daughter on such short notice. I'm sorry, but it has to be this way."

"No." Her head pounded as if it would burst. How could he be so damned arrogant?

"You have to come back. We had an agreement. You promised."

"You broke the ground rules, so I don't have to abide by the agreement." Let him argue with that.

"What happened between us wasn't planned. You know that, as well as I do. You know something else?" he paused, allowing her time to answer.

"What?"

"You wanted it to happen as much as I did. I'm not blind. I know when a woman wants me, especially one I desire as well."

"I just bet you do. Go to hell, you entitled son-of-a-bitch. This conversation is over." She punched the disconnect button and drew her arm back.

Marti grabbed Nikki's arm before the phone could become a deadly missile. "Now, now. Let's not take our anger out on the poor little telephone."

"Not one word of explanation. I'm supposed to keep my end of the bargain and *be there for Alexa*." She mimicked his accent.

"Give it some time. When do you have to give him an answer?"

"He has his answer." She sipped her coffee. "Ugh." Cold and bitter. How appropriate. She felt just like the leftover dregs in her cup—used, then discarded once they no longer suited.

Marti stood and pried Nikki's fingers from the cup. "Fresh cup coming up." She dumped the cold contents into the sink. "You'll feel better after some breakfast."

"No, I won't." Nikki drummed her fingers on the table top. "I'll never speak to him again as long as I live."

"Give it some time. He might have a good reason."

"I don't have time. He expects me to be there when he leaves for Paris tomorrow." Nikki jumped up and started pacing.

"Tomorrow? Then while he's away, hire someone to chaperone Alexa. When he comes back, it'll be a done deal."

Nikki stopped pacing in mid-stride, turning to face her friend. "I suppose I could. I just hated giving him the satisfaction of knowing I caved."

"Yes, just think how he'll feel when he comes back from Paris and finds Alexa with a new chaperone. You'll have won, after all." Marti sat back with a satisfied smile on her face. "It behooves us to keep our men on short leashes. They're much happier that way."

Shocked, Nikki stammered, "I-I thought you liked Max."

"Oh, I do, but I'm a veteran at this. You're still a beginner." Marti gave a chuckle.

Puzzled, Nikki stared at her friend. "How did this turn into a joke? I've been used, and you sit there cracking jokes. Sometimes I wonder if I know you at all."

Marti wrapped Nikki in a warm hug. "Sweetie, I know you're hurt, but it's not the end of the world. It only feels like it. Maybe he's scared of commitment. I don't know what his problem is, but he wouldn't be on the phone demanding you come back, if he didn't want you."

"For *Alexa*," Nikki insisted.

"He could hire anyone from the office to look after his daughter, and they'd jump at the chance. It's you he wants. And whether or not he has the nerve to admit it, I think he's in love with you."

Nikki shook her head and spoke with deliberation. "You've never been so wrong. Dead wrong."

Marti shrugged and gave her a fey smile. "We'll see."

Max replaced the telephone on the kitchen counter. Finally, the aroma of freshly-brewing coffee filled the kitchen. His conversation with Nikki hadn't gone well. At this point, he should consider a Plan B, but still he hesitated. He didn't have a Plan B.

Nikki loved his daughter as much as any sister. And as angry as Nikki was, he was positive she wouldn't let Alexa down. The Sunday deadline gave Nikki twenty-four hours to cool down and reconsider. Time would tell. His business wasn't all that urgent. One of his reasons for leaving was to give her a reason for coming back to the townhouse…and it would give them both some breathing room.

And time.

The tension between them had simmered for days, then boiled over so quickly. Distance would give him some time to clear his head…to make decisions which could affect both their lives.

All this dream stuff was against his pragmatic nature. How could he go to the woman he loved and prattle nonsense about dreams and reincarnation, like some wimpy New Age guru? But was it nonsense? He didn't know, but perhaps in Paris, he would find the answer to the riddle of the mask.

Thirty

Saturday was a beautiful day, and the very beauty of it mocked Max. Rays of sunlight streaked across the office from one corner window to the other. He drummed his fingers on the desk. Whatever made him think he could focus on work and forget about Nikki?

After their argument and his making plane reservations, he spent the next hour planning his trip to Paris. Desperate, he'd called Ted Landry, hoping for a game of racket ball that afternoon. Fortunately his friend was available. Perhaps then, he'd be able to think about something besides a certain willowy blonde.

Yes, he needed to think about something other than her silken ivory skin and rose-tipped breasts, firm and yielding to his touch. Think about anything other than long slender legs wrapped around his waist. And how sweet it had been to hold her in his arms and make love to her for the first time.

First time? Yet it hadn't felt like the first time. There'd been none of the usual first time awkwardness; it was as if their bodies had been together many times.

Dammit! He slammed his fist against the desk. The paperwork could wait. He didn't give a damn. The way he saw it, he had two choices. Either he expended his excess energy soon, or he'd rush to the Aldens' and drag Nikki home by the hair.

His Neanderthal impulses shocked him. Not surprising. On the brink of losing his mind, he'd already lost his heart. And no one to blame but himself. He'd let a damned dream tear him away from the woman he loved. He glanced over his shoulder. Could the little men in white coats be far behind?

Perspiration dripped from Max's hairline, down his forehead and into his eyes. Heart pounding, he leaned against the white wall of the racket ball court and gasped for air. "You win," he conceded. The score had been close, until his focus had slipped in the last set.

"'Bout time I won a game off you." Ted chuckled, then added, "And whipped your ass too." He walked over to the bench and opened his gym bag. He pulled out two fresh white towels and tossed one of them at Max. "Here, wuss, you need this more than I do."

"Happy to be a source of amusement." Max grimaced and caught the towel and wiped his face.

"What's eating you?"

"Nikki—it's not working out."

"Enlighten me. Since when—?"

"We're not." He'd overreacted. Ted would never stop with the twenty questions. "She's staying at the townhouse."

"Hold on. The townhouse, as in *yours*?" Ted's eyes widened; he shook his head in disbelief.

"Yes."

"Living together. Well, well. Will wonders never cease?" Ted's face wreathed in a smile. At the same time, he gave Max a broad wink and patted him on the shoulder.

"It's not like that." Not exactly the truth. He jerked away from his friend's lighthearted attempt at bonhomie. "Nikki is there to stay with Alexa, until school starts."

Ted shook his head again and gave Max a cynical look. "For Alexa—*right*. I was about to congratulate you and tell you I didn't know what had taken you so long. If your agitated manner and attempts at obfuscation are any indication, I would venture a guess that my congratulations would be premature."

Ted's pontificating touched a raw nerve. "You're not in court. Cut the crap."

"Your command of the English language is admirable." Ted's grin widened.

"*Merde.*" He should've known better than to say anything. Ted, being a happily married for over ten years, was unable to comprehend the pitfalls of being single.

"Your French is better," Ted admitted, leaning against the wall, nearly doubled in laughter.

"*Ça suffit.*" Anger always caused him to slip into his native tongue.

"Don't know what you said, but I get your drift."

Max took a deep breath, squared his shoulders and managed to say in his calmest manner, "I'm leaving for Paris tomorrow."

"Business or…?"

"Business, but I may stay for a couple of weeks."

"Running away?"

"Hitting the shower," he said, ignoring his friend's heavy-handed probing. "I have a date with two teenagers tonight."

"Teenagers? Have you lost your ever-loving mind?"

"My daughter and her friend will simply die, if they don't see 'NSYNC." He faked a grin.

"*Bon chance.*" Ted laughed, mangling the pronunciation. He zipped his equipment bag. "You are one brave man, my friend. Or crazy."

Max shrugged. "I wish Nikki were as easy to please as my daughter."

At five AM—for Pete's sake—Nikki paced back and forth in the Aldens' guest room. Max had left another message for her. His flight to Paris left at eight, and he wanted her at the townhouse by six-thirty for final instructions.

Final instructions? Who the hell did he think he was?

Logically, he had every right to leave instructions regarding Alexa, but his condescending attitude infuriated her. One night of passion, followed by morning regrets, and now he had the unmitigated gall to order her around—like a servant.

And an unpaid one at that.

She still hadn't made up her mind if she would go or not. Actually she'd made up her mind, or she wouldn't have been up so early. Showered, dressed and packed, but she'd make him wait all the same. Let him wonder if she would show up. She didn't give a tinker's damn about his trip to Paris or the reasons behind it. She knew the real reason. He was running.

Fine. He could just go to Paris...and to Hell.

Glancing repeatedly at his watch, Max paced the foyer. His taxi was due in five minutes, and still no sign of Nikki. Dammit, if she weren't going to show up, she should've at least called. Canceling his trip was not an option. He could've made other arrangements for Alexa. For that matter, he could've taken her with him. It was his own selfish desire to keep Nikki in his life, but at arm's length. She would never forgive him. In her eyes—and his own—he'd acted like a selfish bastard.

First making love to her. Then telling her, it was a mistake and not explaining why—not that she was in any mood to listen.

The arrival of his taxi screeching to the curb interrupted his train of thought.

Not his taxi—Nikki's. The morning sun glinted off her blond hair as she exited the cab. Dark sunglasses covered her eyes. Had she shed tears over him? The pain he must've caused her hit him like a sucker punch. What could he say? How could he make it better?

Face it. He couldn't.

He picked up his luggage, opened the door and stood on the stoop, waiting for her. She ignored him as she climbed the steps, her face set in an unreadable mask. He reached into his jacket pocket and pulled out a business card. "The number of my hotel is on the back." He shifted uncomfortably from one foot to the other, uncertain what to say next. "Alexa and Bitsy are still upstairs asleep. Email or call me, if you need anything."

"Fine." Nikki took the card and without looking at it, stuffed it into her jeans pocket.

Max grabbed her wrist. "I-I'm sorry." He wanted to memorize her face, anything to delay his departure...except tell her what she needed to hear.

"Forget it." She jerked away and motioned with a nod. "Your taxi's here." She brushed past him and walked into the house without giving him a single glance.

"Thank you," he called after her.

Nikki turned, hesitated a beat, then told him tersely, "I keep my word."

Her words stabbed, the pain physical, but no worse than he deserved. He hefted his luggage down the steps to the curb where the cabby waited.

"JFK," Max told the driver, then jumped inside and slammed the door.

He hoped he'd find answers in Paris, but he hated leaving matters this way. More than anything, he wanted to stop the taxi, rush back into the house, fall at her feet, and beg her forgiveness.

Passion battled with control, and this time, control was the uneasy victor.

Self-control mattered. It was an essential part of who he was.

He couldn't—no, he wouldn't—risk Nikki's life and happiness. Or had he just copped out in the worst possible way?

Nikki walked through the kitchen into the sunroom and tossed her purse in the direction of the nearest chair. Her hands shook from seeing Max face-to-face, her emotions still too raw. She shouldn't have had to face him...not this soon.

Arrogant bastard. But was he really? He'd been responsible for everything good in her life. How could he treat her like this? After they'd made love?

In her mind, the answer was clear. Max didn't think she was good enough for him. He still thought of her as the girl he'd scooped out of the gutter. She should've known better than trust his words of love. They were little comfort in the cold light of day. All men were alike. That was her biggest disappointment.

Always in her mind, Max was different.

She'd put him on a pedestal.

His fall from that pedestal might've broken her heart, but not her spirit. She'd get over him. She would. She had her own life. She had her book. Dammit. She had goals.

Shit. The book. She'd promised Geoff she'd have the first chapter on his desk in a few days. And there was the matter of the first half of her advance—it was time she earned it.

Her laptop sat there, waiting patiently. Nikki sat, opened it, touched the on switch, then leaned back and waited for it to boot. Once the system was up, she signed online and checked her email, quickly scanning the list and deleting anything that looked like spam or porn—or worse.

Dammit. Someone had already discovered her new email address, and since the last time she'd checked, that someone had left her numerous messages, telling her how much he loved her and what he'd like to do her, if she'd only give him the chance.

Fat chance. Apparently, he'd signed in under various screen names. By the time she'd scanned several of them, she'd become familiar with his florid style of purple prose. Not that she'd read more than the initial line or two, after the first few.

Delete. Delete. Delete. So much for the cyber stalker.

She opened one from her editor. Just what she expected—a reminder about the first chapter. After emailing him a quick assurance that the chapter would be ready, she had no choice. She had to live up to her commitment.

No time like the present. She opened her word processing program. Reluctantly, she forced her thoughts back—ten years. She stepped into an alley... The emotions and impressions of that fateful night overwhelmed her as they rushed back.

Cold. Fear. Desperation. Her fingers poised over the keys, she shivered. Could she really bring her story to life? She struck the first key.

Three hours later, she had a revised draft of her first chapter. It still needed some spit-and-polish, but it was a good start. She saved it, backed it up and then printed it out. Writing was difficult enough without losing what she'd already done.

She'd just removed the last page from the printer when she heard a thump overhead. The girls were awake. She sighed and braced herself for the certain onslaught of two teenagers in full throes of 'NSYNC ecstasy.

Thirty-one

Monday morning Nikki and Alexa stood in front of St. Anne's Shelter for Women. It might've been a-beautiful-day-in-the-neighborhood kind of day, but St. Anne's faded sign had seen better days. As if mocking the dim reality of life on the streets, the sun was bright, and the sky, clear. Farther down the block, an optimistic bird sang its piercing song. But by afternoon, the heat would rise in stifling waves from the asphalt and concrete.

The teenager's hesitation was clear. "This place looks kind of—uh, sleazy, Nik. Are you sure we're at the right place?" the she asked, a slight frown wrinkling her young brow.

Nikki grinned at her young charge. "You're safe with me, kid." Alexa was right, of course. The neighborhood was frequented by street people, drug dealers and prostitutes selling their wares. The avant-garde theater was gone, replaced by an adult bookstore. So much for urban renewal.

St. Anne's occupied a former flop house and hadn't changed much in the last ten years. From the looks of it, the funding that paid for its conversion into a shelter had been depleted long ago.

Nikki hesitated. Could she really re-immerse herself in the world of despair? The old feelings of hunger and hopelessness hit her like it was yesterday. Secure in her modeling career, she'd been safe and comfortable far too long. She'd forgotten how bad it really was.

No, she wouldn't run away, not this time. With a lot of help, she'd made it. Others could too.

She waved and caught the attention of the security guard. "I'm here to see Sylvia Moore," she said into the intercom. The burly guard looked the two of them up and down. Apparently deciding they were harmless, he unlocked and opened the door.

Nikki nudged Alexa. "Come on. No time like the present," she said, leading the way. She walked past smudged glass door into the lobby, looked around and sighed. Nothing had changed. Without a doubt, it was still the dreariest place on earth.

The receptionist sat behind a counter leafing through a tabloid, never looking up from her scandal sheet. The clinic was situated to the left of the bleak lobby. Two avocado green sofas covered in cracked vinyl and a limp rubber tree made up the less-than-welcoming décor.

Nikki ran the numbers. She had yet to realize any money from the sale of the apartment. While she'd have to discuss it with her accountant, she would earmark some of the proceeds for the shelter, instead of waiting for book sales. Unfortunately, the apartment wouldn't close for another month. That money was too far in the future. The shelter looked like it needed help now. Maybe she should've sold the beach house as well. She'd received half her advance on the book, but the other half wouldn't be forthcoming until after she delivered the final version.

Her mind reeled with possibilities. Tom Alden, bless him—he was filthy rich and benevolent. She would definitely hit him for some operating funds once she had a better idea how much the shelter needed.

Alexa tugged on Nikki's sleeve. "Are we really going to work here three days a week?"

"Yeah," Nikki said. "We really are." She looked at the teen. Alexa wore jeans and a T-shirt, but the difference between Alexa and the other youngsters at the shelter was readily apparent. Alexa's curly hair and clear skin glowed with health and vitality, both noticeable benefits of good nutrition.

Nikki walked over to the receptionist. "Excuse me."

The receptionist reluctant laid down her tabloid. "Yeah?"

"We have an appointment with Sylvia Moore," Nikki said.

The receptionist shot Nikki a look of annoyance, then nodded with a jerk of her head. "Down the hall, second door on the right," she muttered, then returned to her scandals.

"Thank you." Nikki refrained from growling...barely.

As they continued down the hall, Alexa whispered, "She wasn't very polite, was she?"

"No, but good manners aren't high priority in a shelter." She repressed a grin. Max's protected daughter was in for a rude awakening. While she didn't intend for her charge to be overwhelmed, she hope the experience would broaden the teen's outlook.

They reached the indicated office. Nikki knocked and heard a disgruntled, "Come in."

She opened the door, anxious to greet the woman who'd befriended her so many years before. The social work director sat at the same scarred wood desk covered with tall stacks of paper, which threatened to topple any second.

Sylvia Moore looked up at Nikki, her frown immediately replaced by a wide grin. "Just look at you. I can't believe you're really here." Her chocolate brown skin showed no signs of aging, in spite of the fact that it'd been ten years since Nikki had last seen her.

"Well, it's true. I'm back."

"I couldn't believe it when my assistant told me you planned to do some volunteer work down here. I still don't." Sylvia glanced at Alexa and grinned. "This your daughter? No, it can't be. You haven't been gone that long."

"Sylvia, this is Alexa Devereaux. She's—"

"Right. The guy at the modeling agency—his daughter, right?" Sylvia gave a knowing nod.

Nikki swallowed. Even an oblique mention of Max still caused a lump in her throat. "Yes, that's right."

Sylvia stood and cleared off a single straight-backed chair.

"Thank you." Nikki smiled and sat. "The years have been good to you."

Sylvia beamed. "Me? They've been even better to you. You're more beautiful than ever. I figured I'd seen the last of you—except on magazine covers, of course."

"Thank you." Nikki gave Sylvia a smile and shrugged. "Anyway, I'm not modeling anymore, and I think it's time I gave something back."

"Wonderful. What did you have in mind? We have several programs that could use funding—Crisis Line, the day care program, the clinic. Most of all, we really need money. I know that sounds crass, but there it is."

"I know the shelter needs money. That's pretty clear. My money is tied up in the sale of some property right now, but I have a few contacts who might be persuaded to help, right away." She hesitated, realizing she still had a way out. Could she—should she—plunge into the subculture of the hopeless lives, whose greatest ambition was just to escape the streets?

Raising money would be so simple…and a complete copout. Quickly, before she could change her mind, she added, "I want to do more than raise money. I'd like to establish a mentor program, if you don't already have one. Plus, I'm working on a book about my experiences, and I plan to donate part of the advance and any profits to the shelter."

Sylvia sat back; her chin dropped. "You're serious, aren't you?"

She could almost see the wheels turning in the social worker's mind.

"Yes." Nikki studied her hands, then met Sylvia's direct gaze. "I wouldn't have made it, if I hadn't had a lot of help. I can't promise anyone will have the kind of life I've had, but I can offer hope and a lot of practical advice."

"And Alexa? How does she fit in with your plans?" Sylvia's brows were raised.

"I don't blame you for being skeptical. Alexa's the closest thing to a little sister I ever had. I'm looking after her this summer, and I thought some experience here at the shelter might be good."

Sylvia looked over her wire-rimmed glasses at the teenager. "And how do *you* feel about Nikki's big plan for your summer?"

Alexa shrugged, looked first at her feet, then back at Nikki. "I'm not too sure. I mean I don't know what I could do around here, anyway." She shrugged again, then grinned good-naturedly. "But Nik's the boss, so I guess I'm stuck."

Sylvia rubbed her chin. "Well, it appears to me as if I have two new volunteers, even if one of them is a tad reluctant. I'm glad to have you both, and I think I have just the job for you, young lady. I hope you like kids. There are about a dozen or so here at the shelter. They're too young for school. During the school year we have teaching interns, who come in to tell them stories, teach them their letters and numbers, but right now we're at loose ends. How would you like to be the new Storytime girl?"

The not-so-reluctant teen chewed her bottom lip. "Sounds like fun."

"Sounds ideal to me. Thanks, Syl."

Sylvia stood. "Why don't I show Alexa where the play area is? I'll be right back, and then we can discuss your ideas for the mentor program."

Nikki nodded, watching Sylvia lead Alexa from the office. She let out a deep breath. So far, so good. Alexa had been less than thrilled about spending three mornings a week at the shelter, but that still left two mornings a week for sports and music lessons. She intended to keep Max's daughter busy—very busy. And leave little time for dating a handsome young man who was entirely too old for the teen.

Sylvia's return interrupted Nikki's train of thought. "Okay, now, let's talk."

"You know I'll never forget how kind you always were."

"Oh, yeah, like you were willing to accept kindness. You were such a hard case. Pretending to be so cool, but I saw through that mask you hid behind. Back then, you were just a big ball of hurt. I guess life's a lot better now?"

"Things are okay." She shifted uncomfortably, not wanting to go into detail. "Not modeling is the biggest change. Selling the apartment, trying to make adjustments. Writing."

"So, you're going through some transitions." Sylvia nodded, then gave Nikki a wide grin. "You always had a habit of landing on your feet. Somehow I think you'll do just fine."

"It's a little scary. But actually, once I made up my mind to write, everything else fell into place."

"And…what about your personal life? I mean, do you have someone?" Sylvia asked with a grin. "That's a silly question. I bet you have to beat off the men with a stick."

Nikki hedged. "Not really. I tend to keep to myself." She hoped the flush stealing up her neck wasn't visible.

"I see," Sylvia said with a nod.

The doubtful expression on Sylvia's face told Nikki she hadn't fooled the perceptive social worker. Growing uncomfortable under her old friend's gaze, she insisted, "Really."

"If you say so, sugah," Sylvia drawled, emphasizing her southern accent.

Attempting to change the subject, Nikki asked, "About the mentor program?"

Sylvia pushed her glasses up on the bridge of her nose. "Just what did you have in mind?"

"I'd like to come three mornings a week. Alexa will be with me this summer, but I plan to continue after she goes back to school."

"Who's your target group?

"I'd like to work with any of the women interested in finding employment and any teens interested in finishing school or getting their G.E.D."

"Well, I'll have to check on the scheduling and space availability. We already have several self-help groups that meet here like AA and Crisis Management, but I'm sure we can work something out."

"I've outlined a preliminary agenda." Nikki opened a notebook-sized, leather portfolio and removed a sheaf of papers. "This outlines proposed topics of discussion and possible outside resources for guest speakers."

Sylvia gave the outline a quick scan. "It looks like you've thought this out pretty carefully. Are you sure you're going to have enough time for this project along with your book?"

"Yes, I'll still have plenty of time to write in the evening. I've always been a night owl."

"And chaperone a teenager at the same time?" The social worker gave Nikki a skeptical glance. "You're going to be one busy lady."

Nikki grinned. "I like to keep busy."

"Well, this'll do it." Sylvia glanced down at her watch. "Speaking of the teenager, I'll fetch her for you."

"Great."

Sylvia walked around the desk, leaving Nikki alone with her thoughts. She'd always heard the expression, in for a penny, in for a pound. She would commit her time and energy to this project. Backing out was not an option. Never mind the small fact she already had misgivings about her ability to affect change. But still, she had to try.

Sylvia returned with Alexa. "Here we are."

"Thank you, Ms. Moore," Alexa said, definitely in her polite mode."

"So, how was it? Think you'll like it?" Sylvia asked.

Alexa nodded. "The kids are really sweet." She lost her bored-to-death-teenager expression for a second, but then recovered and shrugged, "It might not be so bad."

"I'll take that as an unqualified 'yes'," Sylvia said with an abrupt bark of laughter.

"Sylvia, thank you." Nikki smiled, offering her hand to her old friend and counselor.

Sylvia accepted with a warm, firm grip. "Thank *you*. I'll call you after I check the meeting schedule, and we'll set a time for you to start." She shoved her glasses up the bridge of her nose, then smiled. "I'm really looking forward to working with you."

"Same here." Nikki picked up her portfolio and turned to Alexa. "Ready?"

"Uh huh." Alexa nodded, then said to Sylvia, "B-bye, Ms. Moore. It was nice meeting you."

"You too, Alexa."

Nikki placed an arm around the girl's shoulder, telling Sylvia, "We're going to leave you to your work now. I hope to hear from you soon."

Sylvia snorted, then said with good humor, "Don't you worry about that, you will."

Seeing the frown lurking beneath the surface, Nikki rushed to reassure Alexa, "It won't be so bad, honest."

Alexa tilted her head to one side and admitted, "I guess it'll be okay…as long as you're around."

"Of course, I'll be around. Wouldn't have it any other way." She hugged the semi-captive teenager.

Reaching the lobby Nikki and Alexa walked past the security guard. Nikki acknowledged him with a brief nod.

"Bye, Nikki," the burly guard said, giving them a wolfish smile.

Quickly eyeing the guard's name tag, Nikki replied, "Bye—uh, Mac."

The guard lumbered to the door and unlocked it. He opened it, then stood aside, allowing them to leave.

"Are we gonna see ya soon, I hope?" he asked.

"Sure thing." Nikki shivered. His smarmy smile jarred her insides.

After the door closed behind them, Alexa turned to Nikki and asked, "Do you know him?"

"No, but every man on the street thinks he knows *me*. That's the price of fifteen minutes of fame."

Alexa shuddered. "I don't think I ever want to be famous."

"Well, it just happened. I didn't plan it."

"Daddy made you famous."

"Yes, he did." She stopped at the curb and raised her arm. "Taxi!"

The taxi screeched to a halt in front of them. Alexa asked, "Do you love Daddy?"

No, I hate him. Not that she could say that to his daughter. Ignoring the question, Nikki gave Alexa a slight nudge. "Get in the taxi. Your cello lesson is in thirty minutes and we're over thirty blocks away."

The girl jumped into the cab, and Nikki followed, slamming the door shut. "You didn't answer my question."

Stubborn child. Like father, like daughter. "No, and I don't intend to, either."

Alexa crossed her arms and gave Nikki a smug smile. "That means yes."

"That means nothing."

Thirty-two

Paris

Max threaded his way through the crowd and walked onto the marble columned balcony of the Rousseau mansion. In moments like these, he craved a cigarette. He hadn't smoked in years, not since before Alexa was born. Social gatherings like this... The sidelong glances he received from former friends, reminded him he'd never been cleared in his wife's death.

He hadn't planned on attending any social functions during this trip; however, his old friend, Gilbèrt Rousseau, had invited him, and rather than offend one of his few true friends, Max had relented.

He stared into the night sky at the thousands of twinkling lights that had given the city of his birth its nickname. In spite of all the bad memories he associated with Paris, he felt centered and at home. His roots were here. For centuries his ancestors had been born and buried here. *Maman* and he were the first of their families to live on another continent. His daughter was totally immersed in American culture, which he considered neither good nor bad. He supposed it really didn't matter, since she seemed happy with her life, or at least as happy as a fourteen-year-old girl could be.

He couldn't change the past... Solange...and dear heaven, most of all Nikki. Whether his decision made sense to anyone else or not, he had to protect Nikki—at all costs—no matter how much it hurt both of them.

"M. Devereaux, is the party too much for you?"

Turning he discovered a lovely woman with wide-set, dark brown eyes and auburn hair, styled to frame her face. A flawless ivory complexion did nothing to hide the feral intensity of her gaze. An inexplicable uneasiness in her presence crept into his awareness.

"*Madame*? You have the advantage of me. I do not think we have met."

"Emilie Balladur, M. Devereaux. I was at school with your late wife."

He stepped back. "You-you knew my wife?" It was possible, he supposed. He hadn't known all of Solange's friends. She'd certainly managed to keep her lover a secret.

"Yes, not very well, but we had some friends in common."

"I see." He desired nothing more than to forget his past, yet here was another reminder staring him in the face. He turned away. Surely the woman would take the hint.

Instead of leaving, she leaned against the balcony railing next to him. "It's beautiful, *n'est-ce pas?*"

"*Oui, madame.*"

"Do you not miss living in Paris, M. Devereaux?"

"Sometimes," he admitted.

"Then why do you not return to live here? Paris is the center of the fashion world."

He shrugged. "It's complicated, madame..."

"The dark cloud still hangs over your head? Yes, I suppose it is complicated."

"*Madame*, if you please, I do not wish to discuss—"

"I see this is still very painful for you, M. Devereaux. Perhaps you need to make some new memories." She cast him a meaningful glance through lowered lashes, before adding in a sultry voice, "More pleasant ones, I mean. It's been a long time, *n'est-ce pas?*"

Merde. Why wouldn't she drop it? "Not long enough. I am in Paris on business, not pleasure. I should not have come tonight."

"But I am so glad you did. This is a wonderful party, but if you would like to leave, I would not mind."

"Pardon, am I not being clear?" The woman was rapacious and oblivious, as well. "If I leave, I leave alone," he said. He had seen women like her before, accustomed to having their way, but he was not interested in her having her way with him.

"*Salaud.* Your manner is aloof and boorish. No wonder your wife fell in love with another man." She folded her arms across her chest and thrust her chin at him in defiance.

He regarded her coldly. "Think whatever you wish." He turned and walked away. He scanned the room, looking for Gilbèrt or his wife Madeline. He would make his excuses to his hosts, but the surroundings suffocated him.

"Maxim? Maxim Devereaux?"

He turned and saw his mother's dearest friend, Florimel Dambasle. "*Madame* Dambasle. How wonderful to see you again," he said, genuinely pleased to see the lovely woman before him. Indeed, the years had been kind.

"I could not believe my eyes when I saw you come in from the balcony. I have not seen you since Renée's memorial. Such a sad a day." The older woman's hands fluttered gracefully as she spoke. "None of us could believe it. Suddenly she was gone...much too young. I miss her so much."

"She always treasured your friendship, *Madame*." he took her graceful hands in his and brushed his lips across the backs. "I shall always treasure your kindness that day. Renée would have been pleased you came to bid her farewell."

"Pierre and I were so pleased you brought her home to Paris. I do not think she would have rested in American soil, no?"

"Probably not, *Madame*." Over his old friend's shoulder, he spied the Balladur woman heading toward him. "I was about to leave. May I drop you somewhere?"

"Maxim, it's early," she protested. "Surely you're not leaving?"

"*Oui*, I fear I am not in the mood."

She noted his distraction and turned to see what had caught his attention. "Well, your lovely companion looks as if she won't mind leaving early." Mme. Dombasle paused, then raised a finely-arched brow.

He frowned, then confided, "I never met her before tonight, but she makes me uneasy, *Madame*."

"Perhaps, you knew her in another life," she suggested, her manner serious.

"Another life, Madame? Do you believe in such things?"

"Why not, Maxim? It explains the inexplicable. Now, I've monopolized you far too long. If you have time, you must visit Pierre and me at *Belle Rêves*, and we will talk more. *Au revoir*."

She waved a fluttery hand, then wandered away to talk to someone else, leaving Max alone...with the Balladur woman bearing down on him.

"M. Devereaux, I have decided to forgive your incivility. You may call me Emilie." She placed her hand on his forearm and smiled up at him."

A flash of light caught Max by surprise.

"I hope you were smiling for the camera, *mon chèr*." she smiled—a satisfied expression that reminded Max of a cat's licking cream from its paws.

"You must forgive me. I am about to leave. I have an early appointment."

"The evening is young, and surely you were not going to leave without me," she said, giving a simpering smile...and still clutching his elbow.

He resisted the impulse to shake her off and stalk away. Her cloying persistence irritated him beyond belief. "My driver will drop you anywhere you wish, but as I said, I have an early meeting. And I am leaving *now*."

"Well, if you insist, we can make an early night of it, this once. Of course, you will want to stop at my place for a drink or espresso."

He scowled and took a deep breath before answering. "I'm afraid not. My business commitments take precedence over personal engagements." He turned and walked toward his host and hostess, along with Emilie who stuck to him like an annoying wad of gum.

Once his *au revoirs* were said, he ushered Emilie Balladur down the grand marble staircase to the foyer of the eighteenth century house. She made a great show of their togetherness. Rather than humiliate her in front of her acquaintances, he allowed it, but her touch sent an unpleasant chill down his spine. Something was not right about her, something beyond her aggressive and clinging behavior.

After leaving the stately mansion and walking into the balmy Parisian night, they stood at the top of another set of stairs. Max nodded to two previous business associates, neither of whom seemed anxious to renew their old acquaintance. Apparently they hadn't forgotten the cloud over his head either. She chattered away, but he barely heard her. He merely wanted the night to end. As his car and driver pulled up, he nudged her. "Ready?"

"*Mais oui*, Maxim."

"Fine."

Together they descended the exterior steps. As they reached the bottom, the woman stumbled. Max caught her... And it was duly recorded for posterity by more annoying flashes from cameras of the ever-present paparazzi. No doubt there would be photos of the clumsy witch in his arms, gracing the morning tabloids. The paparazzi—the plague on civilization—had hounded him unmercifully after Solange's death. How fitting.

"Are you all right, *Madame*?"

"*Oui*, Maxim," she replied, slanting her eyes at him. He ushered her into the limousine and instructed the driver before he settled back into the comfort of the soft leather seats, patently rejecting her attempts at closeness.

Angry he'd allowed her to maneuver him into the uncomfortable position of escorting her home, he determined this was as far as he would permit her machinations to ruin his evening. Her desperate attentions repulsed him. It was a given that he'd been pursued by determined women before. In fact, he'd even responded favorably, if briefly, to some of them, but he felt no attraction to this one—quite the opposite. Some men might be taken in by her sensual allure, but he had pressing memories of a more delicate beauty in mind. Beautiful, warm memories that were confused with an unexplainable foreboding.

"You are so cold. It's difficult to believe you are a true Frenchman," she huffed in a fit of pique, when he removed his arm from her possessive grasp, for the second time.

Perhaps another tactic would work with her. "I'm involved with someone in the States," he declared. It wasn't a lie. Even if he and Nikki were at odds, they were certainly involved.

"And you are faithful to her?" Emilie asked, raising a questioning brow.

"I am." He stared out the window, hoping his blatant disinterest would…frankly, shut her up.

"How quaint and American," she replied, with a sneer, then added, "I knew your wife's lover too."

His back stiffened. His breath caught in his throat. "You knew Destael?" he managed to croak.

"*Oui*, quite well. In fact, I knew him better than Solange."

Max took a slow deep breath. Might as well listen to her. Doubtful anything could hurt more than news of Solange's death. "So?"

"Well it seems that even as your wife was unfaithful to you, he was unfaithful to her. He cut quite a swath among his students." She paused before adding, "I should know, I was one of them."

Still unsure of the reasons for her revelations, he kept silent. He could easily believe the woman had had an affair with Destael…and countless others, if her overtures toward him were any indication of her normal behavior.

"Well?" Emilie raised her chin a notch. "Don't you have anything to say? Don't you care your wife was a fool?"

Anger flashed through him, along with a strong impulse to wring the stupid woman's neck. He choked back his rage and forced a quiet and deliberate response. "I don't see that my feelings in the matter are of any concern to you. My wife and her lover have been dead for twelve years. They are beyond feeling."

"I just thought you should know." Emilie said with a sniff and a toss of her head. "So your lover in America? Tell me about her. Is she a model? She must be very beautiful. You are surrounded by beautiful women, *n'est-ce pas*?"

Another change in her direction of attack. He guarded his response, well aware she had no sense of what was appropriate. "What about you?" he asked, taking the offensive. "Why aren't you involved with someone?"

Emilie's eyes narrowed. "Because the only man I ever loved died twelve years ago."

"I see. Then you know something about pain and disappointment."

"Far too much, *mon chèr*," she replied, her tone brittle.

Max drummed his fingers against the expensive leather seats, while he willed the driver to hurry.

The remainder of the ride passed in stiff silence, punctuated by her intermittent sighs. Finally, the limousine stopped in front of a tall apartment building. "Are you sure you won't change your mind, Maxim? I'm afraid we've gotten off to a bad start."

"As I said, it's quite late, and I have an early morning appointment."

The chauffeur opened the door for Emilie. She turned to Max and huffed. "Fine. You'll be sorry, Maxim."

"Pardon?"

Emilie grabbed her evening bag and jumped out of the limo. "Damn you and your fine manners!"

"Are all women crazy?" Max asked the chauffeur.

"So it would seem, sir. So it would seem."

Thirty-three

Nikki hit the play button and listened to Geoff's message for the third time, in an attempt to determine whether he was pleased with her efforts or not. Some suggestions? Good grief. She'd revised her work until she thought it was ready for publication. Guess not. Well, that's what an editor was supposed to do, make suggestions, but did she have to take them?

Then add Geoff's concerns about the book to the depressing morning she and Alexa had at St. Anne's and it equaled a bad day. A fifteen-year-old girl had shown up at the clinic, homeless and pregnant. She'd refused to tell them anything about the father or her family, except that they'd thrown her out when they learned she was pregnant and HIV positive. How could a family treat their child like that? While Nikki's childhood was no picnic, but her mother was a paragon of maternal virtue compared to one or two she'd seen at the clinic.

The misery she'd witnessed at St. Anne's compelled her to write the book quickly. Her easy life had given her an artificial form of amnesia. Saddened, she realized she'd forgotten more of the pain and despair than she'd thought. Any royalties she received would only be a band-aid on the problems of the world, but she could do something concrete for the shelter.

Encouragement never put food in anyone's belly. A positive attitude only went so far when you could feel your stomach rubbing your backbone. Delays in editing her book would delay the funding St. Anne's needed so badly. She picked up the phone and punched in Geoff's number, ready to do battle. "It's Nikki. What kind of suggestions? Is it going to take much time? I really want this thing published and off my hands." Might as well come right out and tell him the truth.

"Hold on. Hold on. I'd rather go over them with the manuscript in hand."

Over the phone she heard the rustle of paper.

"Okay, what about this afternoon or evening? I'll free up a block of time. Then we can get down to it."

"Not this afternoon. I have to take Alexa for a school uniform fitting, but I'm free this evening. Why don't you come by then? I'll order in something."

"Are you sure that will be okay with your—uh, employer?"

"He's in Paris. Besides, I don't answer to him for my free time," she replied with a distinct huff.

Geoff chuckled. "All right. Seven, okay?"

"Seven's fine. I'll see you then." She put the phone down on the counter and took a deep breath. Hopefully she hadn't made a mistake, inviting Geoff to the house again. His comment told her he'd picked up on some of the vibes between Max and her.

"I hate fittings." Alexa exclaimed as she stomped along the hot sidewalk.

"Really? I never would've guessed," was Nikki's best attempt at good humor. She was hot and tired, and Alexa had been a major pain in the ass all afternoon.

The teenager rolled her eyes at Nikki's remark. "I guess you must've gotten used to fittings and stuff like that."

"Yeah. You're right, they're pretty boring.

"Let's stop by the deli. I'm dying of thirst." The teen grabbed her throat in a theatrical gesture.

"Can't have that." Nikki held back a giggle.

"Are you still mad at me?"

"No, just my usual funk after being at the shelter. And I'm worried about the meeting tonight with my editor."

"I wish I could be there. He's cute, isn't he?"

"Cute enough, but you're still going to Bitsy's."

"I know. Do you think he's as handsome as Daddy?"

"Lexa!" Exasperated, she continued, "Just give up on the idea that your father and I are going to be together. It's not happening."

Alexa pouted. "Don't be mean. I love you both."

Nikki came to an abrupt halt and turned to the teenager. "Honey, your father and I are just friends."

"He does love you. I know he does. I've seen—"

"That's enough! Okay?"

Alexa heaved a big sigh. "Okay."

They walked along in silence for another five minutes. The deli was a short distance from the townhouse. Together they entered Armand's d'Eli. Nikki waved at Gisele, the owner. "*Bonjour, Madame.*"

"*Bonjour, Mademoiselle* Nikki," Gisele replied, looking up from her ubiquitous New York Times crossword.

Nikki strode down the aisles of the store. Armand's was a small tony delicatessen with a coffee bar. The store was lined with shelf after shelf of exotic—make that imported—comestibles, from the finest truffles to wonderful nut-flavored bhasmati rice from India.

"I'm going to check out the spices." Nikki indicated her direction with a nod. "I won't be long."

"Okay, I want a bottled water," Alexa said, heading toward the rear of the store.

Nikki ambled halfway down the spice aisle, but the aroma of fresh roasted coffee drew her in the other direction. There weren't as many choices as there would've been at Starbucks, but there were quite a few.

No, no, she decided, it's too hot outside to drink coffee. She turned away from the shiny self-service area and stumbled into a man standing directly behind her.

"Sorry," Nikki said.

He drew himself up, but fell short of being able to meet Nikki eye to eye. "That's all right. Say, aren't you that model?" He mopped perspiration from his brow with a handkerchief.

"Yes," she replied, wishing she could ignore him. She stood on tip-toe and looked about the store, hoping to spy Alexa. The girl stood at the front counter, watching and grinning widely.

"You're a real babe, y'know."

"Thank you." She clutched her large linen bag close to her chest. Never used to see a stalker in every man who wandered in her path, but after the recent happenings, she couldn't help but wonder if this man was the one who wrote lurid emails and left roses willy-nilly on her doorstep.

"Say how'dja like to have a cup of coffee with me?" he asked, pulling at his collar and stretching his neck.

She smiled. "No, I'm afraid not, I'm with my little sister, and we have another appointment."

"Too bad. Does she look anything like you?"

"Sorry." She tried to walk around him, but he blocked her. "I have to go."

"Listen, if you'd like to go out sometime, give me a call." He reached into his jacket pocket, pulled out a business card and thrust it at her.

Rather than make a scene, she took his card and shoved it in her bag. "Now, excuse me." She pushed her way around him and headed toward the front of the store. Alexa stood waiting, her earlier grin replaced by a peculiar expression. "What's wrong?"

"Nothing."

Over Alexa's shoulder, Nikki spied the tabloid rack. A full-color photograph of Max was displayed on the front page…and he had a very attractive woman in his arms. She mentally counted to ten, but it didn't help. Her mouth grew dry, and tears stung her eyes. She had to get out of the store before she lost it.

She swallowed, then finally trusting herself to speak, she said quietly, "It's none of my concern."

All business, she pulled out her coin purse and paid for Alexa's bottled water. "Let's go," she said to her young charge, then attempted to smile at Gisele. "*Au revoir, Madame.*"

"*Au revoir, Mademoiselle*, Nikki."

She hurried out of the store, striding along in fury, leaving Alexa to catch up with her.

"Nikki, wait. I'm sure it wasn't like it seemed. You know those rags do all sorts of computer things with pictures. Daddy probably hasn't been within ten miles of that woman."

The very idea that Max's daughter found it necessary to comfort her—humiliating. Again, the unshed tears stung her eyes. She blinked them back before they could spill down her cheeks. "Never mind, It doesn't matter."

"Okay, but..."

The girl's tone was so pitiful, Nikki relented and slowed her pace. "Look, I do care about your father, but he doesn't feel the same way. It just happens that way sometimes. Life isn't a romance novel."

"But..."

She placed a finger on Alexa's lips, interrupting her protest. "There's no happy ending here, honey. I'm sorry. I know you want us together, but—" She shrugged.

Damn Max for hurting both of them. He had a lot to answer for...if and when he decided to bring his sorry butt back to New York. She took a deep breath. Time to stop feeling sorry for herself. "Come on. Let's go home and get you ready for your sleepover at Bitsy's."

"Okay." Alexa's expression brightened, then faded again.

"Are you taking your new CD's?" Nikki asked, hoping to divert the girl's attention.

"Sure."

"Well, let's get a move on. The sooner you get packed up, the sooner you can have some fun. At least one of us ought to have some."

"What about your editor?" Alexa asked, her mischievous air returning. "You said he was cute."

"He is, but he's my editor. It's business. Come on here, give me a break. You're not missing out on anything, but some stuffy talk about my book." She patted Alexa on the shoulder. Luckily the teen's usual good nature returned and her face brightened with a smile.

Thirty-four

Geoff McHugh made it a point to arrive at Nikki's exactly at seven. Attention to detail was part of his compulsive nature, part of what made him a good editor. Wearing a pale gray silk suit and a slightly darker gray Egyptian cotton shirt, only his colorful Mickey Mouse tie gave away he might take life less than seriously. Normally, he dressed much more casually, but a command performance at a board meeting had induced him to wear a suit. All the same, he'd enjoyed the raised eyebrows of his grandfather's hand-picked men when they'd noticed his tie.

He rang the doorbell and waited.

Oh, yes, indeed. His newest author opened the door herself, wearing jeans that fit her tall, lean body like a glove and a loose-fitting, pale blue short-sleeved sweater that threatened to fall off her shoulder. No makeup, or at least it had been so artfully applied he couldn't discern it. Her shoulder length blond hair had been cut in layers which she wore in soft waves away from her face. As always her thick-lashed blue eyes were hypnotic, or would've been if he allowed himself the luxury of gazing into them for too long.

"Hey, you're right on time," she said, giving him a smile that hit his mid-section like a linebacker's shoulder.

"I've been looking forward to seeing you again," he said, then hastily added, "email can be so impersonal." She stood aside, and he followed her into the foyer, carrying her manuscript in his briefcase. "We can really get to work now," he said, waggling the briefcase.

"Is it that bad?" she asked over her shoulder, while leading him to the sunroom.

"Not at all. You've a very original voice, but there are some areas that could be expanded." He set the briefcase on the glass-topped coffee-table. "I'd like to go into some of those tonight, rather than focus on some minor grammar and punctuation changes. Those are no-brainers, and you can take care of them easily," Geoff said, opening the leather briefcase with quick snaps and removing the manuscript.

"I see."

Geoff settled back on the sofa and began riffling the pages. "Okay, there's one particular section I feel needs expansion—actually, two."

Nikki nodded and returned a slightly diffident smile. "Uh, not to change the subject, but dinner will be here around eight," she said. "Italian, okay?"

"And if it weren't?" he asked, teasing her, then watched her reaction in amazement. Her face paled, then flushed. Her hands actually trembled.

"I—I'm sorry. I should've asked you what you preferred."

"I was kidding. Italian's great. All New Yorkers love Italian food." He felt like a heel for pushing her buttons. Obviously his fledgling author was feeling a tad insecure. Good God, didn't she realize most men would eat worms just to be in the same room with her?

She gave a sheepish grin. "Nothing like over-reacting, is there?" She looked down at her feet then admitted, "This book has me so nervous. I just want to get it in the bookstores. The shelter needs so much. What if the book doesn't make any money?"

"That's always a chance with a new author, but we we're not in the habit of publishing books we don't think anyone will buy. Let's just get it ready to publish, okay?"

She sat on the sofa across from him. "All right, I'm ready. Hit me. What needs expansion?"

"First of all, you've done an excellent job in your first chapter."

"Why do I think I hear a 'but' coming up?"

"Because I want more depth and more emotion in the next chapter."

"The one before I left home?" She shifted positions as if uncomfortable.

"Yes, you've compressed fifteen years into a tiny paragraph. I'm exaggerating, of course, but you know what I mean?"

He watched Nikki bite her lip and take a deep breath. What was the cause for her uneasiness? "For instance, you've told me very little about your relationship with your mother and nothing about your father."

She frowned. "Some things are best left unsaid." She picked up a pillow and actually punched it. As far as he could tell, she was unaware of her actions.

"My father left when I was two. I don't remember anything about him." She combed her fingers back through her hair in another seemingly unconscious gesture.

"But your mother must have memories of him. She must have told you things about him?"

"Nothing fit to print in a book," she said, then sprang from the sofa and paced. "My mother and I don't get along very well. That's one of the reasons I left home."

"Now we're getting somewhere." He nodded, tapping his fingers on the chair arm. He'd never seen Nikki so agitated. Matter of fact, he'd never seen her as anything other than cool and laid back. Maybe he'd better leave the subject of her benefactor for a later session. Better to err on the side of discretion. She was upset enough, as it was.

"I don't want to rehash all that stuff. I'd rather forget it."

"But if retelling it would keep another young girl from running away from home, wouldn't it be worth it?"

"I don't see how."

"Maybe you don't now, but it could by encouraging more communication with parents or someone else—a teacher, perhaps."

Nikki gave a heavy sigh. "I don't think I can bear to think about all that crap, again."

"Okay, let's try something else. After I leave, try taking a nice warm bath, with soft music and one of those aroma candle things you gals like so much and let your mind drift back."

She giggled. "So, now you're my guru?"

"I'm whatever it takes."

"I see."

A smile played about Nikki's lips...her soft luscious lips. She stopped pacing and placed her hands on her hips. "Okay, Swami McHugh, then what?"

"Take your journal with you, and when the muse strikes—write."

"Write? In the Jacuzzi?"

Visualizing the two of them in the Jacuzzi, he nodded. "Yeah. Forget punctuation, grammar—all that stuff. Just write what you feel."

"You'll be sorry. It's not a pretty picture."

"I'm not looking for a pretty picture. I'm looking for truth." What had happened to this beautiful young woman? What was she hiding?

"Oh, Mr. High-and-Mighty," she said, giving a nervous giggle.

"If the readers want a pretty picture, they can just check out the cover. But if they want a real story, then you're going to have to give them something more than your best come-hither stare."

"I think I heard a compliment in there somewhere. Thanks."

The door bell rang, saving Geoff from making a worse fool of himself.

"Hold on. I'll be right back," She took to the front door. He admired her lissome body as she strode past him. If he'd ever needed all his will power to maintain a professional distance, it was now. Her beauty damn near took his breath away.

While she answered the door, he considered the risk and complications of becoming involved. It would be totally unprofessional, but to be completely honest, he felt a very powerful attraction to his newest author.

He'd never run across the problem before in his career, and he hoped he wouldn't, again. True, he'd had some difficult authors in the last three years. He'd babysat an alcoholic Pulitzer Prize winner, wrenching the necessary revisions from him with the dire threats of a Mafia hit man. Once, he'd even house sat with a wealthy socialite's Jack Russell terrier. The now-famous, and filthy rich, romance novelist still sent him a Christmas card every holiday season.

Yes, he'd handled those situations quite handily, but Nikki, in spite of her unpretentious attitude, was complex and secretive, to boot. For the first time he wondered, if he were up to the task.

She returned, carrying a large cardboard box in her arms. "I hope you don't mind dining informally."

"Not at all." Geoff sprang to relieve her of the burden, but before he could, she caught her foot on the edge of a thick oriental rug. The box flew in Geoff's direction. He caught it by reflex, not skill.

She sprawled, hitting the floor with both knees. "Ugh!"

Casting their dinner aside, he knelt down beside her. "Are you all right?"

"Just embarrassed," she admitted, rolling with great care from her stomach to her bottom. "I don't guess I'll die from it." She rubbed both knees, wincing in pain. "I guess it's a good thing the rug is so thick."

He stood, extending his hand to her. "Here, let me help."

"I'm fine, really." She attempted standing on her own, but grimaced with the effort. "Big mistake. I'm not fine."

Somewhat reluctantly, she accepted his hand and then his arm around her waist. Together they limped toward the nearest sofa. "Here put your feet up," he said. "I'll get some ice for your knees."

"Bossy, aren't you?"

"Bad habit, I know." He grinned, then looked around. "The ice?"

"Well, the ice would be in the freezer…which would be in the kitchen…which you walked past to reach this room."

Her tone implied she thought him dense. "Smart-ass, aren't you?"

"Bad habit, I know," she mimicked.

Geoff shook his head and grinned, then headed toward the kitchen where he rummaged around, making a lot more noise than necessary, hoping for a clue or a suggestion where he might find a soft-sided container for the ice.

"Plastic bags in the first drawer on the right side of the stove," Nikki yelled from the sunroom.

"Okay, found them. One very professional ice pack coming up, or should I make that two?"

"Two. Two knees, remember?"

"Oh, yeah. How silly of me." Two gorgeous knees, how could he forget?

He quickly enclosed the crushed ice into two plastic bags and returned to the sunroom, brandishing them with pride. "Don't you think you should go to the emergency room, or something?"

"No, but I do think I ought to—uh, put on something less restrictive."

"Oh." Geez. Did she expect him to undress her?

"The laundry room is off the kitchen to the right." She pointed. "There should be some athletic shorts on the counter."

"Okay." He was at a loss for words. The situation had deteriorated from an editor/author meeting to an I'm-injured-help-me-get-my-clothes-off deal. Just what he'd hoped to avoid. He wandered in the direction she'd pointed and found the laundry room without difficulty. "Athletic shorts, athletic shorts," he muttered and pawed through a stack of lacy unmentionables, but no athletic shorts. A brief, teasing vision of Nikki wearing only her lacy bits passed through his head. Damn, was she testing him?

Half his laundry usually stayed in the dryer. Maybe hers did too. Oh shit. Spandex!

While her editor rummaged in the laundry room, Nikki unbuttoned the top of her jeans and waited, drumming her fingers on the sofa arm. Men. They could never find anything. And heaven forbid one of them should ask for directions. She gave each knee a cautious poke. Something wasn't right, but there hadn't been that deep stunned feeling that went along with a broken bone. As a child, she'd fallen down some stairs and broken her wrist. Her knees hurt, but nothing like that.

"Will these do?" Geoff asked, holding aloft a pair of lavender bicycle shorts.

"I guess. Now turn your back," she ordered. "I'm not doing this for your entertainment."

"Never thought you were." He squared his shoulders as if indignant.

"Good. Just so we're clear on that point."

"Here." He tossed the shorts, then turned his back.

She struggled, inching her jeans down past her hips and past her tender knees. "Ye-ouch." They were discolored and swollen, already. Ice was definitely in order. With a minimum of difficulty, she shoved her jeans down to her ankles. She stretched and pulled them free, grunting as she did.

"Are you okay? I could help, y'know."

"Don't you dare turn around. I'm fine." She grabbed the shorts and eased them over her ankles, up past her calves and easy, easy over the knees. Then a quick yank and a wiggle, she pulled them over her hips. "Okay, I'm good."

"Damn. Those knees look terrible. You have to go to the emergency room."

Nikki shook her head. "No, the ice will be enough—and maybe some ibuprofen."

"But you can't walk. You—"

"I'll call Alexa and have her come home. I'll be fine."

"Then I'll salvage what's left of dinner and bring it to you."

"Only if you have some too."

"All right. But I'm staying with you until Alexa comes home. I won't leave you alone."

What was going on here? Not that she was attracted to him that way, but he was so damned nice…and cute. And open, nothing like Max.

Actually, that was in Geoff's favor, considering Max was whooping it up on the continent with a redhead while he was supposed to be closing on the last of his mother's Parisian properties.

Nikki grinned. "Bring it on. I'm starved."

Thirty-five

Uninvited and armed with two suitcases, Emilie Balladur stood in Max's courtyard.

"*Madame*, this is most unexpected," he said. What he thought was another matter. What the hell was she doing in Provençe—much less on his family farm?

The woman set her suitcases down and smiled up at him, a true coquette's seductive smile. "I thought you might have reconsidered your rash behavior of the other night and would want to see me."

"I'm afraid you've caught me at an inconvenient time. I'm on my way out…to visit some old friends.

"I could go with you."

"I'm afraid not."

"You could at least invite me in for a moment. I'm quite thirsty after my long drive from Paris."

"It will have to be a brief drink. As I said I'm expected at friends."

Sauntering into the living room, she settled on the nearest sofa. "I would like a glass of wine from your own vineyards, Maxim."

He nodded. He poured a double whiskey for himself and a glass of Sablet Blanc for his uninvited guest, while calculating how quickly he could send her on her way. Fifteen minutes, twenty? He handed her the glass, then positioned himself in a comfortable chair across the room. The greater the distance, the better.

"*Merci.*" She sipped from her glass of wine, raising an eyebrow. "It is quite good. I adore the wines of the south… I adore their men too."

Mèrde. He didn't appreciate being on her *menu du nuit*. "Why are you here, *madame*?" he asked. Subtlety and subterfuge were for people who had time to waste. He didn't.

"I'll have you know I don't give up easily…" She continued her seductive gaze over the rim of the wine glass. "I know when a man is interested in me."

"You are mistaken this time."

Emilie shrugged. "You still maintain that you're involved with someone in the States?"

"Yes."

Without warning, she jumped up and threw her glass at him. "I hate you, you cold bastard. You have no passion. No heart. You are incapable of love."

He dodged the wine, then sighed when he heard it shatter on the terra cotta floor. If an expensive piece of crystal was the price of ridding himself of her annoying presence, so be it. "I think you should leave."

"You've rejected me for the last time. You will be sorry!" Her high-pitched shriek filled the air, then she grabbed her luggage and rushed from the room.

He relaxed his clenched fists, then shouted after her, "I never asked you here. This stupidity is your own doing."

She halted and turned, her eyes flashed at his terse appraisal. "My own doing? You've led me on, made me promises. I thought you loved me!"

Demented—she must be. He took two steps toward her. "You are mistaken. I did no such thing. I told you from the beginning I wasn't interested."

"Ugh." The woman's hand snaked out and before he could move, she raked his jaw with her long nails. Screeching she whirled and fled.

Seconds later, the squealing tires of her Porsche told him all he wanted to know.

Relief coursed through him. The woman's pathetic attempt to initiate an affair with him was eerie, reminding him of a nightmare. And he had no desire to end up with a bullet in his head. Not in this lifetime.

The next morning Max paced the length of his bedroom and considered his next step. He hadn't slept since the Balladur woman's visit the evening before. He stared into the rosy dawn. Soon the sun would rise high, kiss the rolling hills before him with its golden light and sweeten the grapes ripening on his vines.

Nikki. He simply couldn't get her out of his mind. After all, he'd been enthralled by her since she was sixteen. From the first moment, she'd captured his heart. Her youth had been the major stumbling block. Then, but not now.

Now, like a fool, he'd allowed a mere nightmare to destroy the fragile bond he and Nikki had forged during the storm.

She'd damned him for his callous behavior…and she'd moved on. Nikki, who at this very minute, according to the American tabloids, was engaged in an affair with her editor. They even had a photo of her leaving the Emergency Room in a wheelchair. The sight of her in a wheelchair had been enough to stop his heart until he had read further. Her injuries weren't serious, but there was that damned McDuff fellow—

or whatever the editor's name was—at her side. Carrying a pair of crutches. *Mon Dieu.*

More than anything, he longed to call her. But he wouldn't. She wouldn't welcome his call—certainly not now. How could he ever make her understand he'd hurt her only to protect her? Simple answer—he couldn't.

True, he'd had affairs over the years, but they'd all been brief and of little consequence. The disastrous end to his first marriage had left him cautious.

Then along came Nikki. He was so proud of her. She overcame tremendous odds and had a successful career—and could still would it if she weren't so damned stubborn. Yet he found himself excited by her choice of a new career. He'd never doubted her intelligence, just her wisdom.

And he enjoyed her deft way of handling his daughter Alexa. The frequent sight of the two blondes together, plotting and planning their day had touched him as nothing had in years. He couldn't give up loving Nikki. She was a fragile flame that warmed the depths of his heart. A flame he dared not touch, lest the heat consume them both.

For years he'd avoided the very situation in which he now found himself—in love...head over heels...poets...roses... *Mèrde.*

Was it too late? What about his mission to find out more about the mask? Closing his mother's estate had proven more complicated than he'd expected. He recalled *Madame* Dombasle's invitation. Perhaps, she could shed some light on the mask...and the dreams.

He needed answers before he saw Nikki, again. Otherwise, she'd never listen.

Max sped along the twisting, curving road, the vibration of the powerful motorcycle engine energizing him. Florimel Dombasle and her husband Pierre had retired for the summer to their country house less than an hour from his farm. What if she had no answer for him? What if he came away with more questions?

He rounded a sharp curve and eased up on the gas, slowing the old Harley. If he remembered correctly, the entrance to *Belle Rêves* was near.

Ah. Recognizing the stone entrance, he turned into the narrow lane which led to the house. He couldn't help but admire the old farmhouse.

Farmhouse, indeed... Much closer to a mansion than a farmhouse, it rambled about the golden summer landscape. From his perspective, he identified three wings, each with three stories. The flowers in the informal country garden were at their height of beauty and fragrance, their effect heady, reminding him of the summers he'd spent in Provençe as a child.

That was then, he told himself sternly. *This is now.*

He brought the Harley to a stop and parked it. Two Border Collies announced his presence, barking and circling him. Reaching down, he extended the back of his hand toward them, allowing the dogs an opportunity to become acquainted. Apparently he passed muster. The two energetic canines bounded away in search of more interesting prey.

Everywhere he looked, time seemed to have stood still. In a nearby field, he spied a donkey pulling a dog cart carrying two children. A grizzled, stooped man walked beside them, encouraging the donkey forward.

Max removed his helmet and dark glasses, shading his eyes with his hand. "*Monsieur Dombasle?*"

"*Oui.* Young Maxim?"

"*Oui. Bonjour.*" Max walked toward them. "Are they your grandchildren, *M'sieur?*"

"*Non*, Maxim, they are my great-grandchildren."

"*Bonjour*, Maxim," Florimel Dombasle called from the great stone dwelling.

Max greeted his hostess. "*Bonjour Madame, comment allez vous?* You appear younger every time I see you."

A pleased smile spread across her elegant features." I am wonderful and so delighted you are here. Please come in from the hot sun." She turned and yelled at her husband, "Bring the children in and take that animal to the barn."

M. Dambasle smiled broadly and shook his head. "We're fine out here, *Madame.*"

She smiled and turned back to Max. "Pierre—he is so crazy about his donkey. He pretends he is a peasant now he's retired. Just imagine, once he was the president of a large bank, and now he plays with the donkey."

He smiled, thinking Pierre's choice didn't seem like too bad a way to spend his retirement. "I am certain he finds farming relaxing after the stress of his old career."

"I'm sure he does too, but sometimes…well, that donkey does make that sound." She laughed. "They are quite sweet animals, but—"

"They do make that sound," he finished for her.

"*Oui.* Now let us go inside. You must tell me what has you so upset?"

He followed her into the house, grateful for the thick stone walls that kept the hot Provençal sun at bay. The comfortable furnishings, not elegant, but well-cared for, welcomed him. The tension started to leach from his shoulder muscles.

"I must say I would never have known you in your biker costume. The last time I saw you, you wore a tuxedo. I'm not sure which way I prefer you," she giggled, then touched her hair, patting it into place.

Max chuckled, glancing down at his black leather jacket and pants. "I'm afraid the tuxedo would be out of place on my old Harley. I had no idea it would still run, but Raynaud has kept it well-maintained."

"Well, no matter, you look so dashing in all that leather." She gave him a mischievous grin before adding, "And very dangerous too."

"*Merci, madame,* but I don't feel dangerous." Max waited until his hostess seated herself on the sofa, before relaxing into a well-stuffed wing-back chair. He stretched his legs out before him, the tension easing.

Two cats—one black, the other white—sprang to the back of her sofa and prowled from one end to the other, their long tails curling and swishing.

"Ah, my companions Yin and Yang have come to meet you."

"I think they do not accept my presence as easily as your dogs."

"No, as a rule they are quite arrogant." She leaned forward and asked, "Now what is wrong, Maxim? You have been on my mind ever since the party two weeks ago."

"I—uh," he stuttered, bargaining for time. "Dreams." He hesitated again. "Dreams I can't explain."

"Dreams?"

"Yes, the first occurred right after I met Nikki."

"Oh, yes. One of your loveliest models, I always thought. Go on."

He proceeded, haltingly at first, but finally got it all out, not omitting anything, including his terrible behavior after they'd made love.

The elegant woman listened to his rambling tale attentively, then leaned back. "Let me see if I understand you correctly. After making love to the woman you have desired for what—ten years—you have a bad dream, and on the basis of that dream, reject her in order to protect her?"

His heart sank, realizing for the twentieth time just how ludicrous his story sounded. He nodded. "Basically that's it, *Madame.*"

"Then it must have been a very powerful dream…and you were wise not to ignore it."

Stunned by her response, he said, "You agree with me? I should never have been so stupid. She will never trust me again."

Her expression grew sad, and she gave him a wry smile. "From what you've told me about her, she may not."

"How can I fix this? How and why does the mask seem to be mixed up in everything?"

"Consider the possibilities, Maxim. Perhaps, you and Nikki have been together in the past. It is possible that you've had contact with the mask before. From what you told me, it caught your eye and you felt compelled to buy it."

"Past lives? I'm not sure about all this. In spite of the dreams, couldn't they just be dreams?"

"Do you have the mask?" she asked, her expression brightening. "If I could but hold it, I could possibly tell you more."

"No, I gave it to Nikki—as a gift. She collects them." Puzzled, he asked, "Why would you want to hold the mask? What would that tell you, *Madame*?"

"I have a certain gift to sense things through physical contact with inanimate objects. It's called psychometry. I have assisted the authorities myself, once or twice."

"I had no idea."

"No, I don't advertise my ability. People tend to look at me differently when they learn I possess a psychic gift."

"I-I wish I had the mask. I suppose I could ask Nikki to send it to me. No doubt she'd throw it at me, given the chance."

"Do you have anything of hers, anything at all that she's touched?"

The memory of Nikki's hands playing across his body made him smile. "Only myself, *Madame*."

"La, la," she trilled. "I am not sure if my ability extends to warm bodies, Maxim."

"Will you try?"

"Give me your hands."

He extended his hands toward his mother's old friend. He felt a shock as soon as she touched him…and warmth. Energy seemed to flow from her to him and back again.

He eyed her closely. Her eyes closed; her breathing slowed. His hands grew warmer, then actually hot between her slender ones.

After several long minutes, Florimel's eyes opened. "You must go back. Your Nikki is in danger. It surrounds her. It is your mission to protect her. It always has been. You failed before. You must not fail, again."

"Danger? Tell me."

"I cannot. I simply know that it is ever-present. You must guard her well. She is your destiny."

Max shook his head. "I find this difficult. I—"

She straightened her back and jutted her chin at him. "I am not asking you to swallow anything. I am telling you what I sense."

"Yes, but—"

"Heed my warning, Maxim. You met her by chance, but you felt something right away, did you not?"

"Yes—"

"She did as well?"

"I don't know what she felt."

"You are fooling yourself."

He bit back another denial. Yin, the black cat, jumped into Max's lap, stared at him with unblinking green eyes, and yowled, before curling up into a purring ball of ebony fur.

"It seems the female has found you worthy after all, my old friend."

"That bodes well for my future?"

"I would say it does, indeed."

He gently dislodged the cat, stroking its silken fur. Yin promptly stuck her nose and tail in the air and walked away. "I offended her?"

"No, but Yin would allow you to think so."

He stood. "If what you say is true, I'll leave for the States as soon as I can get a flight out. *Merci, Madame*."

"One more thing, the danger to *you* has not passed. I fear she will cause you more grief in this life time."

Max turned, his curiosity piqued by her words. "Nikki?"

"No another woman." She rose from the sofa in one graceful motion. "Just a lingering impression. Do you know of whom I speak?"

He considered, recalling one of the dreams. "Perhaps."

"Then I wish you *Bôn Voyage*." She lifted her face to Max. He inclined his head and kissed her on each cheek.

"*Merci and au revoir, Madame*."

Maxim ran from the farmhouse, jumped on the motorcycle, turned the key and revved the engine. Nikki needed him. This time, she'd have to listen.

Thirty-six

Max threw his clothes into a flight bag. He'd have to hurry in order to reach Orly in time for his flight to New York. He rushed downstairs, taking the steps two at a time.

Before he could open the door, there was a loud pounding.

"What now?" he muttered and flung open the door. A small dapper man stood there with a smug expression on his familiar face. *Mon Dieu.*

"Inspector Parilland? It has been quite some time since I had the *pleasure* of your company." He picked up his flight bag, intending to brush past the dapper inspector. "I'm afraid I am unable to invite you in. I'm on my way to the airport."

"You must make the time, *M'sieur* Devereaux. I am not going away," the Inspector said with a satisfied smirk. He paused and glanced over his shoulder. "Nor will those who have accompanied me."

As if to verify the inspector's words, six gendarmes materialized from behind the poplars lining the walkway. He shrugged. "What do you want? Aren't you a little far from your usual jurisdiction?

"Can you not guess?" A crafty smile spread across the dapper inspector's face. "I am here to arrest you."

"Absurd. I've done nothing."

"But you are running away, again, *M'sieur*." Parilland looked down at the flight bag.

"Running away? No. I'm on my way to Orly. I have a flight to America—my home, now."

"Was it not enough to kill your wife and her lover, that you have now murdered another woman?"

"What? Just one? Surely, since I am your favorite murder suspect, I could do better than just one."

"Do not think you will escape punishment this time, *M'sieur*."

Max folded his arms across his chest. "All right. I give up. Whom have I killed now, Inspector? Isn't Provençe out of your jurisdiction? Why are you involved, at all?"

Parilland ignored Max's questions. "You had a guest only last evening, *M'sieur*. Is your memory so faulty you do not remember Mme. Balladur?"

Energy drained from Max's body. A sense of déjà vu rocked him. He stumbled backward into the nearest chair. "She is dead? How?

When?" Even in death the woman plagued him.

"I ask the questions. I have come to escort you to Paris, but I fear you will not be taking any flights to America for a very long time."

"But I don't understand why you think I— At home—there's an emergency. I must catch my flight," Max protested.

"Cuff him." Parilland order was terse, yet full of glee.

Disbelief swept over Max. Arrested? No. Nikki was in danger, and it was up to him to warn her.

The ride to Paris was a nightmare. No matter how many times Max asked for details, the inspector refused to answer.

He couldn't help but remember his first encounter with the Parilland after Solange's death. He had just identified her broken and bloodied body when the inspector entered the observation area and informed him of the other victim in her car—a man.

Max reeled from the shock; he was escorted home. His second encounter was worse. The detective actually accused him of hiring someone to tamper with the brakes on his wife's car.

Now once again, in an interrogation room, lit by one bright light, Max resisted the inspector's constant badgering.

"For the tenth time, I ask you, how long have you known Emilie Balladur?"

"For the tenth time, my answer is the same, Inspector. I met her at a party last week."

"Surely you do not expect me to believe you met this woman and had an affair with her immediately?"

"We did *not* have an affair."

"The two of you were photographed by the paparazzi, more than once. You appeared quite familiar too familiar for a new acquaintance, *n'est-ce pas?*"

"Photographs are not always what they seem. She was aggressive. I wasn't interested. I had my chauffeur take her home."

"A lovely woman, and what else, *M'sieur*? What are you hiding? Why did she come to your farm in Provençe?"

"She had the mistaken impression I was interested in her."

"Why did you invite her to your summer home if you were not interested?"

"I didn't *invite* her. She showed up at my door. You may ask my servants, if you like."

"Oh, be assured, we will. But you spent the night together?"

"No. She became angry and left." Keeping calm, more and more difficult.

"*M'sieur* Devereaux, I am very tired of your lies and excuses. You could save us all time and trouble if you would confess. What did you do to Emilie Balladur's Porsche?"

"I never touched her or her car."

Parilland swore in disgust. "Sergeant, take this miserable excuse for a man to his cell. I grow weary of his lying face."

Max stood and squared his shoulders. "You wouldn't know the truth if it bit you on the ass."

Parilland leaned into Max's personal space. "I know a liar and a murderer when I see one, *M'sieur* Devereaux, and you are both." Turning to the sergeant again, he ordered, "Take him back to his cell." The inspector spun on his heel and strode from the interrogation room.

The sergeant nudged Max toward the door. "Move along."

Hope fading fast, he tormented himself with one more question. Was Nikki safe?

Inspector Parilland paced back and forth in his office, but could not resist congratulating himself. Arresting this particular murderer was a supreme moment in his career. He had finally brought the high and mighty Maxim Devereaux to justice. At last the wife-murderer would go to prison for his crimes. Too bad the guillotine wasn't still in use. He would have loved to see Devereaux on his knees and pleading for the mercy he had never shown his wife, her lover or Emilie Balladur.

But his reverie was interrupted by his sergeant's rushing into the office.

"Inspector, you must take a look at this. Mme. Balladur left a diary. It was concealed in the lining of her luggage. That is why we did not find it before."

"So she left a diary." He shrugged and waved the officer away. "I suppose we can use it as further proof of Devereaux's involvement."

"*Non.*"

"What do you mean?" Parilland grabbed the slender volume from his sergeant.

"Read the entry for last Monday."

He quickly skimmed the entry. "*Non, non. C'est impossible.*"

For the third time Max looked at his wrist. Dammit. No watch. They'd taken everything from him. Surely they could not think he would—or could—commit suicide with his watch. His friend and the attorney for his mother's estate had been called hours ago. Still Max had heard nothing. Surely Gilbèrt would either obtain his release or convince the authorities he had nothing to do with that woman's death.

He buried his face in his hands. He should never have returned to France. He should've stayed in New York and worked out things with Nikki. Now, if *Madame* Dombasle were to be believed, Nikki was in danger…and he, helpless to save her.

The rattle of keys in his cell door snapped him out of his bout of self-pity. He looked up and met the steady gaze of the inspector. "Ready for another round, Inspector? Will it be the rubber hoses this time?"

The inspector opened the door and stepped back. "You are free to go, *M'sieur* Devereaux."

Disbelief again, rocked Max. "Free to go? Just like that?"

Parilland nodded. "With the apologies of the *Commissariat de Paris, M'sieur*."

Not waiting for Parilland to change his mind, Max stood and walked through the cell door. "I don't understand."

"Mme. Balladur left a diary. It clears you of the murder of your wife and her lover. If you did not have them killed, then there is no reason to suspect you of Mme. Balladur's death."

Max stopped. "My wife—who did kill her?"

"The brother of Mme. Balladur."

"But why? I still don't understand."

"Your wife supplanted Mme. Balladur in her lover's affections. The woman scorned, pure and simple."

"But how does that clear me of Emilie Balladur's death?"

"The accident investigator has ruled her death an accident. Excessive speed, under the influence of drugs and alcohol."

Odd, once freed of suspicion of Solange's death, he thought he'd feel a release, but no. Responsibility for her death weighed heavier than ever. His neglect had caused Solange's death. And Emilie Balladur, poor twisted creature, had been but a tool in the hands of fate.

"I see. So basically, you rushed to judgment, Inspector. You know in America I would sue you.

"Again my apologies, *M'sieur* Devereaux."

"Yeah…" Max muttered under his breath, "Screw your apologies. I have a flight to catch."

Thirty-seven

Nikki glanced at her watch.

Midnight—the witching hour. She yawned and stretched, moving her head from side to side. For over three hours, she'd slaved over the manuscript revisions. And as much as she hated admitting it, her editor had been right. Relaxing in a hot tub had done the trick. And the glass of wine hadn't hurt either.

Once she'd allowed the memories and emotions to surface, they'd overwhelmed her. But instead of crying or sinking into her usual morass of self-pity, she'd grabbed a legal pad and filled page after page. Pages of things she hadn't thought about in years.

Things her mother which would give her mother fits when she saw them in print.

Not that she'd written another Mommie Dearest, but her childhood had been bleak. Lived on the wrong side of the tracks. Never had the right clothes. Left alone while her mother worked low-paying jobs.

Before hitting her rebellious teens, she'd tried to please her mother with good grades or washing the dishes...anything. But mama could've always done it better, or so she said, loudly and frequently.

"Enough of this shit." She'd dwelt in it long enough. Hitting the print icon, she listened with satisfaction as the printer warmed up. She'd send Geoff the latest revisions first thing in the morning. Thankfully, he had given in to her demand for privacy as far as her love life went.

Not that she'd had one. On the other hand, he'd insisted she reveal the circumstances and aftermath of the date rape. She'd eventually agreed, only because she hoped it might keep another naïve girl from the same fate.

Beep. Beep. Beep.

The alarm! Triggered by the front door opening. Heart racing, she jumped up and grabbed the desk lamp.

The beeping stopped. Deactivated. Then footsteps.

"Max?"

"Yes."

She heaved a sigh of relief. Damn the man. Why in the hell hadn't he warned her, let her know he was coming?

When he walked into the sunroom, she was still debating on whether or not to pitch the lamp at his head.

"You scared me to death."

"Sorry," he said with a shrug and wearily set his luggage down. "I didn't mean to frighten you. I should've called."

"Y' think?" She set down the lamp, noting how tired he looked, the dark circles under his eyes. He needed a haircut, his dark hair curling longer on his strong neck. The unkempt curls made her want to—

Nope, not going there.

"I see you're up and around. Recovered from your injury so soon?" he asked, his tone sarcastic.

"Deep bruises, but otherwise just fine. How did you know?" she asked. "Alexa?"

"No, you're big news on the continent. Cable and the tabloids. I saw pictures of you leaving the hospital with McDougal."

"His name's McHugh."

Max shrugged, his gaze never leaving hers. "Whatever."

"Geoff was here when I stumbled and fell. My knees kept swelling so he took me to the ER. No big deal."

"You don't owe me any explanations. Whomever you see is entirely up to you."

"Not that it's any of your business, but I'm not seeing Geoff. He's my editor—period." She huffed to make certain her displeasure was apparent. "Besides, I wasn't the one partying all over Paris. Don't tell me you're tired of the jet set already."

He walked toward her. "It wasn't like that." Instinctively, she stepped back.

"I want to explain what I couldn't explain before. I—"

"I don't need your explanations. We did the wild thing. You moved on. I have too."

"You said you weren't seeing McDuff."

"That's not what I meant. I mean my book is finished, and I have a book tour starting next month."

A quick smile crossed his face. "That's wonderful." He took another step toward her.

She retreated again. "Yes, it is. But I'm afraid it means you'll have to find someone else to ride herd on Alexa. I'll store my things at Marti's while I'm on tour. After that, I'll find a new place to live." She watched...and waited for his response. He frowned; the muscle in his jaw twitched.

Good. At least it was a response.

"I see."

To her confusion, the muscle in his jaw kept twitching. No doubt afraid of losing his baby-sitter.

"Alexa still awake?"

"Maybe." She shrugged, then added, "She went up about twenty minutes ago."

"I'll go up and see her, but I'll be back. I have something important to tell you—very important."

"Not interested." She glanced around the room, anything to distract him." But her curiosity got the better of her. "Okay. What's the big deal?"

He reached out, touching her chin with one finger. Ever so gently, he directed her gaze back to his. His eyes narrowed. "It's important. Be patient."

Trembling from his touch, she watched as he turned on his heel and left the sunroom. "Jerk." She swore at his retreating back. He must have her confused with one of his flavors of the week.

She grabbed the latest pages of her manuscript and straightened them into a neat stack. She'd finish proofing them in bed. Max Devereaux could just kiss her you-know-what.

At the bottom of the stairs, she met him on his way down.

"Alexa's asleep," he said.

"I'm going to bed too. You'll just have to find someone else to discuss things with." She tried brushing past him, but he placed his arms around her. "Please?"

She pushed against his chest, but not before she caught the faint scent of his spicy after-shave. "Let me go."

He released her and stepped back. "I want—no, we must talk. We can't go on like this."

Hands on her hips, she drew back and looked into his damned green eyes, wishing with all her heart, that the sight and smell of him didn't still make her heart race and her body burn. "Let me get this straight. Now, you want to talk? If my memory serves me, we got hot and sweaty, and the next morning you said it was all a big mistake and—"

"I thought I was—"

"I'm not through. Please allow me the courtesy of finishing my own sentences."

He nodded, remaining silent, his expression blank.

"You took off to Paris, stayed for nearly a month. Played around with at least one of your fellow countrywomen. Basically had a high old time. I think that pretty much sums it up, don't you?"

"No."

"No? What little detail did I miss? The one where you ordered me to come back to the house, like a servant?"

"That's not how it was. I-I…" He faltered. "… I know you're angry. I hurt you. I was wrong."

"Wrong? You? Whatever is this world coming to?" Her breathing increased as she battled to remain calm. Damn him. "You think you can come in here say you're sorry and make it all better. What's wrong? Get dumped like I did? Did she crawl out of your bed the next morning and tell you it'd all been a terrible mistake?"

He stiffened. "I can't stand it when you act like this," he said between gritted teeth.

She lifted her shoulders in a casual shrug. "You don't have to stay."

An expression of pure bewilderment crossed his face. "This is my house."

"I don't care. You came home, unannounced, and scared the hell out of me."

"I figured you'd know since I called Alexa from Orly airport." His confused expression was quickly replaced by one of concern. "Why are you so nervous? Has something happened?"

"No." Okay, so she lied. "Don't be ridiculous. And don't change the subject. When I heard the alarm, it startled me, that's all."

"You're sure?"

"Of course." No point in whining about a bunch of creepy emails. He'd just laugh and tell her to stay offline.

"The lamp looked like a deadly weapon when I came in. Are you sure nothing's happened?" His dark brows drew together in a frown.

She sighed, then in a gesture born of nerves, glanced over her shoulder. "The townhouse has a top notch security system. We've been quite safe." She put her foot on the bottom step. "Now, if you'll excuse me, I was on my way to bed."

"There's still something I need to tell you."

"Can't it wait until morning? I'm tired. You look tired too. Actually you look like hell."

"Thank you," was his ironic reply.

She bit her bottom lip, resisting the growing urge to grin. "Did I say that out loud? I must really be tired."

A smirk played about his lips. "You're right, it can wait until morning."

When morning came, Max didn't roll out of bed until eleven, still jet-lagged, pulled on a pair of jeans and stumbled downstairs for his first cup of coffee. Neither Nikki nor Alexa was anywhere to be found. "Just like her—running away again."

Mérde. Nikki'd turned off the coffeemaker. "Bless her passive-aggressive little heart." He grabbed the coffeepot and staggered to the sink. Emptying the cold coffee into the sink, he rinsed the pot, dumped it, then refilled it again.

After a search, which took more energy than he wanted to expend, he discovered Nikki's hiding spot for the coffee beans. He poured them into the grinder, he punched the button and waited.

Seemed as if it took forever, but finally the red light went off. The aroma was almost enough to snap him out of his torpor. Almost.

It took barking his shin on an open cabinet door to wake him completely, that and spilling the newly ground coffee all over the kitchen floor. "Shit."

"Your English has really improved. You daughter will so proud." Nikki said from the doorway.

"I didn't hear you come in." He bent over and rubbed his shin, allowing his gaze to travel up her long red, spandex-clad legs to the white jacket that stopped just above her hips. "Where've you been?" he asked, disgruntled because she looked so damned appealing.

She unbuttoned her jacket and shrugged it off, tossing on the counter. "I took Alexa to her music lesson. Bitsy and her mom are picking her up afterwards for shopping. And I met Marti at tae-bo," she said, flipping her hair over her shoulder.

"Tae-bo? Is that Chinese cooking or self-defense?" he asked, hoping to lighten her mood. Her eyes narrowed. Obviously, he'd failed.

"Cute." She looked down her nose at him. "Are you going to clean up your mess, or do you expect me to do it?"

He straightened up. "I'll clean up. You're not a servant."

"Oh, really? I must have you confused with the crazy Frenchman who demanded I come home and resume my governess duties."

He ignored her bitter tone. She had every right to be angry. He didn't blame her. But what really irritated him was how she used her anger to keep him at a distance. It worked too.

He bent over, giving his shin a final rub. "We need to talk. I discovered some things in France I want to talk to you about."

"Hm, let's see now. What could it be? The franc is doing poorly against the dollar, or French women make better lovers?"

"Euros, not francs," he corrected. Give him something to throw. A wall to punch. "You are, without a doubt, the most infuriating woman I have ever known."

"*Merci*, Maxim, I do try my best to live up to your expectations." she said and turned, ready to storm from the kitchen.

"Don't go. It's important."

She whipped around, raised her chin in defiance. "Our discussion is over. I have to change."

"Dammit, Nikki. Just once will you listen to what I have to say before you flounce out of the room in a fit?"

Stopping in her tracks, she drew herself up to five-feet, ten-inches of blond fury, then raised her hands in front of her, warning him to stay back. "No. You've had your say. I'm here for Alexa, but you would be doing me a large personal favor—one last one, if you please—if you didn't speak to me ever again about our mistake."

"But—"

"Those are my terms. Take it or leave it."

"Fine."

"Fine." She took a deep breath. "And another thing."

"Tell me. I can handle it," he heard himself say, knowing it would infuriate her even more.

"I don't flounce!" Then she awarded him with a fake smile and sashayed from the room.

How could he protect her from whatever danger threatened? She wouldn't listen to reason, much less a warning. Leave it to Nikki to push his buttons with such deadly accuracy.

And all before his first cup of coffee.

PART THREE:
PAST AND PRESENT COLLIDE

Thirty-eight

February 2001

Max stared out the window of the eighty-eighth floor. February in New York City was not the city's best time of year. The night sky, black and starless, was imbued with a sense of foreboding, when he should have been elated—elated by the prospect of seeing Nikki that evening.

Tonight might be different, he thought, away from the townhouse, the scene of all their disagreements…and their single night of passion. The last six months had been a study in futility. She'd avoided him. And he'd done the same, but only because she seemed to wish it.

Stupidity—his own. Insensitivity too. The words—he couldn't take back.

It was a mistake.

Perhaps, tonight she would see him in a different light. Would she remember another night twelve years earlier—the only time they ever danced? Someday, she might even forgive him. He clenched his fists. Not damned likely.

Without warning, the door to his office opened. He turned.

Jolie, his V.P., stood with arms folded, tapping her foot. "We have a crisis."

"What now?" Everything was a crisis to Jolie.

"There's—uh, been another incident with Ian Stark and one of our models on the Monte Carlo shoot."

"Ian Stark? I gave strict orders years ago that we never use him again."

"I know," she replied evenly. "Everyone knows, but apparently Dano became ill and Terry made the substitution without first clearing it with anyone."

"Which model?" He demanded, knowing already what had happened.

"Tonia, the one from Brazil, and pretty much the same scenario as with Nikki. I don't have all the details."

"How is she?" He had a pretty good idea; memories of Nikki's emotional highs and lows after her date-rape were still fresh.

"Tonia's been treated and released. She'll be on the next flight out of Nice."

He shook his head in disgust. "How could Terry have gone against my express orders?"

"I think he was in a bad spot, needed to keep the shoot on schedule." Jolie shrugged. "Stark was available."

"I want a full explanation, but Terry will have to go."

Jolie nodded. "I'll see to it."

"Good."

"One more thing, Tonia's mother is on the line. I'm afraid she's very upset and will talk only to you. How's your Portuguese?"

"Fair." He glanced at his watch. He still had to shower and change for the Mardi Gras gala. He'd planned to have his driver pick him up, then Nikki, but Tonia's mother understandably deserved his time and attention.

He walked over to the desk and hit the intercom button. "Crystal, I'm running late. First, call Nikki and tell her I'll meet her at the gala, then call Randy and have him pick her up. I'll take a taxi. And put Mrs. Alvarado through."

He turned his attention again to Jolie. "Anything else?"

Jolie shook her head. "No, that should cover it."

The intercom buzzed, "Mrs. Alvarado for you, sir."

"*Boa noite, Alvarado de Sra. Como são? Estou tão arrependido...*"

Across town, at Marti's co-op, Nikki grabbed hold of the rice-carved post and looked over her shoulder at Alexa. "Pull tighter."

"You're going to have to suck it in, Nik," the teenager said flatly and pulled on the corset ties.

Taking a deeper breath, she groaned a breathless. "I am."

"Just not enough." The teen tugged again.

"Don't get carried away. This isn't a real corset, kiddo." Just the same Nikki held her breath, while Alexa tied the strings.

"But I wanted to do you like Mammy did Scarlett," she said with a giggle, then fell over on the bed, holding her sides.

"Very funny. I'm not sure I've ever had a nineteen inch waistline, like Scarlett."

"That's what the corset's for, silly."

She looked down at her costume. Why she'd ever decided to go as Marie Antoinette, she'd never know. To think that women actually used to parade around in such garb everyday of their lives—well, it was mind-boggling. At present, the only part of the costume she'd managed to don was the corset and lace-frilled pantaloons—hell, who knew what the French called them? At least there were no whalebone stays in the corset. No point in taking authenticity too far.

"Here, help me with the panniers."

"The what?"

"That wide contraption over on the chaise. It goes around my waist."

"Oh, that thing." Alexa jumped to her feet. "It's going to make your butt five feet wide."

"True." Nikki nodded. "I don't know how they managed to walk down a hall without knocking someone down."

Alexa grappled with the panniers, and together they managed to settle them around Nikki's waist, tying them securely.

Nikki twisted about, trying to see the clock. "What time is it? The limo is supposed to be here at eight."

"You have plenty of time. It's only seven-thirty."

"Plenty of time? I still have my makeup and hair."

"Why don't you do your face, then put on the dress? You're wearing a wig, aren't you?"

She nodded. "Good idea. Don't know why I'm so flustered. This is just another society whoop-de-do."

"Because you're the guest of honor…and maybe 'cause Daddy's your date tonight?" An impish smirk spread across the teenager's face.

"That's just for show. The chairman assumed your father would bring me and seated us next to each other on the dais. I couldn't ask her to change it without making a big deal."

"Sounds like a plan to me."

"Well, it places your father and me in a difficult position. We barely speak."

"Oh, you do better than that, but maybe you just need to get out more…" she paused before adding, "…together."

"Hmph. I think there's a little old matchmaker woman lurking inside that teenage body of yours."

Alexa placed her hands on her hips. "Well, it's pretty obvious to me. You need some help."

"Obvious to me that *someone* needs to mind her own business."

"*Moi*?" Alexa assumed an innocent expression, but the mischief danced in her clear green eyes.

"Yes, you. Just you wait. When you start bringing dates home, I'll be sure and return the favor."

"Oh, does that mean you plan on moving back to the townhouse with Daddy and me?"

Nikki's face grew warm. That was exactly how it sounded. "Well, you know what I mean."

"Uh-huh. Sure do."

"Time to change the subject, okay?"

"You're no fun."

Nikki let the comment pass and sat to do her makeup. She really couldn't blame the girl. Alexa only spoke the truth, as she saw it.

After putting the final touches on her makeup, she straightened and surveyed the effect, then turned to her fourteen-year-old assistant. "Help me with the dress?"

"Sure." Alexa rushed over to where the dress hung.

"Careful," Nikki warned. "We don't want to smear my makeup."

The girl sighed. "You're always beautiful."

"Thanks, brat." Nikki gave the teen a hug.

Together they maneuvered the blue satin ball gown over Nikki's head and settled it on her shoulders. She shook out the ruffled skirt, turning and preening in the mirror. "Is it straight in the back?"

"It's fine. Wouldn't want you to moon anyone tonight"

Nikki giggled. "No, not tonight—or any other night."

She spent another two minutes making minuscule adjustments in the garment's fit. "Now for the wig." She walked over to the wig box, removed the lid and pulled out the wig. Two-feet tall and topped with a gilded bird cage and stuffed canary, the wig was a monstrous powdered affair, with curling tendrils about the face and long sausage curls down the back.

"Tell me you're not going to wear that thing...please," Alexa begged, her face wrinkled up as if she didn't know whether to cry or laugh.

"I am."

"No-o-o," the teenager moaned in mock agony.

"Yes. I've already practiced, and I'll have you know I can balance it quite nicely."

Alexa grinned. "Cool, but ya know it'll make you a lot taller than Daddy."

"What's your point?" She raised the wig and gingerly put it on over her head, pulling and tugging until it felt secure. Finally she was wearing the full costume. She studied the effect in the mirror. A chill slithered up and down her back.

Eerie. For a moment she'd almost stepped back in time. It was as if she'd seen herself before...

"Nik?" Alexa nudged Nikki's shoulder. "Are you all right?"

"What—"

"You just had a weird expression on your face."

"I'm fine...really. What were you saying?"

"I was teasing you about being taller than daddy. Yanking your chain."

"Figures." As aggravating as Alexa could be sometimes, Nikki loved the girl without reservation. "Weren't Bitsy and her mother supposed to pick you up already? I thought you were headed to the ski slopes of Vermont."

Alexa nodded. "Mrs. Elliott called earlier. They're running late, as usual. But the trip's been canceled—not enough powder to suit Bitsy's dad, so we're stuck in the city for the weekend."

"Bummer. Your weekend's spoiled."

"It's okay. Bitsy and I can always find stuff to do."

"That's what I'm afraid—" From the other room, Nikki heard the doorman's buzz, cutting off any further comment.

"That'll be Bitsy and her mom. Gotta go. You and Daddy have fun tonight," Alexa teased, then gave Nikki a swift hug and ran from the bedroom. Her quick footsteps echoed down the hall as she ran to meet her friend.

Relieved Alexa was finally on her way, Nikki sighed. The teenager was a whirlwind, and keeping up with her was more and more difficult.

I'm too young to feel this old.

If truth be told, she dreaded the upcoming evening. She had no great desire to be honored or fêted, nor did she relish the idea of spending a night with Max at her elbow. No doubt, he felt the same. However, the Mardi Gras gala was a great opportunity to bring attention to St. Anne's shelter. That fact alone made all the aggravation worth it.

Marti Alden wandered into Nikki's bedroom. "Aren't you ready yet?"

"I still have some time. The driver's late."

"And your escort?"

"He's still at the office. He's taking a taxi to the gala."

"Bummer."

"Just as well. The less time we spend together, the less chance we'll have a disagreement."

"Well, there is that." Marti stood back and gave Nikki the onceover. "That's some regal costume you're wearing."

"It's fine, if you don't mind being squeezed to death by a corset."

Marti turned in a circle, modeling her costume. "Well, I am a Pilgrim and have no need for such fripperies."

Nikki snorted. "Lucky you."

The doorman buzzed, again, stalling further comment. "Miss Prentice's limo is here."

Nikki looked at her watch—ten minutes after eight. "I'll see you in a bit."

"Yes, your majesty. This pilgrim shall attend you anon, along with her Indian Chief spouse."

Nikki giggled. "Right."

Marti adjusted her white headdress. "I must needs repair my

appearance. My hat doth be askew."

Nikki gave one last tug on her wig and grabbed the antique mask. It made the perfect accessory to her costume, but she'd be damned if she'd risk wearing it again.

Walking out into the frigid February night, Nikki pulled her wrap tighter around her shoulders. A man of medium height stood waiting beside Max's limo, wearing the usual black wool uniform and cap, but it wasn't Randy.

"Where's Randy tonight?"

"Sorry, ma'am, I'm Donald. Randy called in sick at the last minute. The agency arranged for me to take his place."

"Fine." She shrugged, walking down the steps carefully. Tripping and falling weren't in her game plan for the night. Balancing the tall wig on her head was a difficult proposition. How did Vegas showgirls manage it anyway?

The driver proffered his hand; she took it gladly. He opened the car door for her, and she slid carefully into the leather-covered seats. Just enough room for the wig. She arranged the satin folds of her gown, making sure it wouldn't be caught in the door and then laid the mask on the seat beside her.

Before closing the door, the driver leaned into the back seat. "Are you comfortable, Miss Prentice?"

"Yes, Donald," she murmured, still occupied with arranging her costume. "Thank—"

Before she could finish, a smelly cloth was shoved over her face cutting off her breath.

She gasped and struggled. Clawed at her attacker's face. Kicked him with useless kid leather shoes. Couldn't anyone see what was happening?

"Bitch," her attacker hissed and punched her hard in the stomach.

"Nuh—uh." She struggled, more feebly now. And the blackness took her.

Thirty-nine

Aglitter with a myriad of tiny white lights, the ballroom gave Marti Alden the impression of a starlit milky way. All of New York City's famous and near-famous, the rich, both *nouveau* and old, had attended in expensive costumes that could've fed and housed all the homeless in the city for a month. For the life of her, she couldn't think of a better opportunity to exhibit excess and frivolity than at a charity gala for the homeless.

A masked sultan swathed in silk waltzed with an anorexic faux-Madonna in a pointed brassiere, while a Scarlet O'Hara, skirted in yards of crinoline, did the same with a whiskered Abe Lincoln.

The Mardi Gras Masque was in full swing, but the guest of honor hadn't yet arrived. Marti had chosen her Pilgrim attire as a not-so-subtle way of reminding all those around her that her forebears had come over on the Mayflower. She stood next to Max Devereaux, who if she weren't mistaken, was doing a slow burn. He had all the signs, the constant checking of his watch, looking toward the door, and last but not least, a muscle twitching in his sculpted jaw.

"Where's Nikki?" Max asked her through gritted teeth. "How can she be late for a gala given in her honor?" He checked his watch again. "Something's wrong. She's never late. I sent the limo for her. I thought I'd be the one who rushed in at the last moment."

Marti wondered too, since Nikki'd left before she had. "This charity means so much to her. I mean she's devoted most of the last year to the shelter."

Max finger-combed his hair in a nervous gesture.

Marti heard the exasperation and concern in his voice. Maybe it was time for her to mention Nikki's stalker. "I'm a little worried myself. I don't understand it. Nikki left before I did."

"What—?"

He was interrupted by the arrival of the flustered gala director, costumed in a low-cut black dress well known for its appearance in a certain John Singer Sargent painting. "Mr. Devereaux, it's time we proceed with the announcement and the award. Where is Nikki?" she asked, looking around and fanning her cheeks.

"We are very concerned about her. It seems she's missing. We must notify the police."

The gala organizer gasped, "Oh, of course, everyone will be so concerned, but are you sure it's a matter for the police? That will mean negative publicity."

Max's smile tightened. "I fear so," he replied between gritted teeth.

Marti watched him take his place at the podium. Unlike most of the men attending the ball, Max had eschewed a costume and instead, wore a black tuxedo. His wavy hair had been immaculately styled, except for the errant lock on the right temple. It gave him a rakish look. The man looked damned marvelous, and it was no mystery why her friend was crazy in love with him. Nothing would have kept Nikki from a ceremony in her honor, especially since Max was supposed to be her escort for the evening—no matter how she pretended otherwise. No further interruptions—she had to tell Max about the stalker.

Max motioned and the music stopped. The rumble of the crowd hushed. He spoke, "Ladies and Gentlemen, Nikki's apologies to you, since I know how important and personal this charity is to her. Something untoward has prevented her arrival here tonight. I will end my remarks and say thank you again. I know she is honored by this award." He bowed to the stunned and silent audience and left the podium.

When he rejoined her, Marti stammered, "I-I have to tell you something. Someone has been stalking Nikki...since last year."

"What? And why didn't she tell me?"

Marti shook her head. "You know how she is. She refused to take it seriously. I tried. I begged her to tell you or the police, but she said he was harmless and she could take care of herself."

"Damn. Doesn't she watch the news or read the paper?" He brushed his fingers through his hair. "I'm calling the police," he said, pulling his cell phone from his jacket, then hurried from the ballroom.

Marti picked up her long gray skirt and scurried behind him. Hopefully, it wasn't too late to find her friend.

Forty

Cold, so cold. Why was it so cold…and dark…something over her eyes? She tried to open her mouth. She couldn't. Where was she?

She shook her head in an attempt to clear the haze. Slowly, a few details returned. The charity gala…Max sent the limo for her. She stepped into the limo and…

No.

Full-blown panic reared up and threatened to overwhelm her.

Take a deep breath.

At least, she was still alive. She lay on her side, uncomfortable on a cold metallic surface. Rubbing her face against it, she attempted to dislodge the blindfold. If she could just free up a corner—

A metallic screech. Nikki froze, feigning sleep. Then came the sound of furtive steps approaching.

"I see you finally decided to awake up." The voice, male and soft, possessed an underlying harshness.

She refused to move or acknowledge his presence.

"You are my guest now," the stilted voice informed her. "You ignored me, and I don't like being ignored. You see the error of your ways? You'll never ignore again. No one will come to your rescue. I had hoped to make you comfortable, but you'll have to earn your privileges."

Earn her privileges? She shuddered, but listened to her captor's pacing about the room. Who was he? Was this the stalker who'd hounded her for the last year? Why hadn't she paid more attention to his threats? Or was he some other nutcase? Where was she? Oh, God, how would she ever get through this? A woman's worst nightmare—but her reality. Her body betrayed her by an uncontrollable shudder.

Focus. Her life depended on staying calm. She concentrated on absorbing every sound and smell, the cadence and affected formality of his speech while he lectured her.

"I leave you now to consider your fate. Never fear, for I shall return to favor you with my caresses."

He stroked her bare arm, his hand cold and sweaty. She couldn't help it; she jerked away from his touch. A wave of nausea struck. Why did this all seem so familiar?

"Are you cold, my dear, or do I arouse you?" He emitted a soft purring growl, then fondled her neck.

She trembled. He was mere inches from her and reeked of strong cologne. It failed miserably. The combination of his body odor and cologne... Another wave of nausea, hit her. She swallowed dryly. The thought of his doing more...

The waiting grew more unbearable with each passing second. But instead of groping her further, he removed his hand from her neck. His footsteps retreated. Then the door—it opened and closed.

Her relief at his departure was brief. He would return and do whatever he wanted, whenever he wanted.

She twisted and pulled against the cords binding her until her wrists were raw and burned like hell. Whoever he was, he'd bound her with expertise; her efforts were useless. Like a fool, she'd considered her stalker a pain in the butt and nothing more. If only she'd told Max.

Yet there was something eerily familiar about everything.

And his voice? Something in his affected manner of speech tugged at her memory. She replayed his words again and again in her mind, but couldn't pinpoint the familiarity. Hell, it didn't make any difference who he was. He had her.

She wanted to kick and scream and dissolve in great shaking sobs, but resisted. Crying would solve nothing. If she were going to survive, she had to stay focused. And she *would* survive.

Nikki awakened with a jump, at first confused and unable to move. But reality rushed back. She must've slept a little. Still exhausted by her ordeal, her fear had eased. Had anyone missed her? Was anyone looking for her? Of course, someone would be. She was supposed to be given an award that night, for Pete's sake. What time was it, anyway?

Had her captor made ransom demands? Somehow, she doubted it. He wasn't after money. He was after her and always had been. Now he'd won his game of persistence and intimidation with one grand gesture. Whoever he was, he'd planned it all quite well. She was his to command, until she could find a way to escape.

Everyone has a weakness. I'm his. Play on that.

She shivered. She couldn't ever remember being so cold, not even on the streets. As far as she could tell she was still wearing her costume. Must've lost the wig in the struggle. She doubted she'd be returning it to the costumers in the morning as she'd promised. Maybe they made allowances for being kidnapped. Perhaps, they would even give her a discount. The overwhelming need to cry and scream and laugh flooded through her. Instead she kicked the wall behind her.

Concrete. Was she in a basement?

A hot flash of warmth swept over her. First she'd been freezing, now she was burning up. Was she sick? How much time had passed?

After what seemed like hours, she heard the harsh metal scrape of the door opening. Soft footsteps approached her. The familiar voice asked, "Now what is it, my dear? Oh, I see you can't speak can you. Well, let's see if I can guess what you need. Potty break?" he asked with an insinuating whine.

Nikki shook her head furiously.

"How about a change of clothes then?" Her captor broke into a wheezing laugh. "I'm afraid your lovely costume has seen better days."

Again she shook her head. She wasn't about to give him an excuse to touch her, but unable to control her reaction to the idea, she shivered again.

"Oh, we're cold, are we? I suppose," he paused, "I could do something about that." He ran his hand down her cheek. She recoiled.

"Touchy, aren't we?" he said with an evil chuckle. "But then you always were."

His footsteps faded and she almost wept in relief. Once again he had not harmed her.

But this time the door didn't open and close.

Not again, please go away. Why did he keep tormenting her? Who was he?

"There, there my pretty," he said in what was an excellent imitation of the Wicked Witch of the West. He covered her with something heavy and scratchy. "Wouldn't want my little one to catch her death now, would I?"

Forty-one

Max paced back and forth in his study. "Detective Halloran, How long is this going to take?"

The Central Park precinct detective looked up from his note pad and shrugged. "Hard to say. We don't know much, except your usual driver, uh—" Halloran glanced down at his notes. "—Randy Jackson was about to pick up Miss Prentice when he was stopped and accosted by a man asking for directions. The perpetrator knocked your driver unconscious."

"Is Randy going to be all right?"

Halloran nodded, "Good thing too. He was able to give us a description of the suspect, so we're one step ahead of the game." He checked his note pad again. "Middle-aged man of medium height and build, wearing a billed cap pulled down, covering most of his face."

Exasperated, Max threw up his hands. "A middle-aged man of medium height? There must be a million men fitting that description in this city alone." He shook his head. "I can't believe this. There has to be something else I can do."

"You wait. That's all you can do. We need you to stay by the telephone, in case there's a ransom demand."

"I have waited. It's been two hours. There's been nothing."

"It's early yet."

A uniformed officer tapped at the door. "I wanted to let you know the FBI will be here shortly. I just heard it over the radio."

Detective Halloran frowned. "Great," he said, although 'great' wasn't what his tone conveyed.

Fine, so the detective wasn't pleased, but Max didn't care. He'd notified the FBI himself. "What about my daughter?"

"She should be here any minute. We dispatched a patrol car and female officer to pick her up at the Elliotts' residence."

"Thank you. I'll feel better when she's home."

Halloran cocked his head toward the door. "If I'm not mistaken, they've just pulled up."

Max stood and rushed past the detective and the patrolman in the hall. The sight of his daughter as she ran up the front steps sent a rush of relief surging through him.. At least one of his charges was where she was supposed to be.

"Daddy? What's happened? Are you all right?" Panic was written over his daughter's face.

"Let's go inside." He put his arm around his daughter, pulling her close. "Nikki's been kidnapped."

"No!" Alexa cried, an expression of horror crossing her young face.

"She never made it to the gala. Someone knocked out the limo driver and took her. That's all we know. But the police and the FBI—they'll find her."

Alexa looked down at the floor, then back at him. She chewed her lip, never a good sign in his daughter.

"What?"

"Think it was the guy who sent her the nasty emails?"

"You knew about him?" *Mèrde*. Had everyone known Nikki was being stalked, except he?

Alexa nodded. "Uh huh. He used to send her flowers too. She always threw them in the trash." Her eyes brightened with unshed tears. "But she said it wasn't anything to worry about. And…"

"What?" Did his daughter have the key to Nikki's disappearance? "Please, go on. Anything you can tell us might help find her."

"And she said whatever I did, not to bother you about it. I'm sorry. I should've said something. This is my fault." Tears welled in his daughter's eyes.

"No." He reined in the fear and disbelief. Putting his fist through a wall wouldn't help anyone. Instead he replied in the calmest tone he could manage. "No one's blaming you, but she was wrong."

"I-I'm sorry, Daddy," she said, sniffing. "I should've told you."

Max gathered his daughter into his arms. "It'll be all right. There's no way you could've known this would happen. We're doing everything we can to find her. Do you remember anything else that might help the authorities?"

"No, just the emails and flowers." Alexa paused, chewing her bottom lip. "Well—uh, there was this guard at the shelter. He always acted weird around her."

"Weird, how?" Det. Halloran asked, stepping up and taking over the interrogation.

"Oh, you know, he always called her 'Nikki' and grinned like a real dork whenever she was around."

"Can you describe him, Miss Devereaux?" the detective asked, leading them back to the study.

Max appreciated the detective's gentle manner with his daughter. "Tell him whatever you know."

"Sure, he was a big guy, red hair." She sat on the leather sofa, her posture, school-girl proper, with her hands folded.

"How old?"

"Well, older," Alexa frowned, then glanced at Max with a sheepish grin. "But not as old as my Dad. Over thirty, maybe."

Had not the situation been so dire, Max would've been amused.

"All right, we'll check him out. Shouldn't be too difficult. Which shelter?"

"St. Anne's. I have the number in my cell phone memory." Alexa pulled a bright red cell phone from her purse, punched a couple of buttons. "Here it is." She read the number to the detective who recorded it on his note pad, then looked back at Max.

"He doesn't fit the description, and stalkers usually work alone, but we'll check him out. Can't afford to leave any loose ends. You never know."

"Thank you, Detective. We'll cooperate. Whatever you need, it's yours." Max sat with a weary slump, then sprang up again too anxious to sit idly by, while Nikki was in the clutches of some pervert.

"I got a few more questions, if you don't mind, Mr. Devereaux." Halloran arched an eyebrow in Alexa's direction.

He took the hint. "Alexa, why don't you run upstairs and get ready for bed? There's no point in your staying up. I'll let you know if they find her."

Alexa pouted. "But it's early. I'm not tired."

Max sighed. "Please…"

After a token, huff, she relented as he'd known she would. "Oh, all right. I guess I'd better go to bed. Good night, Detective."

"G'night, miss."

"'Night Daddy." She leaned over and kissed his cheek. "Don't worry. The police will find her."

Without another word, she turned and left the room, leaving Max alone with the detective. His daughter's grownup reassurance left him a little off balance. His daughter's reactions were so grown-up. Imagine, her trying to reassure him instead of the other way around.

"Nice young lady. Not like some that age."

"Thank you. She's all I have." Max drummed his fingers on the desk, waiting for the inevitable questions.

He didn't have long to wait. Halloran plunged right in.

"What's the exact nature of your relationship with Miss Prentice?"

"Nikki's a friend of the family. She lived with my mother for several years."

"And now, she lives with you?"

Max shook his head. "No. She lived here last summer…as my daughter's companion."

"Not *your* companion?"

"I don't see what bearing my relationship with Nikki has on her disappearance."

"We gotta investigate every angle."

Instead of raising his voice, Max lowered it, mustering his self-control. "If you must know, I care deeply for Nikki, but we haven't worked it out." He stood placing his hands flat on the desk. "I'm the one who called the police." Dammit. He knew what came next.

"I understand your wife died under mysterious circumstances."

"In an automobile accident. You're wasting valuable time dragging up my personal tragedies. My wife's been dead for twelve years."

"Perhaps I am. But the report here says, someone tampered with the brakes."

"That's true, but I assure you it wasn't I."

"Seems like the French authorities thought it was."

"They did." Max took a deep breath."Surely your report tells you I've been cleared of her death."

Halloran flipped a page on his notepad and gave a sheepish grin. "Yeah, matter of fact it does." He closed his notepad and returned it to his jacket pocket.

The patrolman knocked again. "Feds are here."

A woman's voice, familiar and low-pitched, announced from the hall. "I know my way to the study, Officer."

Forty-two

A moment later, Mario's mother, FBI Agent Lorena Judson, glided into Max's view. He rose and greeted her, "I'm so glad it's you."

"Luck of the draw, I guess," she said, displaying a rueful smile. "Sorry to see you again under these circumstances." She flashed her identification for the detective's benefit. "FBI, Supervisory Special Agent Judson."

Halloran looked first at Lorena, then at Max. "Guess you two know each other?"

"Obviously, Detective." Lorena's tone would have withered a pine tree. "Is the wire tap in place?"

"Yes, SSA Judson."

She acknowledged him with a nod. "There will be three agents in the house at all times. I don't want to risk any further incidents. While we wait, I want you to tell me everything you know."

Walking over to a well-stuffed chair, she sat, crossing her legs at the ankle.

Halloran pulled out his notepad, beginning, "Well, first of all—"

Lorena turned and nailed him with a stare. "You may turn over all your notes, but I want Mr. Devereaux's impressions first. I should mention I'm a profiler, and I'll interview him, his daughter, and Nikki's friend…" she paused, looking down at her Palm Pilot, "…Martha Alden, at length."

"Typical. Thought the FBI had to be called in on a case," Halloran muttered, huffing into his thick mustache.

"This is a special case because of the high profile nature of the victim and the family's request. Get over it."

"Yes, Ma'am. Shall I polish your shoes, when we're through?"

Max watched the territorial skirmish. If the situation had been different, he might've been amused. This was a side of the woman he hadn't seen.

She ignored Halloran's jibe and turned instead to Max. "Now tell me everything you know. Don't leave out anything, no matter how trivial." She pulled a tiny recorder from her shoulder bag. "I'll be recording the interview."

He nodded and returned to his seat behind the desk. "I didn't know anything about this stalker until Nikki went missing. Her friend Marti told me about him. Then I discovered my daughter knew about him too."

"Tell me about Nikki's background. I gather she spent some time on the streets. There could be a link from her past."

Max shrugged. "I suppose it's possible, but she was only on the streets for two or three months. We met shortly after that."

"Why did she run away from home?"

"Didn't get along with her mother. Teenage rebellion."

"Has she maintained any relationships she might've formed on the streets?"

"No." He ran his hand back through his hair. "Wait. Maybe someone from the shelter. She and my daughter do volunteer work there, so I guess it's possible."

"All right. I'll ask Alexa about that."

"My daughter also mentioned emails and flowers. In fact, I saw her throwing away some roses, once. I didn't question her, since she wasn't forthcoming when I commented on them."

"You thought they were from an admirer?"

"Something like that."

"Were you jealous?"

He hesitated, then admitted, "A bit."

"Was she seeing anyone regularly?"

"Not to my knowledge. Nikki is a very private person, and I haven't been around much lately. I've been back and forth to the continent for the last several months, settling the last of my mother's estate."

"Anyone she might've had regular contact with? A newsboy, or delivery person—anyone who made her uncomfortable?"

"She didn't mention anyone. There's her editor, of course."

"Her editor?"

"Geoffrey McHugh. Rafferty's Publications. But they got on well enough."

"Did she ever give any indication he was interested in her?"

Max shrugged. "Nothing she said, but he was interested."

"Really?"

"Definitely."

"And his interest bothered you?"

"Yes."

Alexa eased from her room and tiptoed down the stairs. She sat on the bottom step and listened. The FBI had invaded her home. The phones were bugged. And Mario's mother was installed in the study with her father, and three really cute agents were arguing in the kitchen. She tried to make herself small…invisible would've been better.

Carrying a laptop computer under his arm, a third agent walked by declaring, "We should've brought a computer expert. Mrs. Alden just told me the stalker had sent her some threatening emails."

"Exactly," the second agreed, "we need someone who can access her Internet account and break into her personal files."

"No, that'll take too much time," the third argued. "Let's try it ourselves, first."

"I can do it," Alexa said.

In unison, their heads turned toward her. "You can?"

"It's a piece of cake." Alexa was puzzled. Had these big, smart FBI guys never seen a computer? "It's really simple. Nikki set up a screen name for me on her account. Her password is stored, so you don't have to know it to get in."

"And you've done this before?"

"No, of course not. I've only accessed my files under my screen name, but I figure this is sort of an emergency, right guys?"

"Kid has a point," the red-haired agent agreed.

"Lead on, little Birkoff," the blond agent gestured.

Alexa rolled her eyes. "Birkoff? Who's that?"

"Never mind," the blond replied. "You don't get to stay up that late."

"How do you know how late I stay up?"

"Well, you shouldn't stay up that late," he amended. "By the way, I'm Agent Samuels. The carrot top is Agent Russell, and the tall fellow with no sense of humor whatsoever is Agent Eastwood."

"Eastwood?" Alexa giggled. Maybe she hadn't heard right.

"Yeah, that's right, his name is Clint "make my day" Eastwood."

"I bet you get teased a lot, don't you Agent Eastwood?"

Agent Eastwood stood taller, if possible, straightening his very broad shoulders, and frowned. "We're wasting time. Young lady, if you can get into that computer, do it. Now."

"Y-yes, sir." Talk about no sense of humor.

Alexa walked into the sunroom, followed by the three agents. She pulled out the chair and sat in front of the computer. A double-click and another click and she was in. "It's all yours." She pushed the chair back and stood. "Just click on the files icon to get to her old emails."

Agent Samuels sat and followed Alexa's instructions. "Didn't she ever delete anything?" There's six months of sh—uh, email in here."

She shrugged and smiled. "Have fun, guys. I'm going to check on my dad."

As she headed toward the study, it occurred to her what an awful person she was. Flirting with the FBI agents when Nikki was in danger, maybe even… No. Nikki had to be okay. The FBI would find her.

Forty-three

He'd designed the room with her in mind—an eight foot square, concrete block-walled cellar. It was perfect for stashing away the woman of his dreams.

He watched Nikki on the hidden camera and smiled to himself. The dear girl had no idea she was being watched. He'd never forgotten his early experience with her. Her rejection had irritated him beyond belief. He would've had her had not someone interfered, and now he knew where that someone was. He'd take care of him later.

Under Lorena's endless interrogation, Max felt like a virus under the microscope of her discerning eye. It was obvious she had no intention of going easy on him. Not that he wanted her to, but it took all his self-control not to cringe as her questions grew more and more personal.

"I understand there was an unfortunate incident with a photographer early in Nikki's career?"

"Yes."

"I imagine it was very painful for her."

"I suppose."

"You never discussed it with her?"

"I told you. She's a very private person. She dealt with it the only way she knew how."

"How was that?"

"I'm not a psychologist, but I would say she was in denial. Afterwards, she simply refused to admit she was upset. Refused to discuss it. Wouldn't see a therapist."

"What about her relationships with men, after that?"

"As for other men, I can't say." Although he was positive she'd formed no other attachments. He shook his head. "My mother tried to comfort her, but Nikki refused to be comforted. She didn't want anyone to know."

"But people found out—before she wrote about it?"

"Yes, the photographer bragged to everyone."

"She was humiliated?"

"Wouldn't you be? But she was strong. She held her head up high and ignored the gossip."

"So this photographer—uh, Ian Stark, got away with date raping a minor."

He sucked in a deep breath, then let it out. "Not exactly."

The agent's gaze narrowed as she looked at him. "What happened?"

Max cleared his throat. "He was advised to leave the country and not return."

"And he did? Just like that?" she asked, her expression skeptical. "Who advised him?"

"I did."

A smile played about Lorena's lips. "After you beat the hell out of him?"

"Yes."

Lorena stopped the recording. "Off the record, I'm glad you did," she said with a smile and turned toward the silent detective. "Any problem with that, Detective?"

"Son of a bitch got what he deserved. But why didn't she report it?" Halloran asked.

"Because he used a drug on her." Max's voice grew harsh with emotion. "She couldn't remember anything, except waking up in bed with him. As recently as yesterday, the bastard was in Monaco and up to his old tricks."

Halloran nodded. "We'll check him out anyway. Make sure he didn't hop on a plane and come back to the States for a little personal revenge."

"Daddy? Is everything okay?" Alexa asked.

Max swallowed. He'd been so caught up in reliving the horrible incident he'd not seen his daughter standing in the doorway.

"Everything's fine."

Alexa glanced over at Lorena, giving her a diffident smile. "Hi, Mrs. Judson."

"I'm glad to see you again, Alexa," Lorena said, offering the girl a genuine smile. "If you don't mind, I'd like to interview your daughter, now—since she's here."

"Of course, anything," he agreed. No telling how much information his daughter had unknowingly stowed away.

"I'd like to talk to her alone, with your permission, of course. It might be less distracting."

He glanced at his daughter, judging her response.

Alexa nodded. "It's okay, Daddy. I don't mind."

Max stood and walked to the door. "Coming?" he asked Halloran.

"Yeah, sure."

The last thing Max heard before he shut the study door was Lorena's soft voice. "Now tell me about the flowers and emails—the ones that upset Nikki."

Nikki. He'd been quite angry, when she'd rejected him, then disappeared. For a long time he'd wondered where she'd gone and what had happened to her. He'd even feared that she'd fallen victim to foul play. He couldn't keep from laughing aloud at the concern he'd actually felt for her then.

Imagine his surprise, when six months later he'd seen her photograph on a magazine cover, floating toward the gutter. He'd rushed after it, but lost it when it slipped from his reach down the storm drain. His real search for her had begun then, but she'd remained as elusive as she'd always been. Perhaps, if he'd spent more time at home watching TV, he would've seen her on Entertainment Tonight or on E!, but the very nature of his calling demanded he keep a close eye on business. It wasn't until he'd built his nest egg and retired that he'd possessed the time to search in earnest. He'd purchased a computer and started surfing the 'Net. He'd even started a new enterprise—a porno web site—his own version of a 401K.

If only he'd bought the computer years earlier. Then it might not have taken him so long to find her. And there she was: Nikki, a supermodel and darling of all the photographers. He'd even found multiple web sites devoted to her. Hmm. All he ever wanted to know about his darling. He knew about her glitzy New York apartment and her cottage on Martha's Vineyard.

Yes, indeed, he loved the Internet, but the more he'd read about her glamorous life, the more resentful he'd become. Never once looked back. Washed her hands of all her old friends. It didn't matter to him that she volunteered at a homeless shelter. Who gave a shit about those dregs, anyway?

So, society had thought they would honor darling Nikki for her philanthropy. Well, he'd certainly spoiled their little party when he snared their guest of honor.

Again he laughed. If they could only see her now, all trussed up like a Thanksgiving turkey. She didn't look so super. Now she was his…forever.

Time to torment her again. He couldn't remember when he'd had such fun. He scooted away from the video screen and stood to get a better look. Dear girl appeared to have settled down for a little nap.

Forty-four

Lorena allowed the girl a moment to settle comfortably on the sofa. "Now tell me about the flowers and emails Nikki received—the ones that upset her."

"Where do you want me to start? I already told the detective all I know."

"I know, but you're so close to Nikki, and anything, however small, might be useful."

"Okay." The teenager nodded, twisting her mouth to one side, "Well—uh, I know about the emails because one day, Nikki showed me her email list and told me to delete anything that wasn't from any of my friends. She said if I didn't know the screen name, to delete 'em."

"And did you?"

She watched, making mental notes of Alexa's body language. The girl looked down at her hands, then directed her gaze to Lorena. Wrinkling her nose, the girl admitted, "Uh, one time I opened a couple of them, and they had links to some porno sites. Majorly gross, so I deleted them after that."

"I see." Lorena looked down at her PDA and hid her smile. "Is Nikki involved with your father?"

"No."

"You might not know, if they were discreet."

"Oh, I'd know. "

"How?"

"I'd just know. I mean, Nikki would be happy and not get mad every time I mention Daddy's name."

"Could she be dating someone else?"

Alexa shrugged. "I don't think so. She's been real busy, traveling all over the country promoting her book."

Why someone as lovely as Nikki wasn't dating anyone? Why had Nikki agreed to spend last summer as a teenager's companion? Lorena was pretty certain she knew the reason—Max. She shifted uncomfortably. She'd gone beyond what she needed to know for the case and was on the verge of prying for her own curiosity.

"All right, I want you to think back. Whenever the two of you were doing things together, was there anyone who bothered or harassed her in anyway?"

Alexa gave a huge sigh. "It's hard to say. I mean, almost everybody, especially men, wanted to talk to her. I already told the detective about the guard at the shelter. He always acted like he knew her."

"What did Nikki say about him?"

"Just that she didn't know him, and people acting like that was the price of being famous."

"Was there anyone else, in the last year or so?"

Alexa twisted about in her chair, appearing to consider the question.

"Anyone, no matter how insignificant?"

"There was this geeky guy who tried to get her phone number in the deli one day."

"Describe him."

"Uh, kind of medium tall, pudgy around the waist." Alexa chewed her lip, concentrating. "Brown hair, combed over his bald spot." She shook her head. "That's all I remember."

"What did he say to her?"

"I wasn't close enough to hear, but he gave Nikki a business card."

Lorena slowed her breathing. Keep calm. "Remember what she did with it?"

"Stuck it in her purse."

"Do you remember which one?"

"Uh, let's see. It was toward the end of summer. Hot weather. Hmm," Alexa chewed on her lip again, then smiled. "Yes, it was a big shoulder bag-linen or something like that."

"Do you know where she keeps it?"

"I do if she left it behind when she moved to Marti's." She jumped up. "I'll be right back."

Alexa ran from the room. In less than two minutes, the girl returned, triumphantly carrying the bag in question. Lorena took it from Alexa's outstretched hands.

"I'm afraid to look," Alexa said.

"Well, it's a very long shot, but maybe it's still there." Lorena reached into the depths of the purse and felt around the bottom. She pulled out three pennies, an emery board, an unused tissue...and a crumpled business card. She offered a quick, silent prayer before unfolding it. "MEGALOMANIA COMPUTERS, Stuart Hall President." The card included his address, phone and fax numbers, and an email address. "How convenient."

Lorena jumped up and walked into the hall. "Agent Eastwood," she called, tapping her foot.

The unfortunately-named agent sauntered into the hall. "Yes, ma'am."

"Send a team around to roust this guy." She handed Agent

Eastwood the card. "He tried to pick up Nikki in a deli."

"Sure thing, ma'am." Eastwood turned on his heel, pulling the cell phone from his pocket, and set the wheels in motion.

Not for the first time, Lorena watched the agent's confident strut, while he walked back to the kitchen. What had Eastwood's mother been thinking? Naming her son Clint. She must've been quite a fan. Poor guy. He obviously felt he had something to prove, and she fully intended to enjoy the spectacle.

At Max's townhouse, Marti Alden paced up and down the hall and tried not to stumble over various and sundry police officers and FBI agents. She'd abandoned her white pilgrim's cap, but still wore the rest of the costume. With her husband Tom she'd hurried to the townhouse, mainly for moral support and because she couldn't think of anywhere else she'd rather be. Going home was out of the question. No way could she sit idly by while her best friend was missing. She shivered at the thoughts whirling through her mind. Just let her be alive, that was all she asked.

The FBI wanted to talk to her. If it were anyone but Nikki, Marti acknowledged she might've been excited about the prospect of being interrogated by one of the hunky agents in the kitchen. But no, it was the female agent who wanted to talk to her. Not that she minded being interrogated by Agent Judson, it was just that Nikki...

Oh, God, what if...

The study door opened; Alexa came out. "Hi, Mrs. Alden." Alexa gave Marti a wan smile.

"Hey sweetie, are you okay?" She hugged the teenager, surprised that Alexa seemed to have grown at least three inches in last year.

"I guess so," she sniffed. "But I'm so worried about her."

"Me too, hon. Me too."

A low well-modulated voice spoke, "Mrs. Alden?"

Marti looked up. Agent Judson was of medium height, a trim figure, with shiny dark hair cut short in a style that was attractive and no-nonsense at the same time. Intelligent dark brown eyes, worried eyes, gazed back at her. "Yes, I'm Marti Alden."

"Agent Judson." The woman stood back, motioning for Marti to enter the study ahead of her. "I'm sorry we have to meet under such circumstances."

"Any leads?" Marti couldn't keep from asking. She walked into the study and sank down on the sofa.

"It's early yet, I'm afraid."

Judson's tone of voice was meant to be soothing, but as far as Marti was concerned, it wasn't working. She watched as the agent took the chair opposite and turned on her recorder.

"I'll be recording our interview."

Marti nodded. "I understand."

"How long have you known Nikki?"

Marti grinned, remembering how she'd met Nikki. "Ten years."

"You've been close to her since then?"

"Yes."

"Then you would know if she were involved with someone?"

"Yes."

"Do you have any idea who her stalker might be?"

"Some nut case?" She glanced around the room. Cigarettes? Damn she could really use one right now.

"True, but is there anyone you know in her life who might fit that description?"

"No. Nikki always made it a point not to hang around with nut cases," she replied unable to keep the sarcasm from her voice.

Agent Judson shot Marti a sour expression.

"What about her editor? Have you ever met him?"

Marti shook her head. "No."

"Has she ever said anything about him?"

"Just that he was here one afternoon and Max acted like a junk yard dog when the two of them met."

"Junk yard dog?" Agent Judson raised an eyebrow.

"You know, territorial."

"And McHugh's response?"

"From the way Nikki described it to me, her editor made a strategic retreat. Discretion being the better part of valor, I guess."

"He wasn't angry?"

"Didn't sound like it."

The agent sighed. "Anyone else? For example, was there anyone who annoyed her or seemed to hang around on the periphery?"

"I can't think of anyone." Marti racked her brain. Her friend's life might depend on anything she could remember. "For the last year, she kept a very low profile, you know, trying to stay pretty much out of the public eye until her book was finished. But then the hype took off. She did some talk shows—Leno and Letterman. Then E! did a one-hour special on her career and the book. At one point, there was even talk of a Lifetime movie."

"Weren't there some episodes of stalking before she did publicity for the book?"

"Sure. First one happened at the beach house at Martha's Vineyard."

"That was when?"

"May last year."

"So it hasn't been a full year?"

"No."

"Tell me about it."

"Well, she'd just come back from a walk on the beach and found a note on the table. Outside on the deck, I mean."

"What did it say?"

"Oh, uh—something like, 'you don't need him.'

"And the 'him' it referred to was?"

Marti delayed answering. "Probably Max."

"Mr. Devereaux, I see." Agent Judson paused and made an entry on her PDA. "Why do you think it referred to Mr. Devereaux?"

"Well, he'd just left in a huff. He and Nikki—uh, had a disagreement on the beach."

"About?"

"See here. I don't think whatever they argued about has anything to do with her disappearance, unless you think he has her stashed away in the cellar or something."

"But the stalker incidents date from that initial note?"

"Yes, and there was a rose attached to the note too—and there weren't any rose bushes at the beach house." Marti's indignation grew. The smart and well-dressed FBI agent was ready to pin this on Max.

"Tell me more about Nikki's relationship with Max."

"You're barking up the wrong tree, Agent." Marti couldn't resist a calculating dig. "Or maybe you're prying into their relationship for reasons of your own."

The usually self-possessed agent had the grace to blush. Marti was glad she'd managed to disturb the agent's equanimity.

"My involvement in Nikki's disappearance is purely professional. It's my job to find her, and in order to accomplish that, I sometimes ask difficult questions. So, you and I have the same objective. Let's try to remember that. Truce?"

It was Marti's turn to blush. "Sorry, guess I'm a little protective of Nikki."

"A *little*?"

Marti shrugged. "Okay, a lot."

"What other episodes can you tell me about?"

"I know that the stalker sent her flowers, always roses, several times. I can't remember when, but just often enough to get on her nerves."

"Why didn't she report it?"

"She preferred to ignore him. Didn't take him seriously. Honestly, I tried—but she wouldn't listen."

"When did the emails start?"

"Within a couple of weeks after she bought the computer. I mean, if I didn't know better, I'd think he was watching her when she bought it. Or maybe he saw it delivered."

Lorena nodded. "It's possible." She made more notes on her PDA. "Thank you."

Marti rose and straightened her skirts. "You have to find her."

"We're doing our best."

Okay, but your best better be good enough. Surely with the FBI on the case, her friend would be found before it was too late. Oh, God.

Forty-five

From the sunroom off the kitchen, Max watched the sky lighten and turn the palest pink at the horizon, heralding dawn. Nikki had been missing for over eight hours. He watched her friends, glad for their company. Three hours earlier, he'd had banished Alexa upstairs to bed. She had been drooping with fatigue after her interview with Lorena. Tom Alden had not slept. He sat drinking coffee, the fingers of his left hand beating a tattoo on the arm of the sofa. Marti had finally given up and lay in a fitful sleep, her head resting in Tom's lap. From his doting expression, whenever he gazed down at his wife, the man adored her.

"Max, I'm so sorry this happened," Lorena said, walking toward the coffee maker.

He looked up, surprised by her soft tone. For the first time, he voiced his worst fear, "What are the chances she's still alive?"

Lorena grimaced. "It's difficult to say. The quicker we discover who he is, the better. Somehow this doesn't feel like a traditional stalking. There's been no physical contact, no disappointed suitors. As a rule, a stalker doesn't kidnap his victim. Typically, he or she harasses them, showing up everywhere, and eventually escalates to physical harm…or worse. I feel like I've missed some detail that would fit it neatly into one category or another."

"Then, is it just a kidnapping?" Max shrugged.

"No. As yet there'd been no demand for ransom. No communication at all. Flowers and harassing emails fit a stalker, but the kidnapping doesn't."

"Excuse me, Agent Judson." Agent Samuels looked up from Nikki's computer.

"Yes, what is it?"

"We have a lead on the emails." With those few words, hope flared in Max's chest.

Samuels continued. "We've managed to trace his ISP. We should have his name quite soon."

"Assuming, and there's no reason not to, that the kidnapper sent the emails. Keep me informed, Mick."

Samuels nodded. "Yes, ma'am."

Impatient, Max paced around the room.

Two of the three FBI agents were huddled over Nikki's computer, while the third argued with the internet company representative. "You are impeding an official FBI investigation. A young woman has been kidnapped and you're jerking me around about confidentiality." He paused, listening. "You'll have your subpoena any minute. They should be knocking on your door right now." Another pause. "Right. Then call me back with the name and address."

Agent Samuels turned to Max. "God, I detest computer geeks."

"Do you think it'll take long?" Max asked, looking from Agent Samuels to Lorena.

"Not once we have his address, presuming it's his real address," she replied, taking a sip of coffee. "It'll be a start, if it's not a false lead."

"I hope so." Max said, collapsing into his chair. Waiting made him feel powerless. "Nikki's... I..."

"Did you ever tell her?" she asked, her tone gentle.

Max shoved his hands in his pockets. "No."

"Just a word of advice, the next time you have a chance, *tell her*."

"If there is a next time."

It had taken him two months of back-breaking labor to prepare Nikki's special accommodations. The concrete block basement of his new house was perfect. The metal door had almost been more than he could install by himself, but driven by the desire to have everything just right for his guest, he'd managed.

It had taken almost as long to research the drug he planned using on his lovely visitor. Once he'd decided, it had been a simple matter to obtain it. He'd simply called in a few favors...carefully, because he didn't want to be connected with the purchase. In fact, he'd dispatched the only contact who could trace it to him. The dosage was tricky. Too much and Nikki would quit breathing—that wouldn't suit him at all. Just enough and she would be powerless before him, unable to resist his attentions. He could do whatever he wanted...for as long as he wanted.

He picked up the syringe, checked that the needle cover was in place, then smiled. He did love it when a plan came together. Placing a ski mask over his head, he eased down the steep basement steps and opened the heavy steel door.

The squeaking of the door had awakened her. Good. He didn't want her too comfortable. "Good morning, my dear. Did you spend a comfortable night? No, I don't suppose you did." He watched as she moved stiffly about. The costume she'd been wearing at the time of her abduction was torn, apparently from her struggles. "I see you're not happy with your accommodations, and I've taken such care too. You always were an ungrateful little wretch. However, I have something new for you to wear. I wouldn't want you to be less than stylishly dressed. After all, this is going to be your film debut."

"My what?"

Forty-six

Lorena Judson walked into the large airy kitchen. Samuels sat at his computer. Eastwood stood at parade rest, his dark eyes seemingly taking in everything. Over in the corner Russell, leaning his elbows on the counter, spoke softly into a cell phone.

She touched Samuels on the shoulder. "I want full dossiers on the deli guy Stuart Hall, her editor Geoffrey McHugh, the shelter guard and the pimp. And I want them yesterday. Don't forget the photographer. Make sure he's still in Europe. Check local and federal records. I want to know anything which points to whomever might have Miss Prentice. Interview the doctor who brought them into the world, if you have to, but do it."

"Yes, ma'am." Samuels returned to his computer.

"Eastwood, maintain contact with perimeter surveillance and be available in case there's a ransom demand."

He nodded, never changing his dour expression or position.

"Russell, you're my liaison with Detective Halloran. We need to know everything the police know before they know it."

Russell nodded his understanding, continuing his hushed conversation.

She turned, intending to return to Max's study.

"Ma'am," Russell spoke. "The shelter guard is Malcolm Dodd. His record is a little dodgy, but—"

"No buts, get on him."

"That's what I'm trying to tell you. He's been in the hospital for the last three days—ruptured appendix. He can't be our guy."

"You're sure he's still there?"

"Talked to the charge nurse. He's still hooked up to I.Vs."

"All right, we can eliminate him." She shrugged. "Didn't fit the description anyway."

Max stared at the telephone, willing it to ring. Even a ransom demand would be preferable to this interminable waiting.

"Max."

He looked up at the sound of Lorena's voice. "Have you heard something?"

She walked over to the sofa and sat beside him. "No, but we've ruled out the shelter guard. He's been in the hospital for the last three days."

He nodded. Fatigue had long ago sapped his energy. All that kept him going now was adrenaline and caffeine.

"What about Nikki's editor, Geoff McHugh? Why wasn't he at the gala? I should think he'd be there to see her honored."

Max shrugged. "I'm sure he was invited. I never—you don't think he kidnapped Nikki, do you?"

"How long has he been her editor?"

"I don't know. Nikki already had the initial offer when I came back from Paris, but I don't know if they met before she moved into the townhouse or not."

"I see."

"I didn't care for him, but he didn't strike me as the stalker type." He shook his head, still doubting the editor was a viable suspect. "On the other hand, if Nikki rejected him…"

"Until he's cleared, he's still a suspect."

"Am I still a suspect?"

"Not in *my* book," she admitted with a smile.

"I guess I should be relieved." He leaned forward, his head in his hands. "But I'm too worried."

"We're doing everything we can to find her."

"I know. It's not knowing whether she's—" His voice broke. Panic overwhelmed him. His hands shook. Dragging air in and out of his lungs became a chore.

Nikki twisted and turned, attempting to loosen the cords binding her wrists. Every time she felt it give, hope flared…quickly followed by despair when nothing seemed to work. No matter how hard she tried.

She couldn't see them, but her wrists were raw. No skin left. Still she had to be making some progress. Sooner or later the bindings would give.

The small matter of getting out of where ever the hell he'd taken her could wait at least until her hands were free. One step at a time, she told herself. One step at a time.

Max paced back and forth in his study. Located on the west side of the townhouse, the study was dark, lit by a single lamp. Agent Eastwood had manned the telephone all night, sitting upright, at attention. Lorena Judson sat at one end of the sofa, her head back, eyes closed, but he knew from her tense posture that she wasn't asleep.

Still no ransom call. Nikki could be anywhere. He refused to believe she was dead.

Agent Russell tapped on the door. Max stopped pacing, held his breath, his heart literally pounding in his throat. Lorena sat up, appearing alert and all business.

"Agent Judson, the police have located Stuart Hall. They have him down at Central."

"Does he look good for it?"

Agent Russell shook his head and shrugged. "Dunno, better than the security guard, anyway. He has a rap-sheet—small time stuff and a complaint against him for sexual harassment..." Russell paused, "...but it was dismissed. Locals are going to have a chat with him anyway."

Lorena stood. "Russell, we're going down to the precinct where they'll hold Stuart Hall. I need to see him, get a feel for his quirks." She turned to Max. "I'll let you know if I learn anything." Nodding in Eastwood's direction, she said, "Agent Eastwood will stay here just in case of any contact by the kidnapper. Agent Samuels will continue searching the local and federal data bases."

She frowned. "Anything on the editor?"

"Still no sign of him at his office or condo. Maybe he went out of town for the weekend."

"Or maybe he has Nikki," Max suggested, even though he didn't really believe it.

"McHugh's record is clean," Lorena admitted, "but I don't like loose ends."

"What about the photographer? Still in Europe?"

Russell snickered. "Definitely. He's a guest of the Monegasque authorities...date rape."

"*Mèrde!*" Max swung around and punched the wall with his fist. How many young women had the photographer raped in the intervening ten years?

Lorena's eyebrows rose. "If you feel that strongly about it, why didn't you prosecute before when he raped her?"

"Nikki wouldn't hear of it," he snapped. "I told you that already."

Again the absolute helplessness of the situation galled him. He hated sitting back, waiting for the FBI or the police to find Nikki. He should be out there turning over every rock, looking for the slug who'd kidnapped her.

Max walked Lorena and Agent Russell to the door. "Just one thing."

She turned. "What?"

"When you find her, I'm going along."

Lorena shook her head. "No. It's against procedure. We're still eliminating the possibilities."

"Damn the possibilities! I will go."

"It's against procedure." Lorena shook her head. "But I understand how you feel. Let's just wait until we have a solid lead."

Forty-seven

"Now, I'll give you a choice. If you promise to behave, I'll unbind you and allow you to change clothes." He watched for her reaction, seeing only a sullen shrug of her shoulders. He added, "If you don't behave, I'll be forced to undress you myself."

In spite of himself, he giggled at the thought of touching her flawless ivory skin. Whether she cooperated or not, his pocket contained a syringe filled with a drug which would immobilize her. He hoped she would struggle, just a little. More fun that way.

"Which shall it be? Oh, dear. You can't talk, can you? Well, I'll fix that for you." He eased the duct tape from her cheek and mouth. As her mouth was released, she attempted to bite him.

"Ouch." He moved away from her. Little hell cat. "You know I warned you to behave. Now I shall have to undress you myself." Nikki shrank against the wall and shook her head furiously.

He slapped her. "I told you. I am in control here, not you." He grabbed the neck of her gown and jerked her to her feet. The more she cringed, the better he liked it...no, he loved it. It was time to teach her exactly who was in charge. He took both hands and gave a savage rip, parting her fragile costume to the waist. Another rip, and the gown lay at his feet. "There, there. Now my viewers will be able to see how lovely you are."

"No, please, no," Nikki cried as his hands began an intimate exploration of her body. Vertigo overtook her...and a terrifying memory...

Stumbling in the gloomy darkness on rough cobblestones, she picked up the hem of her tattered gown, ripped off the lace and tossed it aside. The exquisite trim would do no good in the Temple Prison. The dress would never be the same. Her life would never be the same. Condemned by the Citizens because of her station. It would have been laughable, if she were not so afraid of dying. Maxime had prevailed on her to leave Paris several months before. Now, she wished she had listened to him.

Why had she been so stubborn? To stay near him? No, that was not the real truth. The real truth was that she had truly believed the Royal Guards and the King's Army would handily defeat the riffraff clogging the streets of Paris. She wanted to stay in Paris and enjoy the balls as if nothing were happening outside the gates.

Now, she was truly up the Seine without a paddle. Her mother had fled their country home at Maxime's suggestion, but at the last minute, Nicole had changed her mind. She had decided to remain with her aunt, unaware that her beloved aunt was already on her way to England. Maxime had been duty bound to defend the king. All alone, she was thrown into prison and condemned.

Granted there were other aristocrats in the Temple Prison, even the King and Queen, who reportedly had comfortable apartments, not like the pest-ridden cell into which she was confined. Something skittered in a corner, and a cold chill passed through her. Rats, no doubt. She folded her arms and backed away from the sound. She bumped into a rude cot and sat on it, drawing her feet up off the floor. Almost immediately, she began to itch. The bedding was infested with heaven only knew what kind of vermin.

Tears stung her eyes. She huddled on the cot for what seemed like hours listening to the skittering sounds, fending off the rats' exploratory excursions, until she heard the key in the door. Freedom? She knew Maxime would try to free her. Had he not promised in his last note? She had only to be brave. He would save her.

The rough door scraped open. She held her breath. Two figures entered.

"*Bonjour*, Citizeness," one of them said in guttural street patois.

"*Bonjour, M'sieur*," she replied politely, standing.

A vicious backhand knocked her back on the bed, and one of the figures advanced toward her. "Your fine manners won't do you any good in this place, royalist whore."

Unable to speak for the pain, she touched her lip and felt the blood as it welled. *Why me?*

"Quiet. You have no rights in this place," the larger of the two men shouted.

She withdrew into the farthest corner of the cell, but the men advanced again. The taller man grasped the front of her gown and ripped it, exposing her breasts. "No. Please," she moaned. "No!"

"No. No, no. Not this time. Never again." Nikki screamed at her captor. An adrenaline-induced rage pumped through her. Summoning all her strength, she kicked him backward, causing him to stumble. At the same time, she broke the last strand of her bonds.

"Stupid bitch!" He came at her again, his fist drawn back.

"No!"

Surrender? Never. She drew her hands into claws and raked down his face.

"Bitch!" he screamed, coming at her with a fluid-filled syringe.

She scanned the cellar for a weapon.

Nothing. She pummeled his head with her fists and kneed him in the groin.

"Umph." He collapsed, moaning and clutching his genitals.

She sprang from the cot and headed for the steel door, praying he hadn't locked it. Damn thing was heavy, but no matter. She had to get out. Behind her, she could hear him already scrambling to his feet.

"Come back here, bitch," he screamed.

She gave a final jerk on the door and it opened. Freedom. She struggled up the steps, stumbled, then caught herself.

It was only a second's delay, but one she couldn't afford. "Ugh!"

Nikki felt the bite of a needle jabbed into her shoulder. She elbowed him in the abdomen—too late—the stinging of the drug told her. Using the last of her strength, she kicked backward and sent him sprawling down the stairs.

Her breath caught in her throat. What had he given her? Panic flared as she collapsed.

I can't breathe.

Forty-eight

Max looked up as Lorena and Agent Russell returned from the Central Park precinct. "Well?"

Lorena's cell phone rang. "I need to get this," she said, then answered, "Okay. Okay. I'm on the way."

He jumped up. "I'm coming too." He said reminding her of her earlier decision.

She frowned. "You'll be in the way." She looked back at him over her shoulder. "Stay here. I'll let you know as soon as we know something definite."

"Like hell. This is it. I know it." He grabbed his jacket and ran after her. "I'm following. You can't stop me."

"I can, but I won't. Come on."

Together they ran to her government-issue car.

"Buckle up," she ordered.

"Where are we going? Who is he?" He tightened the seatbelt across his midsection. He didn't want to risk her changing her mind again.

"He's Donald Stanley, a Brit with a long history of pandering, supposedly retired. Started out as a college professor, but he ran afoul of authorities for rape."

Mon Dieu. Max shuddered. A rapist. "You don't think he's already...?"

She cast him a quick, pitying glance. "Who knows? He's had plenty of time." She maneuvered the car swiftly and expertly through the early morning traffic.

"Where are we going?"

"Queens."

"You think he's the one?"

"Best lead we have. You get a feeling sometimes."

"Do you have it now?"

"Yes. My stomach is tied in knots."

Mèrde.

Lorena shot him another look of pity, but ignored his fears. "We'll hit the Queensborough Bridge in another twenty minutes if traffic doesn't get any worse." She spoke into her com unit. "Charley-Robert-X-ray ten, we're heading east on Sixty-fifth Street. Our ETA is thirty-five or forty minutes. I want Stanley's house surrounded, clear the entire block, I don't want a milkman or a paperboy stumbling into this operation. I want it done now."

If the agent's stomach was tied in knots, Max could see no indication of it. On the other hand, his gut twisted and turned worse than the route of the Tour de France.

Helpless. Dammit. He'd been warned, but he'd failed to prevent fate's latest blow to their relationship.

One more chance. Just give me one more chance.

Forty long minutes later, Max and Lorena reached Stanley's quiet neighborhood. She opened the door and jumped out. "Stay here," she ordered.

"No." Right behind, his long strides quickly caught up with the agent.

She flashed her badge at the patrolman on perimeter control. "He's with me."

The patrolman nodded and allowed them through.

She turned toward him, her face stern. "You will stay outside. You will not go past this point. I've allowed you inside the crime scene tape, as a favor. Do you understand?"

"Of course." Like hell. He'd play a tame dog, but only until it was verified that Nikki was inside. After that, they'd have to handcuff and chain him to keep him away.

He marveled at Lorena's swift personality change. She was certainly all business now. He followed behind her as she made her way over to an unmarked van. It was filled with high-tech surveillance equipment—multiple viewing screens, each with a different display. He could make neither head nor tail of it. He listened, hoping he'd hear they'd found Nikki.

She gestured toward one of the screens with two yellow glowing dots. "Heat sensors picking up anything, Detective?"

"Two heat signatures, neither moving," Halloran said. "Could be he knows we're here."

"What about the floor plan?"

"City records show he built a new basement. My guess is that's where he has her stashed."

"Any sound from the microphones?"

"Nothing."

Max eased away from the two of them. Neither moving? No sound. It was early. Maybe the kidnapper was asleep. Maybe Nikki was hurt or... He straightened his shoulders, tried to look like he belonged—no mean feat in a tux. Why the hell hadn't he changed clothes?

"Hey you, where do you think you're going?"

"Interpol," Max bluffed. "I've been after Stanley for over a year." He stared the patrolman straight in the eye...and held his breath.

"Okay, just stay back. Full-scale assault about to go down. Wouldn't want your fancy suit mussed up."

He cursed the light. Daylight made it damned difficult to sneak around to the back of the house. If Nikki was in the basement, then perhaps he'd find a small window for access.

A commotion sprang up behind him. He glanced over his shoulder. Someone was attempting to cross the crime scene tape.

Taking advantage of the diversion, he streaked for the rear of the house, his heart hammering in his chest. She had to be nearby. He sensed her presence.

He crept along the rear of the small one story cottage. One small window in the back. That had to be it. He grabbed a rusting lawn chair and hit the window with it. So much for being quiet.

No good. He kicked the window.

It cracked.

Crouching he kicked out the rest of the glass. Slipping his legs and hips through the window didn't pose a problem, but his chest and shoulders did. Damn. There had to be a better way to get inside than turning himself into a human pretzel, but he didn't have time to find it.

He exhaled as forcefully as he could, rolled his shoulders forward and slid the rest of the way into the basement. He fell hard on a cold concrete floor. But he was in. That's all that mattered.

The light dim, Max blinked as his eyes adjusted to the lower light level. He made out an open door...

Mon Dieu, a body. He rushed over and knelt beside it. Felt a grizzle of beard.

Male. Where the hell was Nikki?

He found the door, bounded up the stairs to the first level...and tripped over Nikki sprawled at the top of the stairs.

Breathless with fear, he touched the side of her neck feeling for the pulse that would tell him she was alive. There, but barely.

"Nikki." He put his cheek next to her mouth. She wasn't breathing. He placed his mouth over hers and exhaled.

How many times? Why hadn't he ever taken courses? Everyone should to know how to do this. He continued, desperate for her to respond.

Breathe, dammit. Breathe.

The front door crashed in.

He kept forcing air into Nikki's lungs.

"Hands up!"

He heard the order, but ignored it. "She's...not...breathing," he said between breaths of air.

"Get the paramedics." The first officer dropped down on his knees beside Max. "Here let me."

"No...down...in the...basement."

Chaos reigned as the house filled with the SWAT team, officers, paramedics and the FBI.

A soft hand touched his shoulder. "Come on. Let the paramedics take over."

He looked up and saw Lorena, then fell back, giving the paramedics room. In a matter of seconds, two intravenous lines were started and a tube was put down Nikki's throat and attached to a portable respirator. "So she can breathe," one of them explained unnecessarily.

For the first time, he realized that Nikki was nearly nude. He pulled off his jacket and covered her.

Carefully the paramedics lifted her to a stretcher.

"Holy shit," the paramedic exclaimed, "She's got a needle in her shoulder. He drugged her." He removed the syringe, wrapped it in a plastic bag and stuck it in his uniform pocket. "We'd better keep this. The doctors will need to know what he injected her with."

"Is she going to be all right?" Max asked, dreading the answer.

"Too soon to tell, but she's still with us. There's still some drug in the syringe. Whatever it is, she didn't get all of it."

He glanced over his shoulder and down the stairs. "He's down there."

Another paramedic stood and clambered down the stairs. "We've another one—in the basement," he called out. "Need another stretcher and a back board."

The two remaining paramedics lifted Nikki, stretcher and all. "We're taking her to Long Island Jewish Medical Center. You can ride with us, if you want," the small redhead told him.

"Thank you." He turned to look at a frowning FBI agent. "I can go with her, can't I? You're not going to arrest me, are you?"

"That's still under consideration," she said. "Go on. Get out of here, before someone decides that's exactly what we need to do."

He followed behind the paramedics, afraid to let Nikki out of his sight. Another team of paramedics rushed by him. Personally, he hoped the SOB was dead. As they neared the ambulance, multiple flashes dazzled his vision.

The press. Couldn't have a rescue without them, he thought bitterly.

As soon as the paramedics had secured Nikki, Max climbed into the ambulance. The last thing he saw was her editor, standing handcuffed and yelling at a police officer. Had McHugh something to do with

Nikki's kidnapping, after all?

Forty-nine

After the desperate ambulance ride to the hospital, Max paced in the hallway outside the intensive care unit. Fear gripped his gut. By his reckoning, Nikki had already been unconscious for at least two hours. Concern for her welled up and threatened to choke him. The neurologist had been with her for more than forty-five minutes. The longer the physician took, the greater Max's apprehension.

Alone he waited. Nikki's mother was on her way from Florida, but he'd refused Alexa's plea to come to the hospital.

The electronic double-door, separating him from Nikki, swung open. Finally, he thought. He walked forward to meet the neurologist, a short man, immaculately dressed in a starched white lab coat. The doctor emanated an air of God-given authority, leaving Max feeling like a penitent before a priest. The physician extended his hand. Max took it. Should he kiss the ring, genuflect, or would a bow be sufficient?

"Doctor DiSilva, how is she?"

"Mr. Devereaux, Miss Prentice is stable for the present," the dapper physician assured him.

"May I see her?"

"Not yet. Let me explain first what we've done and what we know…and what we don't know."

"I'm listening." His tone was impatient, but he didn't care.

"First of all, the electroencephalogram shows normal brain activity, which means that she hasn't suffered any irreparable brain damage."

"That's good, then?" He hoped for an affirmative answer. Why can't the man use simple words? Why drag it out? The waiting room wasn't a stage, but the neurologist acted as if it were.

"Yes, of course. Now, we've taken body fluids for drug screens, and the results are pending. Whatever she's been injected with hasn't shown up on any of the more common panels. In addition, we are checking out the residue in the syringe. Without knowing the actual drug used, I can't give you any estimate on how long her recovery will take, or if there will be other organ damage."

"Make an educated guess." He wanted answers, not equivocations.

"I told you we'll know more when the spinal fluid screens come back, and that won't be for eighteen hours, at least. You'll have to be patient. We've given her every drug antagonist we can safely give her.

Her vital signs are stable, and her respiratory status is improving. At this rate, she'll be off the ventilator soon."

"How soon is soon? Will she be conscious?"

The physician sighed and continued his pedantic explanation. "She already has some spontaneous respirations. We're weaning her off the ventilator. I would expect her to start awakening within the next several hours. Again," he paused, emphasizing, "until we know what drug was used, I can't predict anything for certain."

"Perhaps, the FBI or the authorities have faster labs."

"That's entirely possible, but our tests are already underway. Right now, my concern is the young woman in the ICU. The hospital toxicology department and the authorities will do their jobs. And I would appreciate it if you would allow me to do mine."

"Fine, then see that she doesn't die." Max shoved his hands in his pockets and continued pacing.

On hearing Max's response, DiSilva's eyes narrowed. He pivoted on his heel, leaving Max to his pacing.

"Maybe you should've been nicer to him, Daddy."

"Alexa?" He whirled in the direction of his daughter's voice, then sighed. He should've known she would come, anyway. She was as stubborn as he was. He hugged her to his chest, and stroked her hair, glad to have the unexpected warmth and comfort of her presence. "I'm glad you came."

She hugged him back. "Is Nikki going to be okay?"

He looked down into his daughter's upturned face, tension and worry furrowing her brow. "The doctor thinks so."

"You were really giving him a hard time. You must be worried about her."

"I am."

Alexa looked up at him. He saw a calculating gleam in his daughter's eyes. He waited.

"You—uh, love her, don't you?"

He swallowed. It was time he admitted it aloud. "Yes, little one. I do."

Alexa flashed him a wide grin. "I knew it. I told her you did."

"You did? When?"

"Well, let's see. Hmm, several times while you partied around in Paris."

"Oh?"

"Yeah, she was really upset over all those tabloids. She tried to pretend that she didn't care, but she did. I could tell."

"Really, how?" A feeling of well—smug relief passed through him. Nikki did care about him, no matter what she'd said.

He stopped pacing and sat on the nearest vinyl-covered sofa. Alexa sat beside him, close to his side and still clasping his hand. Her features grew animated as she talked.

"Yes, her face would get red, then she'd chew on her bottom lip. She'd stick her nose up in the air and tell me she wouldn't discuss it."

"I know. Those damn photographs. I couldn't stand that woman. The tabloids blew it all out of proportion. That's how those rags make their money."

"I tried to tell her that, but she wouldn't listen. "Her grin grew wider. "She's even more stubborn than you are, Daddy." Then her expression turned serious. "Is her mother coming?"

"Yes, I called Mrs. Prentice as soon as we found Nikki. A neighbor answered and said she was already on her way to New York."

She nodded, then asked, "So what did he do? Who was he?"

"The police are checking him out, and he's not talking. He was found at the bottom of the stairs with a neck and head injury. They took him to Bellevue. We won't know what he did until some of the tests come back."

Max's worst fear, beyond losing her, was that the stalker had harmed her in a more devastating way. She was almost nude when he'd found her, bruised with scratches and terrible marks on her wrists where she'd been bound. In the emergency room, the doctors had refused to tell him if she'd been raped. After all, he wasn't a relative.

Alexa squeezed his hand. "She'll be okay. She just has to."

Max looked at the tears welling up in her eyes. "She will," he reassured her. "The doctors here at LIJ are excellent," he told her, then added mentally, even if the neurologist is a first-class prick. However, DiSilva's personality was of less consequence than his skills, and his reputation was among the best.

On the opposite side of the lobby, the elevator door whooshed open. Nikki's mother rushed toward him, her face pale and drawn. He'd never seen the woman with less than perfect make-up or coifed hair. Now, she stood before him, wringing her hands, casually dressed and without a single piece of jewelry.

"Where's Nikki? Where's my baby? Is she going to be all right?"

He nodded toward the double doors that led to the ICU. "She's in there, but Dr. DiSilva said she would be conscious soon, maybe."

"My baby's in the intensive care unit. *Maybe* she'll be all right? Oh my God, what have I done to deserve this?" Jessie collapsed into a fit of weeping and wailing…and into Max's arms. He eased her toward the sofa where Alexa scooted over to give room.

He cringed, wishing he could slap some sense into the woman, but she was only giving into maternal guilt. Instead, he patted her hand and attempted to console her. "Mrs. Prentice, the doctor said there was no brain damage. Apparently, the stalker injected her with something just before we found her. She's still unconscious, but the doctor is hopeful of her recovery."

"W-was she..." Jessie hesitated, glancing at Alexa at the far end of the couch, then dropped her voice before adding, "...hurt any other way?"

He shook his head. "I don't know. They wouldn't tell me, but I'm sure they'll tell you."

"I *am* her mother after all." Jessie folded her arms across her chest and cast a baleful look in his direction. "This is all *your* fault. You should've taken better care of my baby."

A flash of white-hot rage blazed through him, laced with a heavy dose of guilt. More than once, he'd thought the same thing. He understood Jessie Prentice only too well. Upset and powerless, she needed a scapegoat. He'd always been her favorite target. So be it.

He bit back his anger. "I'm sorry. I didn't know about the stalker, until it was too late."

Jessie appeared to consider his words, then nodded. "Nikki always kept things to herself. I don't guess she's changed much. Stubborn too."

"Yes."

"Will they let me see her?"

"Soon, I'm sure."

Mrs. Prentice leaned back and heaved a sigh. "I guess I'll have to be patient."

Alexa reached over and patted the older woman's hand. "She'll be okay. I just know it."

He watched in amazement. A small smile flickered over the woman's face. He'd never seen a genuine smile on her face, however tiny.

"Thank you, Alexa. I'm sure she will too."

If only he knew for sure.

"She's been in there for hours," Max said to no one in particular. He sat wearily on the sofa outside ICU. He'd given up pacing, but not watching the clock. The adrenaline rush of the early morning had dissipated. More than twenty-four hours had passed since he'd slept, and his tuxedo had seen better days. Dr. DiSilva had announced that Nikki was coming around and allowed her mother to see her, but Max hadn't...yet. Frustrated and afraid, he waited. Nothing the doctor said could reassure him. Only seeing Nikki for himself would.

"No, Daddy, it just seems like it." Alexa handed him another cup of coffee; he'd lost count long ago. She sat beside him and patted his knee.

His chest swelled with love. His daughter, nearly a woman, was comforting him. Her ski trip had been spoiled, and she hadn't mentioned it. He couldn't help but wonder how many teenagers would've handled the disappointment so maturely.

The moment of father-daughter bonding was interrupted by Agent Judson's emerging from the elevator. Along with her was Nikki's editor McHugh—no longer in handcuffs.

Out of habit, he stood, nodded at Lorena and McHugh.

"How is she?" the editor asked.

"Still in the ICU, but coming around, the doctor says. Her mother's with her now."

"I'll have to debrief her, but not until she's stable," Lorena said. "I've already interrogated her kidnapper."

"He's still alive?" Max raised a brow, his fists clenched at his side. "I hoped he was dead."

"Alive and—uh, talkative."

Max nodded at McHugh. "Why is he out of handcuffs?"

McHugh gave a wolfish smile. "One of my better moments, I thought."

"Really?" Max glowered at the editor. "'Better moments'?"

"Really," Lorena added with a frown. "The diversion he created allowed you to make your heroic rescue."

"You tried to break through the barricade to help me?"

"Anything for Nikki," McHugh said. "Friend of mine on the force gave me a heads up. When I arrived, I saw you edging toward the house, somewhat conspicuous in your tuxedo, and figured what you were up to. Just thought I'd give you a hand. You can thank me later—or not."

Max stared at the editor and nodded. Perhaps, McHugh wasn't such a jerk, after all.

McHugh stuck his hands in his pockets and leaned against the wall. "You're welcome."

"Later." Max turned back to Lorena. "What about the kidnapper?"

"He has a spinal cord injury. The neurosurgeon is uncertain whether or not it's permanent, but he won't be stalking or kidnapping anyone else for quite a while."

"Good!" Max and the editor said together.

"Did he tell them what he used on her?"

"Yes, he used a type of paralytic agent. She's very fortunate that it was injected into her shoulder and not a vein. Apparently, he had diluted it as well for his purposes. Full-strength and Nikki wouldn't be coming around, ever."

"*Mon Dieu.*" He sank back on the sofa, overwhelmed by how close he'd come to losing Nikki forever.

"Another minute or two and—"

"I get the picture," Max said with a groan.

"Your intervention saved her. She's very lucky." The agent's tone said she approved of his actions.

"It should've never happened. I should've protected her."

"But you didn't know about the stalker."

"True, but I'd been warned she was in danger."

The agent's eyes widened. "Warned? I thought you—by whom?"

Shifting uncomfortably on the couch, he considered just how much he should reveal. "A friend of my mother's in France—she's a bit of a psychic. Anyway, she warned me Nikki was in danger. I left as soon as I could, but there were complications before I could come back to the States."

Lorena smiled wryly. "Complications would be your arrest."

Restless, Max stood and started pacing again. "Yes, yes. I was detained briefly. It's all been straightened out. You know that already."

"Yes." Lorena stood with her arms folded across her chest. "Go on."

"When I returned, I tried to warn her, but she was still angry with me and wouldn't listen."

"Angry?"

"It was a personal matter. Personal."

"I see." She nodded with a hint of a smile.

"I thought Nikki would be safe as long as she stayed in the townhouse. The security system is excellent, however, after my return, she left on her book tour. Before she left, she insisted on moving most of her things to the Aldens'."

"Basically, you lost control of the situation."

"Control? There is no controlling Nikki."

"Apparently."

The door to the ICU opened and Jessie Prentice walked out, wiping her eyes and sniffing. "My poor baby."

Fear of the worst hit him in the midsection. His heart pounded. He rushed to the woman's side. "Tell me. Is she conscious?"

Mrs. Prentice took his hand, leaning on his arm for support. Again, he resisted the impulse to shake the silly woman and led her to the sofa.

"Oh, Max. My baby's going to live. That's what that nice Dr. DiSilva said."

A wave of relief washed through him. "What else did he say?"

"Well, they took that awful tube out of her throat. She's still groggy, and very hoarse, but she knew me." She leaned back, placing her forearm to her head in an overly dramatic gesture.

"May I see her now?"

DiSilva walked up behind Mrs. Prentice. "Of course, Mr. Devereaux, if her mother doesn't mind.

Max leveled his gaze on Nikki's mother. "Mrs. Prentice, please. There's so much I need to tell her." He'd get down on his knees and beg if necessary.

"Well—" she said, obviously trying to torture him.

DiSilva cleared his throat. "I would suggest a very brief visit. Nothing to upset my patient, of course."

Jessie batted her eyes at DiSilva. "Whatever you think is best, Doctor."

"Thank you," Max murmured. Nerves and anticipation roiled in his stomach as if he'd eaten something spoiled. A brief visit was better than nothing at all. Certainly long enough to tell her he loved her.

Fifty

Lights…too…bright…beeping… Would it never stop? Pain…everywhere. Mama's voice. Gone. Alone, again. Nikki groaned, tried to open her eyes once more, then squeezed them shut.

Someone was holding her hand, stroking it.

"Nikki? Darling, you're in the hospital."

"Max?" *Darling*? What did he mean by that? She took a deep ragged breath. "You're here?" Had to be hallucinating. Her lids were too heavy.

"*Oui, chère*. I am here. You're safe. He won't hurt you again."

"Dead?"

"No, but paralyzed when he fell down the basement stairs."

"I-I kicked him. He tried to—"

"Don't talk. Save your strength."

She attempted opening her eyes again. A very fuzzy Max Devereaux stood beside her bed. "You really are here. I thought I was dreaming."

"I am really here, and I will never leave you."

"Okay." She sighed. Without a doubt, she was dreaming again, but it was a nice one.

"Sorry, Mr. Devereaux. Miss Prentice needs her rest," a woman's voice warned.

"One more minute," Nikki's dream man said. "I have to tell her something important."

Dream man's pressure on her hand increased. She even dreamt he kissed it.

"Nikki, *Je t'aime*," he murmured. "I love you."

"Love you too, Max. Love you." The effort too much, she fell asleep.

Max left the ICU, his heart lighter and his step buoyant. Nikki would live, and she loved him. In all his life he couldn't remember a more supreme moment. He took in the scene in the waiting room. His daughter sat on one side of Mrs. Prentice, while Agent Judson sat on the other. Nikki's editor leaned nonchalantly against the wall. All of them looked exhausted. Of the three women, only Alexa had had any sleep in the last twenty-four hours.

Alexa jumped up. "Daddy?"

Max swept his daughter into his arms for a big hug. "She's going to be okay. I talked to her."

"I told you that, already," Nikki's mother said with a huff.

"I didn't doubt your word. I-I just needed to see for myself." He swallowed, his mouth dry as cotton. "Why don't we all go home and get some rest?" he suggested. "Nikki's asleep again. The nurse said we can come back for evening visiting hours."

"Sounds like a plan." McHugh said, turning to walk away.

Jessie shook her head. "No, I want to stay nearby. The doctor said she might be moved to a private room later today."

Lorena shook her head as well. "I can't leave. I have to debrief her as soon as the doctor gives the okay."

"Alexa?" He asked, looking down at his daughter.

"Sure, Daddy, let's go home. You look like you're about to crash."

He shook his head and smiled. "No, little one, I have never felt better."

Nikki opened her eyes, just a tiny bit. The god-awful lights were dimmed. She yawned and wondered what time it was.

"Nikki, it's Mama."

"Mama?" she croaked, opening her eyes wider. "Where am I?"

"They moved you to a private room. There's a fold-out cot for me to sleep on. I won't leave you."

"Oh." Just Mama, not Max. Well, it had been a lovely dream while it lasted.

"They kept you pretty sedated. Even the FBI agent gave up. She'll be back tomorrow morning."

"She?" Surely not.

"Agent Judson was very nice. She said you were very lucky Max got to you as soon as he did."

"Max? What do you mean?"

"Well, the FBI found the house where that awful man had taken you, but while the FBI was preparing for a full assault, Max broke into the basement and found you."

"He did?"

"Yes, he saved your life. He did that breath-of-life thing. The doctor said another minute and they wouldn't have been able to revive you."

"H-has Max been here?"

"Of course he has. He saw you in intensive care, right after I did."

Nikki smiled, remembering her dream.

"Then he took Alexa home until it was time for evening visiting hours. When they came back, he wouldn't let anyone disturb you. Said you needed your rest."

"Good."

"You know how I hate to admit when I'm wrong, but I think Max really loves you."

"Really?"

"Uh-huh, I sure do. You better grab him now."

"Now, Mama."

"Well, he did save you. That must mean something."

"Okay, I'm gonna go back to sleep now." She stifled a yawn, smiled and rolled over on her side. Max loved her. That's what he'd said. It wasn't a dream..

The next time Nikki awakened, a nurse was taking her blood pressure. To keep from waking her mother, she whispered, "I'm starving. When's breakfast?"

"Not till seven and it's five now. By the way, I'm Betty, your nurse for the night shift."

"Five? Any chance of getting rid of this contraption?" she asked, waving her arm with the intravenous line.

The nurse grinned. "Not until you've eaten."

"But that's two hours from now. I don't remember the last time I ate something."

Betty stopped and placed a finger to her lips. "You need to go light at first. I happen to know there're some popsicles in the refrigerator. How's that sound?"

"Sounds great. Bring me two, please?"

The nurse grinned, showing deep dimples. "Two it is."

"Then can I take a shower? I feel god-awful grungy."

"Sure, but we'll need to protect the bandages on your wrists."

"Anything to feel clean again."

Nurse Betty waved and left the room. Nikki looked over at her mother, who was still asleep and snoring softly. With any luck at all, she should get out of the hospital today.

Two popsicles and one shower later, she sat cross-legged on the bed. And she even felt human. Her hair, still damp, but clean. Nearly seven. Breakfast time. Now she knew how animals in the zoo must feel, waiting for their keepers to feed them. Her stomach growled and she let out a chuckle.

Mama sat straight up. "Nikki?"

She giggled. "Sorry, Mama. I'm hungry."

The door opened and the nurse walked in with a breakfast tray. "I grabbed yours off the cart first."

"Great. You're the best, Betty." She swung her legs over the side of the bed, ready to dig into the tray full of heavenly food. Her stomach growled and her mouth watered at the smell.

Nurse Betty positioned the over-bed stand. "It's a regular diet, but go easy on it. Small bites, chew them well. Stop when you feel full."

"Yeah, yeah. Whatever you say. Just let me at it."

The nurse turned to Nikki's mother with a wide grin. "I think she's almost well."

Her mother giggled. "So do I."

The aroma of scrambled eggs wafted up. Grabbing the small glass of orange juice, she drank it down without stopping, then gave a little burp. "Sorry, guess I went too fast."

"Slow down or it might come back up," the nurse warned.

She shook her head. "It wouldn't dare." She reached for a piece of buttered toast, bit into it and savored her first bite of real food in two days. "I've died and gone to heaven. Thank you so much."

"You're welcome. Have to give report now. My shift's ending."

"Thank you again. You've been wonderful."

"Yes, wonderful," her mother piped in.

Nikki polished off the second piece of toast, the scrambled eggs and a muffin, barely stopping to take a breath. She pulled the top off the coffee and took a sip. "Ah, this is fabulous. I don't know when I've had such good food."

"Nikki, this is just hospital food. It can't be that good."

"It is if you're just glad to be alive." A new thought popped into her head. "I suppose all this has been on the news?"

"Why I guess so. To be honest, baby, I haven't even turned on the television. I've been so worried about you."

Nikki reached over and punched the TV button on the side rail. "Well, let's just see what CNN has to say. Think I'm important enough for CNN, Mama?" she joked. "If it bleeds, it leads. That's what television journalists say—even the prestigious CNN."

"Of course you are."

"Well, I'd just as soon not have my problems aired all over the TV, but somehow I have a feeling they will be." She hit the power button a second time and the television flared to life.

Sure enough, there she was. Not a very flattering picture, either. And there he was. The Professor—no-good pervert pimp. The news anchor intoned, "Donald Stanley, the stalker…"

She didn't hear the rest. Her mother gasped, "No, no," and grabbed her chest.

Nikki scooted off the bed and rushed to her mother's side, pulling the IV pump with her. "Mama, what's wrong?"

"I—I, no, no…" She sank back on the fold-out bed.

Her mother's face, so pale and drawn, scared Nikki. She jerked the I.V. pump back so she could reach the call button.

"Yes?"

"Come quickly, I think my mother's having a heart attack."

Thirty minutes later, the house physician gave Nikki the news. "Your mother just hyperventilated. She's fine."

"Thank you. I'm sorry. I panicked. I've never seen her like that before."

"It's no problem, Miss Prentice. Hyperventilation is quite dramatic, both for the victim and anyone around. Let me know if I can be of assistance again."

"I will. Thank you."

The house officer nodded, turned and left Nikki and her mother, who still appeared drawn and pale. At least Mama wasn't dying.

She walked over and sat on the fold-out cot. "Okay, let's have it. What upset you?"

Her mother gave a weak shake of her head. "Oh, baby. I-I'm so sorry. Oh, God."

Nikki wanted to scream, but held it back. "What? There's something you're not telling me."

"I-I don't know how to tell you. You'll hate me."

Baffled, she pressed her mother. "You have to tell me. I don't care what it is. Nothing can be as bad as what I've already been through."

Her mother hid her face in her hands. "Oh, baby, the stalker—I knew him."

"How? He was a pimp. Tried to recruit me when I was a runaway, but don't worry. I never did anything like that."

"No, no. That's not what I mean." Her mother shook her head furiously. "He—he's your stepfather."

Her mother's words didn't register right away. "What?"

"Donald Stanley is your stepfather, Nikki."

A sick numbness spread through her body. She swallowed. "M-my stepfather? The Professor…?" As much as she tried to process it, she couldn't. "Did he know?"

"I don't know. I mean I took back my maiden name after he left. Baby, I'm so sorry. I've blamed *you* all these years."

"Yes, you always blamed me for his leaving. Told me what a burden I was. I remember." Anger flashed, replacing the numb disbelief.

Her mother started sobbing. "No, no. It's much worse. I-I kicked him out b-because I found him trying to—"

"What?"

"Trying to m-molest you."

"What?"

"No, I stopped him in time. At least I think…"

A wave of nausea hit Nikki without warning. Her stomach clenched in enormous cramps. She clapped her hand over her mouth and barely made it to the waste basket. She doubled over and heaved.

After losing her breakfast, she collapsed on the floor. Her mother stood over her, wringing her hands. "I'm so sorry."

She looked up at her mother, unable to disguise the hatred raging through her. "All these years, you told me *I* was the reason he left us. Now you tell me *you* kicked him out because he was molesting me. How could you treat me that way—all those years. I thought it was my fault we had it so rough. Why you had to work so hard."

"I know it was stupid. I couldn't help it. I—really loved him—until that night." Tears ran down her mother's cheeks. "But every time I looked at you, I saw him."

Nikki stood, ripped the tape off her arm and pulled out the needle, ignoring the blood oozing from the site.

"Baby, stop it! You'll hurt yourself."

"I'm getting out of here. All those years. All those lies. You make me sick. You're pathetic!"

"Oh, baby…" her mother wailed.

She walked over to the cupboard and jerked it open. Good thing her mother—no she'd never think of the woman like that again—had brought her something to wear.

Once dressed, she turned to Jessie. "I never want to see you again." Legs trembling, Nikki walked to the door. "I'll never forgive you. Never."

She ran.

Fifty-one

Max strode through the hospital lobby, looking neither left nor right. Stopping at the elevator, he jabbed the UP button...and waited. He jabbed it again. Finally, the doors opened, and Nikki's mother emerged and walked toward him. "Is she being discharged?"

The woman looked away, refusing to meet his gaze. "Nikki's gone."

"Already? Why didn't she wait? Surely you didn't allow her to take a cab by herself?" An uneasy sensation in the pit of his stomach told him something wasn't right.

"She ran out Max. It was awful. I had no idea it would upset her so."

Dammit. He to shake the stupid woman until her teeth rattled. "What?" Why couldn't the woman just spit it out?

"Let me sit down a minute. I've had a very difficult morning."

Max reined in his frustration, then led her to a comfortable sofa in the main lobby. She settled on the sofa, smoothing the wrinkles from her slacks. He took a deep breath. Five more seconds of her delaying tactics and he would strangle her.

"It's like this," she said, her gaze still averted.

He took another deep breath. Clenching his fists at his sides, he sat beside her. "Go on."

"Nikki and I were watching the news when they flashed a picture of the man who kidnapped her, that pimp, you know?"

"Yes. Please continue."

"Well, I nearly choked on my coffee. I mean, I couldn't have been more shocked."

"Please, Mrs. Prentice, tell me."

"Well, if you'd stop interrupting me, I would. He's Nikki's stepfather. After Nikki's real father ran out on us, I moved in with Donnie. We got married as soon as my divorce went through."

"Nikki's stepfather?" Every muscle in his body tensed. *Mon Dieu,* but he wanted to strangle the woman.

"The kidnapper, the pimp—he's my ex-husband. Nikki was so young. She never knew her real daddy."

"Donald Stanley...is...Nikki's stepfather?" Somehow he couldn't quite wrap his brain around the idea. The very pimp he'd rescued her from so many years ago. The same man who'd kidnapped her and done

God knew what.

She nodded.

He jumped to his feet and faced the woman. "Let me get this straight. Does Nikki know? What did you tell her?"

"Yes, I told her. I mean she knew something was wrong when I saw his picture. I had to tell her, besides—oh, it's just so awful." She wrung her hands, gazing up at the ceiling.

Sickened, he asked, "What else?" He forced himself to sit down again. No matter how distasteful, he had to hear the rest.

"I'd always told Nikki that her Daddy run out on us, because he didn't want the responsibility of a child, but that wasn't quite the truth. I kicked him out."

"You blamed your daughter for her stepfather's leaving, but *you* kicked him out?" The woman should be executed for stupidity, but not until she told him everything.

"Well—uh, I," she stammered, then the horrible words came in a rush. "I found him fondling her. She was only two—a baby. And he had the nerve to tell me she asked him to touch her, but I knew better. I kicked him out, divorced him and took back my maiden name. She never remembered any of it."

"But you blamed her for his leaving all this time? Do you have any idea what you've done to her? Any idea?" Repressing the rage collecting in the back of his throat, he forced himself to remain calm.

"I-I know you can't understand. I was in love with him back then. He was very handsome, charming, such wonderful manners. He was a professor at the junior college. I heard he got into trouble later with one of his students and the college sacked him. I lost track of him after that. You know, we moved around a lot trying to keep ahead of the bill collectors.

"I see."

"No, I know you don't. I don't understand it myself. There were times when I'd look at her and see how she'd ruined my life. I tried to love her. I mean, I do love her, but there were times when I couldn't stand the sight of her. After all, if it hadn't been for her—I wouldn't have had to work so hard."

Unable to listen to another word, he jumped up again. "Where was she going? I have to find her."

"I don't know. She wouldn't talk to me. She just threw on her clothes and ran out.

"Her computer. She won't go anywhere without it. I'll check with the Aldens first."

Desperate, he dashed from the hospital. He had to stop Nikki before she ran away from him forever.

Fifty-two

Max shoved his way past the doorman of the Alden's luxurious co-op. "They're expecting me. There's an emergency." The elevator door had just opened and Max ran for it, repeatedly punching the button for the twenty-fifth floor. He swore softly, willing the car to move faster. Missing Nikki wasn't an option.

The elevator stopped. He bounded out as soon as the door opened. "Twenty-five A, twenty-five B," he called off the numbers as he strode past them. He needn't have worried. Marti Alden stood at the door, waiting for him. "Is she...?"

She nodded. "She's here. But she *says* she doesn't want to see you."

"Where?"

"Second door on the right." She stepped aside, giving him a rueful smile and patted his shoulder. "Good luck."

"I'm going to need it." Thank God he hadn't missed her.

"Nikki?"

No answer. Damn. Taking long hurried strides, he reached the open door of her bedroom.

She stood in the middle of the room, hair in disarray. Clothes were piled everywhere, an open suitcase, as yet empty. She turned toward him, her eyes puffy and red from crying. Her air of devastation broke his heart.

She cringed at the sight of him, hands thrust forward as if to ward off his presence. "Go away."

"You can't run away," he said. "We'll face this together."

"I don't want to face it." She sagged and collapsed onto a chaise.

"You have to." He fell to his knees before her, taking her hands in his. He had to convince her to stay. "I can't live without you."

"Sure you can." She swiped her nose with the back of her sleeve. "You've managed so far."

"I've never known you to run from anything. You're not a coward. I can't change what happened when you were a baby. Dammit, you were just a baby! It's not your fault your stepfather was some kind of sick bastard."

"Leave me alone." She began to cry, her shoulders shaking with the sobs. "You don't know what kind of wife or mother I'd make. You'd want me raising your children?" Her voice rose to a shriek.

"You forget, I've known you for ten years. I've seen you with my daughter. She loves you. She'll be devastated if you leave. Hell, *I'll* be devastated. Please, don't go."

"I-I have to."

She kept her face averted from his gaze. "Please listen to me," he begged. "You've overcome so much, when anyone else would've been crushed. You're a wonderful woman. You've written a beautiful book. You've given your time and money to the shelter. *Ma chère*, any man would be honored to share his life with you. And I've loved you from the first moment we met."

His desperation grew. The unyielding expression on her face told him he hadn't reached the damaged child she'd hidden so deeply inside the beautiful woman. He wanted to shake her, to rid her of her self-delusions.

Instead, he marshaled every ounce of self-control he possessed and gazed into her tragic face. "Look at me. I love you, Nikki. You are my heart, and I nearly lost you. It was your age and my pride that kept me away from you for so long…my stubborn pride that left you vulnerable. Can you ever forgive me?"

"Forgive you?" she asked in obvious disbelief. "You haven't done anything. I'm such a fool." She turned away from him again and looked out the window, as if she couldn't bear to face him. When she spoke again, her voice trembled with emotion. "You know, somehow, I convinced myself I'd managed to live a charmed life. Yeah, that's right. In spite of growing up with a mother who seemed to hate me for reasons I couldn't understand."

Her tormented eyes locked with his. "Now I know the truth. Instead of being Cinderella, I'm…" she paused, "…what—a statistic? I don't know who I am anymore."

Her bare declaration cut him like a knife. He took her hands in his. "You are my love…my heart…my soul. I don't want to live without you. I can't. Fate has put us together before and has seen fit to do it again."

"You believe in fate?" She wiped the tears from her eyes. "You?" Arching an elegant eyebrow, the beginning of a mocking smile played about the corner of her mouth.

He ignored her derision. "I do now. I'm looking at her. You're my future as surely as you've been my past." His desperation mounted; he simply had to reach her. Yet with every word he spoke, she grew more remote.

"No." She pulled her hands from his. "No. All I am is a face…a mask with nothing behind it."

"Dammit! You can't give up now," he shouted. "You're not a quitter. We can do this, together. Please, give us a chance."

"No." She shook her head. "I need some time to m-myself."

His common-sense arguments weren't working. Exasperated, he tried another tack, jumping up from his knees, he paced and waved his hands in the air.

"*Mèrde!* You are the most stubborn woman I have ever known. Just once, I wish you'd listen to me." He waited for a response and was immediately rewarded by an angry flush that spread up her neck and face.

She turned on him, her blue eyes flashing. "Listen to you? *Now*, you love me?" She stood, hands on hips, her voice thick with emotion. "You've left it a little late, *mon ami*. I needed to hear that precious little speech of yours months ago." She shook her head furiously. "Instead of your it-was-a-mistake-morning-after speech."

She assumed a fighting stance, her fists clenched. Another second and she might actually take a swing at him. Everything about her body language dared him to answer.

He dared. "Better late than never, they say."

"Agh!"

She sprang at him, and he caught her in his arms. "You want to hit me? Go ahead. Hit me."

"Turn me loose, and I will." She floundered in his arms, grappling for her freedom.

He shook his head. "No, I like holding you, and I'll keep on holding you."

"Let me go, you—you asshole!"

He drew back, clucking his tongue in amusement. "Ah*, ma chère*, such bad language. I thought *Maman* taught you not to say such words."

"Don't you dare bring up her name. You're a pig—a controlling, asinine—"

"Asinine. Yes, that's much better. *Maman* would've approved of that one." Her body began to relax; she stopped struggling.

"Yeah, I guess she would." Again, she pushed him away. This time he allowed her. She sank to the floor and leaned back against the chaise. He followed her lead, sitting beside her, not touching, but there…if she wanted him.

"I was yours that night—totally yours—and the next morning you rejected me. I felt used."

"I tried to—"

"Explain? What was there to explain? You got what you wanted, and how I felt didn't matter. I was so hurt…and disillusioned. All those years I'd thought of you as—well, my knight in shining armor. You rescued me, showed me a new world. A part of me believed you were waiting for the right moment—for me to grow up or become perfect—or whatever. Just goes to show how naïve and stupid I was."

"But—"

"After we made love, yeah, I thought my dreams had really come true. We shared everything that night…" She paused and took a ragged breath before continuing, "… then you tossed me aside like a used tissue." Tears streamed down her cheeks; she buried her face in her hands.

"I know it seemed that way." Would she never let him explain? No, he'd remain quiet and listen to whatever else she had to say. He owed her that much; he'd caused her so much pain.

"Seemed? Hmph." Nikki raised her head and gazed into his eyes. "I thought you really cared when you beat up Ian Stark after he raped me."

"I did. I hated what he did to you, what he took from you."

"But what you did was even worse. I'll never understand how you could treat me that way." Tears abating, she rested her head on her drawn-up knees and looked at him with a weary, sad expression. "Tell me why, Max. Tell me why you broke my heart."

Max shifted until he stood on his knees before her. "I-I did it to protect you."

Her eyes widened. She folded her arms across her chest. "To protect me? Please, go on. I have to hear this."

Now she was ready to listen, but what could he say that made sense?

"Haven't figured it out yet, have you?" Her voice trembling, she turned away, refusing to look him in the eye.

Frantic to reach her, he grasped her shoulders. "It sounds bizarre. It started with a dream." *Mon Dieu*, but he sounded stupid even to himself.

"A dream?" She turned back, giving him her full attention.

"Several dreams, but—"

She reached out and touched his cheek, desperate to know. "When—what did you dream? Tell me, it's important."

He frowned. "I—uh, don't—"

"Start at the beginning. With the first dream." She leaned forward, intent on hearing him out. Had he had the dreams too?

"The first night I took you to *Maman's*. It was brief, just an impression of being at a costume ball…and the mask. You wore it."

"The mask?" Her heart tripped into overdrive.

"Yes. The one I sent you from Paris. It was the same one. I just didn't know it at the time."

"I dreamt of a masked ball that first night too." She shut her eyes, reliving the images and emotions from her first. "You saved me from being raped by your brother. Quick, tell me, more. Don't leave anything out."

"After I bought the mask, that same night, I had a nightmare. It was during WWII, I was—"

"In the French Underground," she finished for him.

"Yes, how did you know?"

"I tried on the mask before I put it away. I passed out, or fell asleep. I had the same dream."

He slipped his arms around her and pulled her to him. "I died."

"Yes, because you came to me in the night. It was my fault you died." She buried her face on his chest. "I'm sorry."

"Not your fault, *Chèrie*."

He pulled away, his green eyes full of emotion. "Is this real?" he asked. "The mask's provenance told of such an event."

"I-I don't know. It feels like it. Were there more dreams?"

"Another? Yes, I was a ship's captain. I seduced you." He met her gaze and grinned. "I couldn't help it. You were so desirable."

"I remember too well," she said. "You were a wonderful lover that time too."

He looked down, shame-faced. "And then that night, that beautiful night when we made love—during the storm—you remember?"

Nikki cast her eyes down, then looked back at him with her bravest smile. "Not likely to forget it."

Swallowing, Max said, "I'll never forget. It was the most beautiful night of my life."

Tears formed in Nikki's eyes. "Then why?"

"I had another nightmare. Only this time I saw *you* die."

"How?"

He shook his head as if unwilling to tell her the details. "The French Revolution—no, it doesn't matter. That time I failed. I didn't rescue you. When I woke up with you in my arms, I was confused...so I left. I needed to clear my head. But all I could see your death over and over. And all I could think was that I-I was bad for you, and our being together would hurt you once again."

"But it was a dream," she told him softly, stroking the side of his face.

"No, yes—I don't know. Maybe we've been together before. I love you—"

"You do?"

"I told you I did. I couldn't risk losing you, but I didn't know how."

"So you dumped me instead," she said with a sigh, beginning to understand.

"I tried to tell you, but..." Max shrugged.

"I threw the clock."

"You did," he said wryly.

"Now go back to the I-love-you part."

He grinned. "*Oui, Chèrie*. Let us go back to that. I love you with all my heart." Max lowered his head and pressed his lips to hers.

"I love you too. I always have." She slipped her arms around his neck and pulled him closer. He skimmed his hands beneath her shirt and cupped her breasts, teasing the peaks with his thumbs. He deepened the kiss, his tongue sweeping and mating with hers, then he pulled away.

Breathless, she demanded, "What now?"

"You will marry me, have my children?"

Nikki bit her bottom lip, to keep from laughing. "Asking or telling?"

"Pleading with all my heart."

"Then yes, I will."

"My love—"

"Sh—you talk too much." She pulled the shirt from his pants and fumbled with his belt buckle.

"You interrupt my sentences."

"The door…" she whispered.

Max turned and looked over his shoulder and saw the bedroom door standing open. He extended his leg and kicked it shut.

He turned back with a broad smile across his face. "You are the love of my life, all my lives. I don't care about the past. All we really have is right now…and the future. My future has to be with you."

"No matter what happens?"

"No matter what."

Epilogue

Spying her husband leaning his elbows on the wrought-iron balcony, Nikki eased from the bed and joined him. From her vantage point, she could see the elegant lines of the Eiffel Tower in the distance, lit by a myriad of lights.

Max turned and placed his arm around her waist and pulled her to his chest. Love and contentment suffused her entire body. She sighed, then smiled into his crystal green eyes. Reaching up, she winnowed her fingers through his wavy hair. "Do you know how many times I've wanted to do that?"

"Do you know how many times I've dreamt of having you here with me—just like this?" He placed a kiss on her forehead. "*Je t'aime, Madame Devereaux.*"

"*Je t'aime, M'sieur Devereaux.*" Nikki smiled at her husband. "But surely you can do better than a fatherly kiss on the forehead."

He grinned. "You think so, *Chèrie?*"

"I know so." She raised her chin, daring him.

"That sounded like a challenge."

"Oh, it was."

His eyes darkened. "Then you expect me to prove myself again?"

"Uh-hm… again."

"Then I must not disappoint my bride."

"No, you absolutely mustn't disappoint your bride. It's the first rule in the honeymoon rule book."

He rubbed his chin, his expression thoughtful. "Honeymoon rule book?" Slowly, but deliberately, he took her hand and led her from the balcony back to their bed. "Is there anything in this rule book about how I may keep disappointment at bay?"

Slipping her arms around his neck and pressing against him, she winked. "Suggestions on every page."

"Really?" he asked, his accent deepening.

"Really."

Hi lowered his lips on hers for a long, drugging kiss. Her knees buckled, but his strong arms held her fast. Max was actually her husband.

"Is this how I start?" he asked, ending the kiss.

"Oh yes, but you can't stop now."

"I wouldn't think of it."

Together they toppled onto the bed. Once more, they spiraled into the giddy heights of love. A love that transcended time.

In the cool, early dawn hours, Nikki awakened in his arms. He was still asleep, allowing her a moment for quiet reflection. Joy had filled every waking moment since he'd asked her to marry him. He even managed to broker a truce between her and her mother. Her heart was so full, she wasn't sure she could bear it. The man lying at her side loved her, loved her as no one had ever loved her. His acceptance and love wiped away the pain of her past and allowed her heart to heal.

About the Author

Marie-Nicole Ryan is an award-winning author of romantic suspense. *See You in My Dreams* is the first book she completed and her second published. If any book can be called the book of her heart, it's this one.

She lives in Western Kentucky with Cassie the Wonder Sheltie.

To learn more about Marie and her work, visit her web site: http://marienicoleryan.com.

Facebook: https://facebook.com/marienicoleryan.author

She has a Yahoo News group which is currently announce-only. You may subscribe by sending an email to Marie-NicoleRyanNews-subscribe@yahoogroups.com.

Read more of Ms. Ryan's work:

Romantic Suspense Novels

Broken Promises
Love Me If You Can
Holding Her Own
One Too Many, Sequel to Love On The Run
Love On The Run
Too Good To Be True
The Man For The Job
See You In My Dreams

Erotic Historical Western Novels

Loving the Lawman Series
Taming Talia: 2 *(Coming 8/14/12 from Samhain Publishing)*
Seducing the Sheriff: 1

Holiday Interludes
Novelette
Valentine's Gift: 3
(Nikki and Max ten years later)

Short Stories
Pillow Talk: 2
(Prequel to *Broken Promises*)

Mistletoe and Mario: 1
(Alexa and Mario ten years later)